THE B[...]

Title

A. B. GOODMAN

When discussing well-known public figures and other matters, the subjective opinions of the characters do not necessarily represent the viewpoints or conclusions of the author or the publisher. Except for well-known public figures specifically referred to by name, any similarity to real people, living or dead, is coincidental and not intended. Other than the section on real world facts that inspired the book, references to actual or imagined commercial banks, central banks and the "banking cartel" are part of a "what if" fictional universe. Nothing in this work of fiction should be taken to imply or infer that any real world bank(s), banking executive(s), central bank(s) or groups of banks is engaging or has ever engaged in any conspiratorial or nefarious activity as described in the novel.

Copyright © 2025 by Planetary Book Company, Las Vegas, NV, USA

Support Creative Rights!

Authors and artists deserve to earn a living from their work. Copyright protection exists to encourage the creation of books, art, and other works that enrich our culture. When books are pirated instead of purchased, creators and publishers struggle to continue their work. Scanning, uploading, or distributing this book without permission is illegal. Such actions violate copyright law and the author's rights. You may, however, use brief excerpts (up to 2,500 words) for reviews. For permission to use more content, contact the publisher at

info@planetarybooks.com

To Readers Who Downloaded The eBook Version From Unauthorized Sources!

If you enjoyed reading this book, please consider supporting the creators fairly. Please send 50% or more of the regular eBook price via PayPal to info@planetarybooks.com. If that's not possible, contribute whatever amount you can afford. If you're unable to make any payment, at least leave positive reviews on retail websites. Your support will be appreciated. All financial transactions will remain confidential. Thank you for helping sustain the work of authors and publishers.

Chapter 1 – MURDER

Charlie Bakkendorf considered himself an ordinary man. Neither virtuous nor villainous, he lived a life driven by simple wants and needs, with no space for malice. His title, "vault manager" at the esteemed investment bank Bolton Sayres, carried prestige but little meaning; in reality, Charlie managed nothing. A high school graduate with no special credentials, he had drifted into the role without fanfare.

At 32, Charlie was single and ached with loneliness. That, however, was about to change—or so he believed. In just two weeks, Maria had turned his world upside down. Her face lingered in his mind, vivid and irresistible. He was smitten.

He hoped his insistence on sending her home by taxi had made an impression. It was a small gesture, but one he felt conveyed his sincerity. Smiling to himself, he replayed the memory of their coffee date, which had unexpectedly blossomed into a charming dinner. On Saturday, he would see her again, treating her to an evening designed to dazzle: dinner at an exclusive New York City restaurant, followed by a Broadway show.

The lavish night would cost a fortune—perhaps over $1,000—but for once, Charlie wasn't concerned. He had hit the jackpot. Two million dollars. Enough to fulfill his every dream. Spending a fraction of it to treat Maria like royalty felt not only doable but right. The 21 Club and prime Broadway seats were just the beginning. Adjusting to his new wealth might take time, but starting Saturday, he was determined to embrace it.

The taxi ride back to Brooklyn jolted him from his reverie. He reached for his wallet, calculating the fare. Old habits lingered; the thought of paying another $50 for the rest of the trip made him cringe. Why spend so much when the subway costs a mere $2.50? With a sigh, Charlie paid the cabbie and stepped onto the platform at the 181st Street station.

2

The subway, mercifully quiet, was a world away from its usual chaos. A few scattered passengers milled about as Charlie boarded the train. He welcomed the solitude, envisioning a future where he could afford to leave this grind behind. Soon, he would buy an apartment in Lower Manhattan and stroll to work—or perhaps leave work altogether.

Switching lines mid-journey, Charlie made it home in under thirty minutes. Emerging from the station, he stepped onto a dimly lit street. Pools of weak light spilled from scattered lamps, barely illuminating the surrounding shadows. Something about the darkness unsettled him, a feeling that grew sharper as he noticed a figure emerge from the gloom.

The man, short and stocky, appeared abruptly at Charlie's right. His arrival was jarring, and Charlie's pulse quickened. Encounters like this were rare in his mostly white neighborhood. Though Charlie prided himself on being open-minded, the sight of an unfamiliar Black man triggered a pang of unease. What could he possibly want?

The stranger had been waiting, impatiently, for hours. Frustration tightened his jaw as he stepped closer.

"You Charles Bakkendorf?" he asked, his voice edged with a thick street accent.

Charlie stiffened. How did this man know his name? He kept walking, quickening his pace, hoping the stranger would lose interest. But the man followed, easily matching his speed.

"I'm talkin' to you, brotha'! You Charles Bakkendorf or not?"

Charlie hesitated. If the man knew his name, he probably wasn't a mugger. That thought calmed him—slightly. Stopping, he turned to face the stranger. The dim streetlamp made it difficult to make out the man's face, and recognition didn't come. "What do you want?" Charlie asked cautiously.

"You Charlie Bakkendorf?" the man pressed.

"Yes," Charlie admitted.

Before he could say more, a second figure stepped from the shadows. This one was enormous—a towering, six-foot-nine giant with a ponytail of salt-and-pepper hair and a thick mustache. The bandanna wrapped around his forehead gave him the air of an aging hippie, though his demeanor radiated menace rather than peace.

Before Charlie could react, the giant slipped a garrote around his neck and pulled tight. Panic erupted as Charlie clawed at the thin nylon cord, desperate for air. But the man's grip was unyielding. Positioned slightly behind him, the giant thwarted any attempts to fight back. Kicks missed their mark; his fingers found no purchase between the rope and his throat. Oxygen dwindled. The world blurred. Within moments, Charlie's body went limp.

The Black man and the White giant worked quickly. Each looped an arm under one of Charlie's, propping him up like a drunk friend. To anyone watching, the trio appeared to be a group of rowdy pals heading home after a night out. No one would guess that Charlie was already dead.

They reached a waiting BMW and maneuvered Charlie's lifeless body into the backseat, tucking his legs neatly in place. Once the doors shut, the car's heavily tinted windows concealed its grim cargo. Even if someone had looked closely, Charlie merely appeared to be asleep—save for the telltale red line across his neck.

The giant, seated in the passenger seat, peeled off his mustache and wig, revealing a clean-shaven face with a military-style buzz cut. With practiced efficiency, he retrieved a fresh license plate from under the seat. Surveillance cameras would scan the car as it passed, but the new plate would send them chasing ghosts. Confident and methodical, the men drove into the night.

Chapter 2 – EYES OF A SPY

OUTWARDLY, IT WAS INDISTINGUISHABLE from the many commercial structures near Wall Street, its above ground spaces bustling with businesses. But 90 feet beneath its foundation, embedded in Manhattan's ancient basalt, lay a clandestine surveillance hub, actively operational on July 24, 2008—the night Charlie Bakkendorf was murdered.

This underground facility housed an extraordinary electronic surveillance system known as THEATRES, masterminded by Adriano Navarro, a middle-aged former soldier turned tech architect. Navarro had designed it ostensibly to protect New York City from terrorism, but it also served the financial interests of a few mega-banks. These institutions used the system to monitor competitors and customers alike, consolidating power through omnipresent surveillance.

The heart of THEATRES was a network of three supercomputers connected via a dense web of fiber-optic links. Tens of thousands of cameras, microphones, drones, and other devices streamed data into the system, their inputs processed by cutting-edge algorithms capable of outpacing an army of analysts. From his vantage point above the control floor, Navarro marveled at the system's scope—an achievement once deemed science fiction. With a mere keystroke, he could extract intimate details about any resident's life: employment, finances, health records, and even personal relationships.

Despite his pride, Navarro was a man marked by both physical and emotional scars. Of Italian and Greek heritage, he liked to imagine himself a descendant of the ancient Spartans, warriors renowned for their discipline and agility. Yet, time had diminished his actual physical prowess. Once a lean and formidable fighter, his reflection now revealed graying temples and a bald crown. A bad limp, the result of a military ambush during the Gulf War, reminded him daily of his vulnerability.

The ambush had left him with a shattered hip, a broken arm, and two fingers amputated. Though he'd survived, thanks to Kurdish rebels and subsequent medical evacuation to Germany, the ordeal reshaped his life. Declared unfit for active duty in the field, rather than going into quiet retirement from the military, Navarro had been reassigned, at his request, to defense intelligence, where he honed his skills in wiretapping and counter-surveillance—a pivot that eventually drew the attention of Wall Street.

In the post-9/11 chaos, Navarro's tactical brilliance shone. His emergency plans earned the support of New York's financial elite, culminating in the birth of THEATRES. To sidestep constitutional challenges, its operations were privatized, ensuring no civil rights lawsuits could claim government overreach. By 2008, the system was an omnipresent force, logging faces, vehicles, and conversations with unparalleled efficiency.

Navarro leaned back in his office chair, sipping coffee brought by his assistant, Susanna Maloney. Smart, efficient, and charming, Susanna had been his trusted aide for years. While her presence sometimes stirred sexual thoughts in his mind, he kept them suppressed, Navarro valued her professionalism.

The routine evening was interrupted by a young operator with troubling news: a partial blackout of surveillance feeds in downtown Brooklyn. Navarro limped his way forward, following the young man as they exited to the control room. Moments later, they stood at the operator's monitoring station. As expected, the monitor displayed a blank screen.

Navarro sat down, adjusted the controls, and engaged the touch-sensitive zoom feature. The console was user-friendly, akin to a video gaming machine. He zoomed out until the display reverted to a map covering a large section of Brooklyn.

"There..." the young man suggested, pointing to a specific area on the map.

Navarro zoomed in, and clicked on "street view," but the screen filled with static instead of a video feed.

It was impossible to see or hear anything. Navarro typed the reset protocol and waited. The subsystem computer rebooted rapidly, but it didn't resolve the issue. The screen and speaker remained filled with static.

Navarro looked at his watch again. It was now reading 10:40 PM. Five minutes had passed. Soon, the system would restore itself.

"We might need to reboot the entire system," he noted. "In the meantime, send an NYPD team and a repair crew to the area."

"Yes, sir," the young man replied. "But it'll take at least 10 to 15 minutes to get people there..." As it turned out, however, the time factor quickly became unimportant. Suddenly, at 10:41 PM, as if by magic, the relevant video feed flickered back onto the screen. Although the area was dark, the infrared imaging made it relatively clear. A drunken man staggered down the street, mumbling incoherently. The young operator shook his head, confused.

"I don't understand it... should I still send the NYPD?" he asked.

"Go ahead and do that," Navarro replied, smiling, as he made his way back to his office, his walking stick helping him along the way.

He turned back to the young man and added,

"And email the programming team. We'll see what they have to say..."

Chapter 3 – FIVE YEARS LATER

Jim Bentley grabbed his coffee and headed to the bank's car loan office at 9:30 AM sharp. Another day at Bolton Sayres, another assignment no one else wanted. As a young lawyer working at his father-in-law's bank—a position secured through his marriage to Laura Stoneham, the CEO's daughter—he'd jumped at the chance for courtroom experience. But, a real estate foreclosure case seemed bizarre for an investment bank.

In the fourth sub-basement, Leroy White was just finishing waxing a burgundy BMW 528i. The 60-year-old transplant from Mississippi managed the bank's fleet of luxury cars with meticulous pride, his position secured through his own son-in-law's political connections in New York's Black community. Though illiterate, Leroy knew every vehicle like the back of his hand.

"Morning, Mista Bentley," Leroy called out with a broad smile. "She's all ready fer ya."

After a quick check of Jim's paperwork, Leroy handed over the ignition token. "Don't forget me at Christmas now," he added with a wink.

The BMW's silent cabin made Jim think of his own 2002 Chevy Cavalier. It was still gathering dust in a Manhattan garage. He hadn't touched it since moving to the city. What was the point? Most bank employees relied on subways and taxis; many didn't even have licenses. But Jim liked driving, even if opportunities were rare these days.

Laura's words echoed in his mind: "Money doesn't matter."

That was easy for her to say—she'd never known anything but wealth. She'd drawn him to New York despite his hatred of city life, and he'd followed for love. But everything had changed since their marriage, especially after their daughter's birth. His wife's dramatic weight gain had transformed her into someone he barely recognized.

What choice did he have? Their daughter needed him, and he wouldn't abandon his responsibilities as a father. Still, he couldn't help but wonder what remained of their relationship beneath the weight of all these changes. They hadn't had sex for months.

By 10:00 AM, the BMW was cruising north on the New York Thruway toward Clarksville, the county seat of Verde County. The journey took him from Manhattan's concrete jungle to the pristine Catskill Mountains, where 76,000 residents lived among rolling farmland and tourist destinations. The courthouse—a 19th-century Roman-style building of red sandstone—dominated the small town of 20,000.

At 1:40 PM, Jim slipped into the traditional courtroom, taking a seat several rows behind the other pinstriped lawyers. Before Judge Floyd Van Hewing sat two attorneys: Jeb Knight, a respected Kingston lawyer known for representing big businesses, and Albert Bennington, a local sole practitioner.

Knight rose to speak.

"Your honor, as my colleague admitted in his paperwork, NY Code Section 3212 provides that creditors have no claim upon life insurance if the named beneficiary survives the deceased."

"Doesn't that mean I have to deny your motion?" Judge Van Hewing interrupted.

"No, your honor. Our bank is one of Thomas Mattingly's creditors, but as you know, back in 2009, the bodies of three members of the Mattingly family were found dead in their home in Paradise. A forensic investigation proved that the cause of death of the wife and son was murder, followed by the father's suicide..."

"Why would the insurance company pay out on a suicide?" the judge cut in.

"The policy was purchased over two years before the suicide," Knight explained. "Suicide exclusions are active for 2 years. After that, it's assumed that a suicide wasn't done for financial gain."

"I see..."

"No one disputes that his wife, Sarah Mattingly, was the named beneficiary of the policy and that she died 2 hours before her husband."

"What difference does it make?"

"It means that Sarah did not survive him. Therefore, her beneficiary status never kicked in. The only surviving heir is Thomas Mattingly's grandson," Knight pointed out. "But, since he was NOT a named beneficiary, and New York law protects only named beneficiaries, the money must be paid into the estate."

"And, then, of course, to the creditors, which means to your bank, right?" the judge finished.

"Exactly, your honor."

The judge leaned forward. "If I grant your motion, the boy will, in practical terms, be left with nothing, because your client will take every penny, minus administration costs."

"Maybe, your honor. But, that's the law, and we're all sworn to uphold the law."

"How do we know that the omission of the boy was not an oversight by his grandfather on the insurance policy?" The judge asked.

"It doesn't matter," the lawyer argued, "because there's no basis for a potential heir to receive life insurance proceeds, in preference to the Estate of the deceased, unless he is named in the policy."

"How much is the debt?"

"The line of credit was $25 million. Of that, Thomas Mattingly had drawn down $1.4 million. The appraisal on the house comes to $738,000. The remaining balance is $642,545.34, including foreclosure costs."

"Mr. Knight..." the judge's voice hardened. "Part of this court's job is to protect widows and orphans..."

"The appraisal, I might add, is very generous," Knight continued, undeterred. "The bank will almost certainly get less money on the subsequent sale...but we've agreed to take ownership at the appraised value."

The judge flipped through his file.

"I don't like taking away an insurance policy from an orphan..."

"Your honor," Knight stated proudly, "You won't be taking it away, because he never had it. Bolton Sayres provided a line of credit of $25 million, on very thin collateral. They have a right to be repaid."

"Why would they do that?" the judge pressed. "Why would they loan someone up to $25 million–dollars, based on collateral consisting of a farm worth only $700,000?"

Knight paused before responding.

"Your honor, this wouldn't be the first time the bank's helped someone achieve a dream, even at great risk. That's what banking is about. That's why we've got to collect this money. We work hard to reduce our losses, to make sure we can help more people."

"Oh, please...spare me..." the judge commented.

"Thomas Mattingly's dream," Knight continued, "was to build a ski resort. My client tried to help him achieve that dream. It must recoup what it can and, even after we collect this money from the Estate, we'll still have lost a great deal of money."

"I represented Catskill Bank of Commerce, before it was taken over," the judge grumbled. "Lending so much money, with so little collateral, well, frankly, it seems like a serious violation of the executive's fiduciary duty to shareholders. You don't give away money to back crazy schemes..."

As Albert Bennington prepared to respond, Jim frantically reviewed the file he regretted not reading thoroughly earlier. Something wasn't right. Bolton Sayres was an investment bank that packaged mortgages into bonds—it never actually wrote the mortgages itself. The case made no sense. The bank dealt in stocks, bonds, and derivatives, not personal loans. Official policy explicitly prohibited ownership of any illiquid assets, that is, any property that couldn't be quickly traded on the exchanges. Real estate loans, generally speaking, are one of the most illiquid assets known to man.

Lost in thought about Bolton Sayres' business practices, Jim's attention snapped back as the opposing lawyer stood up for his chance to speak and Bennington's voice rang out:

"Your honor, it would be outrageous to award life insurance to a greed mongering bank!"

Bennington pointed to a woman in the third pew. "This young mother is a widow, made so by a terrible tragedy. Her young and innocent child, an orphan boy, less than 4 years old, has no father. He did have a grandfather who, no doubt, would have expected the life insurance proceeds to go to his grandson. Is this young boy going to become a ward of the state?"

"Objection, your honor!" Knight jumped to his feet.

"Overruled," the judge barked.

"But, Mr. Bennington is appealing to emotion and suggesting that you ignore the law!"

"You've been overruled!" Judge Van Hewing barked at the bank's lawyer, and then turned to his nephew, Bennington, "Are you suggesting that I ignore the law?"

"Of course not."

"What legal citations support your position?"

"The rule of fairness and equity prohibits unjust enrichment, and the rule of pretermission of unborn children."

"Objection, Your Honor," the bank's lawyer exclaimed, "there is no rule of pretermission of unborn children!"

"Overruled." the judge said, and then asked his nephew, "Do you have some cases or statutes that support your argument?"

"No," Bennington admitted and, then, added, passionately, "But, we all know what's right and wrong."

"That doesn't hold up on appeal," the judge muttered. "Anything in rebuttal, Mr. Knight?"

"There's nothing to rebut. The law is clear. Mr. Bennington can't make a decent legal argument, because there are none to be made. The boy is not a named beneficiary. His client has no case. It's as simple as that."

The judge scribbled some notes, as he spoke:

"Gentlemen, I won't be deciding this today. As you know, I've ordered mediation, and I expect both sides to engage in good-faith negotiations. Can I trust you both to do that?"

Both lawyers agreed, and as they gathered their papers, Jim rummaged through his own. Among the documents in his briefcase, he caught a glimpse of the foreclosure judgment: "In re: The Estate of Thomas Mattingly – Bolton Sayres Holding Corporation v. The Estate of Thomas Mattingly." The loan documents attached to the complaint caught his eye. The borrower's signature line showed both a clear signature and typed full name. But the bank's signature was entirely illegible, with no typed name underneath. Who at the bank had authorized this irregular loan?

Jim intercepted Mr. Knight, the bank's attorney, as he headed for the door.

"My name's Jim Bentley," He explained, "I'm with the legal department at Bolton Sayres."

"Hi, Jim." Knight's welcome was hearty. "They told me you were coming. Let's talk for a moment, outside..."

In the hallway, Knight whispered, "As I told your colleague, Tim Cohen, this case is a slam dunk."

"The judge didn't seem too enthusiastic about finding in our favor..."

"If he decides against us, we'll win on appeal. Even if the law wasn't on our side, he should have recused himself—Bennington's his nephew."

"How about mediation?"

"Just a formality," Knight waved dismissively. "The judge wants his nephew to make money. We won't offer anything."

"But then..." Jim hesitated, already planning to seek settlement authority, "Why am I here? What's the point?"

"Actually, there isn't any particular point, never has been. The judge ordered mediation. Corporations have to be represented by someone, and I can't be the representative, because I'm the lawyer. So, you're here. Simple as that."

"Sounds like a waste of time."

"Might be, but it's the law." Knight shrugged. "Mediation's at three, across the street in Bennington's office—the Lawyer's Building."

In the courthouse café, Jim mechanically ate his egg salad sandwich while trying to reach Murray Sachs, his supervisor. The idea of offering nothing in mediation just didn't sit right. Even a small settlement would be better than leaving the boy with nothing. But Murray was a stickler for rules and hated risk—he wouldn't budge without approval from above.

Desperate after being rebuffed by Murray, Jim tried calling his father-in-law, the highest authority at the bank. It was a risky move. Jeremy Stoneham had never hidden his contempt for the man who'd won his daughter's heart. Everything—the job, the salary—was done solely to keep Laura in New York City. But, his father-in-law's secretary had long since been trained to stop putting Jim's calls through during business hours. So, with 3:00 PM approaching, Jim gave up and headed to mediation.

Bennington's office sat right across the street. Inside, five people had already gathered around a long polished conference table when Jim arrived slightly late: Mr. Bennington, Mr. Knight, the widow Sandra Mattingly, and the court-appointed mediator.

"Sorry, I'm a bit late..." Jim apologized.

The woman didn't match the expectations he had of grieving widows. Sandra Mattingly was slim and fresh-faced, like an untouched maiden off the farm. Her soft smile when they shook hands, combined with her brown hair, green eyes, wide hips, and narrow waist struck him immediately. At barely 22, wearing a low-cut dress that accentuated her curves, she looked nothing like a grieving widow. Jim did the math—she must have become pregnant at 17, just before her husband died.

What sort of widow dressed so provocatively? Of course, many years had passed since her husband's death. No one could grieve forever. Still, any competent lawyer would have ensured his client wore more appropriate attire. Bennington was clearly riding on his uncle's coattails. He was incompetent for letting her dress this way for a mediation. Her delicate perfume drifted across the table, and, as he looked at her, the feelings she stirred, inside him, made him uncomfortable. How could a woman on the opposing side—a widow, no less—affect him this way?

He loved his wife, didn't he? But they hadn't been intimate in a very long time. Their baby's endless crying kept them up at night, and Laura wasn't very interested now that she was breastfeeding. If he was honest with himself, though, it was mainly his choice—the intense attraction he'd once felt for his wife had faded along with the expansion of her waistline.

The mediation dragged on, and Jim found his sympathies growing alongside his attraction. As a Bolton Sayres employee, he was duty-bound to represent the bank's interests. But a strange idea took hold. He had no settlement authority. What if he offered money anyway? His father-in-law was CEO of the bank. Sure, Laura's father didn't like him, and Murray Sachs might complain to the personnel committee, maybe even try to get him fired. But in the end, Sachs was powerless—he couldn't risk his own job, and Jeremy Stoneham wasn't going to let him get fired, leaving his daughter with an unemployed husband. That was the beauty of nepotism.

The thought made him uncomfortable. Using his connections this way would make him everything he despised. Normal lawyers got fired for such things, but he was protected. His father-in-law might despise him, but loved his daughter and granddaughter. Any rule violation would be swept under the rug. Even if the worst case scenario actually happened, and he got himself fired, what was the harm? He didn't like his job anyway, hated New York City and wanted to leave. Getting fired would give him that opportunity.

After more than an hour of fruitless discussion, and seemingly endless excessive demands from Bennington who should have known he had no case, and no offers from the bank, Jim couldn't take it anymore.

"On behalf of Bolton Sayres, I can offer you $50,000 maximum," he blurted out.

Silence fell. The face of the bank's trial lawyer, Jeb Knight, lost all color. If accepted, the case would end, along with his juicy fees. But Bennington simply shook his head, taking the offer as a sign of weakness.

"Not a penny less than $200,000," he repeated. "As you know, there's no way the judge will put this family in the poorhouse."

"You've got a 100% chance of losing, because the law is against you," Jim pointed out, not considering the fact that the Judge was Bennington's uncle.

"I suppose you're making the offer, then, out of the goodness of your heart?" Bennington snapped.

"Actually – yes," Jim replied. "I'm just trying to close this case, so the family will have something. Because even if your uncle decides in your favor, you'll lose on appeal."

"I beg to differ!"

"You've got no statutes or case–law to back you up. The language of the statute is clearly against you..."

This back and forth banter went on for a while longer. But, by 4:30, much to the relief of the bank's local counsel, they had reached no settlement. During breaks, the local litigator's anger about the unauthorized offer had become clear. He would certainly report it to Murray Sachs with a disciplinary recommendation. But Jim didn't care. He knew that $50,000 was meaningless to the bank, which would earn $20 billion in annual profit that year. Of course, unauthorized settlement offers violated bank rules and legal ethics. But, Jim wasn't concerned with that. He just wanted to do the right thing.

The drive to the tiny town of Paradise took over an hour through winding Catskill roads. The region was beautiful, but not all mountains make good ski resorts. Jim knew enough about skiing to see through the scheme. The mountains near Paradise were foothills—too low, too close to the Hudson Valley, and had insufficient snowfall to stay white for long. Competition from established resorts like Hunter Mountain, with infinitely better slopes, made the plan's foolishness even clearer. Only an idiot would approve such a loan. He wondered about that as he drove. It wasn't clear who had signed off on it because there was no typed bank representative's name on the contract and the signature was illegible.

The Mattingly farm was beautiful from afar—rolling acres against three heavily forested slopes. Up close, however, the reality set in: wild overgrown fields, a termite-infested picket fence, and a large but deteriorating house built in 1886. Its white wood shingles hadn't seen paint in decades, and the paint that remained was peeling off in large sections. The winter-browned grass was so high it had gone to seed. The place was rotting away.

Finding no real estate agent waiting, Jim used his key. Inside, darkness and musty air greeted him. All furniture lay draped with coverings, even the mirrors, prepared for a long absence. Years of emptiness had let cobwebs grow large enough to block corners of the foyer. The polished oak floors had lost their shine beneath thick dust.

Upstairs, he found three bedrooms. Two looked untouched for a century, but the boy's room stood out with modern Ethan Allen furniture—not cheap, he knew from shopping with Laura. Was it the former room of the four-year-old boy? Unlikely, since he would have been less than one when the family left after the initial foreclosure. A worn baseball bat and mitt rested in one corner, with Yankees and Mets emblems on the walls. Jim guessed this had been the dead father's boyhood room, not his son's.

The stink in the air drove Jim to wrestle with a stuck window. As he struggled with it, his foot caught an uneven floorboard. The window finally opened, but he heard a loud cracking sound underneath his foot. Looking closer at the floor, he found that there was no damage to the wood. Instead, there was a tin, hinged opening, a secret compartment. Inside lay a thick red leather-bound book with golden edges. Dusting it off revealed the title:

"DIARY OF ROBERT MATTINGLY"—the murdered father of the boy now fighting for his grandfather's insurance money.

He hesitated. This was private, carefully hidden from prying eyes. But what harm could reading a dead man's diary do? He opened to a random page:

"July 24, 2008

Dear Diary:

Two nights ago, near the road, we saw two men carrying a bag that looked like it had a body inside..."

"Hello?" a woman's voice called from downstairs.

Jim quickly closed the diary and slipped it into his briefcase.

"I'm up here!" he called back.

The real estate agent, Jane Simon, waited below—a middle-aged, blonde, blue-eyed woman whose layers of fat masked former beauty. She seemed like an older, more worn version of his own wife. Beauty is fleeting, Jim decided, and just like Laura's, Jane's had been worn down—in her case, not just by age or childbirth, but by a string of former husbands and lovers, none of whom had given her children. Well into her mid-40s, she'd learned not to depend on men, making her way selling rural real estate despite her minimal education.

They exchanged awkward handshakes and pleasantries before getting down to business.

"We normally provide the listing contract," she noted before signing his paper.

"I understand, but remember, we're a bank. Big bureaucracies have big rules, and one of those is that we always write the contracts."

It was true and not true. The bank did try to write its contracts. But this was different. There was no standard form for a listing agreement in the legal department's database. He'd had to search the Westlaw database to find a template to use, and he had drafted a custom agreement himself.

After pleasant conversation and a thorough tour of the bank-owned house, it was time to leave.

"I'll be in touch," she promised, heading out.

As they walked to their cars, Jim's stomach rumbled.

"Is there a decent place to eat around here?"

"Paddy's Diner," she suggested. "A lot of tourists go there. It's in downtown Paradise."

Later, sitting in the diner, Jim checked his watch: nearly 8 p.m. He pulled out his phone.

"Laura? Yeah, it's me... I know, I know. It's late. I don't want to wake the baby but, frankly, there's nothing I can do about the timing now. The meeting ran overtime, and I had to check out this property..."

He sighed, wondering if he should mention the diary now burning a hole in his briefcase. No, this wasn't the time. And given the contents, he certainly didn't want to discuss it over the telephone.

Chapter 4 – MARCUS DUNLOP

On March 19, 2008, the morning sun glinted off New York Harbor, casting long shadows across the luxury office suite high atop the Bolton Sayres Tower. Five years before Jim Bentley's drive north toward the tiny town of Paradise, NY, another man was very busy doing what he did almost every morning, as the Statue of Liberty stood as a silent witness to his morning routine.

At twenty-five, Marcus Dunlop represented banking royalty. He was the son of Christopher Dunlop, the patriarch of the powerful family behind W.T. Fredericks Bank. Though his door carried the modest title "Quantitative Investment Analyst," his true role ran far deeper. In banking, titles mean little; the size and placement of one's office told the real story. Dunlop's office was large, well-appointed with fine furniture, and commanded a sweeping view of the harbor. These were all the marks of genuine importance.

The young woman in his office zipped up her tight jeans with practiced grace, adjusting her silver belt buckle before pulling on her pink top.

"You turn me on... you, handsome man," she cooed in accented English, running her fingers down his chest.

Dunlop's perfectly chiseled features twisted into an amused smile. With his impressive height, dark hair, and light brown eyes, he could have attracted any woman he wanted. But traditional relationships came with complications he preferred to avoid.

"You're so beautiful, baby," he said, reaching for his wallet. "But I need to work."

Her eyes tracked across the office, searching. "Tell me vat you do, again?"

"It's too complicated..."

"I understand lots of tings." Her smile widened as she watched him take out the first hundred-dollar bill. Finding her missing hairpin, she pressed, "Smart girl, I am... tell me vhat you do..."

He studied her for a moment, knowing he would share nothing—not even the sanitized version of his role.

"Yes, you're not only smart," he said, drawing out ten one-hundred-dollar bills one by one, "You're expensive, too..."

To the outside world, Marcus Dunlop was a habitual liar, cheat, drunkard, and whore monger. But within the banking cartel, where traditional values held little sway, he was the golden child—a rising star with a perfect pedigree. His true power, however, lay not in his lineage but in the software running on his computers.

Through "wash trading" and other techniques, his programs orchestrated an elaborate dance of buying and selling between cartel member banks. They reimbursed each other's gains and losses, manipulating market prices at will through carefully choreographed transactions. These artificial prices were then reported on public exchanges as if they were legitimate market movements, with only the highest-ranked banking officials aware of the deception.

The alliance between Bolton Sayres and W.T. Fredericks ran deeper than anyone outside the inner circle could have suspected. While business journals described them as competitors, they had evolved into branches of one shadowy organization, their interests so deeply intertwined with each other and with the cartel that separation would bring down the entire system. For all intents and purposes, the two huge banks were actually one.

"You have to pay for top qvality, darling..." she purred, her previous questions forgotten as she stuffed the bills into her purse.

She settled onto his lap for one last embrace. Dunlop glanced at the clock—6:20 AM. Beautiful as she might be, the girl had overstayed her welcome. His morning visits from prostitutes typically happened in the early morning hours between 4:30 and 5:30, and the girls normally left no more than an hour later.

"OK," he said, "But I do have a lot of things I need to start working on..."

She took the hint and sashayed to the door, throwing a flirtatious look, smile, and blown kiss over her shoulder.

"Good riddance," he thought, watching the clock tick to 6:30.

Marc Dunlop's special secure phone buzzed right on schedule. Time for the daily London call. The phone was military-grade hardware – the kind spies use, impossible to hack or break.

"Hello..."

"Hi, Marc!"

"What's going on in London?" Dunlop asked his cousin Jennett, who'd taken over his old job at the London desk of Bolton Sayres.

"Nothing unusual. Everything's normal this morning." Jennett replied.

Dunlop held back a smile. His cousin was an idiot, but that's exactly why he'd picked him for the job. Someone smarter might figure out that what they were doing was a violation, not only of the law, but of the banking cartel's governing rules, and report it. If British officials, for example, ever caught on, the bribes to keep them quiet would cost a fortune.

"What did the Bank of England say?"

"They said 'no.'"

"That's exactly what I expected."

"Why do we even need them?" Jennett asked, confused.

"Because they've got real gold in their vaults, and we don't," Dunlop explained like he was talking to a child. "When we mess with gold prices on paper, it often stimulates a lot of physical demand. Some people, especially in places like India and China, demand real gold. The Bank of England needs to have enough real gold on hand, or our whole plan falls apart."

"But they said no. Something about the US Treasury not signing some papers..."

Dunlop decided to explain it to his dim cousin.

"Look, it's like this: It's called a 'swap lien.' The Bank of England will lend us gold, but only if the US promises to give them gold from Fort Knox if we can't pay it back. It's like having Uncle Sam co-sign a loan. The whole thing gets arranged through a Swiss bank called the Bank of International Settlements, and that helps keep it all secret."

"But who actually owns the gold, then?"

"Lots of people – small countries, banks like us, rich folks. They all store this gold at the Bank of England, but here's the trick: they just get a piece of paper that says they own some gold – not specific gold bars. So the Bank of

England can legally do whatever it wants with the actual gold until someone demands it back."

"Why can't we just take the gold from Fort Knox?" Jennett asked, "The Treasury is our customer, isn't it?"

"Congress would throw a fit. It's political suicide."

"What if the Bank of England demands the gold back from America?"

"Then there's trouble," Dunlop admitted. "But usually, after we drive down the price, we can buy back the gold back, cheaper, from mining companies."

"What if it doesn't work? I've bet almost everything I have on this..." Jennett complained.

Dunlop smiled at his cousin's naïveté and nervousness.

"Listen," he said, "this is why we do it through Switzerland. Everyone pretends they're not involved. The US Treasury doesn't like promising gold as backup, but they know they have to. Without these deals, they couldn't control gold prices. And if they can't control gold, people might start thinking it's more trustworthy than dollars."

Then came the bombshell.

"Marc..." Jennett's voice shook. "I need to tell you something... I... I didn't place the bets like you said..."

"WHAT?!"

"We seemed to be losing so much money!" Jennett tried to explain.

Dunlop wanted to reach through the phone and strangle his cousin. The whole plan involved losing money on paper, at first! The two men were front running, that is, trying to make a nice profit from a US government supported gold price suppression event. Betting that gold prices would crash wasn't just a bet. It was a certainty. Dunlop's own software would ensure that prices crashed, just as they had done so many times in the past. But, you had to place the downside bets, that is, the "puts" while prices were still high – that was the way you made big money.

"For Christ's sake," he finally exploded, "our people run the god-damned Treasury and the Federal Reserve!"

But it was too late. His idiot cousin had just cost them millions in profit. But, in spite of what he had done, all the man could think about was lunch!

"I'm heading to Jersey's Steakhouse," he said cheerfully, completely missing his cousin's fury.

"Yeah, sure," Dunlop growled, slamming down the phone. "Fucking idiot!"

It was now 7:07 AM.

He tried to think through the problem. What if he quietly added some puts on the regulated exchanges? No—too risky. This close to the operation, it would draw attention from regulators or the banking cartel itself. Within the cartel, one rule governed government-sponsored market manipulations: banks as entities could reap huge profits, but individual profiteering was prohibited.

He walked to his door and surveyed the sea of cubicles beyond. Out there was the domain of the line traders—all simpletons. None understood their role in the upcoming operation. They'd blindly follow his supposed technical analysis, never guessing they were part of a vast scheme orchestrated by him and sponsored by the government.

The bots would paint a new price picture. Bank-based and independent traders, including those associated with Bolton Sayres, would join in the momentum, not because they wanted to participate in corruption, but because of the chart patterns created by Dunlop's bots. Most of the traders were just true believers in chart patterns, blind to how easily the tape could be painted. Federal Reserve money would back the operation, but the well-painted chart was the key. False momentum and their reaction would kickstart everything. If convincing enough, the story would become a self-fulfilling prophecy. A successful operation always generated more than enough profit to repay the seed money and reward the banks. Regulators looked away regarding institutional profits—everyone understood banks had to profit. Personal side bets, like the ones he was making with his cousin, were frowned upon.

Another glance at his watch. Not quite 7:30.

His Treasury contact, Wolff Grubman, should have called already. Doubt gnawed at him. His cousin had acted unpredictably—what if this public official did too? One change in timing could implode all their side bets, leaving him in debt.

He began thinking. What was it like to not have money? He couldn't imagine it. From childhood allowances to yearly banking bonuses, Dunlop had always been wealthy. But what if everything fell apart?

He opened an investment spreadsheet and stared at the screen. He'd already put down $500,000 on a Caribbean island—just the deposit. The full $10 million purchase price loomed ahead, plus millions more for development. Wave breakers, sea wall, mansion, Olympic pool, tennis courts, landscaping, helicopter pad—it would all require money. Money he had counted on being generated by this market manipulation. Jennett's stupidity had jeopardized it all.

7:37 AM. Should he call Grubman? No—that would reek of desperation...

Then, the phone suddenly rang and he lunged for it.

"Hello."

"Marc?"

Relief flooded through him at hearing Grubman's voice. The man specialized in currencies for the Exchange Stabilization Fund, a Treasury division housed at the New York Federal Reserve on Liberty Street. The man was a middle-aged Brooklynite who had never lost his thick accent.

"What's the scoop?" Dunlop asked eagerly.

"I'm not sure you're gonna' like 'dis, but..."

Dunlop's hand trembled slightly on the receiver. Thank God for audio-only calls!

"What, what is it?" He asked.

"I jus' got off da' phone with Treasury, a few minutes ago."

"Treasury?" Dunlop thought to himself, *"You ARE the goddamned fucking Treasury!"*

"Dey needs you ta' staut right away."

Dunlop exhaled, realizing he'd been holding his breath. It was a relief to hear that.

"Excellent! I'm set to start. I just need the cash and the gold."

"You got it," Grubman stated, "but dere only lookin' for a $150 drop 'dis time. Dey wanna' prove a point but not spend too much gold, ya undastand?"

"Anyways, you got $460 million in cash, fer da performance bonds."

"That's only half what I asked for..." Dunlop complained.

"Don't worry," Grubman replied. "We can give ya more cash if ya need it."

Of course, they could. The Fed printed unlimited money, handing it out through various "loan windows." Any well-connected bank could perpetually renew these theoretical "overnight" loans—they were essentially gifts. But it wasn't cash he needed. It was gold.

"Having cash to buy performance bonds isn't what I'm worried about..." Dunlop stated.

Performance bonds are the required deposits that are demanded by futures exchanges before they will allow a trader to control a set amount of a traded commodity, including gold. The bonds represent a tiny fraction of the commodity's real value. Fed cash was always abundant at a big bank like Bolton Sayres. The cash covered such requirements.

Having cash was crucial for market intervention, but after a certain critical amount of cash, his bots didn't need much more. The bots primarily dealt in wash trading. Cartel member banks traded futures between themselves, reimbursing each other for losses per prior agreement. The fake trading network was carefully designed to fool non-connected traders.

But, even the fake network needed "seed cash" because to make trades appear legitimate, third parties had to be allowed access. Human hands couldn't keep up with trading bots. Neither could most lesser trading bots deployed by independent traders. But, on occasion, real third-party traders did end up in-between fake trades. When this happened, money had to be paid to settle the small number of wash trades gone wrong. Given the size and number of the transactions, this often ended up mounting into tens of millions of dollars.

Because the Fed printed unlimited cash at the request of any big bank, the only real check against Dunlop's brand of fraud has always been the physical gold market. In theory, any commodity traded on a futures exchange could see its price set anywhere from zero to infinity. But for goods like gold, which are ultimately real physical products, if too low of an artificial price were set, it triggered real-world demand spikes, especially in China and India. Banks, like Bolton Sayres, hold only enough physical gold in their own vaults to satisfy less than 1% of the amount pledged. That meant that running out of gold was a persistent problem.

Price manipulators walked a tightrope—finding the lowest price that wouldn't trigger systemic collapse through physical demand. U.S. government-guaranteed physical gold supplies were crucial to smoothing out pricing errors. Without it, the whole system would collapse, as the nature of the game required extreme highs and lows. Extremely low prices could never be maintained indefinitely, but periodic price crashes could create sufficient volatility to scare conservative investors away from gold and into government-preferred paper investments. That was the ultimate goal.

"I need physical gold, not just cash," Dunlop barked.

"You know, yous guys ain't returned even one gold bar in 28 years!" Grubman complained.

"Returning the gold bars isn't part of my job description," Dunlop insisted, "Protecting the ability of the government to borrow is."

"I was just tryin' to explain what's goin' on." Grubman excused himself.

Physical gold scarcity had driven a 2001–2008 price surge. Previously, European governments had been convinced to supply the gold needed for price suppression. Europe had tired of selling, and the Bush administration had grown wary of gold swap liens.

"Shrinking gold supplies are taken seriously, you know," Grubman continued. "How could we eva explain dis if de outside woyald ever discovered it?"

"There's always a price for stability," Dunlop countered.

Both were standard arguments within their circle. Stability justified sacrifice—continued depletion of government gold reserves to suppress prices. But everyone was becoming concerned about the depletion, just in case Congress ever demanded an audit of US gold reserves.

"Some are feelin' dat' da cost of intervening is getting too high."

"Look," Dunlop warned, "if they're not willing to put up the gold, we're out of business."

"You're speakin' to da choir, ya know, but deys' got priorities above my head."

"Alright, so what's the bottom line?"

"You get tirty' five tons."

"Only thirty-five tons?" Dunlop questioned, his disappointment evident. "You expect me to get a $150 price reduction on the back of thirty-five tons? I've got to deal with London, Switzerland, India, and China!"

"Look, no one expects the reduction ta hold. It's just for show, ya know, now, because of all dis' stuff about banks failing and all dat..."

"I can't wave a magic wand!" Dunlop complained.

"Look, I'm not really 'autorized to tell ya dis, but, uh..." Grubman hesitated.

"Tell me..."

"Des actually got 60 tons allocated. I'm supposed to tell ya only tirty' five, ta keep ya on dee up and up, understand?"

"No problem," Dunlop replied. "I never heard it from you."

"Good," Grubman said, "'Cause ifen ya did, I'd lose my job fer tellin' ya sometin like dat."

Silence hung between them for a moment before Grubman spoke again, his Brooklyn accent thicker than ever. "Dere's somethin' else I wanna' to talk ta you about..."

"What?"

Dunlop tensed. Wolff Grubman was a disgusting little man—someone he had to deal with. The man was too old, too Brooklyn, and frankly too low-class to be more than a necessary business contact.

"I always treated ya right, haven't I?" Grubman continued.

"Sure."

"I always give ya some extra stuff, just like today..."

"Yeah." Dunlop couldn't deny that Grubman was helpful, despite being a disgusting little man.

"I don't gotta' do dat, ya know," Grubman added meaningfully.

Dunlop's heart rate quickened. What was the man getting at? Did he know about the front-running? The arrangement was strictly confidential, protected by a trusted Bahamian lawyer. Breaking Bahamian banking secrecy laws carried serious criminal penalties—the government there took such violations seriously, given how vital the black money banking operations were to their economy.

"I need somethin' from ya..."

Dunlop's stomach clenched. Sharing the cash with Jennett was bad enough—he didn't have a choice, even though his imbecile cousin didn't deserve a dime after what he'd done. But sharing with Grubman? Being blackmailed by him? That was entirely unacceptable. Just thinking about it almost made him want to scream. But he swallowed his rage and said carefully,

"Yeah, of course, if there's anything I can ever do for you, I'll certainly do it."

"Well, I'm figuring it's about time I got somethin' fer me for a change..."

"Here comes the blackmail," Dunlop thought, *"How much is Grubman going to demand?"*

"I applied for a position with W.T. Fredericks," Grubman finally said. "I wanna get on ya' dad's staff."

Relief flooded through Dunlop's body like a soothing balm. The man knew nothing about his side bets. If he did, he didn't care!

"Of course, you've got my highest recommendation," he said quickly.

"Tanks..."

The banking cartel always rewarded its friends—even slimy little men like Grubman, and every government servant understood this. That's why they passed inside information so readily. Former Treasury Secretaries and Federal Reserve Chairmen would look forward to multimillion–dollar consulting gigs or even CEO positions. Or, if they preferred to maintain appearances, they could earn hundreds of thousands or even a million dollars for a single hour's speech.

The revolving door between public and private sectors is perfectly legal. The stench of graft and cronyism runs all the way up into the highest levels of power. But Grubman was not a power player. He was no Fed Chairman—just a small cog in the wheel. The cartel's rewards scaled with the importance and usefulness of the government servant. For someone like Grubman, though, it usually meant a cushy job, a nicely decorated office, and a high six–figure salary without many actual responsibilities.

Still, the thought of Grubman working on his father's staff turned Dunlop's stomach. Would the man still be there when he inherited W.T. Fredericks? No, thank God...he was pushing 60. He would likely be dead by then. That thought provided some comfort.

Ending the call, Dunlop turned to his computer to check the bots' readiness. They were good to go. Before day's end, the portfolio that he and

Jennett had accumulated would shift from deep loss to substantial profit. Within days, all his private positions would be heavily in the money, though because of his idiotic cousin, far from as lucrative as they might have otherwise been.

He glanced at his watch again: 7:55 a.m.

There was still extensive reprogramming needed—there would be no time for the usual prostitutes over the next few days. Crashing the gold market $150 with only 60 tons of physical gold would be challenging, but he was up to the task.

Chapter 5 – MANHATTAN AGAIN

The drive back to Manhattan took all evening. When Jim finally pulled into the Bolton Sayres' Tower, the massive building stood mostly dark, inhabited only by security guards and a few late-working stragglers. The parking garage echoed emptily—unusual for a banking center, until you considered the weekend.

"*Every single loaner car is gone,*" he thought wryly.

Executives were joy-riding against company policy. He seemed to be the only one using a vehicle for actual company business. He wondered if the absence of the BMW he was driving might have been noticed. He could almost hear complaints from the myriad of spoiled, overpaid brats, of all ages, whining about their favorite vehicle not being available for their weekend getaway to the Hamptons.

After depositing the ignition transmitter in the "late return" box, he made a quick detour to a 24-hour mini-mart. Experience had taught him well: angry women required candy or flowers as peace offerings. Laura preferred candy, though he felt a twinge of guilt about giving that to her. Her growing weight problem... Well, he couldn't deny his role in it anymore. Might as well make her happy.

He caught a cab ride, and soon the five-story red brick apartment building in midtown Manhattan that he and his little family called home, welcomed him. It was just after midnight. As he eased the front door open, a soft melody drifted through the apartment to his ears—it was Laura's voice, singing a lullaby, trying to put the baby back to sleep. Following the sound, he carefully pushed open the nursery door.

Laura sat in a rocking chair with little Jenny, and when she saw him, she shot him a pointed glare that needed no translation. She was obviously pissed off at the fact that he was arriving so late. He quietly backed out, closing the door with practiced care.

In their bedroom, he stripped down to his underwear, draping his clothes over a chair. Then, he laid down, and the exhaustion pulled at him, as he stared at the ceiling. Suddenly, he bolted upright, remembering.

"*The diary!*" He thought, as he shot out of bed and made his way to the foyer.

He retrieved the book from his briefcase, studying it thoughtfully.

"*I probably ought to give it to Sandra Mattingly...*" He thought to himself, "*She's the executor after all...*"

But, it wasn't so simple. The diary was obviously the property of the deceased, but the writing inside it was potential murder evidence. The police needed to see it first. He returned to bed, found his place again, and continued reading where he had left off:

"*...Our suspicions were confirmed when the bag tore as they were carrying it, and a man's arm came dangling out. The bigger man stuffed it back in, but then we knew for sure that the two men were burying a body in the woods...*"

It was the diary of the murdered young man—father of the orphaned boy, whose mother was fighting the bank in court. But who was the "we"? He turned the page:

"*It was my first date with Sandra, and this was the last thing I wanted her to see. I just wanted to show her my special glen in the woods...*"

The same Sandra Mattingly, he assumed, as the one fighting Bolton Sayres over the insurance proceeds of her supposedly suicidal and murderous father–in–law. The dates aligned perfectly—July 24, 2008, referencing events from July 22.

Jim would have continued reading uninterrupted were it not for the fact that the bedroom door creaked open, and his wife walked in.

"What are you reading?" Laura asked, stepping inside.

"Nothing important." Jim set the diary on the floor beside the bed.

Laura's eyes caught the red–ribboned box on the dresser. "What's this?"

"A gift," he smiled.

She made a beeline for it, unwrapping it eagerly. Two chocolates disappeared into her mouth with lightning speed, before the box was carried with her toward the bed. Pausing just short of climbing in, she posed in her new Victoria's Secret lingerie—a sight that, given her weight, stirred mixed feelings in Jim. She leaned down, planting a chocolate-flavored kiss on his lips before nuzzling against his shoulder, gazing up at him with devoted eyes.

"I can't stay mad at you, you know..." Laura's voice softened as she snuggled closer. Then, more seriously: "You remember we're going to the zoo tomorrow, with Jennifer?"

Jim nodded. Actually, he hadn't remembered. But, experience had taught him to keep such lapses to himself, if at all possible.

Her hand wandered lower, offering intimate caresses—an apparent reward she was willing to provide him with, as thanks for the candy. Her expensive perfume wafted between them, and Jim realized she must have spent hours planning this seduction. But no amount of perfume, pleasant as it was, could stimulate his interest in her. This ritual for feeling "sexy": elaborate makeup, costly perfume, provocative lingerie might work for her, but it didn't work for him.

What might look alluring on some Victoria's Secret model took on a very different character when it was worn on someone twice her intended size. Like many women who love their husbands but are at a loss at how to please them, Laura seemed blind to the simple truth that only a strict diet would cure what no amount of packaging could disguise.

"*Like mother, like daughter.*" He thought to himself.

When it came to shopping, Laura and her Mom, who was also seriously overweight, were like peas in a pod. They would spend hours shopping together, leaving baby Jennifer with Isabel—the same Hispanic nanny who'd raised Laura. Then, they'd return with various frivolous purchases like tonight's nightgown, as if silk and lace could work transformative magic.

"*If only they'd put that energy into dieting,*" he thought bitterly.

But, neither of them ever would. Could he tell Laura his true feelings? No. It was impossible. The slightest hint about her weight brought tears. Yet, it was a simple fact. The changes toward obesity, which had come since she'd given birth, repelled him. His body might momentarily respond to her touch, but revulsion flooded back as soon as he felt the fatty folds of flesh. Making love to her was like embracing a walrus.

He couldn't help feeling guilty about the way he felt. Love was supposed to be blind, wasn't it? He still loved her, but he didn't want to be with her. It was wrong. But there was nothing he could do about it. Feelings aren't about right or wrong—they simply are what they are. He squeezed his eyes shut, conjuring images of the striking young widow he had met, that morning, from upstate New York. He was imagining Sandra Mattingly naked. It was a twisted fantasy. He felt guilty about it. But, at the moment, the only way he could make his body respond to his wife's touch was to close his eyes and dream about that young woman.

The act itself, once finished, left him feeling empty. What had his life become? How had things devolved to this? Needing fantasies about another woman just to satisfy his wife? He stared at the ceiling as Laura drifted off to sleep. Then, he carefully extracted himself from bed, retrieved the red diary, and slipped off into the living room. Settling onto the sofa, he opened to where he'd left off:

April 8, 2010

"*I finally told Dad. What else could I do? There's a man buried in the woods, right under our soil, and only I know. Who better to go to than Dad? Sandra won't understand...*"

Jim paused, mind racing. Was the corpse he spoke about still buried on the Mattingly farm? Apparently, that seemingly innocent widow was more than just a hottie. She knew a lot more than she had told anyone about. This diary could change everything! The police had it all wrong. A secretly buried body suggested foul play, perhaps a staged suicide. But why target the entire Mattingly family? And, why was Sandra Mattingly hiding what she knew?

He skimmed past mundane entries until another relevant passage caught his eye:

April 17, 2010

"*Sandra's angry at me for telling my father. She says I promised I wouldn't say anything to anyone. But, I had to tell him. He's my dad. Anyway, there's nothing I can do about it now.*"

The clock read 2:30 AM.

Tomorrow's zoo visit loomed. He ought to go to sleep. But, he couldn't stop reading. As a long term fan of murder mysteries, with this one being thrillingly real, he was fascinated. But solving this murder wasn't his job—he needed to hand the diary over to the proper authorities. That was his obligation. And, as an attorney, he knew that. But, if he gave it to the police, afterward, it would be gone, forever...

Or, would it? Not necessarily...

The last thought spurred him into action. Using his desktop scanner, he carefully copied each written page, saving the files to both his laptop and a USB drive. After nearly an hour of painstaking work, he returned the diary to his briefcase and crept back into the bed. Now, he could give the original to the police and keep the copy for private reading. It was a violation, but as long as no one knew, he could indulge himself.

He went back to bed. Yet, sleep eluded him. Instead, his thoughts drifted to his first meeting with Laura at UCLA. He'd been studying at the law library when he'd spotted her. She was stunningly attractive, back then—one of many female students who studied at the law library during finals week. Many of her peers went there because of practical reasons. They'd been instructed, by their older and wiser mothers, that, if you're going to fall in love, you might as well fall in love with someone who would make a lot of money. And, most of them thought hunting for husbands at the law library fulfilled this advice, because many lawyers eventually make very good money. The irony was that Laura did not need a breadwinner.

Unknown to Jim, back then, was that her father's net worth ran to the hundreds of millions of dollars. But her family's wealth didn't insulate her from being heavily influenced by her peer group. She followed the lead that her friends provided, and adopted their shared impression that landing a law or medical student was an ultimate prize.

At first, Jim had been too absorbed in reading to even notice her. But, when he looked up, a pleasing sight caught his eye: a floral summer dress, silky brown hair, sparkling green eyes. Her petite figure was lithe and tanned—perfect bikini body, he'd thought absently. When she caught him staring, she stretched and smiled, speaking that ancient unspoken language that needs no translation. Every movement, every expression—they all screamed invitation without a single word. He accepted that invitation by opening a dialogue.

"Good book?" he whispered.

She giggled, holding up her text.

"You think Physics 101 is a good book?" She laughed.

The title surprised him—in his experience, beautiful girls rarely ventured into hard sciences. He had presumed it was some liberal arts book she was reading. Maybe, about art or culture or something like that.

"I see," he managed to say, scrambling for something more clever, "You'd be surprised at how many people like physics..."

"Maybe, but they'd be nerds for sure..." she teased with another giggle.

"I like physics..."

"If the shoe fits..." She laughed, "I'm taking physics because it's part of the science requirement. Otherwise, I wouldn't go near it. What are you, a physics guy?"

"Do I look like a physics guy?"

She pretended to study him, then shook her head.

"What do I look like?"

"A law student," she answered without hesitation.

"Good guess," He laughed, "I assume that you're not a law student?"

"Bingo!"

"What's a beautiful girl doing in a boring law library like this?" He delivered the line with deliberate cheesiness.

"Boring is exactly what I need right now. I've got finals... I need to cram!" She replied.

Their flirtation was interrupted by a sharp voice from two tables away.

"The problem with undergraduates," snapped Wilma Valdez, "is that they're not mature enough to stop making noise!"

Wilma was well-known in the law school. She was a short, plump girl, with shoulder-length black hair and acne-marked skin. Despite being an exceptional student—President of the Women's Law Society, University Senate member, and winner of the moot court competition—Jim, like many male students, saw her as an unpleasant presence. She and others like-minded women had recently spearheaded a crusade to ban undergraduates from the law library. The campaign had never really been about quiet study. It was about jealousy. It was about preventing pretty co-eds from poaching on the limited supply of male law students. No one would ever admit that, of course, and to say it like it was to invite being labeled a misogynist or worse.

"Wilma, chill out...will ya?" Jim started.

"Oh, go ahead...flirt with your little friend, Jim." Wilma's voice dripped venom. "Flirt as much as you want! You'll just be sorry later, when you fail the Bar...God! You'd think we were in a singles bar or something! You're so disgusting!"

Before Jim could retort and, most likely, get himself in trouble with the far left administration of the school, which forbade such commentary as he was about to make, his new friend intervened and saved him.

"Let's go somewhere and get something to eat..." She said,

She was already packing her physics book, confident of his answer.

"Uh, sure..." he stammered, fumbling with his own books.

Outside, on the law school patio, she turned and extended her hand.

"My name's Laura Stoneham, by the way. What's yours?"

He took her hand awkwardly—handshakes with beautiful women always felt strange.

"I'm Jim."

She giggled, holding his hand longer than necessary.

"Nice to meet you, Jim."

Finally finding his footing, he asked,

"Do you know the origin of handshaking?"

"No." She replied.

"Oh, it's really very interesting..." he began.

As they walked, he explained about warriors and sword arms, about how the gesture meant 'I won't kill you today.' She seemed genuinely entertained by the impromptu history lesson.

"How do you know all this stuff?" She asked.

"I read a lot." He replied.

"I don't really like to read," she admitted.

The campus café was only three minutes away, and Jim struggled to maintain a clever conversation to keep her entertained. They ordered identical meals—burgers, fries, and Cokes. When Laura reached for her purse at the checkout, Jim shook his head.

"It's on me." He declared, "I've got this one..."

"No..." She objected, "I don't believe in that. I can pay for myself."

But, he ignored her and paid anyway.

"Next time, I'm paying..." she insisted.

Over lunch, their conversation meandered from finals to the bar exam, until Laura dropped: "My dad's a lawyer..."

"Really?" Jacked asked.

"But, he doesn't practice law. He works for a bank." She commented.

Jim immediately assumed her father had failed the bar like so many would-be lawyers who end up becoming bank managers or insurance adjusters. So, he tactfully avoided the subject from that point on, not wanting to upset her with any insinuation that her father couldn't be very smart or capable, or that he probably failed the bar exam or anything like that.

"That's interesting," He said, instead, and then, "My goal is to become a trial lawyer. Because I want to fight for the little guy. For what's right and just."

"You mean, like, an ambulance chaser?" she laughed.

"No." He grew serious. "Why do people say stuff like that? I'm talking about doing the right thing; represent honest people who've been screwed by the system, fighting against crooked corporations."

"You're funny," she giggled.

Then, abruptly, he posed a question,

"Have you ever thought about living in New York City?"

"No," he answered honestly. "Never been there. Never want to go. I don't even like the idea of New York City...too big...too crowded...too dirty. Worst of all possible worlds..."

"It's where I'm from," she declared.

Realizing his mistake, Jim tried to think of a way to backpedal.

"Oh," he said. He couldn't think of anything better, but he realized that he might have screwed up in a big way, "Uh...why did you go to UCLA and not, you know, Columbia or NYU?"

"Because I'm studying acting," She replied, "I went to NYU for the first two years. But, I want to do film. The choice was between USC and UCLA. And, USC is in a bad neighborhood, so my Dad wanted me to go to UCLA."

They discussed her film ambitions, and then she asked,

"So, if you want to be a lawyer, why did you go to UCLA, and not, for example, Berkeley?"

"I never applied to Berkeley, but I did apply to Stanford."

"OK, then why not Stanford?" She asked.

"Too expensive. Even with financial aid, I'd have hundreds of thousands of dollars of student loans to pay off after I got out. UCLA is cheap. With financial aid, I'll be less than $100,000 in the hole when I graduate."

"That's still in the hole, isn't it?" she'd commented with practiced concern.

"Yeah, but, hopefully, I'll be able to pay it back," he said.

She hadn't finished more than about half of her burger and a few fries, as she glanced at his empty plate. She laughed.

"Well, good that you're going to be a lawyer because no burger joint will ever hire you...you'd eat up all the profits!"

He joined in her laughter.

The conversation flowed more easily after that – comparing New York's weather to California's, debating Miami versus Los Angeles as warm places to live, exchanging views on countless topics. Finally, he gathered his courage.

"Want to go to a movie tonight?"

Her smile was warm but apologetic.

"I can't." She said, "But don't take that as a 'no.' Just not tonight..."

"Okay," he said, trying to mask his disappointment. "What about tomorrow night?"

She shook her head.

"I can't," she explained. "It's finals week and if I don't do well, my dad will make me go back to NYU."

She pulled out a piece of paper and wrote something down.

"Here, it's my cell number." She said as she handed it to him.

That night, her smiling face had haunted his thoughts. The next day he called her, but she didn't answer or call back. Days passed. He tried again repeatedly, after that. Her image was carved into his memory. But, he never saw her at the library again. Finally, the day after undergraduate finals, his phone rang. It was Laura, calling him back.

"Do you like opera?" she asked.

He didn't like opera at all. The thought of enduring hours of incomprehensible falsetto singing, in some language that he couldn't understand, made him cringe. But seeing her again would be worth the suffering.

"I love opera," he had lied.

Laura, as it turned out, was fluent in both French and Italian. She understood every word of the opera, tears welling in her eyes during the emotional passages.

For the next two weeks, they were inseparable. The cool, dry California summer nights seemed made for young love. They found their own private spot on Malibu beach, where the sea breeze carried salt and promise. Walking barefoot, hand in hand, they paused to watch the sunset paint the horizon. The beach was empty except for them. He turned to her, cradling her face in his hands. Her blue eyes were deep pools, her lips waiting. The faint scent of her perfume mingled with the ocean air. As he pulled her closer, he could feel her warmth. With that kiss, they melted together, sinking into the sand, and their passion crested with the waves. Neither of them suspected that this union had created new life.

As he drifted toward sleeping on the sand, Laura's voice pulled him back.

"Jim?" She asked.

"What?"

"Do you love me?"

He hesitated, hating such questions. But this time, the truth came easily.

"Yes." He replied immediately.

She kissed him again, quickly, and settled beside him.

"I have to leave for New York," she said suddenly.

He sat up, fully awake now.

"What?" He asked, confused.

"I should have told you earlier," she whispered. "I'm sorry."

"I don't understand..."

"I'm going for the summer. You should come with me..."

"I've got to take the bar exam..." He replied.

"After that," she pleaded.

His mind raced. Of course, her parents would expect her home for summer break. How would he stay in touch with her? How could he make sure that she didn't meet someone else? Phone calls and video chats would be fine, but they wouldn't be enough. Nothing could replace her physical presence, her kisses, her touch.

"Can you wait until after I take the Bar?" He asked.

She shook her head.

"My Dad's got all this stuff scheduled," She explained, "But I'll only be gone for three months... and then, I'll be back, and we'll be together again, in the fall."

Three months stretched before him like an eternity. A familiar sadness washed over him. It wasn't just a fear of losing her. There was also the old grief of losing his own parents. Others, like Laura, went home to see family. But he had nowhere to go. His parents' death on the Pacific Coast Highway when he was eleven years old had left him growing up in foster homes. No family, no home, no one.

"Jim!" Laura's voice, in the current real world, cut off his dream about the past, "Wake up! We're going to the zoo. Remember?"

He opened his eyes to find her holding the diary.

"What's this, by the way?" she asked.

"It's a diary."

"Whose diary?"

"It's a complicated story." He explained.

She set the book on the dresser.

"Well, don't tell it to me now. No time. Get dressed!"

Chapter 6 – IMG V. BOLTON SAYRES

The Daniel Patrick Moynihan Courthouse, which is located at 500 Pearl Street, New York, NY is twenty-seven stories of granite, marble, and oak, towering over Foley Square. It is America's second-largest courthouse, home to 60% of the world's banking litigation. Inside one of its modern courtrooms, Jim Bentley and Timothy Cohen sat quietly at the defendant's table, two in-house lawyers along for the ride, a learning experience. Neither of them had much litigation experience.

Cohen leaned over to whisper to Bentley,

"Funny how in-house lawyers never get to handle any of these big cases."

"That's what thousand-dollar-an-hour trial lawyers are for," Bentley offered some wisdom, nodding toward their lead counsel.

The two young men felt lucky to be in the company of such a prominent lead counsel. The man had a wide reputation throughout New York's banking community. He was considered one of the best attorneys in town. Top of the list, with a long list of power connections and an even longer list of successful trials and favorable settlements. That's why Bolton Sayres and others were happy to pay extraordinarily large fees.

The hearing was not a trial. It was a pretrial discovery dispute—an unglamorous process preparatory for the trial, where most cases are truly won or lost. The case of International Megatron Group (IMG) v. Bolton Sayres had dragged on for nearly two years now. Today's motion to compel document delivery was simply another step in what had become a seemingly endless process.

Bentley glanced at Cohen. The latter was now officially serving as Bolton Sayres' official corporate representative. It was a role that had previously belonged to Bentley, but as a result of his unauthorized settlement offer in Verde County, he had been removed from it as part of his punishment. His connections to the top of the bank had saved his job, but his ability to attend matters that were interesting to young lawyers, like this hearing, had been stripped away.

Jim Bentley was attending the hearing on his own time, at the expense of sick leave. Otherwise, he would have been relegated to the unpleasant task of document drafting, which was the only work he was now given, in light of his transgressions. It would be a while before he was allowed to do anything else.

At the podium stood opposing counsel, Dillon Higglestrom, who was representing IMG in the litigation. Despite his unimpressive physical appearance—short pudgy legs, a pug nose, and a prominent bald spot—like his opponent, Higglestrom's reputation preceded him. He also commanded over $1,000 per hour and, again, only the corporate elite could afford his services.

"Your honor," Higglestrom began, nodding to his old Yale classmate, "my name is Dillon Higglestrom. I represent the plaintiff, IMG."

"Go ahead..." the judge prompted.

"My client is a large American multinational corporation," Higglestrom continued. "Three years ago, we made a successful bid for Pan–Euro Bank. However, the EU Competition Commission ruled against the combination."

The judge raised an eyebrow.

"Fair competition rule? Compared to unfair competition?"

"The European Fair Competition Code is their version of our anti–trust statutes," Higglestrom explained. "It prevents monopoly power."

"I see... Go on..."

"We reached an agreement with the EU to buy Pan–Euro, but only if we divested IMG Financial's European operations. So, we hired Bolton Sayres as our investment banker, to find buyers." Higglestrom paused, "After ten months, they found German Fatherland Bank, but then, Bolton Sayres' executives claimed the German bank had decided it wasn't interested in buying our $800 million consumer loan division anymore."

"How much time was left on your EU selling deadline?" the judge interrupted.

"About a month, your honor." Higglestrom explained, "It was a last minute cancellation and, unfortunately, there was no penalty clause in the contract, so they could pull out at will."

"I see..." The judge commented.

"Bolton claimed that the second-highest offer they had received was only $250 million," Higglestrom continued, "And, then, they suddenly found a private equity fund offering $450 million—still a $350 million discount against face value, but $200 million more than the highest offer they alleged that they had ever received for our division."

The judge nodded thoughtfully.

Higglestrom leaned forward, his voice tight with controlled anger.

"My client sold those loans for $450 million, believing there were no better offers. Then we discovered the truth—the 'fund' was actually composed of Bolton Sayres' executives! A week later, they flipped those loans to new buyers, for $700 million."

He paused, letting that sink into the judge's mind.

"Now, during the process of discovery, we took the testimony of the German Fatherland Bank's Vice President. He testified, under oath, that he always wanted the consumer loans. They never withdrew their offer. Bolton's people lied to both them and us. They told them we had refused to sell! Those lies netted the Bolton execs about $250 million in profit in just one week, when they flipped the portfolio."

The judge raised an eyebrow.

"Based on this testimony," Higglestrom continued, "we've amended our complaint to include fraud, breach of fiduciary duty, and unjust enrichment. We're seeking both compensatory and punitive damages."

"That's all very interesting," the judge interrupted, "but what do you want me to do today?"

A slight smile crossed Higglestrom's face—he'd been waiting for this question. Everything the judge wanted to know was already in the file, but it was all in writing, the judge's clerk was ill, and he hadn't personally read the motion. So, the lawyer carefully began his oral explanation.

"The German VP testified that every meeting took place on the premises of the London branch of Bolton Sayres, and that every meeting was recorded by consent of the parties. He provided this consent agreement, marked as exhibit 'A.'"

Higglestrom moved swiftly, distributing copies to Bolton's counsel and the judge via the bailiff. "Your honor, Bolton Sayres has recordings,"

Higglestrom continued, "They will prove that the Bolton executives lied both to German Fatherland Bank and to us. The recordings are crucial to proving our fraud case, but they refuse to hand them over. Our motion is for an order compelling production—and if they fail to comply within 30 days, we seek a default judgment against them, for destruction or concealment of evidence."

The judge's face remained carefully neutral.

"Anything further?" He asked.

"Not at present, your honor," Higglestrom replied.

"What says the defense?" the judge asked.

All eyes now turned to the defense table. James Hunter rose—tall, gray-haired, a member of the prestigious Surrey & Clark firm. Despite his usual confidence in working with banking giants, he seemed unusually nervous. The judge's personal background, a scion of one of the wealthiest families in New York, made him unbribable. Meanwhile, the opposing attorney, Higglestrom, had deep family connections in New York's legal community greater even than his own. To make matters worse, the actual facts weren't helpful at all.

Adjusting his reading glasses, Hunter began speaking,

"Your honor, I won't dignify each detail proffered by my colleague with a response. Suffice it to say, he has a vivid imagination. The requests that have been made are overly broad and burdensome—nothing more than a fishing expedition for a weak case."

"How can asking for specific recordings, arising out of specific meetings, be a fishing expedition?" the judge challenged. "I'm looking at signed releases, right here, right in front of me. Why won't you produce the recordings?"

Hunter avoided the true answer—that the recordings would doom Bolton's case. Instead, he argued,

"A release, signed by a German Fatherland Bank executive, doesn't prove the recording exists. Our records division says it doesn't. Even if it did, it would be privileged under work product doctrine and attorney–client privilege."

"How can pre-litigation recordings be work product?" The judge asked, "And, since there was no case at the time, how can they be covered by attorney-client privilege?"

"If any recordings were made, they were made to deter litigation," Hunter admitted.

"Is German Fatherland Bank a defendant here?"

"No."

"Do you intend to sue them?"

The words hung in the air, undermining Hunter's entire argument, and it was one of those rare occasions when the man didn't know how to respond. Instead, all he could manage was a rambling response,

"Well, I, uh..."

"So, if that's so, it's certainly not work product." The judge cut through Hunter's fallback argument. "Now, tell me why it's covered under attorney–client privilege?"

"Numerous Bolton executives, many of whom are attorneys, licensed in the State of New York and New Jersey, were present," Hunter said, his usual confidence wavering.

"Mr. Hunter, the fact that there happen to be people with law degrees present doesn't mean anything, and you know that."

Hunter could see that his usual dance was working with the judge, so he shifted tactics.

"Well, regardless, your honor, no such recordings exist. Releases are simply obtained, as a matter of routine, from anyone who meets on the Bolton premises."

"You're saying that your client gets a signed recording release for every discussion?" The judge's skepticism was evident.

"Well, I can't really say for sure... but it's often done." Higglestrom insisted.

"Then I'd like to see all the signed recording releases for that year..." The judge countered.

"Let me clarify..." Hunter said, nervously, "What I meant to say is that they sometimes get releases they don't need. Finding all the releases that were signed that year would be almost impossible. Extremely time–consuming to say the least..."

"According to the plaintiff's brief," the judge said, demonstrating that he was a quick read, because he had just skimmed the documents in the courtroom, for the first time, "German Fatherland Bank's Vice President testified that Bolton's executives specifically asked him to wait while they turned on the recording devices that day."

The exchange continued, with the judge methodically dismantling each of Hunter's arguments about document storage and search burden. Jim was impressed—all judges were political appointees, to one extent or another, and a lot of them were incompetent. This one, however, knew the law cold.

"The SEC and FINRA require your client to keep redundant copies for six years," The judge insisted, "And, I think, you know that..."

"Well, yes, your honor. But, in a big company, even if a document exists, it can get lost over three years."

"If that's the case," The judge snapped back, "It's your responsibility when the evidence is lost."

After more challenges and further attempts at evasion about backup tapes and search burdens, the judge finally issued his order. He ordered Bolton to find the recordings within 30 days, with detailed documentation of search efforts required if unsuccessful. He also implied that a failure to find the documents would likely result in the issuance of a default judgement against Bolton Sayres.

Later that day, at the scheduled mediation, the opposing sides faced each other across a long walnut conference table. Hunter sat with his two young in-house associates assisting him. Tim Cohen, who was serving as the official representative of Bolton Sayres and Jim Bentley, who was along for the ride. Across from them were Higglestrom, his paralegal, IMG's legal chief Lloyd Falton, and unusually, IMG's CEO Sam Parrington.

Parrington's presence was notable. The tall, thin 66-year-old had spent decades building IMG from his father's small radiation sensor company into a multinational conglomerate. Known for his volatile temper, he'd remained surprisingly cordial through the first hour—until Hunter made his play.

"Since we value IMG as a client, we're ready to offer $30 million in full settlement..."

At that, the calm shattered completely.

"You're a son of a bitch!" Parrington erupted. "What the hell is that supposed to mean?"

Hunter maintained his measured tone.

"Mr. Parrington, I am simply pointing out that Bolton Sayres values you and IMG as a customer..."

"Bullshit!" Parrington's eyes flashed with fury, "If Bolton's people valued me, they wouldn't lie, cheat and steal from me! Your client stole hundreds of millions of dollars! $30 million is peanuts—it's a joke. They walk off $220 million richer. That money belongs to my shareholders! You're going to pay the full $250 million, plus fees, minimum, or we're going to trial, and you'll pay billions!"

"I understand how you feel, but my clients won't pay anything near $250 million. They don't feel they've done anything wrong."

"That's because your clients have no moral compass," Parrington snarled, turning to his lawyer. "Let these banksters tell it to the jury! Let them hand over a couple of billion in punitive damages. Fuck 'em!"

Higglestrom placed a calming hand on Parrington's shoulder and began trying to do what he did best, which was to persuade the other side, namely the Bolton Sayres' people.

"Bolton's exposure is huge," Higglestrom warned, "The German executives are all eager to testify against you. It'll be devastating—remember, they're angry about being cheated too. Once a jury finds fraud, it's going to award hefty punitive damages. And, on top of that, other companies won't want to do business with Bolton after all the facts come out in the Wall Street Journal. My client simply wants what's rightfully his. Pay the $250 million and fire the executives, or it's corporate suicide."

Hunter smiled.

"I can make one final offer: $50 million. That's it."

"No," Higglestrom replied. "That's not enough money and, on top of that, the firing of every Bolton executive involved is non-negotiable. Frankly, they should all go to jail."

"We don't think your case has merit," Hunter responded.

"This is an open and shut case," Higglestrom insisted, "You don't have a leg to stand on."

"What's open and shut one day can change dramatically the next..." Hunter responded cryptically. "You'll be surprised. We'll hold this offer open for a few days. But, before we pay any money, we'll require a strict confidentiality clause. Because, frankly, there are other potential litigants who also want to win the lottery..."

Parrington exploded again.

"Lottery?" He shook his head, cursing under his breath, and then continued aloud, "Fuck you! I'll have this on every news channel! Every newspaper! I'll destroy your fucking bank!"

"You overestimate yourself," Hunter said wryly.

Parrington stormed out, his entourage following. Only his lawyer paused to shake the mediator's hand, pointedly ignoring the team from Bolton Sayres and its outside counsel for fear that his client might see him. After the mediator left to file an impasse, Bentley was confused. He'd read the entire file—the smoking gun documents, the angry witnesses ready to testify. Higglestrom was right. It WAS an open and shut case. The Bolton Sayres executives should go to jail. At the very least, they were guilty of fraud. It was beyond question. The smallest punishment the Bolton executives deserved was firing. Why would anyone want to continue employing such fraudsters?

"Parrington isn't likable," Jim said to his colleagues, finally, after only the Bolton team was left in the room, "but the evidence shows our people were bad actors. Given our exposure and the potential reputational damage, we can't afford to go to trial..."

Hunter finished clicking his briefcase closed and laughed.

"Who says we're going to trial?" He quipped.

"Well, that's what it sounds like..." Cohen chimed in.

"Not everything is as it sounds." Hunter insisted.

"OK, I think I get it," Bentley said, "But, if you're intending to make a better offer, why antagonize them? Why not just make the offer and settle the case?"

"Who says we're making a better offer?" Hunter said, once again, cryptically. "We won this case fifteen minutes after the discovery hearing. The settlement's already been arranged."

Jim shook his head in disbelief.

"What?" He questioned in disbelief.

"You heard me," Higglestrom stated.

"I respect you, Mr. Hunter," Jim said, "And I know you've got a pretty big reputation. But, you and I seem to be living in different universes..."

"No, Jim. It's the same universe, same understanding, same everything...just different levels of expertise," Hunter replied. "You don't understand how things work. But you will..."

"Well, if you've arranged a settlement, Parrington deserves an Oscar," Cohen suggested.

Hunter just smiled and shrugged.

Jim wrestled with trying to make a decision. Bolton Sayres faced certain defeat, a multi-billion dollar defeat, most likely. Yet, the decision-making power lay with Hunter, who seemed dangerously unhinged. How could he remain silent?

The case wasn't scheduled for trial yet. There was still time to act—but what could he do? Go to his boss, Murray Sachs? No, that wouldn't work. Sachs was already livid about the unauthorized settlement offer back in Verde County. Also, even if he was willing to help, he simply lacked the authority to fire outside counsel as important as Mr. Hunter.

Maybe, John Farley, head of legal? No. Farley resented Jim's unconventional hiring, which had been at the direct order of Jeremy Stoneham, bypassing normal channels. Going over Farley's head to Laura's father would deepen the resentment? And, besides, it would result in yet another complaint against him, this time from Hunter, and that would further strain the already weak relationship with his father-in-law to the breaking point.

But, it was Hunter's ego that interrupted Jim's deliberations. As he was walking away, he suddenly turned back to them and spoke,

"You both think I'm crazy, don't you?" He said, "Here's what I suggest. Go watch the news over the next couple of weeks. Our fiery friend Parrington is about to learn a lesson he'll never forget..."

"What are you talking about?" Jim asked.

"Everything," Hunter said cryptically. "Mr. Squeaky-Clean is in big trouble. Watch and learn."

Despite his year and a half at Bolton observing the revolving door between banking and regulatory agencies, Jim didn't fully grasp Hunter's meaning—not until the news broke a few days later.

The Times reported that Parrington was now under investigation for undisclosed accounting discrepancies. Within days, he was arrested. Then, a few days later, he was removed as CEO by the Board of Directors of IMG, for "poor health," and replaced by Frank Caligari—a former Bolton Sayres fund manager named in the original fraud complaint.

A week before the deadline to hand over the documents, IMG's board also approved a confidential $50 million settlement—exactly Hunter's offer. The new CEO promptly hired Bolton's investment banking division for a new stock and bond offering.

"It's obvious what happened," Jim told Cohen. "Hunter is totally corrupt. We need to do something..."

"Are you crazy?" Cohen replied, "I'm not going up against him. He'd crush us both, the same way he did with Parrington."

"He's corrupt!" Jim insisted.

"Yeah, well, Parrington was an asshole anyway," Cohen mused, "Why stick your neck out for him? And, besides, I'm not married to the boss's daughter, and I happen to like my job."

"You're not going to back me up on this?" Jim asked. "Three weeks ago, we agreed that Bolton would get destroyed if the case ever went to trial."

"Yeah, well, but it's settled now. So, there won't be any trial. Just let sleeping dogs lie."

"If we don't do something, knowing what we know, then we're complicit," Jim insisted. "We should testify for Parrington's lawyers."

"Are you fucking nuts?" Cohen recoiled. "I need my job."

Jim saw that his friend's cowardice would ensure that he got no help from him. He changed the subject.

"Remember that upstate foreclosure case?" He asked.

"Yeah, sure..." Cohen replied.

Jim described finding the diary with its account of a dead body.

"Send it to the Verde County Sheriff," Cohen suggested immediately, "You can use our Albany courier service. Or better yet, just give it to one of those FBI agents, you know, the ones who are always fishing for leads..."

Both suggestions were solid.

Chapter 7 – STONEHAM GOES TO D.C.

Jeremy Stoneham gazed out the helicopter's window. At 55, his gym-honed physique suggested youth, but his sparse gray hair, a wide bald spot in the middle, and deep facial lines told a different story. The black-rimmed glasses he'd worn for four decades had once earned him the nickname "Clark Kent," though he'd never been anyone's superhero.

"ETA?" he called through his headset, cutting through the muted roar of the rotors.

"Less than 10 minutes to Washington," the pilot responded.

Stoneham nodded, his mind fixed on the impending meeting. As CEO of Bolton Sayres, one of the Street's savviest and most prestigious trading firms, the media had nicknamed him with the unofficial title "King of Wall Street." What they didn't know, however, was that his success, as was often the case with respect to the top echelon of America's financial industry, did not primarily arise out of any form of financial expertise. It was dependent upon his political acumen and his ties to sources of information in Washington DC, most particularly at the Treasury and Federal Reserve.

In the great game, kingship comes with a price. Todd Bolton's premature death three years before, had elevated Stoneham to the top of the most important investment bank on Wall Street. However, it had also sparked an intense power struggle, leaving him with a network of enemies within Bolton Sayres and throughout the banking cartel.

"You can't make an omelet without breaking eggs," he had once muttered to himself.

He couldn't help giving thought to the ongoing process. He was still systematically replacing opponents with loyalists. It would take years, but he had plenty of patience. It was a virtue he'd cultivated carefully throughout his career. He would bide his time. When the perfect opportunity came, he would strike with devastating ruthlessness and efficiency. His ability to hold off from immediate action and wait for the right moment was the key personality trait that had brought him to the top of the totem pole.

This morning's unexpected interruption by his son-in-law, Jim Bentley, still rankled him. Margaret, his trusted secretary, was home sick, and a temp girl was in her place. The temp hadn't known any better. She'd let the boy breach his carefully guarded sanctuary. Jim's complaints about James Hunter, one of the bank's top contract lawyers, demonstrated his fundamental misunderstanding of how everything in the world worked. The boy had continually annoyed him ever since his daughter had first introduced them.

"Political connections are the lifeblood of this business," Stoneham had tried explaining to Jim, "Hunter's influence is precisely why we hired him and why we're paying him his ridiculously high fees."

But, as usual, pragmatism had made little impression on the young man, whose naive idealism would be a huge liability and an impediment to his daughter's long term financial security. Jim Bentley would never succeed unless he smartened up. He couldn't help thinking about Laura's ridiculous transfer to UCLA, which he had discovered months too late. He blamed himself for her relationship with that loser, Jim Bentley. He'd been too absorbed in work to even notice her absence. He'd learned about it, for the first time, at a revealing dinner with his wife and daughter after her return from LA.

"Daddy, I've met someone special," she'd announced, launching a chain of events that had forced him to seek help from Adriano Navarro, the one man he trusted least.

Navarro was one of Todd Bolton's creatures, and had built an intelligence network that penetrated every major banking and government office. Because of that, and because he had a lot of supporters within the banking cartel, generally, he was nearly untouchable. Navarro answered only to the eight-member cartel Council, where Stoneham served. But, he held just one vote on the Council, no more, and he was powerless to fire the man, who had grown, frankly, too big for his britches.

"But he does get results," Stoneham acknowledged silently, arguing with himself.

He remembered the thick dossier Navarro had built on Jim Bentley, at his request.

As the helicopter began its descent, his thoughts turned to most immediate concerns, most particularly, the real reason for this Washington trip. The gold price manipulation scheme had finally hit a wall. The New York Fed's vault, long the source for fulfilling physical gold and swap liens, was now nearly depleted, though no one would ever admit it. To do so would be treason. Access to Fort Knox was now critically important. He expected, however, that the President would be very unhappy about the idea. He wasn't sure that even generous campaign contributions would be enough to sway the man.

"Mr. President, you must understand what's at stake," he rehearsed mentally.

And, there was a lot at stake! Two of the world's largest banks teetered on the brink, their derivative obligations so interwoven with those of all the other members of the club that their failure would unravel the entire financial system. The Bank for International Settlements was ready and able to run interference, and the Bank of England had confirmed that it could provide thousands of tons of physical gold to back up the save. However, without the secret signature of the President of the United States on a pledge of Fort Knox gold, the swap liens would never happen.

There were, of course, political ramifications. For their role in frittering away so much of America's gold, if the truth became known, there would be a huge amount of bad press against big banks. Someday, he knew, the truth would get out. It was only a matter of time. For now, however, his goal was to get a Presidential signature. With that in hand, everything would be fine for many years...

"When the real scandal hits, years from now, I'll be dead anyway," Stoneham reassured himself.

The upcoming meeting would test every political connection he'd cultivated as one of the current President's earliest and largest fundraisers. Bolton Sayres had flourished during the 2008 Great Recession precisely because of such government ties, even as its rivals collapsed. Now those same connections were needed again.

Washington's landmarks emerged from the morning haze. The helicopter's approach route avoided the worst of the traffic and airport delays that made jets impractical for this short hop from New York. Bolton Sayres owned several helicopters and two private jets, but time was too precious today for anything but the most direct route.

"Final approach," the pilot announced.

Stoneham straightened his tie, pushing aside thoughts of family drama and internal politics. The immediate crisis had to be defused by convincing the President that there was no other choice but to raid Fort Knox. Not necessarily physically, but through paper liens. It was critical for the banking system's survival. The magnitude of what he was about to request settled heavily on his shoulders. His position atop Bolton Sayres, his influence within the cartel, perhaps the entire financial system itself – all hung on the outcome of this meeting. The helicopter touched down, its rotor wash creating miniature whirlwinds on the helipad.

"Sometimes," he thought, adjusting those trademark glasses, "being King of Wall Street means selling your soul one piece at a time."

He stepped onto the helipad, leaving behind the relative sanctuary of the helicopter cabin. Ahead lay a meeting that would either save the hidden financial empire or expose its foundation of shifty sand. Either way, there was no turning back. His thoughts drifted away from the impending meeting again, and back toward the interaction with Navarro and the dossier the man had created about his daughter's future husband.

"What did you find out about the boy?" Stoneham had asked so long ago, as he ignored the file folder Adriano Navarro had slipped across the desk.

"It's all in the report," Navarro replied, his olive-skinned face impassive beneath dark-ringed eyes.

The slight downward hook of the man's nose completed an appearance that Jeremy Stoneham found repulsive. Navarro seemed to him to be the caricature of a Mafia enforcer. He fancied himself a Greek, but he looked like a Sicilian mafia Don. Stoneham would have fired Navarro long before that fateful day, if he had been able to. But, the man was untouchable, a favorite of forces that had always been more powerful than himself. He was backed by powerful figures within the cartel, particularly Christopher Dunlop, the powerful CEO of W.T. Fredericks.

As the chief architect of the THEATRES scheme, the most sophisticated surveillance system ever designed, Navarro had graduated from running Bolton's in-house reputational risk division to overseeing the cartel-wide reputational risk office. The political reality was stark: no individual bank official, regardless of position, could fire an operative like Navarro on his own. Such terminations required full Council approval—an impossibility given his support network and the highly damaging information he maintained on everyone of any importance. More than a few careers and marriages had ended after mysterious information leaks. He was sure, however, that the man had nothing on him.

"I don't have time to read your reports," Stoneham had stated roughly. "I've got a bank to run. Just give me an oral summary..."

Jim Bentley, as far as Jeremy Stoneham could tell, was nothing more than an ambitious social climber. The young man had latched onto Laura for financial advancement. White trash trying to marry up—a tale as old as society itself. The thought of his daughter being scammed by a scumbag made his jaw clench. He'd failed to protect her, being too absorbed in business to notice her escape from NYU, where he wanted her to be, to UCLA, until months after the fact.

"The boy comes from a modest background, economically speaking," Navarro had begun.

Stoneham nodded impatiently.

"I can't fathom why she refuses to date Marc Dunlop," he muttered angrily.

The comparison was inevitable. Bolton Sayres and W.T. Fredericks bank formed the banking cartel's founding core. Their fortunes were intertwined through generations of obligations and agreements. Marc Dunlop, heir to the Fredericks empire, was currently proving his worth at Bolton Sayres, working for Bolton, in theory, but on behalf of the entire cartel. His proprietary trading algorithms had revolutionized the conduct of market manipulation. Bolton Sayres provided cutting-edge hardware. The rest he did himself.

"The Dunlop boy is a good-for-nothing spoiled brat," Navarro stated flatly, "She's smart to avoid him."

The comment jolted Stoneham.

"What are you talking about?" He objected, defending the architect of his most profitable trading system, "He's a genius!"

"Who's spent time behind bars," Navarro noted.

"A few hours. He was only 14!"

"He would have spent much more time behind bars, if not for Judge Watkins," Navarro replied. "Hacking an FBI database, and releasing a virus that crippled half of Europe's computers...it's not minor mischief."

"Watkins only helped straighten out some unfortunate mistakes," Stoneham defended.

The judge was one of several on the cartel's payroll. The clerk's office also made sure that sensitive cases landed on the right desks.

"You don't go arresting young men from good families for no good reason!"

"Of course not," Navarro said sarcastically.

"As I recall, old Todd Bolton rescued you from an FBI sting operation, yourself," Stoneham countered, but immediately regretted the unnecessary jab.

Antagonizing Navarro served no purpose, despite the satisfaction it provided. The man's past – including his paid work for the cartel while supposedly serving in government – was better left undisturbed. He gained nothing by bringing it up just to antagonize the man. So, he backpedaled.

"Look, I'll admit he made some mistakes, but young Marc has grown into a fine young man," Stoneham continued, shifting tone. "He's a self-taught expert in artificial intelligence, the best at everything he does. When you compare this LA boy, Jim Bentley, that Laura apparently prefers, well, I don't think he can stand in Marc's shadow."

"I didn't say young Dunlop was stupid," Navarro replied.

The memory of Laura's debutante ball now surfaced. She had been introduced to Marc Dunlop, and both families had maintained high hopes of getting them together. It was a shared optimism. But, her inexplicable decision to break things off, and her refusal to explain it, even to her mother, saddened them.

"What else did you find out about Jim Bentley?"

"No family, no pedigree, as you might call it," Navarro continued. "No connections. But he did graduate from UCLA Law School. His grades were fairly good."

"I knew all that already," Stoneham dismissed the information.

UCLA was a respected law school, but it wasn't Harvard, Yale, Columbia, Penn, or even NYU. Those were the law schools that mattered to top New York City law firms. But, it really didn't matter what law school he'd graduated from. Jeremy Stoneham despised lawyers, especially trial lawyers, especially ones who specialize in suing banks. The fact that he'd graduated from NYU Law School and was a lawyer, himself, didn't reduce the dislike. And, the thought of Jim's stated ambition to become a trial lawyer, fighting for the little guy, made him sick.

"He's only a student," Navarro pointed out. "How much money do you expect him to have?"

"Don't make excuses," Stoneham grumbled.

"Don't you want to know why he's poor?" The man had asked him.

"Not really."

"It's because he's an orphan," Navarro told him anyway, "His parents died when he was eleven."

The statement hung in the air, and he had found himself searching for something negative to say, but couldn't come up with anything. So, Navarro continued,

"He was bounced through foster care until seventeen. Lived in the UCLA dorms from barely eighteen. Several academic scholarships help him pay his tuition, but it's not enough for expenses—hence the student loans. He's also been working part–time, full–time during summers and holidays."

Stoneham dismissed the work ethic. Social climbers always worked hard. He admired that, and had put a few such people on his own staff for just that reason. But, with his daughter's future involved, a willingness to work hard couldn't redeem a total lack of good connections, family and background.

"Everyone who claims poverty gets scholarships and loans," he scoffed. "That's nothing impressive. It's called welfare state politics."

"I said academic scholarship," Navarro emphasized. "Perfect grades, National Merit Scholar, near–perfect SATs. LSAT scores in the top half–percent. Graduated from UCLA College and Law."

"If he's so brilliant, why not Harvard?" Stoneham challenged. "Our legal department's full of Harvard, Yale, and Columbia graduates."

"He could have gone to Harvard, I think," the man replied, "But, he never applied."

"Why wouldn't he apply to Harvard?"

"Maybe, he wanted to stay in L.A."

"Bottom line? No family, no connections, no pedigree, not even enough ambition for an Ivy League application!" Stoneham concluded. "I want this boy out of my daughter's life."

"What do you expect me to do?" Navarro asked, his tone deliberately ambiguous, "Kill him?"

"Just get him away from her."

Stoneham's own past flickered through his mind—his mother, a distant relative of the Bolton family, marrying down for love to a postal clerk. Subsidized housing in the Bronx. He wouldn't let Laura repeat that mistake.

"The boy has a criminal record, doesn't he?" Stoneham probed.

"One arrest," Navarro confirmed.

"Assault and battery with a deadly weapon—that's enough."

"There's context," Navarro countered. "He's trained in martial arts since twelve—black belts in Karate, Jujitsu, and Kendo. Youth champion. The 'deadly weapons' were his hands."

"What?" Stoneham didn't want to be, but he couldn't help being slightly intrigued.

Navarro continued:

"At seventeen, in a rough LA neighborhood, he encountered two kids being attacked by gang members. Two with knives, one attempting rape. Jim intervened. Got slashed himself, but disabled all three attackers. One ended up paralyzed by his own knife."

"Then why the arrest?"

"Standard procedure with violence. The victims initially fled. Once they came forward, charges were dropped. Two juveniles got detention, the paralyzed one got a suspended sentence. His family couldn't even find lawyers willing to sue."

Stoneham examined the report's cover before tossing it aside.

"What about gang retaliation?" He asked.

"Social Services moved him to San Luis Obispo for a while. By the time he returned to attend UCLA, the threat had passed."

"How do you know all this detail? Aren't juvenile records sealed?"

"It's all in the database," Navarro explained. "Just blocked without proper access."

"Which you have?"

"Of course."

Stoneham had noted Navarro's illegal database access—a potential leverage point, though too valuable to the cartel to risk exposing. It exemplified why Navarro was indispensable. He was the master of whispers and a source of crucial intelligence. Meanwhile, his thoughts returned to Jim.

The boy had courage – that was worth something. Academic prowess too, evidenced by his grades and Merit Scholarship. Yet, the impulsiveness troubled him. Taking on three armed gang members alone wasn't a clever strategy, regardless of the fact that he had ended up prevailing. A smart player stacked the odds in his own favor and carefully played them. That is what he had done all his life. Jim had won in the end, apparently, but his survival had hinged on luck, not cleverness.

Still, raw courage commands respect in the hearts of everyone, even cynical people like Jeremy Stoneham. It couldn't be helped. Hero worship has been an integral part of human nature since the beginning of time. Human beings admire heroes. It's the same instinct that draws young boys to superhero stories. Even a hardened old banker was subject to it.

"His parents?" Stoneham asked, interest rekindling. "Before they died?"

"Father was an aerospace engineer for a defense contractor near Torrance. Mother had a master's in anthropology, and became a housewife."

The details had progressively softened his stance against the young man. However, he couldn't imagine allowing his beloved Laura to vanish into obscurity in Los Angeles. He needed her in New York. She needed to be in New York. That left two options: buy Jim off or lure him in. To do that, he enlisted Laura's help. He had her offer the young man an all-expenses–paid invitation, asking him to visit her in New York.

In the end, Jim arrived in New York City in August 2011, surprising everyone with his refusal of the offer of financial assistance. The surveillance footage showed him giving genuine reactions as he was shown around: amazement at the Mercedes limo, and astonishment at the family's huge Central Park West penthouse. Despite learning of Laura's wealth, he chose to bed down in the cramped Brooklyn apartment of a friend who had just moved to the City, over the offered Waldorf suite.

Still dubious about the match, he had privately offered Jim $100,000 to disappear. The boy's initial negotiating stance impressed him, but subsequent offers – up to $2 million – met flat refusal. After that, he had been forced to backpedal and claim it was merely a test of character. Jim was gullible enough to believe him and, by necessity, the game had moved to the next phase.

He hadn't wanted his daughter to leave NYC, so he'd figured out a way to maneuver her future husband into voluntarily moving to New York instead. The job offer wasn't pure nepotism—the bank's litigation surge demanded the hiring of several new lawyers. Finding them would have been easy, of course. Nearly every executive working for the bank had some relative, fresh out of law school, desperately in need of work.

Not surprisingly, given the intense competition for law jobs, despite graduating in UCLA Law's top quarter, Jim had no job offers. He'd assumed, therefore, that he'd leap at a Bolton Sayres position. It was a dream opportunity that most Harvard graduates coveted. Yet Jim initially refused, his words still echoing:

"I've stood on my own since eleven. Can't take my first job through nepotism."

It was the same type of foolishness that drove him to face armed thugs with three to one odds against him. Book-smart but real-world stupid was the young man's fatal flaw. When Jim's rejection of the job offer prompted Laura to announce her return to Los Angeles, he'd been forced to secretly orchestrate something more. He prevailed upon the director of a major Broadway play to give her the musical lead. She believed her talent alone had won the role. But, it hadn't. The scheme worked. It gave her a reason to stay in New York, and she'd convinced Jim to join her.

Ultimately, however, it was her pregnancy that had forced his hand. Honorably, Jim insisted on taking responsibility and since he had no prospects, no other job offers and plenty of new responsibilities and obligations, he reluctantly accepted the position. The Legal Department VP was very upset about it. He'd been forced to surrender his nephew's promised spot to accommodate Jim. It was something the man continued to hold a grudge about.

If Jim were a more practical young man, it might have been possible to groom him as a successor or, at least, his career at Bolton Sayres could have been fast-tracked. But, the young man's idealism would eventually prove career-ending. James Hunter, Bolton's longtime counsel, exemplified this weakness. Jim completely failed to grasp the idea that there was a huge financial exposure at risk. Outside lawyers were selected for their political influence, not legal expertise. A well-connected attorney could transform a loss into a win. Hunter's $1,000 per hour rate was worth every penny. His connections had just saved the bank from a payout of hundreds of millions of dollars or a trial where the verdict would have likely been in the billions, after punitive damages were awarded.

Would this reality ever be understood by an idealistic son-in-law who continued to live his life inside a bubble, in spite of Stoneham's best efforts to make him understand? Jim needed to be a leader because he was Laura's husband. But, no one in the cartel would support elevating an unrealistic dreamer into leadership. The boy was clearly unfit for investment banking. What was he fit for? That was the question. Some more traditional banking service? Credit cards or mortgages? Bolton Sayres didn't handle such business, but other cartel banks did.

The helicopter pilot's voice interrupted his thoughts.

"Sir, we'll be landing in about two minutes,"

Stoneham nodded.

As one of the President's top fund-raisers, his helicopter would normally touch down directly on the South Lawn. But today was different. Fifteen CEOs from the financial industry were arriving from New York. To avoid the inevitable jealousies among them, his own helicopter landed a few blocks away.

A sleek black Mercedes limo was waiting. It would drive him the short distance to the White House. The ride was so smooth that it felt as though they weren't moving at all. Then, suddenly, the car came to a halt, and the door swung open, flooding the cabin with bright light. A woman stood there, smiling warmly, arms outstretched.

"Welcome to the White House," she said. "Please follow me."

He climbed out of the limo, a sense of familiarity washing over him. He and the Treasury Secretary, for example, had known each other a long time. The Secretary, twelve years his junior, had climbed the ranks to become a pivotal figure, moving back and forth, from the bank to and from the Treasury and Federal Reserve. Now, he would be instrumental in persuading the President to open up the U.S. Gold Reserve.

Many of the CEOs, including those associated with the cartel and those who were not, were already gathered. It was 10:30 a.m., and their meeting was scheduled for 11:00. Stoneham knew everyone by first name. They all stood on the patio, shaking hands, chatting, and sipping refreshments. Most of them were idiots, in his opinion. But, it was what it was. The meeting of the so-called "Plunge Protection Team" was about to begin.

"Just a few more minutes of this bullshit..." Stoneham promised himself, annoyed at feeling forced to engage with people he didn't want to engage with.

After about fifteen minutes of mingling, Tanya Sorbo, the White House's conference coordinator, called for attention.

"It's time," she announced graciously. "Please follow me, gentlemen."

Tanya led the group through the lawn and into the West Wing. Soon, they entered a large conference room adorned with Thomas Chippendale and Queen Anne-style furniture. Although it was on the first floor, the room felt elevated due to a false skylight. Portraits of former Presidents Theodore and Franklin Roosevelt graced the walls, giving the room its famous name: the Roosevelt Room.

The companies represented were among the most significant in the world, with eight of them, including Bolton Sayres, being members of the secret banking cartel. All were on edge; a collapse of W.T. Fredericks' London gold operations could spell disaster. The bank owed a lot of physical gold to a lot of different creditors, many of whom were suddenly insisting on taking physical delivery of the gold they purchased. It didn't have nearly enough gold in its vault to meet the demand.

"Did you know," one CEO murmured, "that most people who think they own gold don't own any?"

He was one of those whom Stoneham viewed as an "idiot" and he worked for a non-cartel member bank,

"It's true," another non-cartel bank CEO replied. "Every bar has multiple claimants. W.T. Fredericks has been playing that game. That's how it got into this mess! If it wouldn't bring down the whole system, I'd just assume let them go bankrupt..."

It was not the kind of talk that Jeremy Stoneham wanted to hear, especially not from a member of the Plunge Protection Team. W.T. Fredericks and Bolton Sayres were joined at the hip. The bankruptcy of one meant the bankruptcy of the other. The tension in the room grew palpable as others shared unspoken fears. The crisis had been precipitated by a clever trader who knew the banks didn't have enough gold to make delivery. He had bought call options in vast numbers, over-the-counter. Instead of selling back the calls at their expiration, he demanded that they be converted to futures contracts and was forcing delivery of the physical gold they represented. But, W.T. Fredericks didn't have the physical gold. Like Bolton, it was playing the paper gold market, and never expected to be forced to make a massive physical delivery.

Everyone in the room was nervously anticipating the arrival of the President and his cabinet members. If W.T. Fredericks couldn't deliver, it could settle with cash. Bankruptcy really was never on the table. However, if it did that, although it would not be a legal default, it would expose all gold bullion banks to similar runs. The fragile truth of the gold market would be on open display, and the whole scheme would come crashing down, with repercussions that might cause bankruptcy as the markets lost confidence in the banks in all areas of trading.

As the group settled around the long walnut table, polished to a reflective sheen, the atmosphere changed abruptly, as the focus shifted. The President entered, flanked by the Secretary and Undersecretary of the Treasury. In a show of respect, everyone stood, even though every one of the bank CEOs were on a first-name basis with all three men.

When the President took his seat, everyone dutifully followed suit. The meeting was officially called to order. Stoneham could feel the weight of the moment. What all the men in that room knew, but what the public did not know, was a dirty secret shared between the titans of finance and the US government. In attempting to carry out a government mandate to protect the US dollar and suppress the price of gold, one huge mega-bank had screwed up.

Stoneham's task was to convince the President, with the help and urging of the other bank Presidents, to shore up the gold market, by allowing them to tap into the US gold reserves at Fort Knox. If they were successful, they would preserve the status quo that the bankers depended on. Failure was unthinkable. The stakes had never been higher. The fate of the world, at least the financial world, which was really all the bank CEOs cared about, hung in the balance.

Chapter 8 – FRIENDS

It was about 6:00 pm but, most importantly, it was Thursday night, which was the night that many younger employees in Manhattan mingle with co-workers at various watering holes around NYC. Therefore, Timothy Cohen found a reason to walk by Jim's cubicle, knowing that his friend would still be hard at work. Sure enough, even though few others were still working, Jim was still there, juggling several assignments. For all the complaints that his father-in-law might have about him, laziness was not one of them. He was engrossed in his research and writing, and hadn't even noticed that someone had arrived at his cubicle, leaning over the edge of the divider.

"Earth to Jim..." Cohen said, facetiously. "Earth to Jim... Come in Jim..."

Startled, Jim looked up.

"Tim!" he said, surprised. "What are you doing here?"

"It's more appropriate for me to ask you, why are you still here?"

Jim turned back to the screen.

"I'm just trying to finish stuff..."

Cohen pointed to his watch.

"You know that it's after six, don't you?"

Jim nodded, but kept fixated on his screen.

"Time for both of us to quit, my friend..." Cohen continued. "Tomorrow is only a day away!"

"Yeah, well, I've got too much stuff to do, and not enough hours in a day..." Jim replied.

"That's because you do too much. Don't keep volunteering. Anyway, what's the story with that Florida firm? And, what about the dead man's diary?"

"The Florida case wrapped up yesterday. They just wanted to settle. As for the diary, I took it over to 26 Federal Plaza; to the guy we work with over there."

The address, 26 Federal Plaza, is the FBI building, an address that needed no further identification.

"What did he say?"

"He told me he'd take a look, but that the FBI probably doesn't have any jurisdiction. He says he'll probably send it over to the Verde County Sheriff."

"That's exactly what you wanted, isn't it?" Cohen noted.

"Yeah..."

"You did the right thing."

"Yeah," Jim replied. "Now that the FBI's got it, it's out of my hands. I won't worry about it anymore."

Jim rubbed his eyes, which were aching. He's just received a new case file, it was hefty, and it was already getting late in the day. According to the paralegal summary, the SEC was taking "administrative action" against seven of Bolton's investment bankers. The regulator accused them of insider trading and manipulating an initial public offering (IPO). His assignment involved scrutinizing the case more thoroughly than the paralegal's capabilities allowed.

Management expected a lawyer's recommendations. Yet Jim harbored no illusions—his analysis would likely gather dust, or if reviewed, carry minimal weight. As one of the firm's junior attorneys, he wielded no influence or authority.

"Have the SEC people said how much they want for a consent decree?" Cohen inquired.

"What are you referring to?" Jim asked, puzzled.

Cohen ignored the question, pivoting to a topic he found more interesting.

"Are you aware what day this is?"

"No."

"It's Thursday," Cohen declared meaningfully.

"And that signifies...?"

"That too much work and too little play makes Jim a dull boy!"

Jim smiled at the wordplay.

"Clever..."

"The Odysseus Club's happy hour beckons!" Cohen urged.

But Jim didn't particularly like nightlife and, unlike Cohen, he was a married man with a child. He might not be extremely attracted to his wife anymore, but he wasn't looking to meet girls either. And, on top of that, he was feeling somber. He redirected the conversation back to the case he was working on.

"The more I read these documents, the more disgusted I am that we employ people like this."

"We certainly have our share of bottom-feeders!" Cohen concurred. "But, then, think of it this way...figuring out how to get them out of trouble is what keeps our lawyer paychecks coming!"

"Your cynicism has reached a new height!" Jim exclaimed. "These violations are outrageous."

"Are they?" Cohen responded flatly. "I'm not surprised. What surprises me is the SEC. They typically turn a blind eye. Suggests they're under pressure to generate revenue."

"What?"

"Oh, come on, Jim, you know these IPO manipulations are commonplace," Cohen insisted, "The SEC rarely gets involved."

Jim elaborated on the facts of the particular case, which he viewed as egregious.

"But our traders explicitly promised several major hedge funds preferential treatment—early exit options, if they committed to purchasing fifty thousand additional shares within minutes of the opening bell."

"It's just the classic pump and dump strategy," Cohen declared, "Totally routine. After you spend two years at Bolton, as I have, you'll have seen it a hundred times."

"But, the SEC says it was a coordinated effort to artificially inflate short-term prices, disadvantaging smaller investors," Jim continued, "The hedge funds orchestrated a synchronized exit, capitalizing on a buying frenzy that our team manufactured through aggressive promotion."

"Just a time-honored Wall Street tradition." Cohen insisted.

"A Bolton investment banker even appeared on CNBC, and fabricated claims about overwhelming demand when he knew that only the cooperating hedge funds were buying."

"It's just standard operating procedure," Cohen discounted the information, "If they can manage to get to a talking head, they do."

"Why doesn't the SEC do something about it regularly?" Jim asked.

Cohen's lips curled into a knowing smile.

"Because it's all about money..."

"What?" Jim asked, "The SEC's investigation? Or, our traders' collusion with hedge funds?"

"Both..." Cohen insisted.

"What are you implying?" Jim asked.

"Simple," Cohen expounded, "The public has the money. The banks take it from the public. Then, the government takes it from the banks. In the end, the banks and the government earn a profit. A 'quid pro quo.' The government gets its share by initiating lawsuits and feigning regulatory oversight. We pay a few penalties, pledge reform, and pretend contrition. Compare the fines to the profits, Jim—the mathematics speaks for itself. The profits dwarf the fines. So these strategies get recycled endlessly with minor variations, and both the banks and the government keep making money."

"That disgusting," Jim protested, shaking his head. "And, it's also ridiculous. If the government just wanted revenue, it could make the penalties severe enough to get more money and also deter the conduct in the future."

Cohen's expression reflected amused disbelief.

"Why would they do that?" he exclaimed. "You're so incredibly naive, it's endearing! You don't understand what quid pro quo means or what? The Feds make us pay a million-dollar payment for a consent decree. That's why I asked, at the beginning, how much do they want? To the average citizen, whatever they demand sounds like big bucks. But, in the context of the constant violations, it's just chump change, at least compared to the profits. Our role as corporate counsel is to negotiate the smallest possible settlement. That's it. The government agencies take their share. That's the game..."

"That's impossible for me to accept," Jim protested.

"The hell it is!" Cohen shot back with conviction, "We have to accept it, because we don't have any choice. You may be married to the boss' daughter, but like me, you're just a cog in a big wheel."

"You're suggesting universal corruption? The perpetrator execs, the banks themselves, even the regulators—everyone!"

"Precisely." Cohen's tone conveyed it as self-evident. "Even me and you, of course. We sanitize the messes before they get too smelly. The innocent parties are the small investors who pour their hard-earned savings into these elaborate schemes, dreaming about getting rich quick—and silly idealists like you, who'll end up getting themselves fired, if they don't wise up, in spite of being the boss' son-in-law!"

"If that really is what our job is, I'd prefer to be fired..." Jim muttered, shaking his head.

"With you and your family out in the street?" Cohen stated, now a bit annoyed, "It's easy for you to say, I guess. Given you're the boss' son-in-law..."

"What's that supposed to mean?" Jim shot back, getting irritated.

Nepotism got him his job and protected it, but he didn't want to hear that, especially from someone he considered a friend.

"Jim," Cohen apologized, seeing the reaction his words had created, written all over Jim's face, "I never intended to fight with you, or imply anything other than the fact that I'm your friend. I'm just trying to be realistic, and tell you how it is. Remember Parrington? Remember, his fate? And, he had wealth and power himself. Imagine what it's like for people who don't..."

"Like you?" Jim asked.

"Exactly," Cohen agreed, "This stuff is too big and entrenched for me, even for you, to fight against. If you do it, they'll destroy you. It's bigger even than your father-in-law. And, it's been going on for ages. It just is what it is."

"Parrington was one case involving one corrupt attorney," Jim insisted, "And, I'm working to correct things."

Cohen's lips curled into a knowing smile.

"And, how, exactly, did that conversation with your father-in-law unfold?" He asked.

"He's promised to respond."

"How long ago was that?" Cohen's voice dripped with skepticism.

"A while..."

Cohen laughed softly and shook his head.

"You'll hear back from him when hell freezes over—and that's optimistic." He commented.

"He'll respond after returning from Washington," Jim countered.

"Perhaps you'll get lucky," Cohen said, "But, I'd simply lose my job...if I did what you're doing."

"I don't agree with that..." Jim responded.

Cohen shook his head while saying: "Anyway, I don't want to talk about this anymore..."

But, Jim didn't want to stop.

"I don't know how you reconcile working here when you think this way..." He commented.

"How do you?" Cohen countered.

"Because I reject your cynical worldview," Jim explained, "I think I can make a real difference."

Cohen's head shake and smile conveyed his skepticism.

"I'm giving you the unvarnished truth. Frankly, if I could maintain this income elsewhere, I'd leave. But with the legal job market saturated, the way it is, I prefer being employed to being out on the street."

"Oh, come on," Jim countered, "There are other jobs. There are even lawyers who specialize in suing us, and some of them make a fortune."

Cohen nodded enthusiastically.

"That's true," He agreed, "So, I'll share something with you. Working for Bolton isn't my endgame. I'm just here gathering intelligence. Once I've got the knowledge, I'll switch sides and litigate against these bastards. I'll devastate them by exposing the truth! I'll be their worst nightmare—just wait and see! They'll settle with me, for big bucks, rather than face me in court. I'll make a huge profit for myself, and I'll help regular investors against these guys. That's my long term strategy. We could even do it together, you and me. What do you say?"

The proposition stirred something in Jim. He didn't like his job. And, deep inside, as much as he wanted it to be untrue, he strongly suspected that his friend's cynicism was based on reality. The idea of leaving the bank was appealing.

Without waiting for Jim's response, Cohen pressed on.

"Meanwhile, stop obsessing! Let's go to the Odysseus Club tonight!"

With an infant at home, Jim had nearly forgotten what social interaction even felt like. Sharing a beer or two with colleagues appealed to him. Unlike a majority of Bolton Sayres' younger employees, he'd never been to the Odysseus Club, but he knew it by reputation—a popular spot, primarily for singles.

"I'm not sure..." Jim hesitated. "Laura's probably expecting me."

But, even as he said that, he realized that, most likely, she wouldn't mind. She'd told him, just the other evening, that he should socialize more with his colleagues. If he didn't come home too late, she might approve.

"Call her," Cohen urged. "Get clearance."

A quick call saw her initial soft resistance melt into a request for a reasonable return time.

After that, Jim turned to his friend again.

"I need thirty minutes to wrap up here." He said.

"No problem," Cohen replied. "You know the location?"

"Yes."

"OK, then, I'll be there, waiting for you!"

Jim nodded farewell. After Cohen's departure, he dispatched pending emails, finished his remaining work and logged out of his computer.

Chapter 9 – The Odysseus Club

The Odysseus Club is one of the premier watering holes catering to Wall Street's 20 and 30 "somethings." It is especially good in the spring because the outside terraces open up in April. The food is tasty and reasonably priced, at least when viewed under the lens of the usually overpriced New York City standard. The place livens up right after work, especially on Thursday nights, because it is "happy hour" that night, when they serve half-price drinks from 5 until 8 p.m.

It wasn't hard to find. Everybody knew its location. When Jim arrived, Cohen was already sitting at a table with several other employees, and as soon as he was spotted, he heard a voice call in his direction.

"Jim! Over here!"the man called out to him.

Standing now, Cohen beckoned him to the table. Jim approached, and exchanged handshakes when he arrived. Two other men occupied seats. The one to Cohen's right, appearing slightly older—perhaps mid-thirties—wore a perpetual smirk.

"Hey, Jim, I want you to meet Marc Dunlop," Cohen announced. "He's one of Bolton's top quantitative analysts. The proprietary traders revere him..." He turned toward Dunlop, "Jim Bentley is a lawyer, like me, Marc. We both work in the legal department."

The handshake with Dunlop left Jim with an inexplicable sense of the man's immediate hostility.

"I've heard about you," Dunlop stated icily.

Jim found that surprising, having no recollection of previous contact with the man.

"Pleased to meet you," Jim offered. "So, you're doing quantitative analysis for proprietary trading? I thought the Volcker rule eliminated prop trading?"

"Fuck the Volcker rule..." Dunlop snapped.

He turned to Cohen, laughing derisively while indicating Jim.

"Is this guy really a lawyer?" Dunlop said derisively, "How can you be a bank lawyer and not know what's going on with the Volcker rule?"

The comment irritated Jim, but he maintained composure during the ensuing silence. A slight man with brown skin, seated left of Dunlop, eventually spoke.

"The Volcker Rule remains pending," the small brown man stated authoritatively, his Indian accent pronounced. "Its implementation has been delayed until 2017."

"Why?" Jim inquired.

"Because we requested it," he explained. "But, even after they put it into effect, plenty of workarounds will still exist. Banks can still maintain market-making operations in stocks, bonds, and commodities. At W.T. Fredericks, for instance, we trade exclusively for clients—many being hedge funds operated by former executives..."

Cohen made another introduction.

"Jim, this is Sandip Gupta. He's the personal lawyer for W.T. Fredericks' CEO, Christopher Dunlop, Marc's father. For any FINRA or SEC regulatory matters—interpretation or modification—he's your man."

"It's a pleasure to meet you, Jim," Gupta said with a smile, extending his hand while taking a deep sip of his beer. "You can call me Sandy, by the way."

Sandy was born in India, but was naturalized as an American citizen. His family belonged to the Kshatriya caste, descendants of the Maharajas of Uttar Pradesh—a large Indian state that was once an independent kingdom. In South Asia, family connections are crucial for business success, a principle that holds true in the Western world as well, although we don't like to acknowledge it. India is more forthright about such realities.

Sandy's family had immigrated when he was just three years old, leaving him few memories of India other than his accent, which he had acquired in childhood, talking to his mother and father, and never lost with age. But, the bottom line for W.T. Fredericks was his political connections. They were strong and inherited from his family. Such connections were vital because Fredericks maintained a significant presence in South Asia. Its hiring practices reflected that. It leveraged influence peddling to gain significant money-making opportunities.

"Sit down, Jim..." Cohen motioned, and Jim sat down.

"I hear you're spending much of the year now in the Caribbean..." Sandip said to Dunlop, attempting conversation.

Dunlop merely nodded and pointed at a pretty blonde at the raw bar.

"You see her?" he announced brazenly. "I'm gonna fuck her tonight. Watch and learn, gentlemen..."

He rose suddenly, swaggering to the bar with a mix of bluster and drunken confidence. After tapping her shoulder and whispering something, he waited. The woman promptly turned away and left, abandoning him there. He lingered briefly, before returning to the table, dejected.

Jim laughed innocently.

"I guess that didn't work out for you..." he noted with a smile.

"Fuck you!" Dunlop snapped, his face contorted with anger. "Do you know who I am?"

Jim wasn't sure what to make of the hostile tone of the question, so he just kept his cool, and answered truthfully.

"Well, let's see, I think your name is Marc Dunlop, and you're a quantitative analyst at Bolton Sayres, and Sandy just said your Dad is Christopher Dunlop...how am I doing?"

"That's right! I'm a Dunlop," the man boasted. "And, my dad's the CEO of W.T. Fredericks Bank!"

Jim wasn't sure how to respond to that. He didn't care if the man's father was President of the United States. Whatever his pedigree, Dunlop, simply put, was drunk. Then, suddenly, Dunlop stood up, smiling now, and raised his pint of beer.

"Funny, isn't it?" he proclaimed. "Here you are, a nobody, and here I am, a somebody, and for some strange reason, you didn't really know me, but I knew exactly who you are! Let's toast to that!"

No one joined him in the toast, but he took a long draught of the beer and wiped his mouth on his sleeve.

"And, who, exactly, do you think I am?" Jim asked quietly.

"The man who's been banging Laura Stoneham, of course," Dunlop shouted. "You knocked her up, got her pregnant, and then married her for her money. Everybody knows you!"

Jim fought to control himself.

"Ha!" Dunlop laughed, "I heard she got fat. There's a price to pay for everything, you know!"

"Who the hell do you think you are?" Jim demanded, rising.

"I'm somebody talking to nobody!" Dunlop laughed. "Everyone can see that... right, guys?"

He gestured around the table. The others looked at each other, questionably. He turned back to glare at Jim, before suddenly smiling and breaking into laughter again.

"Can you believe this idiot doesn't know who I am?!" he shouted. "Everyone in this bar knows who I am!"

"Marc..." Sandip tugged at Dunlop's clothing, trying to guide him to his seat. "Sit down... man..."

Dunlop yanked away violently.

"No!" He snapped.

"Hmm... I saw the reaction of that girl at the bar," Jim observed dryly. "They may know you, but they certainly don't like you..."

"You think you're special, don't you?" Dunlop continued. "You're not. You're Mr. Nobody. But it's America. A country where a Mr. Nobody can fuck the boss' daughter and nothing bad happens to him! Instead, he gets his job by fucking her! That's how you got your job, isn't it?"

He offered a mock salute before extending his palm in an offer to slap his hand.

"Gimme five, Jim!" he laughed.

Jim's anger was now showing plainly on his face. He was always ill at ease when people, even a friend like Cohen, mentioned the nepotism that had gotten him the job. Being taunted by someone like Dunlop was much worse. But, the visible anger on his face only encouraged the man.

"Sometimes, I miss that sloppy wet cunt, you know," he sneered, "It was nice. Too bad she has a weakness for sissies like you. I wouldn't mind fucking her again, like I used to but, then again, maybe not...when I was fucking her, she wasn't so fat!"

Jim's fist clenched. Cohen noticed it immediately, raising his hand in warning and shaking his head.

"Ignore him..." Cohen whispered.

"I heard you, dirty Jew!" Dunlop redirected his venom toward Cohen. "That Stoneham chick was once the most fuckable piece of ass in all of New York. She liked sucking dick, Jim...does she still give the best blow jobs? It was her favorite thing, you know, and she was great at it!"

He thrust his hips suggestively.

"Oh, yeah..." he continued, "I miss how she used to scream. She's such a screamer. I remember..."

Despite his rage, Jim responded with icy control.

"You're drunk, and oddly, that's the only reason you're still standing."

"You hear that, folks?" Dunlop crowed. "He just threatened me...wow! What a sniveling weakling. He's going to let it pass! Give me a fuckin' break..."

"You're an asshole, with a capital A!" Jim snapped.

"Ooh, hoo, hoo..." Dunlop chuckled maniacally. "He's angry...so it must be true love! That's what I thought, too, when I was fucking her..."

He thrust his hips again.

"We've both fucked the same girl, Jim!" he taunted. "Still has decent tits, doesn't she? Hmm..."

Jim lunged up, but Cohen grabbed him, pointing discreetly,

"Those two men at the tables, over there, are his bodyguards," He whispered.

Jim noticed two very large muscular men drinking beer. Both seemed absorbed in their own activities. Neither was paying attention at the moment.

"If you lay a hand on him, they'll be all over you," Cohen warned.

Jim registered their imposing size. Then, he was distracted. Dunlop grabbed a passing busty redheaded waitress, and pulled her close.

"Tell him who I am," he commanded.

"You're Marc Dunlop, of course," she replied.

"And, what does that mean?"

"That you're the richest guy around?"

"Right!" he exclaimed, stuffing a one hundred–dollar bill down her blouse. "She loves me... don't you, honey."

The waitress smiled as she walked on, his hand lingering.

"Sure, Sweetie!"

"How much do you love me?" Dunlop called after her.

"Plenty," She replied, smiling.

"You want to come home with me tonight?" He asked.

"You got a couple of thousand bucks in that wallet?" she joked, freeing herself and retrieving the hundred from her shirt.

She happily pocketed the cash and continued on her way, toward the kitchen, with her order book.

"You see how it works?" Dunlop declared. "Everything is for sale. You buy, you sell, love is no different. Understand?"

"Didn't work so well at the oyster bar..." Jim commented.

Dunlop dismissively waved his hand, and staggered, nearly falling over his chair before catching himself.

"That girl was an idiot," He said, "Probably, a lot like you."

"Sit down, Marc!" Cohen suggested.

"Fuck you, Jew boy!" Dunlop spat, then pointed at Jim. "Is Jim your boy-toy? So, you're a homo, huh? Swinging both ways, eh, Jimmy baby?"

"Marc, sit down, please." Sandip urged.

But, he refused to sit.

"Her Daddy gave you a job after you knocked her up..." he taunted.

The claim was met with silence. Dunlop nodded.

"That's what I thought..."

"The company, I think, is getting old," Cohen said, holding onto Jim's arm, restraining him. "Let me buy you a beer at the bar..."

As they turned away, Dunlop took the opportunity. He lunged forward, attempting to strike Jim's upper vertebrae with his elbow. His drunkenness, however, caused the blow to land on Jim's shoulder instead—painful enough to bruise him, but it caused no serious damage the way it might have if the elbow had landed on its target.

Instinctively, Jim spun around. As Dunlop attempted to punch him, Jim deflected the blow easily, with a practiced sideways movement. Blocking the drunk man's attacks proved simple. Dunlop kept lunging, but each strike was easily parried. Finally, frustrated, Dunlop gathered all his strength and launched into a full-force tackle.

The movement registered in Jim's muscle memory. Acting on instinct honed through countless kata practices, he pivoted right, using his hips as a fulcrum to redirect Dunlop's momentum. The man's mass carried him forward, translating into an aerial spin that sent him flying through the air, only to crash hard against the floor. He landed on his side, dazed.

His bodyguards had finally noticed the commotion, and they arrived almost instantly. One tried to grab Jim, who slipped away. The other—larger, standing six-foot-five with a bodybuilder's physique—approached from behind, attempting to put Jim into a full Nelson hold. Jim escaped that also. As the bigger man tried to gain a grip, Jim dropped low and suddenly swept the man's forward leg under him. The massive brute toppled like a falling tower.

The smaller guard—only marginally smaller, mind you—pounced immediately. But, his fate was to fly through the air, much like his employer had, and he landed heavily, a little bit beyond Dunlop, himself. However, unlike his ward, the bodyguard wasn't entirely intoxicated, and his body was built of pure whalebone and muscle. In spite of being injured, he laboriously regained his feet, and prepared for another attempt. Jim assumed a defensive stance, ready for the next engagement.

The two massive men approached more cautiously this time, moving as a unit and clearly prepared to escalate. The smaller one had already parted his jacket, reaching for a revolver in his waistband holster. That's when the little Indian man intervened.

"Wait!" Sandip screamed, bravely stepping between Jim and the armed guard. "Enough!"

His authority was clear. The huge men hesitated. Club bouncers, nearly as large as Dunlop's guards, were also converging on the scene. The bodyguards, knowing they already faced trouble for failing to prevent the incident, waited to hear what the Indian man had to say.

"What did he do to Marc?" the slightly smaller guard demanded.

Their charge still lay senseless on the floor.

"He didn't do anything to him," Sandip insisted, "They were simply talking. Marc wanted to say something. He tried to reach this man, tripped, fell and hit his head. And, that's all there is to it. That's the report I'll be giving to Christopher Dunlop."

"I don't know about that..." the bigger guard protested.

The two muscle-bound men exchanged confused looks, but the smaller guard's hands moved away from his holster, his jacket falling back to conceal the weapon. The Indian's words seemed to carry a heavy weight of authority. The fate of their employment might well depend on what the little Indian man told Marc's father, so they were inclined to follow his orders.

"Don't worry," Sandip assured them, "I will tell his father exactly how this happened, and how you did everything you could. Understand?"

That's when the club bouncers arrived.

"What's going on?" the lead bouncer demanded, clearly wary of confronting the two bodyguards, both of whom were even larger than himself.

"It's just a little misunderstanding," Cohen explained, indicating the prone Dunlop. "Our friend got himself drunk, tripped, and fell. And, these nice men will take him home now."

He turned to Sandip. "Isn't that right?"

"Exactly so," Gupta confirmed.

The two sets of muscled men eyed each other suspiciously. Gupta addressed the bodyguards.

"All right, boys, let's take him home..."

The guards grunted agreement. The smaller one hoisted Dunlop like a rag doll across his shoulder and headed for the door.

Meanwhile, Cohen slipped hundred-dollar bills to the bouncers.

"Let's forget about all this unpleasantness..." he murmured.

The bouncers smiled, quickly pocketing the cash.

"Anything you say, Mr. Cohen," one replied, seeming to know him, "You're the man!"

The other nodded in agreement.

The odd procession—two massive men, one carrying the limp Dunlop, accompanied by the diminutive Indian—made its way out and vanished.

Jim turned to Cohen.

"I guess I owe you some money," he said, reaching for his wallet.

Cohen waved him off.

"Buy me a beer instead," He suggested. "Better yet, I'll buy you one. It was my fault that all this happened."

Without waiting for a response, he steered Jim toward the bar.

"I didn't intend to throw Dunlop that far..." Jim explained apologetically when they reached it, "But, he's such an asshole..."

"What about his bodyguard?" Cohen asked, "You threw him even further."

"Actually, I intended to throw him harder, but he didn't cooperate." Jim laughed.

"I've never seen anything like it!" Cohen exclaimed, shaking his head.

"Instincts die hard, I guess," Jim replied.

"What instincts? Who has instincts like that? Where did you learn that shit? It was like watching a fucking Bruce Lee movie. What kind of Kung Fu was that?"

Jim laughed again.

"It's not Kung Fu," Jim explained, "It was Karate, with a little Jujitsu mixed in.

"Could you have beaten up those two bodyguards with your Kung Fu, in spite of their size?"

"The bigger one was slow, but I'm glad I didn't have to find out," Jim replied.

"Teach me some of that shit!" Cohen said eagerly.

"It takes a long time to learn," Jim replied.

"I don't care how long it takes," Cohen insisted, "But, let's forget about it for the moment. Right now, it's drinking time!"

Cohen settled onto a bar stool, and Jim took the seat beside him.

"Dunlop's nothing but trouble," Cohen mused.

"Why were you sitting with him?" Jim asked.

"Connections," His friend replied, "I met him through Sandip, who I went to law school with. You're right about him being an asshole. He is. But, W.T. Fredericks' CEO is his dad, and he's the appointed successor. Plus, when he's in a good mood, drinks are on him. The Dunlops are one of the richest families in the world!"

"But, he called you a dirty Jew..." Jim protested.

"Yeah, but he doesn't hate Jews," Cohen dismissed with a wave, "He's really just a drunk asshole."

"You said you wanted to sue people like him and his Dad?"

"It's easier to reach good settlements when you know the top people," Cohen insisted, "And, that's in my future clients' interest. Besides, this asshole is destined to take over W.T. Fredericks bank. I don't know what tomorrow will bring, so I keep my options open."

"But, you said he works at Bolton, not Fredericks..."

"Yeah,"

"Why not W.T. Fredericks?" Jim asked.

"Not sure, exactly. Some of the heirs make rounds through different banks."

"That first blonde obviously wasn't swayed by his money..." Jim pointed out.

"I know her," Cohen explained. "She only dates jocks. She doesn't care about money. She probably would have fucked his bodyguards, but not him. Still, she's the exception. That's probably what set him off tonight—he's not used to rejection.

"Was he telling the truth?" Jim asked, "Did he date my wife?"

"How should I know?" Cohen replied, "What do you want? Dark or light? Guinness maybe?"

"I don't drink," Jim stated.

"You're joking!" Cohen exclaimed, "It's happy hour—drinks are half-price!"

"I'll take a 7-Up."

"7-Up?" Cohen asked, incredulously, "What? Are you a Mormon or something? It's Thursday night. I'll buy you a beer. It'll help you relax."

"7-Up relaxes me..." Jim replied with a smile.

Cohen shook his head and laughed.

"You're a strange one," he said, "That's for sure."

But, he dutifully ordered a Guinness for himself and a 7-Up for Jim. When the drinks arrived, Cohen raised his glass in toast.

"To us—to getting richer than a Dunlop!"

Jim chuckled and sipped his soda.

Cohen drained his Guinness in two long gulps, while Jim nursed his 7-Up. Another beer quickly appeared.

"Come on! You can't stick to 7-Up all night..."

Jim's 7-Up glass remained half-full, and he seemed perfectly content with that arrangement.

Midway through Cohen's third beer, a group of derivatives traders from W.T. Fredericks arrived at a nearby table. Unlike Bolton Sayres, which was exclusively an investment bank, Fredericks maintained traditional banking divisions—savings, lending, and credit cards. However, like Bolton and other cartel members, the serious profit came from derivatives trading: interest rate swaps, futures, forwards, options, credit default swaps, and synthetic securities.

The banking cartel's monopoly over derivatives made it nearly impossible for outsiders to compete. Their decades-old agreements had transformed markets into an enormous casino. Customers could legally bet on virtually anything—pork bellies, iron ore, oil, precious metals, interest rates, Chinese tea, even weather patterns. Weather futures traded openly on the registered futures exchange.

Their influence over major central banks—the Federal Reserve, European Central Bank, Bank of England, and others—guaranteed tight control over derivatives, especially interest rate products, the most lucrative sector. Exact awareness of what the central banks will do with interest rates, long before anyone else knows and long before they do it, allows the "house" to make informed bets that it never loses. It is not that different from a Las Vegas casino, except that, in the banking casino, an occasional unexpected conflict and/or a rogue trader can disrupt the system.

The Fredericks traders were young professionals who liked to drink heavily and party without restraint. When the inevitable drinking challenge emerged, Timothy Cohen, despite being a lawyer who should have known better, dove in enthusiastically. The next day's work schedule didn't deter the young traders, nor did it discourage him.

The contest began with six competitors but quickly narrowed to three serious contenders, one of whom was Cohen. The audience, mostly junior Fredericks bankers, cheered impartially for their colleagues and for the Bolton Sayres lawyer. Another contestant collapsed, leaving just Cohen and a heavyset Fredericks trader.

The opponent's substantial girth suggested greater alcohol capacity. Yet Cohen persisted, refusing to concede.

"Drink, drink, drink, drink..." the crowd chanted as fresh whiskey shots appeared.

Jim checked his watch: 11 P.M.

Despite his sobriety, even Jim found himself caught up in the festive atmosphere. His friend's determination kept him fixed in place, in spite of the fact that he had promised Laura he was going to be home early. He had no choice but to stay until the contest's conclusion. Cohen had consumed five beers prior to entering the competition, and had added countless shots of whiskey since it began. Both finalists took a brief bathroom break before resuming. Cohen returned with bloodshot eyes and clutching his stomach. Yet, he remained determined.

The crowd behaved like teenagers at a sporting event. Jim pondered the irony: how could prestigious institutions like W.T. Fredericks entrust such people with investor funds? The rowdy traders controlled $78 trillion in gross derivatives, capable of destroying billions in shareholder value instantly. Only the influence exerted by their employer, on central bank actions, prevented catastrophe.

These were members of the same privileged class who had collectively crashed the global economy in 2008. It was inevitable that, sooner or later, the same thing would happen again because nothing much had changed. Things had stayed the same because the same top players were still in charge. Some outsiders were nearly ruined by the market losses in 2008, but cartel members had all received central bank bailouts at the expense of taxpayers and savers, worldwide.

"I'm winning!" Cohen slurred triumphantly.

Jim whispered, "This is stupid. Let's go home."

He tried pulling Cohen from his chair, but the man wouldn't budge.

"I'm winning!" Cohen repeated.

The crowd's chanting intensified. More whiskey shots appeared. Both men drained them instantly.

"Drink! Drink! Drink!" The spectators persisted.

Neither competitor wanted to disappoint or surrender. They continued drinking until the Fredericks trader swayed precariously. However, it was Cohen who collapsed first. Jim caught him, but he still bumped his head against a wall tile.

Jim propped him upright on the floor while the crowd hoisted their champion. They chanted his name:

"Gimme an M! Gimme an A! Gimme an R! Gimme a T! Gimme an I! Gimme an N! What does it spell? Mar–tin, Mar–tin, Mar–tin, Mar–tin..."

They paraded their victor toward the bathroom, where he promptly vomited just prior to passing through the door. Two colleagues carried him inside.

Meanwhile, Cohen groaned,

"I think I'm gonna be sick."

He, too, began retching. In between the episodes of violent vomiting, Jim escorted him to the men's room, where both finalists expelled part of the evening's excess. It was already past midnight by the time Jim helped Cohen into a cab. The journey home featured continued stomach upheavals, earning a serious cleaning surcharge from the driver.

At Cohen's walk-up apartment, Jim carried him up the three flights to his tiny efficiency unit. Cohen attempted to drink water, but he couldn't keep that down either. The 15×12 foot space that was the man's Manhattan apartment contained a Murphy bed and sofa. Jim lowered the bed, settled his friend into it, and covered him with a blanket.

"Need to sleep this off..." Cohen mumbled semi–consciously.

As Jim reached the door, Cohen called out weakly.

"Jim..."

"Yeah?"

"Thanks."

Cohen drifted off, and Jim locked the door from inside before leaving, using a key he'd found in his friend's back pocket. Then, he clicked the door shut, and slipped the key back into the apartment, underneath the door. He'd already called Laura to explain the situation, but in spite of that, he knew that returning home after 2 AM would typically trigger an intense argument. Only the sleeping baby would prevent a major confrontation.

Chapter 10 – THE FUNDRAISER

The Ritz-Carlton Central Park Hotel, formerly known as the Hotel St. Moritz, stood proudly at 50 Central Park South. After its 2002 reopening, it maintained its reputation for luxury, boasting spectacular park views and a coveted location near Fifth Avenue, Broadway, and Rockefeller Center. Most importantly for our story, it was within walking distance of the Stoneham's penthouse.

On Friday, April 19, 2013, the hotel hosted the prestigious Bolton Benefit for the Arts Dinner, the Bolton Sayres' annual gala. While the event itself ran smoothly, the weather proved uncooperative. Rain pounded mercilessly from the heavens, forcing attendees in their formal attire to seek refuge in taxis and limousines.

Jim arrived by taxi directly from work, waiting beneath the protective canopy of the drop-off area for his wife. When Laura's taxi pulled up, they entered together. Neither of them was particularly enthusiastic about such social functions. Their attendance stemmed from obligation. Laura's mother traditionally organized the event.

Throughout the venue, New York society women gathered in small circles to do what they did best. Which was gossiping. Rumors spread like wildfire through these social conduits, each story growing more elaborate as it passed from person to person and group to group, with truth becoming increasingly irrelevant with each retelling.

Servers wove through the crowds with elegant precision, offering champagne and wines in delicate glasses. Others carried trays of appetizers – steaming egg rolls, franks in blankets, salmon tarts, and miniature Coney Island knishes. Jim had long ago decided these hors d'oeuvres were the only redeeming feature of such social obligations.

"Oh, Jim, look!" Laura exclaimed, spotting a passing tray.

She quickly intercepted the waiter and loaded her plate with egg rolls – her favorite. She devoured them almost immediately, drawing a polite smile from her husband. He'd addressed her weight concerns too many times to mention it now, especially since she typically ignored his concerns anyway.

"I know it's gross," she admitted between bites, "but I'm so hungry..."

Jim couldn't help but notice, yet again, how dramatically slim beauty he'd married turned into the fat woman who was now by his side, less than two years later. Her pretty face had grown puffy. Her figure now resembled that of the wife of the ogre "Shrek" from the cartoon. And, most importantly, although she was well aware of his feelings about the matter, she was also apparently indifferent to them.

Laura suddenly brightened, pointing out Leon and Anna Sikovsky, middle-aged immigrants who'd defected from the Soviet Union in 1986 during a Moscow Ballet tour. Now, the pair had both become successful Broadway choreographers and built new lives in America. They chose never to return to Russia, even after the fall of communism. She eagerly guided him toward the pair, greeting them with European-style kisses on both cheeks.

"This is my husband, Jim!" she announced proudly, before turning to him and explaining, "Mr. Sikovsky choreographed our musical..."

"Dis is da boy I hear so much about, eh?" Sikovsky's thick Russian accent colored his words as he extended his hand.

"It's a pleasure to meet you," Jim responded, shaking it firmly.

"Such a handsome boy..." Mrs. Sikovsky stage-whispered to Laura, ensuring everyone heard.

"Ah," Leon added, "dis young lady, my little Laura, vill' someday be a star. I am sure of it."

Laura beamed at the praise.

"You're too kind, Mr. Sikovsky..." She said, appreciating the sentiment and smiling broadly.

As Jim reached for a glass of pink champagne from a passing waiter, a strong arm wrapped around his shoulders. It was Jeremy Stoneham, Laura's father, who proceeded to kiss his daughter's forehead.

"Daddy!" Laura exclaimed, embracing him. "I thought you were still in DC?"

"I was," he confirmed. "But that ordeal is over...thankfully."

After exchanging pleasantries with Sikovsky, Jim broached a previous discussion with his father-in-law:

"Mr. Stoneham, I'd still like to talk about what we started to discuss before you left..."

Stoneham knew exactly what his son-in-law was referring to, but dismissed the request with a wave of his hand.

"This is not the time, Jim..." He said.

"When is the time?" Jim asked.

Ignoring the question, Stoneham instead turned his attention to the Sikovskys.

"You two are looking fabulous! Thanks so much for coming." He said, courteously.

"I should tank' you," Sikovsky responded warmly, "for all you've done in support of da' arts."

"We do what we can," Stoneham replied, clearly pleased.

As new guests approached, Stoneham guided Laura away from the pair of choreographers, with Jim following behind. Their progress was interrupted by an elderly man. Admiral Stark's deeply lined face was offset by sharp, intelligent eyes and a ring of sparse gray hair that rimmed his head.

Stoneham made the introductions, and the Admiral immediately recognized Laura.

"Ah! Little Laura. As pretty as ever..."

Laura's attention was quickly diverted by Patricia Aubrey, however, one of her old boarding school friends. The two women fell into animated conversation, leaving the men to their own discussion.

"Jeremy," Admiral Stark said, "I want to thank you personally for bringing Clyde Gibbons into the loop. His middle eastern experience has been helpful, given the threats we're facing..."

Stoneham introduced the Admiral to Jim as the Chairman of the President's Commission on Homeland Security. The group was, in theory, purely advisory only, but in truth, it wielded enormous power and influence. The Admiral leaned in, conspiratorially, and said to Jim,

"Your father-in-law is a lot more important to national security than I am..."

"That's not true..." Stoneham demurred, though clearly pleased at the statement.

"It is true," the Admiral insisted. "All the stakeholders know it. The streets are safe from terrorism, in large part, thanks to Bolton Sayres and the other banks."

"I don't know what to say," Jim admitted.

"You haven't told him, have you?" the Admiral asked Stoneham.

"No."

"Don't you think he ought to know?"

"I suppose he ought to," Stoneham conceded. "You do want to be in the loop, don't you, Jim?"

"Well, yeah, of course." Jim agreed.

"Good. But everything we're about to discuss is confidential. Understand?"

"Jim, my boy, the company you work for plays a much more important role in national security than you probably realize," Admiral Stark suggested.

Though confused, Jim remained diplomatic.

"I'm all ears..."

"We need more than just your ears..." Stoneham pressed. "We need a solemn pledge from you to the effect that you'll keep everything we discuss today in complete confidence. Is that agreed?"

Jim hesitated. He took such promises seriously. His curiosity, however, won out.

"Of course. I'm a lawyer," He asserted, "That's what lawyers do. They keep stuff confidential. And, besides, even if that weren't the case, I would never risk national security. I can assure you."

"Good. That's why I can accept your word of honor," The admiral asserted, "But, you still have to promise that no matter what your view is about what you're about to hear, you'll keep your word. You'll keep everything we're about to discuss strictly confidential. Do I have your word on that?"

"Yes, of course," Jim confirmed.

Stoneham nodded to the Admiral.

"Let's find a place more discreet..." He said.

Turning to his daughter, who was still engrossed in her conversation with Patricia, he announced,

"We've got company business to discuss. We'll be back in about twenty minutes. Okay, little sweetheart?"

Laura acknowledged the statement, with a distracted and disinterested smile. Her focus was not on what the men were doing, but on the continuing animated discussion with her friend. In fact, she barely registered the fact that the three men departed. They exited the main ballroom, traversing a long hallway until they reached a specific conference room. Stoneham opened the door with a key and, then, he and the admiral conducted what appeared to be a careful inspection of the space with an electronic device of some kind.

"It's still clean, I'd say," Admiral Stark concluded, closing the door behind them.

Jim felt uneasy about discussing matters requiring sworn secrecy in a publicly accessible conference room, but the others appeared comfortable with the setting.

"It's OK," Stoneham said, anticipating Jim's concerns. "The moment that door closes, this room is soundproof. We sweep it for bugs every hour on the hour."

"You do?" Jim asked.

"Of course," Admiral Stark confirmed. "It was swept for bugs just a few minutes ago, and my personal electronic detector didn't find any, just a second ago."

Jim realized then that this seemingly chance meeting during the gala had been carefully orchestrated. The room's recent sweep for listening devices indicated that this was planned, not spontaneous. Admiral Stark began, speaking in measured tones, as he spent the next fifteen minutes explaining the details about the THEATRES surveillance system and how it worked. When he finished, Jim was so stunned he didn't know what to say.

"Not exactly what you expected, eh?" Stoneham asked.

Jim struggled to find words.

"It's... well, Orwellian. You're watching everybody, 24 hours a day, 7 days a week... everybody, every day?"

The Admiral nodded proudly.

"Not everywhere, not inside people's houses, of course," He said, "Not without a court order, that is, but, generally, yes. It's the only way to keep the country safe."

Jim shook his head in profound disbelief.

"We really have no choice," Stoneham insisted. "If not for this detailed surveillance, New York City would be a radioactive waste by now."

"Incidentally, just to correct what may be a misunderstanding..." the Admiral interjected. "We are not watching anyone. We simply log it all and file it in case it's needed."

"What's the difference?" Jim challenged.

"The difference is huge," Admiral Stark insisted, "The word 'watching' implies that some human being is spying on another human being. Our system doesn't do that. Not at all. Instead, we use digital scanning. Everything is anonymized, unless an alert is triggered. So, no human being ever sees any identifying information on anyone else, unless the computer detects a serious threat."

"Big brother is still watching," Jim countered. "That's the bottom line."

"It's a give and take," Stoneham insisted, "The trade is hard, but keeping America secure is a hard job."

"The implications are terrifying," Jim argued.

"That's an extreme way of putting it?" Stoneham responded, "We're just keeping everyone safe."

"I don't think so," Jim insisted.

His father–in–law then took another 10 minutes or so to explain how they'd obtained proper permits and documentation, all technically available in public records but effectively buried among countless other documents.

"Does the media know about it?" Jim asked.

"Of course they do," Stoneham confirmed.

"Isn't their job to disclose this kind of thing to the people affected?" Jim asked.

"Well, if they did that, all the terrorists would also be aware of everything." Admiral Stark insisted.

"We have agreements..." Mr. Stoneham noted.

"What kind of agreements?" Jim asked.

"Oh, nothing formal," Stoneham explained. "It's just that the press isn't going to make waves, since they live here too."

"How can you silence every newspaper and news channel in the country?" Jim marveled.

"Jim, ninety-five percent of all English speaking mass media is owned by just 5 major media companies..." Stoneham explained, "It so happens that we, along with other banks, control most of their shares. But, we don't try to silence anyone. Smart people understand that this is for their benefit, too."

"You've created a spying conspiracy, with tens of thousands of pinhead cameras and microphones, covering every inch of the City, and the press has agreed to cover it up!"

"Conspiracy is a harsh and very inaccurate term, conjuring up all sorts of private gain concepts," Stoneham deflected. "But, there's no private gain. We're doing our patriotic duty. And, so is the media. It's a tacit agreement to do the right thing."

"It's a conspiracy!" Jim wouldn't back down, "No one can walk, talk, eat, drink or do anything else without being recorded, and the media shuts up about it because they've been sucked in, and are deliberately keeping the issue away from public debate. People have a right to decide whether they want this or not. Whether they're willing to trade their right to privacy for additional security."

"We're not hiding anything," Stoneham countered.

"You're hiding everything," Jim countered, "If the public ever found out, it would be a huge scandal."

"I don't think you get it, son," Admiral Stark interjected, suddenly.

"What don't I get?"

"We're at war," the Admiral declared.

"Congress is supposed to declare war. That hasn't happened."

"There's a Presidential decree," Stoneham noted.

Jim pressed on with his opposition, and you could see in the faces of the older men that they were anything but pleased with him.

"Who programs the computers?" Jim asked, pointedly, "Who stops the system from being deployed for blackmail? If someone disagrees with the people who run this system, that person can be destroyed. It's unconstitutional."

"Incorrect," Stoneham replied immediately, "The Constitution protects against unlawful government searches, but the government doesn't run THEATRES. We do!"

"What?" Jim exclaimed.

"The banks collectively run the system," His father-in-law explained, "No one's constitutional rights are violated. There's no governmental intrusion at all."

"That makes it worse!" Jim exclaimed. "It's a privately controlled surveillance system, backed by US military technology, and tacitly supported by the US government, under the control of a handful of banks! I don't know what to say..."

Stoneham suddenly shifted the conversation.

"Do you remember that girl you saved from being raped, when you were 16 years old?"

"How do you know about that?" Jim asked, startled.

"I know about a lot of things," Stoneham replied. "You were 16 going on 17, but your age doesn't matter. The point is that the police were not there to help. They didn't even know what was happening. You saved that girl and her brother. What if you weren't there? What if the knife that gave you that big scar on your arm, plunged into your heart instead? You'd have been killed..."

"What does that have to do with what we're discussing?" Jim asked.

"Everything," His father-in-law insisted, "I'll pose a question to you...why did you do it? Why did you put your life at risk to save someone else?"

"It was a calculated risk," Jim responded, "I did what I thought I had to do at the time, under the circumstances."

"Exactly," Stoneham agreed, "And, that young girl and boy were lucky you saved them."

"What does one thing have to do with the other?" Jim asked.

"Simply this... THEATRES ensures that no innocent girl, facing a rapist, will face him alone. Once we perfect the system, muggings and rape will become a relic of the past. Our computers will immediately detect all threats to innocent life and limb. When they do, the police will be sent out, automatically, immediately. It's for the public good."

"That's a severely stretched argument..." Jim warned. "You could go further and say we ought to bug everybody's house? That would make it possible for cops to arrive automatically and immediately whenever domestic violence occurs. But, that's not the kind of world I want to live in."

The heated conversation continued with more revelations. Jim was told about the National Security Court, its secret appointments, and its funding details. In response, Jim suggested targeting specific groups instead. His father-in-law immediately cited constitutional concerns about the targeting of ethnic groups, particularly those connected with the Middle East. Finally, Jim summed up his view of the matter.

"I think the whole thing stinks!" He exclaimed, "You've created a real world version of George Orwell's 1984."

"Not true," Admiral Stark corrected him, "The Orwell book is about government surveillance,"

"Alright," Jim pressed, "You claim it's all private. But, who put up the money?"

His father-in-law gave him the answer, instantly,

"New York City contributed $150 million for the construction of the operations center. That was matched by the Federal government. But, it's the banks who pay rent on the facility. We also pay the salaries, utilities, maintenance, repairs, and so on."

Jim shook his head in response. He remained unconvinced.

Admiral Stark cut in sharply.

"It's about patriotism, son!" He claimed, "As long as the people running the system are honest, decent patriots, no one has anything to fear."

"Yeah, well," Jim replied, "running a system like the one you've just described, without having it devolve into destroying all basic freedom, requires persons of higher moral fiber than anyone who exists. Human beings are all corruptible, and..."

"I know one who isn't." Stoneham interrupted him mid-sentence.

"Yeah, right," Jim stated, skeptically.

"No, you'd be surprised," His father-in-law stated with confidence, "But, I really do know someone who is entirely incorruptible, who ought to run this system."

"Who?" Jim challenged.

"You!" His father-in-law immediately replied.

"Is that a joke?" Jim asked, taken aback.

"No," Stoneham repeated emphatically. "I've considered it carefully, and talked with other people, like the Admiral here. Your unique abilities and character make you perfect. Even your reaction today makes you even more perfect. You, Jim, are going to run THEATRES!"

Jim stared at the man for a moment, not knowing exactly how to respond, but finally he found the words,

"Are you serious?" Jim responded, "You expect me to run a system like that?"

"I'm entirely serious," Mr. Stoneham said calmly, "I want you in charge of the system. And, I'm not the only one. The world NEEDS you in charge of the system. The current director is a man by the name of Adriano Navarro. We're going to retire him. Many of us want him gone. Unlike you, he's a man of weak moral character. We need someone exactly like you... incorruptible."

"My wife's your daughter..." Jim pointed out, "Why would others agree to it?"

Stoneham ignored the question.

"You'd get a big raise in pay, of course," He pointed out. "It would be commensurate with your additional responsibilities."

"Didn't you say that a Committee exercises authority over this?"

Stoneham nodded.

"So, why would they agree to having your son-in-law run this overwhelmingly powerful system?"

"There are ways to convince people," Admiral Stark interjected, "And, your father-in-law is not talking about you taking charge tomorrow. It would be a slow process of learning, but it has to start soon. We need Navarro out of there as soon as possible..."

"Look, Jim," Stoneham stated, "This system's already been quietly challenged in court, and we've won. It isn't going away. But under your leadership, the problems you fear could be minimized."

"Why would they agree to me?" Jim asked, again.

"Because whoever is in charge of the system needs to be above the fray," Stoneham said, "Frankly, Jim, there's not a banker in the system who'd hire you for their investment banking team. You're too damn honest. Everybody at Bolton Sayres already knows that. You've gained a wider reputation than you know, and in a very short time. So, instead, we'll be grooming you to take Navarro's place. In a few years, everyone in the system is going to know you and trust you."

"I... I don't know what to say," Jim stammered. "In theory, I'm very opposed to this entire concept. I'd like to see it dismantled. I don't want to run it."

"There's no rush," Stoneham said smoothly. "You'll be introduced step by step. Soon, you'll realize that we've got no alternative."

Jim remained silent, still processing the unexpected proposal.

"We desperately need someone totally trustworthy," Admiral Stark added.

"So, as of next week, I've issued an order, transferring you from legal to compliance," Stoneham announced. "It'll be the start of your new role."

"I didn't agree. I never said I was willing to do it." Jim pointed out.

"That's okay," Stoneham commented, 'You don't have to. Not at this point. You may even turn down the job eventually, but I think you won't once you realize how important it is. I hope you don't. But, I'm the one who decides where my employees work, and you're moving to compliance. After that, we'll move you through various positions until you learn everything necessary. Within two years, you'll be ready to take full control."

"What happens to the current director?" Jim asked.

"He gets to retire," Stoneham replied.

"Does he know this?" Jim pressed.

"Is that relevant?" Stoneham deflected.

"I'm still at a loss for words," Jim admitted.

"That's fine," Stoneham replied, knowing that Jim's failure to reject the offer outright meant he was considering it, "But, remember, THEATRES will continue to exist. If you're serious about protecting people's rights, if you're in charge, you could take steps to ensure that the public's trust is never misused?"

Jim wrestled with the moral implications. He wanted to expose it all. The public deserved to know. Yet he had given his word. He couldn't break it. Perhaps, his father–in–law was right, after all. Maybe, there was a middle path? By accepting the position, he could ensure that power was never abused...

"If you didn't see this kind of system as objectionable, frankly, we wouldn't want you so badly. We need men like you! Your country needs you..." Admiral Stark added, enthusiastically.

Jim remained silent.

His response aligned perfectly with his father-in-law's expectations. Putting Jim in charge of THEATRES would accomplish two major goals: first, it would neutralize Adriano Navarro's growing power and influence and, second, it would ensure his daughter was married to an influential cartel figure, even if Jim's nature prevented him from becoming a proper investment banker.

The THEATRES operating agreement gave shared operating authority to four American banks. But, though all four were allied together inside the cartel for now, allies could become rivals instantly. Control over THEATRES represented leverage over everyone who lived or worked in New York City and, eventually, since there were plans to take the system nationwide, over the entire nation. There was no candidate who didn't have existing biases and relationships. Jim might be perceived by the others as supporting the interests of his father-in-law and Bolton Sayres. But, the other CEOs were searching for a person of unimpeachable integrity. It was a matter of self-protection. Jim was uncompromisingly honest, and this characteristic would be played up by the best publicists. He was perfect for overseeing the surveillance system.

Stoneham shook the Admiral's hand, satisfied with the meeting's outcome, despite the initial objections voiced by his son-in-law.

"It's been a pleasure," he said contentedly.

"Likewise," the Admiral replied, beaming.

He turned to Jim.

"Young man, I like you...you clearly have a bright future, and I know you'll serve your country well."

Jim found the certainty of the two old men rather strange. They acted as if his acceptance was a foregone conclusion. That level of presumption bothered him. What if he declined the offer, as he was inclined to do?

After the Admiral departed, Stoneham spoke again.

"A word to the wise," He whispered, "You should never express doubts about national security to men like Admiral Stark. Understand?"

Jim didn't understand, but didn't feel like arguing the matter. He simply nodded and let that be that. His mind was swimming with the implications of their previous discussion. They returned to the main ballroom together until someone intercepted Stoneham.

Jim spotted Laura where he'd left her, still chatting with her childhood friend. He approached and interrupted their endless conversation.

"Let's go home..." he whispered.

She shook her head.

"We can't," She said, "We have to stay for Mom's auction..."

He briefly closed his eyes in frustration.

"OK. But afterward, we leave..."

She nodded and resumed her conversation. Jim noticed some colleagues nearby and walked over to join them. While his back was turned, an unwelcome visitor approached Laura. Marc Dunlop wore a Cheshire cat grin.

"Mind if I speak with Laura?" he asked politely.

"Of course not," the other girl giggled, then turned to Laura. "My Mom's over there, and I need to speak with her anyway. You have my new number now – so, let's stay in touch..."

Laura nodded. Her friend departed. She was left alone with Dunlop.

"What do you want?" she demanded coldly.

He shrugged.

"Just saying hello. Is that wrong?"

Her silence prompted him to continue.

"I don't know why you can't see what a complete loser this Jim Bentley of yours is?" He burst out.

"The only loser I see, right now, is YOU!" she shot back.

"Face reality, Laura," he pressed. "Leave the slums. You really need to dump him."

"You're a delusional scumbag," she replied. "Please leave."

"I'll forgive that comment," he said magnanimously.

"Go away," she repeated.

"Whatever drove you to that trailer trash, I'm willing to work through it," he continued. "The baby doesn't bother me, and you know as well as I do, that we were meant to be together, if only in terms of dynasty..."

That's when Jim finally noticed what was going on behind him. Though distance and noise prevented him from hearing the exact words, he saw Dunlop confronting Laura and immediately walked over to intervene.

"Get away from my wife!" he demanded.

Dunlop turned, assessed Jim, then laughed and faced Laura again.

"It's his caveman act that you find so attractive, isn't it?" he remarked. "That's the appeal, right?"

Jim turned to Laura.

"You know this guy?" He asked, "Is that true?"

"Of course she knows me..." Dunlop interjected.

"Unfortunately, yes," she replied.

"He's bothering you?"

"No," she said, shaking her head. "But he's leaving now, aren't you, Marc?"

"Not really..." Dunlop replied.

Suddenly, Jeremy Stoneham hurried over.

"Ah, Marc!" he exclaimed, enthusiastically shaking Dunlop's hand. "Wonderful to see you!"

He gestured to Jim.

"I've been wanting to introduce you two. Young Mr. Dunlop here is barely thirty-three, and he's already one of our youngest managing partners!"

Jim glanced between Laura and her father but remained silent.

"One of the few analysts who is always consistently correct on his market predictions," Stoneham continued.

He turned to his daughter.

"Laura, have you formally introduced these two?"

"No," she said.

"This is Marc Dunlop, Jim," Stoneham announced.

Dunlop offered his hand, which Jim ignored.

"What exactly does managing partner mean?" Jim asked Stoneham.

"Historically, it meant sharing in the firm's profits," Stoneham explained. "Now that we're public, though, it just signifies exceptional contribution. It comes with certain voting rights and bonus structures. This young man generated nearly a billion in revenue last year. He's compensated accordingly."

"We've met," Jim stated flatly.

"Wonderful!" Stoneham exclaimed, missing Jim's refusal to shake hands. He drew Laura away to meet someone else, calling back to the two men: "Get better acquainted..."

Left alone, they stood in silence until Dunlop spoke.

"I hold no grudges."

Jim matched his conciliatory tone.

"Neither do I. I assume you had too much to drink."

"I did," Dunlop agreed, "Which is the only reason you got away with it."

"Got away with what?"

"Sucker punching me," Dunlop explained.

"I didn't sucker punch you," Jim insisted. "I defended myself when you attacked me, nothing more."

"The hell you didn't!" Dunlop snarled.

"You hit my shoulder from behind," Jim said, "Just barely missed my neck, which you were clearly aiming for."

"Your memory's faulty," Dunlop replied. "But as I said, no grudges. I rather admire you, actually."

"What?" Jim asked, baffled by the man's strange behavior.

Dunlop simply smiled.

"I really do..." He insisted.

Jim turned and was starting to walk away, but Dunlop walked after him while continuing.

"I mean, well, here you are, a poor boy – not a penny to your name...low class, plebeian, you might say," Dunlop sneered. "But, in spite of that, you managed to knock up a rich girl, get her pregnant, and get her daddy to give you a job to save her reputation. Clever, clever..."

Jim continued to walk away without answering, but Dunlop followed.

"I know a lot about your wife, you know," Dunlop declared. "I've known her far longer than you have. In fact, I know her inside and out. Literally. But, I wouldn't want her now, not with all that extra weight and all."

That was enough to stop Jim in his tracks, and he turned to his tormentor.

"What the fuck is that supposed to mean, asshole?" He hissed.

"Oh, temper, temper..." Dunlop smiled.

"You really are a piece of shit..." Jim snarled.

And, with that insult, Dunlop's face darkened.

"You don't have any idea who you're talking to, do you?"

"You already told me who your daddy is," Jim said. "I'm not impressed. Having a rich daddy doesn't make you any less of an asshole."

Dunlop's false smile now twisted into a scowl.

"Look at you, getting all red-faced," he taunted. "Looks like the caveman's getting ready to attack me again..."

"YOU attacked me!" Jim insisted, for the second time.

"Excuses..." Dunlop drawled. "Everyone has them. Doesn't matter though. I gotta hand it to you. You've positioned yourself well. You'll be going after that Stoneham money soon. Planning to knock off the old man? Or, I suppose, you'll say you married for love, right."

"That's right, asshole," Jim said firmly, "I did marry for love."

"Ah, love!" Dunlop's voice dripped venom. "Do you know how much richer I am than you are? What do you make? $100,000? $150? $200,000 max? I can buy and sell you!"

"Go fuck yourself," Jim replied.

"I can buy and sell you!" Dunlop insisted, again.

Jim decided to end the pointless exchange. But as he turned to leave, Dunlop lunged forward to block his path.

"Don't get mad, Jim," he taunted, laughing. "I like you! I really do! There you were, without a pot to piss in, but I guess, you must have some major equipment. Laura likes big dicks, you know. She liked mine too..."

The taunts were finally penetrating Jim's defenses. He wanted to hit the man, but he knew that, to do so in the middle of the gala, was impossible. Beyond causing a scandal and risking jail time, Dunlop was probably being as bold as he was because his bodyguards were hiding nearby. There were probably more than two of them this time. If he laid a finger on their employer, they'd have an excuse to pounce on him. They might jointly beat him to a pulp, and even if, by some miracle, he prevailed, it would be a disaster.

Jim tried again to walk away, but Dunlop grabbed him.

"Don't walk away from me!" The man exclaimed, "I'm not finished."

"I think you are..." Jim replied.

He stopped, turned, and caught Dunlop's thumb, twisting it and his hand, into a painful but controlled wrist lock. Dunlop was searching the room for his guards but, apparently, they were too far away or positioned incorrectly, so that they could not see the pain on his face. The move was small and subtle but incredibly painful. Then, after inflicting extreme pain for an instant, Jim released him.

"Fuck you!" Dunlop snarled, nursing his wrist, and threatening, "I'm gonna have you beaten to a pulp and none of your Karate shit is going to help you!"

But, beyond those words, he did nothing.

"You'd need another million or so losers like yourself," Jim snapped, happy with himself at having inflicted such a small but controlled and extremely painful injury on his enemy, "And, by the way, the next time you grab me, I'm breaking bones. And, it'll happen way too fast for your guards to intervene."

"Fuck you!" Dunlop shouted, but now he kept his distance. "They'll be on you in an instant if you ever touch me again!"

"Whatever..."

With that, he walked away, leaving Dunlop behind him, seething.

"Watch your back, Jim!" Dunlop screamed after him.

Jim ignored it and moved across the ballroom, finding Laura speaking with someone new. She gestured him over as he approached. Her companion was an elderly man who appeared to be in his late sixties.

"This is Senator Collins," she said. "Senator, this is my husband, Jim..."

"It's an honor, Senator."

"Senator Collins is one of Daddy's oldest friends," Laura explained.

"I've known little Laura since she was this high," the Senator said, gesturing to indicate a child's height. "She's all grown up now. You're a lucky young man."

"I know," Jim agreed.

When the Senator turned to greet another guest, Jim drew Laura aside.

"How well do you know Marc Dunlop?" he asked.

Laura rolled her eyes. "I just know him, okay?"

"Did you date him?"

"For a few weeks," she admitted.

"Why?"

"Our parents have tried pushing us together since I was born."

"Did you sleep with him?" he asked directly.

"What?" she startled.

"Did you?"

"It was a long time ago..." she whispered.

"Why did you stop dating him?"

"Because he's a pervert and an asshole."

"But you slept with him?"

"It wasn't my choice," she insisted. "He forced himself. I was only sixteen."

"Why didn't you report it to the police?"

"Because... I don't know... it would have caused trouble," She replied, "His father, you know, he's the CEO of W.T. Fredericks."

"I take it you never told your father?" He asked.

She shook her head, and there were tears streamed down her cheeks. Jim took her in his arms and hugged her.

"You should tell him." He advised quietly.

She shook her head violently.

"Are you crazy?" She said, "He can never know, Jim. Don't you dare tell him! Promise me you won't tell him..."

"It's up to you to tell him, not me," Jim replied.

As her strength crumbled, his resolve and rage intensified. Dunlop had been born rich and irritating – a nuisance and a jerk. Now it was personal, deeply personal. Jim's hatred consumed him. His thoughts turned murderous; he imagined strangling the man, watching the life drain from his eyes. Would that be enough? No, it wasn't.

"Take me home..." she pleaded.

He asked nothing more. He'd tortured her enough, and he recognized his own dark thoughts were dangerous. There would be time to learn the rest of whatever full story she might tell in a different setting. Right now, the emotions were simply too raw. Leaving the gala was the sensible choice. They made their excuses and left.

They caught a cab to their nearby apartment. The elevator carried them up, and they walked the carpeted hallway to the door. Jim inserted his key and flipped on the lights. The scene before them was shocking. The entire apartment lay in shambles, ransacked completely except for the walls themselves.

Much of the destruction appeared beyond repair.

Chapter 11 – RANSACKED!

A home is sacred—a sanctuary where people seek refuge from an uncertain world. Psychologists say that when a burglary occurs, the emotional trauma extends far beyond the loss of possessions. The violation of a home leaves deeper scars. Once burglarized, a home never regains its feeling of safety. It never truly feels like home again.

When Jim entered his apartment, there were no signs of forced entry—no broken locks, no shattered windows. Yet someone had clearly been inside. The evidence was overwhelming. Kitchen cabinets gaped open. Their contents were scattered across counters and floors. Pots, pans, and cutlery lay strewn about, some upright, others overturned, a few visibly dented. The living room was worse: couch and armchair cushions had been sliced open end-to-end, exposing raw foam underneath. The destruction was complete and methodical.

Shattered cups and saucers littered the floor, fragments mixing with broken glass from other items. Books lay scattered everywhere. Even Laura's prized collection of Lladro ceramic sculptures hadn't been spared—they lay in pieces beside a broken curio cabinet, which had been toppled onto its side, its glass panes shattered. Jim motioned for Laura to stay outside while he investigated further.

At least their daughter Jennifer was safe. Isabel, Laura's former nanny, was babysitting her at the Stoneham's penthouse, nearby. The little girl was undoubtedly playing and smiling, blissfully unaware of her parents' distress. The elderly woman would keep her fed, bathed, and entertained in a secure environment, far from this scene of destruction.

Jim moved cautiously through the apartment, wondering if the intruders might still be present. He checked Jennifer's room first. The door stood slightly ajar, and he pushed it open carefully. Toys were scattered everywhere—though that wasn't necessarily unusual for a baby's room. The crib appeared untouched, but the rest of the room hadn't escaped the destruction. Dresser drawers had been pulled halfway out, their contents dumped onto the floor.

Something felt wrong about the whole situation. The front door had been locked when they arrived, its deadbolt secured. What kind of burglar locks up after themselves? The windows were still bolted shut from the inside. If someone had entered through the windows, somehow they'd managed to secure them perfectly afterward.

Leaving Jennifer's room, Jim saw Laura still waiting outside. He gave her an "OK" signal but motioned for her to stay put. Then he crept toward the master bedroom, his heart pounding. By now, he'd checked everywhere else. It was the last place. If any intruders remained, that's where they'd be. He hesitated at the door, then quickly grabbed the handle and burst in, ready to dodge or confront whatever awaited him.

The room was empty—at least of people. Like the rest of the apartment, it had been thoroughly ransacked. A sudden rustling sound made him jump, but it was just their Persian cat jumping down from the windowsill. Seemingly oblivious to the chaos, she rubbed against his leg, purring. The dresser drawers had been emptied onto the floor, clothes strewn everywhere, and the mattress had been sliced open, exposing springs and foam padding.

A touch on his shoulder made him spin around, ready to defend himself—but it was only Laura, who had ignored his instructions to stay outside.

"I told you to stay outside," he scolded.

"What am I, a dog?" she retorted.

Fresh tears were smearing her recently-fixed mascara—the makeup she'd repaired after their earlier discussion about Marc Dunlop. Seeing her fear and distress, Jim realized how foolish his scolding had been. He pulled her into a gentle embrace.

"I'm sorry," he said softly. "I'm just on edge."

"We should never have rented in a building without guards," she said through her tears.

It was a point well taken and one that she'd made repeatedly in the past. Their choice to rent a simple flat in an old brick building without doormen or security had been Jim's idea. Manhattan rents were astronomical, and he was determined to avoid accepting more help from her parents. It was already difficult enough that he owed his father-in-law for his job at the bank. He wanted to live within his means as an in-house lawyer. Getting a special salary hike, ordered by his father-in-law, and imposed upon the legal department's budget would have simply made him even more unpopular with his bosses than he already was.

It would have been a lot cheaper to live in a nice area in Brooklyn or Queens, but Laura had insisted on staying within walking distance of her parents. That meant paying Manhattan rents, among the highest in the world. Being close to Central Park meant the highest rent cost per square foot, even within Manhattan. She'd refused to consider anywhere else. The current apartment had been a compromise.

The flat was no more than a modest 1,100 square feet, but it cost nearly $8,000 monthly. Facing the break-in, Jim found himself questioning his stubborn decision. Had his pride put his family at risk? He walked back to the entry foyer and double-checked the lock, leaving the key in place to prevent anyone from entering from outside by jimmying it. Returning to the bedroom, he found Laura picking things up, tears still flowing.

The sight nearly broke his composure—he hadn't cried since his parents' funeral when he was eleven, fourteen years ago. But, for a moment, that emotional dam threatened to break. He fought to maintain his composure. He needed to stay strong, if only for Laura's sake.

That's when he spotted a familiar white envelope on the floor—one he remembered locking in the top dresser drawer months ago. His heart pounding, he tore it open. The $3,000 in cash was still there, untouched. He pocketed the money and moved to the living room, where he found their electronics—TV, microwave, radio, and Laura's new iPod—scattered on the floor. Almost everything in the apartment was badly damaged. Yet, nothing appeared to be missing. It made no sense. What kind of burglar leaves behind an iPod?

Suddenly, he noticed his laptop was on the kitchen floor. He picked it up. It felt unusually light. He turned it over. The back cover had been partially removed. The screws around the hard drive compartment were gone. The hard drive itself was missing. Otherwise, the laptop was intact and undamaged.

"It doesn't make any sense," he said aloud.

Laura hugged him from behind, dabbing at her mascara-stained eyes with a tissue.

"It makes perfect sense," she insisted. "I told you we never should have rented here!"

"That's not what I mean," he explained. "Burglars steal things—that's why they break in. Nothing is stolen and nothing is missing except the hard drive from my laptop. Who steals a hard drive and leaves the laptop behind?"

She looked at him, confused.

"What?" She said,

"Can't you see they didn't steal anything?" He asked her.

Laura surveyed the room, absently picking up a torn cushion. After a moment, she set it down and nodded with new understanding.

"You're right," she agreed. "My jewelry is still in the bedroom."

"This wasn't a robbery," Jim declared. "They were looking for something..."

"What would we have that they'd be looking for?" She asked.

"I think I might know what..." Jim replied.

He began searching through the scattered books and papers.

"They only took a few things: my laptop's hard drive and..." He continued searching before finishing his thought, "...a hard copy of the red book."

"The what?" Laura asked.

"The red book," He explained, "The diary I brought back from the upstate New York case. From that foreclosure and insurance proceeds case. You know, the one you found in my briefcase."

"A hard copy?" she wondered. "What about the original?"

"I gave it to the FBI," he said.

"The FBI?"

"It describes a crime that occurred about five years ago," Jim explained. "So, I felt obligated to turn it over to law enforcement. And..."

He started to search on the cabinets, on the floor, everywhere he could, and then, looked at her.

"And, they also took my evidence receipt..." He said, finally.

"Your what?" She asked.

"My evidence receipt," He replied, "The paper they give you when you turn over evidence to the FBI. It describes each and every item you've handed over to them."

They exchanged worried glances, each considering the implications but reluctant to voice them.

"It's hard to believe..." he began.

"Could the FBI do this?" Laura asked.

"It's hard to believe," he admitted. "But who else would know about the diary. Up until I handed it in, it was hidden in a compartment, inside the floor of the deceased's home."

Their conversation was suddenly interrupted by approaching sirens.

"I called the police while I was waiting outside," Laura explained.

He nodded.

The NYPD arrived on their floor shortly after, and detectives began dusting for fingerprints. Finding no signs of forced entry and only the couple's prints, they began asking questions about insurance coverage, implying the possibility that Jim or Laura might have staged the event to collect insurance money. A quick call to headquarters, however, changed their tone—once they learned Laura's identity, that line of questioning abruptly ceased.

About ninety minutes after the fruitless investigation began, it ended. The police departed. Jim suspected they'd never find the perpetrators—professionals like the ones who would be able to do something like this – enter an apartment with no signs of forced entry or exit, were sure to leave no traces. That evening, Laura spoke with her mother, and it was decided that the family would temporarily move into her parents' home.

Jim was anything but enthusiastic about the idea of living with his in-laws, despite their luxurious lifestyle. Laura had once suggested it, when they had first married—the place was enormous and mostly empty—but he had firmly refused. But, now, the choice wasn't his to make and his ego had to be shelved. His family's safety came first, and whoever had ransacked their apartment had done so in broad daylight, showing no fear of detection or consequences. They were dangerous.

The Manhattan penthouse was much smaller than their Hamptons estate, but it still sprawled across 10,000 square feet, atop one of the few modern buildings on Central Park West. It featured 24/7 armed security and multiple security systems. No one would be able to break through that level of high-security building without triggering an alarm, no matter how expert they were.

Jim's mind kept returning to the break-in. He was certain the intruders were connected to the murder described in the diary. But who even knew about it? The list was short: Tim Cohen and Laura, obviously, but both were above suspicion. The only other person was FBI Agent Peter Barkley, who had received the original diary and had ordered the issuance of the evidence receipt. But, that receipt was now gone. Agent Barkley had said he was going to review the case for possible federal jurisdiction, but expected to forward the diary to the Verde County Sheriff, since state law would normally apply.

He decided to call the FBI office. He asked to speak with Agent Barkley, but the receptionist was evasive. Then, he asked to be connected to the evidence office, where he asked for a duplicate of the evidence receipt. But, they claimed they couldn't duplicate it because no original existed, and there was no evidence that the diary had ever been delivered into FBI custody. All the records had vanished.

After that, Jim found himself questioning everything.

For example, Agent Barkley was actually assigned to investigate bank misconduct. Yet, he had become incredibly friendly with the lawyers who worked in Bolton Sayres legal department. In retrospect, that seemed highly improper, even though it had seemed perfectly normal at the time. He reprimanded himself for having ever trusted Barkley. Now, he concluded, he couldn't trust the FBI or the bank. He couldn't trust anyone!

The next day was a Saturday, and Jim walked the seven minutes that separated the Stoneham penthouse and their now abandoned apartment, for the purpose of gathering some additional belongings. He noticed a pair of jeans on the floor and suddenly remembered something. Reaching into the small watch pocket, he found that what he was looking for was still there. It had been missed—a tiny USB flash drive.

Smiling triumphantly, he transferred the drive to the watch pocket of the jeans he now wore. The vandals weren't infallible after all. The tiny USB drive contained an encrypted copy of not just the diary, but also copies of his research notes. He was sure that both the diary and his research threatened someone. Whoever had killed the widow's husband had somehow learned about the diary. Could it involve the unknown person at the bank who had arranged the odd loan on that upstate farm? Someone at Bolton Sayres was involved. He was now certain of it.

As he thought about it, the pieces were falling into place. The diary spoke of a BMW 528i—that was the same model that dominated Bolton Sayres' fleet of loaner cars. The bank replaced them every two years, but almost all of them were always BMW 528i models. No license plate had been recorded, making a direct connection impossible, but the bank's detailed vehicle records might reveal something. Dead people couldn't tell the tale of their demise, but the database might.

Using the new laptop he had just purchased the night before to replace the one that had seen its hard disk removed, he connected to Bolton Sayres' virtual private network using his employee credentials. Within minutes, he was searching the bank's internal records as if he were at his office. After about thirty minutes, he found what he sought. He tried to download the relevant information. But, it was impossible. He kept getting an error message.

SYSTEM CANNOT COMPLETE REQUESTED OPERATION

After several failed attempts, he closed the laptop and headed to the downstairs deli. He had often picked up a snack there on the way to and from work, and they had a good Wi-Fi connection. He tried again, using their connection, and successfully downloaded the files containing a record of all Bolton Sayres' BMW 528i loaners over the past six years, including thousands of names, dates, and times.

Examining the data for July 22, 2008, he found sixteen loaner cars had been checked out that day. Twelve were BMW 528i's, and eleven had been taken before noon. He copied all the files to his flash drive, and transferred a scanned copy of the Mattingly diary from the USB drive to the new laptop, putting everything under lock and key, in an encrypted folder. This time, he would make sure that the documents were not only on his laptop and on the USB drive, but also in many more places. He made redundant copies and put them into encrypted cloud storage everywhere he could think of.

Reviewing the diary, he confirmed the details: two men burying a body around 1 or 2 AM. Given the roughly three-hour drive from Manhattan to

Paradise, and assuming the killing occurred in New York City, the murder likely happened between 10 and 11 PM. The absence of decomposition details suggested the body hadn't been in the trunk very long.

Scrolling through the vehicle records again, he noticed most cars were checked out before noon. Only one person had taken a BMW late that afternoon—at 5:32 PM. While earlier than the estimated murder time, someone planning a killing might have secured transportation well in advance. The name jumped out at him: Marcus Dunlop.

After the incident at the Odysseus Club, Jim hadn't bothered following up with Laura about her possible relationship with Dunlop. He had initially been angry at the thought of it, but he'd soon been too distracted by subsequent developments. Too many other events had simply moved too quickly for him to pay much attention. Yet here was Dunlop's name, again, like a bad penny. He was clearly a scumbag. Was he also a murderer? It seemed plausible—a spoiled rich kid might think he could get away even with murder.

But, there were big holes in the theory. What was the motive? Why would a wealthy banker's son want to kill a simple farmer or innkeeper in upstate New York? On top of that, neither man described in the diary matched Dunlop. But, did that really matter? Dunlop wouldn't do the dirty work himself. He would hire thugs to do it for him. He recalled Dunlop's words to him during the incident at the club. "Watch your back" The man had warned ominously. Was he next?

Such evidence was tenuous at best. Such speculation would never hold up in court—too many assumptions based upon no hard evidence. And, possibly, Jim thought to himself, his own personal dislike for the man was coloring his judgment. There were innocent reasons to borrow a company car, and who would be foolish enough to use a company vehicle for transporting a murder victim?

The key to resolving these questions lies in identifying the first victim. If Jim's theory was correct, the person would have been reported missing from the New York City metro area. He opened a web browser and searched: "New York City Missing Persons, July 2008"

Several sites appeared, including the New York State Division of Police, but his search yielded nothing useful. Through the bank's VPN, he accessed

Westlaw, one of the main legal research portals containing nearly a century of news archives. Still no success. But, those lack of results raised his suspicions even further. In a metropolitan area of almost 30 million people, surely some missing persons had been reported around that time period. Was his search technique flawed? If so, he knew someone who could help.

He reached for his cell phone but stopped mid-dial. Mobile calls were too vulnerable—it was like shouting in public. Anyone could tap a cell phone signal. In the absence of encryption, anyone could listen in. He needed a landline. Fortunately, the old building still had a payphone. He'd read some of the information his father-in-law had sent to him about state of the art technological surveillance systems. And, he'd learned that, unless specifically targeted for tapping, landlines were still fairly safe. The call could only be flagged if it were made from a landline that was already tapped. Unlike his personal cell phone, which could be tapped by anyone with the proper equipment, a random payphone would not be monitored.

After getting a few dollars worth of quarters from the deli counter, he dialed his contact's number—which, thankfully, was also a traditional wired phone. He checked his watch, hoping he'd be able to reach him. He waited as the phone rang.

Chapter 12 – A Gigantic Problem

Madison Avenue between 55th and 72nd Street is Manhattan's premier shopping district. It is the "Gold Coast" for the wealthy elite. Among its luxurious offerings sits the Giorgio Armani store at 760 Madison, where only the truly affluent dare to venture. And, at the precise moment Jim attempted to access Bolton Sayres' vehicle records, a mountain of a man emerged from that Armani store.

Fyodor Khasan was his real name—though he hadn't used it in years. Fyodor Khasan was a favorite alias that he was now very fond of. He stood six-foot-nine, about 206 cm tall, with shoulders as broad as a heavyweight boxer. His blonde crew cut, and sharp features, suggested a military background, while his impeccably tailored suit spoke of more recent affluence. A smile playing across his face—satisfaction from purchasing three expensive custom suits. Back in Russia, his peers struggled with paying for necessities. Many turned to corruption to make ends meet. He didn't have to do that. A contract killing, from time to time, kept him flush with cash.

He smiled while thinking about how easy his job was. A bit of arson here. A well-timed explosion there. All in a day's work. He had done the same thing for the Russian state, year after year, and never been properly paid for it. America was the land of opportunity. By the standard of most people in this world, though not by the standard of those who employed him, the man had amassed considerable wealth since he'd come to America.

His sense of satisfaction vanished, however, when he heard the sharp whistle from his pocket. That particular alert tone meant trouble. He withdrew what appeared to be a standard, but tiny, Android phone, with a 4-inch screen. The device was anything but standard. It was the newest model of a phone whose operating system, RuMos, began as Russia's military-grade modification of Android. Originally developed in Moscow's cyber warfare division, Russian programmers had stripped out Google's surveillance capabilities, and replaced it with a protocol that sends information back to Moscow.

But, when Khasan had moved to America, and entered the private sector, being sponsored for immigration by his employers, American technicians gutted the Russian additions, and changed the operating system even more. For example, they redirected the entire data stream back to his handlers in New York.

The screen displayed a glowing five-pointed star within a pyramid, complete with the all-seeing eye. It was reminiscent of the Great Seal that is stamped on all U.S. currency, the symbol of Free Masonry, yet not exactly the same. It was the symbol of the international banking cartel, which the group had adopted due to its appearance on the US currency. Their very existence was known only to a select few.

The phone vibrated insistently—its automatic alert system activating without human intervention. Something had triggered a sensitive monitoring program that had been established five years earlier, by his employer, and that was disconcerting. Khasan traced his finger around the star's points in a precise pattern. With the pass-pattern confirmed, a snippet of text flashed across the screen:

"WARNING!! CONFIDENTIAL DOCUMENT DOWNLOAD REQUEST!"

Another gesture activated a complex handshaking protocol, establishing an encrypted connection to THEATRES—the massive surveillance network headquartered in New York City.

More information began to populate the screen:
CRITICAL DATE: JULY 22, 2008
DOCUMENT: CAR LOAN LOGS
IDENTIFICATION OF PERSON: JIM W. BENTLEY
BANK NAME: BOLTON SAYRES
DIVISION: IN-HOUSE LEGAL
Then came the two buttons. ALLOW and DISALLOW.

His finger hovered over the "DISALLOW" button before pressing it decisively. Somewhere in the city, Jim Bentley would be seeing error messages. Meanwhile, Khasan opened his contacts and scrolled to an unmarked number, and selected "ENCRYPTED" when prompted.

"Why are you calling me?" a cultured voice demanded. "I told you not to contact this number for anything but Priority One issues..."

"This is Priority One," Khasan replied, his Russian accent more pronounced under stress.

A pause filled the encrypted connection.

"Priority One?" The voice carried both skepticism and concern.

"Someone downloading documents about July 22, 2008," Khasan said.

The spoken date's significance would need no explanation.

"Who?"

"Someone named Jim Bentley." Khasan checked another window on the phone, where a real-time background check had already been running.

"Jim Bentley?" Surprise colored the voice.

The gigantic man rarely heard his handler caught off guard.

"Da."

"What records is he trying to download?' the voice asked.

"He works in Bolton Sayres' legal department," The gigantic Russian responded, in a worried tone.

"I know where he works," The voice snapped, "I asked what records?"

"Attempting access loaner car index for dates," The big man replied, abandoning his English lessons.

"What did you do?" The voice on the other end was calm, measured – a stillness that even made the otherwise ruthless Khasan uneasy.

"Disallowed access," he replied, thick fingers hovering over the touch screen to push the button again.

"That'll only make him more suspicious," The voice hardened. "He won't give up..."

A pause followed. Khasan imagined that he could almost hear the mental gears turning on the other end of the line.

"How many attempts has he made?" the voice finally asked.

The giant pulled up the system logs, eyes scanning the timestamps.

"Seven."

"Interesting..." The word hung in the air like smoke, heavy with implications Khasan couldn't quite grasp.

His hand drifted unconsciously toward the shoulder holster beneath his jacket.

"I kill him, yes?" Khasan asked.

"No." The response cracked like a whip. "Just wait exactly ten minutes, then allow the download."

"Allow?" Fyodor couldn't keep the shock from his voice, his thick accent becoming more pronounced with his agitation. "But—"

"You heard me. Allow it."

"This is not good idea..." Khasan's distress was so acute that his English continued to slip.

The article 'a' vanished in his diction because it does not exist in the Russian language. Five years of intensive English training were forgotten, and the reshaping of his tongue was undone. The man had spent his entire career following orders without question. For him, doing so was as natural as breathing. But, this order was worrisome – it felt wrong – dangerously wrong. Yet, the voice of his handler on the phone took on a glacial quality, smooth and polished on the surface, and steel hard beneath, and simply said,

"You're not paid to think, That's my job. If anyone else requests those documents, notify me immediately before allowing access. Is that clear?"

The last word left no room for discussion or argument. Khasan's jaw clenched, but he knew better than to protest further.

"Da." He replied simply.

"Good." The voice said.

"Should I increase surveillance on—" Khasan tried to add, but couldn't, because the connection had died.

He stared at his phone for a moment before programming the delayed permission. As he slipped the device into his pocket, a young woman leaving the store caught his attention. There was something in her movement, in the way she scanned the street, that looked suspicious. He made a mental note to have her followed. In his line of work, a bit of paranoia could mean the difference between life and death.

Forty minutes later, his phone chirped again:

CRITICAL DATE: JULY 22, 2008

DOCUMENT: LOAN LOGS

IDENTIFICATION OF PERSON ATTEMPTING: JIM W. BENTLEY

BANK NAME: BOLTON SAYRES

DIVISION: IN-HOUSE LEGAL
ALLOW? DISALLOW?

This time, he authorized the download. As he did so, however, he opened a secondary app that would allow him to trace the IP address. His handler hadn't forbidden him from doing that.

The giant Russian resumed his shopping, but his mind churned with possibilities. His handler's reaction seemed too calculated and precise. Was Jim Bentley a genuine threat or not? Because in his world, as he had learned long ago, coincidences usually weren't.

Chapter 13 – SILICON ALLEY MAN

Silicon Alley is an affectionate nickname for New York City's high-tech industry. Unlike its West Coast counterpart, Silicon Valley, which is actually inside a physical valley, Silicon Alley, in New York, is not a physical "alley" – the tech companies are scattered throughout Manhattan and its boroughs. Silicon Valley in California dominates hardware, telecommunications, and game design, Silicon Alley has carved out its own crucial niche, becoming the undisputed champion in one vital area: FINTECH.

FINTECH means financial technology. That is the beating heart of Silicon Alley's dominance. The software it develops is the backbone of world finance. Almost all global financial transactions are conducted with software originally designed here, and that means everything from ATMs to credit card processing and international money transfers. The physical proximity to Wall Street and the world's largest banks ensures New York's continued dominance in banking and e-commerce software development, creating an ecosystem where financial innovation thrives.

Among the many brilliant minds is Jose Arias, a top computer development engineer and Jim's longtime friend. Their connection dated back to when they were both 16, when Jim had saved him and his little sister from gang members – an act of courage that left Jim with a permanent scar from a knife cut, and with Jose forever indebted to Jim. This had created an unshakable bond between the two men, and it had lasted through the years.

Jose was an introvert. He was not a great lover nor a great fighter, but he was unmatched in his technical expertise. Within FINTECH circles, he was the "walking textbook." His academic achievements spoke volumes: a Bachelor of Science in systems engineering from UCLA (summa cum laude), followed by a master's degree that was normally supposed to take two years to finish, just a year later. Despite being about the same age as Jim, Jose had graduated three years earlier, partly because of his rapid academic progress, and partly because computer engineering requires less study time than law school.

Unlike law graduates who struggle, competing for the few available positions in a heavily oversaturated field, computer science specialists are highly sought after. He'd had his pick of lucrative positions and a myriad of high-paying opportunities. Ultimately, he chose New York City, drawn by the financial possibilities. By the time Jim arrived, Jose had already been established in Brooklyn for two years. That was how Jim had declined the offer of a free room at the prestigious Waldorf Astoria Hotel from Laura's father, back when he was still dating her. When she invited him to New York, he chose to crash on Jose's sofa, in a modest flat across the river from Manhattan.

An hour after Jim's phone call, the two friends met at a Starbucks. Jose had transformed significantly from his teenage years – once gaunt and acne-prone with thick black-framed glasses, he'd filled out, cleared up, and traded those frames for contact lenses. He was what many would call a "late bloomer," but in recent years he'd made impressive strides in both appearance and confidence.

Jim carefully shared everything he knew and suspected not only about the diary and all it implied, but also about the THEATRES spying system, breaking his promise to his father-in-law and Admiral Stark. He didn't do so flippantly. The gravity of the situation – now a matter of life and death – had forced his hand. He had to trust someone, and Jose was beyond trustworthy. By swearing his friend to secrecy, Jim felt he was still honoring the spirit of his promise while gaining crucial assistance.

"Phone lines aren't secure," Jim explained, his voice low. "For all we know, we're being monitored even now."

"That sounds paranoid..." Jose remarked, then smiled with unexpected warmth. "But it's funny... because you're more like me now."

Jim returned the smile, acknowledging the irony.

Jose was drawn to conspiracy theories. He was a lover of both science fiction and everything fringe – from alien abductions to Illuminati plots. Even reptilians living inside the Earth. An avid X-Files fan, he couldn't resist quoting his favorite line:

"The truth is out there."

Jim, as usual, let it all pass without comment, maintaining a comfortable dynamic of mutual acceptance.

"I need to identify the murder victim," Jim pressed, steering the conversation back to urgent matters. "That's the key to finding the people who ransacked my flat, as well as the killers."

"Do you want to find them?" Jose asked, "Maybe, you shouldn't even try...what if you do find them? What will you do then?"

"I figure it out when it happens, but at least I'll know who and what I'm dealing with," Jim replied.

"Listen, Jim," Jose said, "If I were you, I'd drop this thing. You've got your father-in-law, whose pockets are filled with money. He can afford to pay for whatever extra security you guys need now."

"I don't want to be beholden to him," Jim replied.

Jose shrugged.

"You won't be," He pointed out, "Because he'll be doing it for his daughter, not for you."

"I need to know what's going on," Jim countered, "I need to know who is behind this."

"You're way fixated," Jose warned, genuine concern in his voice. "Have you considered how dangerous it could be if you actually succeed and find out who they are?"

"They invaded my home," Jim responded, his determination evident, "I can't just sit idle. They could end up targeting me and my family for death, just like they did to that family upstate."

"You might be increasing the chances of that happening by pursuing this," Jose pointed out soberly, "So far, all they've done is ransack your apartment. That's bad, but if they could do that, they would have targeted you personally, if they wanted to. Why not let the police handle this?"

"I don't trust the police anymore," Jim declared. "I'm not going to be a passive victim. Based on what I know now, everything seems to trace back to someone at Bolton Sayres Bank. I'm sure of it."

"But, your father-in-law is the CEO..." Jose pointed out, weighing the implications.

Jim nodded grimly.

"That's right." He agreed.

"Why not discuss it with him?" Jose asked.

"Too risky," Jim replied, shaking his head.

"You think he's involved?"

"No, but who knows...what if he talks to someone who is?" Jim said, "I need more information before I do anything. That's why I need your help."

"What can I do?"

"I need your computer expertise."

Jose nodded thoughtfully and reached into his pocket, producing a pair of unusually thick glasses. They resembled his teenage eye wear but were even more substantial, with a clear carbonite extension protruding from below the frame in an oddly technical way.

"I thought you'd switched to contacts," Jim said, studying the exceptionally large pair of glasses.

"These aren't for me – they're for you."

Jim fought back an instinctive laugh, not wanting to seem ungrateful for whatever his friend was offering.

"I don't need glasses," he said carefully.

"You do need these," He insisted, "Because they're not for vision – they're for hiding your identity. They distort facial features from the perspective of surveillance cameras."

As Jim examined the strange device, Jose revealed something significant:

"Did you know my company designed part of the THEATRES operating system?"

"No."

"Neither did I until you described it. Now I think I've got a pretty good idea how it works." Jose admitted.

Jim carefully stored the glasses in his backpack, trusting their utility despite not fully understanding the technology behind them. He recognized that Jose's expertise often manifested in unexpected ways.

"Where's the original diary now?" Jose asked, his expression serious.

"I left it with the FBI, but they don't have a record of receiving it anymore."

"You think the FBI is involved?" Jose asked, "That agents raided your home?"

"Maybe, but maybe, also, that someone has a few FBI agents on their payroll."

Jose's expression turned grave, shaking his head with utmost seriousness.

"This is dangerous shit, man...if even half of what you suspect is true, you should run away as fast as you can."

"I can't run."

"You never could, could you?" Jose mused, a mix of admiration and concern in his voice. "I guess I might still be alive because of that same quality..."

"Oh, it's not that," Jim insisted, "I'm a target now. It wouldn't matter where I run. They'd always be able to find me."

"Maybe, they'd just forget about you if you forget about them..." Jose suggested.

But, Jim shook his head.

"I don't think so," Jim stated firmly. "At this point, I'm the hunted. With your help, I want to become the hunter. But first, I need to know the identity of the dead guy they buried upstate. I need you to help me with that, too..."

Jose nodded as Jim explained the timeline – July 22 or 23, 2008 – and showed him relevant diary excerpts mentioning a BMW 528i. They meticulously examined the possibilities.

"Bolton Sayres' loaner fleet is almost completely stocked with BMW 528i's," Jim noted, building his case. "Only employees can check them out."

"There are, like, a few million BMWs in the world," Jose countered, playing devil's advocate.

"But Bolton Sayres also gave this relatively modest farmer a huge line of credit – a loan that should never have been made. We're an investment bank..."

"We designed Bolton's database so that it's impossible to put anything into it without listing a responsible person," Jose explained, his expertise showing. "That might give you a lead..."

"There's no one's name listed," Jim pointed out.

"Impossible," Jose stated, "It might not be the true name of the person who took the car, but some employee's name has got to be listed."

"But it's not," Jim insisted.

"Then someone tampered with the programming," Jose declared. "It can't happen the way we originally set things up. If the transaction is on the computer, there's a responsible person listed."

They explored various theories about the timing of events, discussing whether the body might have been stored elsewhere before burial. Jim applied Occam's Razor, arguing for the simplest explanation: the murder occurred the same night as the burial.

The conversation turned to the subsequent loan and the delayed murders of the farmer's family, theorizing about witnesses and payoffs. The gravity of the situation weighed heavily on Jim.

"I wouldn't blame you if you don't want to get involved," he offered. "There's danger here..."

"If you thought I'd crap out on you, why did you come to me?" Jose asked pointedly.

"I didn't know where else to go," Jim admitted honestly.

"Well, you came to the right man," Jose declared with conviction. "I owe you. And, this is a chance to repay the debt. I might never have another chance. So, I won't let you down."

Jose beamed with pride at Jim's trust in his expertise, determined to prove worthy of it. They began exploring various search approaches, discovering disturbing evidence of internet manipulation across all major platforms, even on international ones like Russia's Yandex.

Jose then shared a crucial secret: his company had built a backdoor into the banking software at the insistence of the big banks, including Bolton Sayres. This could potentially allow external control of any bank's systems, including THEATRES, without internal security clearance. Finally, after exhausting digital options, Jose suggested one overlooked old-fashioned possibility:

"The public library."

"You're joking..." Jim replied.

"No, not at all," Jose explained thoughtfully. "All electronic data can be manipulated. The data probably exists somewhere on the web or on a backup tape, but you may never be able to find it. With hard paper or film archive copies, they would have to find each one to destroy it all, That would require a tremendous amount of man-hours. They'd have to burglarize every library in the country."

"Brilliant!" Jim exclaimed, seeing the logic. "They still print physical newspapers, even though most people use the web for news. An article about a missing person would get printed in a physical newspaper somewhere."

"Bingo!" Jose agreed.

They agreed to meet at the New York Public Library the next day at 1 p.m. After some additional conversation covering various subjects, Jim insisted on paying for the coffee and then, he headed to Midtown Manhattan. He returned to his apartment, just to gather his remaining belongings, packed everything he needed into a suitcase, and took a taxi to the Stoneham penthouse to spend the night with his extended family.

Chapter 14 – THE PUBLIC LIBRARY

The New York Public Library, with its vast collection of books, periodicals, and newspapers, ranks as the world's third-largest repository behind only the British Library in London and Washington DC's Library of Congress. Though the building housed countless resources, Jim and Jose's interest focused solely on the periodicals section. Fortunately, they found the general librarian immediately available for consultation.

"What can I do for ya?" she asked in a pronounced Brooklyn accent.

"I'm looking for newspaper articles from 2008," Jim explained. "How do I find them?"

"The fastest way is wit' da' library database," she offered. "Dere' surchable..."

Jim cut her off. "No. I'm looking for physical copies. Do you store the physical newspapers?"

"From 5 years ago?" She seemed amazed that anyone would request physical copies in the digital age.

"Yes."

"We got about a month and a half of da' New York Times," she explained. "About six months off-site on advance notice..."

"Nothing physical from 2008?" Jim pressed.

"Not that far back..."

"What happens if the internet breaks down?" he inquired.

"We've got a local database on DVD that's updated every week," she responded, then added thoughtfully, "And, of course, we've got the microfilm."

"That's what I want –– the microfilm," Jim said eagerly.

"Reference Rm. 100," she directed, pointing the way.

As they walked toward their destination, Jim and Jose conversed in hushed tones.

"Is it possible to tamper with microfilm?" Jim wondered.

"You can tamper with anything..." Jose acknowledged. "But analog is harder to mess with, because it's arranged chronologically, like pure paper."

They found the microfilm room empty, its readers standing idle. Selecting two adjacent machines, they began their methodical search, pulling rolls of film from the gray metal drawers. The work proved tedious, but by 3:00 p.m., their persistence paid off.

"Jose!" Jim called out excitedly. "Look!"

His friend leaned over to view Jim's screen, which displayed an article dated July 26, 2008:

BROOKLYN MAN MISSING FOR THREE DAYS

Manhattan Island, New York (KXAN) — The New York police are looking for a Brooklyn man who they say has been missing since July 23. Authorities say he expressed suicidal thoughts in the past.

Charles Bakkendorf, Jr., 32, worked for the well-known international investment banking powerhouse, Bolton Sayres, as a vault manager. He was last seen leaving work. His disappearance was reported by his landlord. According to authorities, the man was wearing dress jeans, a white button down shirt with tie, and black dress shoes. He is a white male, 6-foot-1, with brown eyes and brown hair, and believed to weigh around 200 pounds. The New York Police Department have conducted both ground and aerial searches in and around both the area in which Bakkendorf lives and where he works, but with no success. Anyone with information of Bakkendorf's whereabouts should contact the New York Police Department at (212) 334-0742.

"There he is!", Jose whispered excitedly, "You've got your name..."

Jim nodded, a satisfied smile crossing his face. The pieces were finally falling into place. A glance at his watch caught Jose's attention.

"We've got 'till 4:45," Jose noted. "Then this section closes."

"We need to work faster," Jim urged.

"I'm gonna' find the next one!" Jose declared enthusiastically, returning to his reader with renewed vigor. Both men intensified their search efforts.

"I found it!" Jose announced shortly after. Jim leaned over to read:

POLICE SAY BROOKLYN MAN SUICIDAL

New York, NY (KXAN) — The New York police have been looking for a Brooklyn man for over a week, since he was reported missing, but with no success. A police spokesman says that the man appears to have no immediate family. A co-worker, who wished to remain anonymous, disclosed that the man had become very depressed and expressed suicidal thoughts immediately prior to disappearing.

The Brooklyn man, Charlie Bakkendorf, 32, was last seen leaving work on July 22nd with only his wallet and the clothes he was wearing. He was employed as an assistant vault manager at the well known international investment bank, Bolton Sayres. His disappearance was reported by his landlord on July 23rd. Authorities continue searching for a body, but assume that the man might have succeeded in his desire to commit suicide.

"Who do you suppose that co-worker was?" Jim mused.

"Good question," Jose agreed, checking his watch. "We've still got a little less than an hour to find out..."

They ultimately uncovered 37 articles, some duplicates from different news organizations sharing the same generic news feed, but representing at least 10 distinct sources. When the library's lights flashed their fifteen-minute warning, the men concluded their search. Jim carefully gathered the printouts and secured them in his briefcase.

They made their way through the main reading room, past the towering stone lions guarding the entrance, and down the steps to the street. Jim's mind raced, thoughts tumbling over one another as he walked, making it difficult to focus on any single idea. The picture was becoming clearer now. The dead man had been a vault employee at Bolton Sayres Bank. As Jim had suspected, all paths lead back to the bank.

But the physical newspaper articles had revealed something even more disturbing: someone wielding immense power and near-complete control over the internet had systematically erased certain facts from virtually every electronic database. Who could possess such capability? And why target a vault employee? This wasn't a robbery gone wrong—the man had vanished after leaving work. The only logical conclusion was that he knew something dangerous, something so explosive that keeping it hidden was worth committing murder. What secret could be that deadly?

Jose's whispered voice broke through Jim's thoughts. "We should stop at Staples on the corner of 5th and 39th. We need to scan these documents. Once they're digital, we can distribute them everywhere if necessary."

Jim nodded, but suddenly a cold realization struck him. They were exposed! The city was blanketed with surveillance cameras. According to everything he'd read about the THEATRES program, cameras were monitoring all public spaces, every street, recording everything, everywhere, constantly. Why would the library or Staples be any different? The implications were staggering. Jose was now at risk too...

Anyone sophisticated enough to scrub all mentions of Bakkendorf's disappearance could likely access the THEATRES surveillance system. If that was the case, their attempts at secrecy—even using a pay phone—had been futile. Jim had led his friend straight into danger. He scanned the streets nervously, looking in all directions.

Would the killers strike again? He tried to dismiss such thoughts, but couldn't. As they crossed 5th Avenue toward 39th Street, he gently touched Jose's shoulder, bringing them both to a stop. He leaned in close to whisper.

"Remember that surveillance system I mentioned?"

"Sure."

"There are thousands of hidden cameras and microphones everywhere. Some might be watching us right now."

Jose nodded, adjusting his peculiar black-rimmed incognito glasses he'd worn since their meeting.

"I'm sure they are," he whispered back with a slight smile. "We'll discuss it inside Staples."

They entered the office supply store, and Jose pointed toward the laptop section. "Over there."

Jim followed. As they browsed the computers, a store clerk approached immediately.

"Can I help you find something?" the employee asked.

"No, thanks. Just looking," Jose replied promptly.

"If you need anything, I'll be over there..." The clerk retreated.

"We can talk now," Jose said quietly.

"They know about our library visit," Jim whispered. "They probably know we're here, too."

"No," Jose countered softly. "They know YOU went to the library. They know someone was with you. But they don't know who. Remember these?" He pointed to his unusual glasses. Jim recalled having an identical pair in his backpack from yesterday—the ones Jose had given him, claiming they could fool surveillance systems.

"They can't automatically identify me while I'm wearing these," Jose explained.

"How can you be certain?" Jim asked.

"See these tiny lights?" Jose indicated the glasses' rims, where Jim noticed minuscule LEDs. Some were visible, others apparently dark.

"All the LEDs are actually lit," Jose continued. "You just can't see them all. They span the entire light spectrum, including near–infrared wavelengths invisible to human eyes."

Jim nodded in understanding.

"Electronic video systems use infrared sensors for facial recognition. The software can't process my face with these on."

Jim felt relief wash over him. Jose had thought everything through. Teaming up with his old friend had been wise after all. Jim himself was the only one truly at risk—a comforting thought, as he hated endangering others, especially friends.

"How do you know all these details?" Jim asked.

"Partly from your description," Jose replied. "But also because I realized I designed some of it. I programmed the auto–identification system, though I never knew what it was, or who I was really working for."

"Are you sure about this?" Jim asked.

"Yes," Jose replied. "Even if they've been watching everything we've done together, they have no idea who I am. I simply disappeared into the masses a few miles from my home."

"Wouldn't these unusual glasses give you away?" Jim wondered. "Not many people wear anything like them."

"That might become true once they get the system's ID failure rate below 1%," Jose acknowledged. "But right now, it's running around 5 or 6%. Many people regularly vanish from the system's view."

"Couldn't they identify you through the process of elimination?" Jim pressed.

"Not really," Jose explained. "In a city of 8 million, about 160,000 New Yorkers are off the grid at any moment just due to the failure rate. People constantly fade out and reappear. I'm just one more face in that crowd of 160,000, temporarily invisible to the system."

"Could they be monitoring us right now?" Jim asked, glancing around nervously.

"It's possible," Jose admitted. "But all the programming was designed for outdoor surveillance, operating in natural light and darkness. There was never a protocol developed for interior lighting. I think they don't want to get sued for violating Constitutional rights or something, but you'd know more about that, as a lawyer. But, anyway, the system isn't designed to monitor inside homes, offices, or stores. If they need a surveillance tape from inside a store, usually the store itself can provide it, but they'd have to request it, which is a process in itself, right?"

Jim spotted a package of four USB drives on the shelf and picked it up.

"Get a prepaid smartphone too," Jose suggested.

"I already have a phone," Jim replied.

Jose leaned closer, lowering his voice.

"Every call you make on that one announces who you are. With a no-contract phone, you can disappear into the signal traffic. Buy it with cash, invent a name and an identity for activation, and get prepaid cards with cash too. Use that one for sensitive calls—the computers won't trace them to you. Keep making ordinary calls on your regular phone, though. You don't want the algorithms noticing you're using another device."

Jim selected an affordable prepaid Samsung smartphone and a recharge card.

"Time to scan these documents," he suggested.

They headed to the empty copy center and converted all the articles to PDF files, downloading copies onto the four new USB drives. Jim paid cash for everything, kept one drive for himself, and handed the other three to Jose.

"Store them in different locations," he advised, "just in case..."

Jose nodded. "I'll also upload them in encrypted form. That way, I can release them instantly if necessary." He continued, "I'll leave first. Stay here, browse around for ten or fifteen minutes, then find someone roughly my size and leave with them."

Jim nodded gratefully.

"I don't know how to thank you..."

"No need," Jose replied. "I'm still in your debt."

"Not anymore..." Jim insisted.

Jose shook his head.

"You saved my life back then. That debt isn't settled yet." He smiled and added, "Although you might end up owing me before this is over..."

Jim returned the smile.

"Here," Jose said, discretely passing a CD–ROM from his jacket pocket to Jim's hand. Jim examined the mirrored disk, turning it over with slight confusion.

"Is it blank?" he asked.

"No," Jose replied. "It contains an encryption app we developed for the military called Zambo. Install it from your CD drive and follow the setup instructions. It works with Wi-Fi and smartphones, letting us communicate in complete privacy."

Jim nodded. "Thanks."

Thirty minutes after Jose's departure, Jim left too. He waited near the window until he spotted a man generally matching Jose's height and build walking by. Then, he immediately left the store, walking close beside him. After a few hundred feet, they parted ways, and Jim headed home.

Chapter 15 – MORE EVIDENCE

On Monday morning, Jim worked frantically to finish his assignments before lunch. At 11:20 AM, he set everything aside and headed for the nearest police precinct, just a short walk from the Bolton Sayres building. The information officer on duty – a tall Black woman who seemed to have cultivated a permanent scowl – greeted him with barely concealed impatience.

"What can I do for you?" she asked.

"I need to find records on a missing person," Jim said. "How do I do that?"

"Check the missing persons section of our website," she stated flatly.

"I did that," he replied.

"Everybody who's missing is on the website unless they've been found," she insisted.

"He hasn't been found," Jim stated.

"Then, he's on the website," she repeated, paused, then added, "Unless his case is solved, but then he wouldn't be classified as missing anymore. But, if he were missing..."

"How do I know if his case has been solved?" Jim asked.

"Because he wouldn't be missing anymore, and he's off the website," the woman replied.

Jim felt like he'd stepped into some kind of absurdist play.

"I'm not trying to find out whether he's missing," he explained. "I know he's missing. What I need is whether there's an investigation and, if there is, what's the status?"

"There would be a detective in charge of that," she offered.

"Who?" Jim asked.

"Who's your missing person?" she countered.

"A man by the name of Charles Bakkendorf," he said. "He went missing in 2008."

"The case is too old," she stated. "Unless there's a restriction on the file, you'll have to order it."

"Would there be an investigation?" he asked.

"Only if he's reported missing," she replied.

"That's what I'm trying to find out," Jim exclaimed, frustration mounting. "Can you pull a copy of the file, please?"

"No," she replied.

"Why not?" Jim asked.

"It's not available at the precinct level," she insisted.

"Where is it available?" he asked.

"By mail," the woman stated. "Only mailed requests are accepted."

"How long will that take?" he asked.

"A few days, maybe a few weeks... it all depends," she responded.

"Depends on what?" he inquired.

"On how many requests; how busy they are. I'm not in that department."

"Can't you just give me a case number?" he asked.

"No," she replied dryly.

"Why not?"

"I'm not authorized," she replied. "You have to make your request by mail. Here's the form..."

She reached beneath the counter, retrieved a form, and slid it toward him.

"Fill it and mail it," she said.

"To where?" he asked.

"To the address on the form," she replied. "Two copies, and a check or money order for $15. Cash isn't accepted."

Jim examined the document, titled VERIFICATION OF CRIME/LOST PROPERTY. It demanded information he didn't have – a case number, the reporting precinct, and more. He'd come here hoping to gather exactly that information.

"Can I just go physically to wherever this form is supposed to be mailed?" he asked.

"No."

"Why not?"

"Not open to the public," she reported.

"But, I don't have all the information requested by the form," he protested.

"Put in the information you have," she said. "They'll tell you if they need more."

"Do I get a refund when they don't find it?" he asked.

"No," she replied.

"Can't you just look up the case number?" he pressed. "Just to see if there are some records. I'm not even sure it's been reported."

"We don't do that," she insisted. "There are many people behind you, sir. Please fill out the form and mail it in. Thank you."

The dismissal was clear. Jim glanced behind him – indeed, three people waited in line.

"Next, please..." she called out.

Recognizing defeat, Jim left the precinct. His watch showed 11:54 – Timothy Cohen would be waiting at Marvin's deli. He caught a taxi and arrived just ten minutes late.

Marvin's Deli, New York City's most famous delicatessen, operated under its own peculiar rules. The door attendant handed Jim a numbered ticket – a vital document in the Marvin system. You needed it stamped at each food station, and it served as your record of purchases when leaving. Lose it, and you'd face a steep fifty-dollar penalty.

He spotted Cohen at a distant table.

"I was beginning to think you'd never get here," Cohen said.

"Sorry, Tim," Jim apologized. "I got held up by an idiot bureaucrat."

"Welcome to the lawyerly life, Jim!" Cohen said with a smile.

Jim recounted his frustrating experience at the precinct. Cohen set down his celery seed soda and shook his head.

"It's just city bureaucracy," he explained, "and the same reason the cops are always giving out petty citations for stupid stuff like J–walking. It's all about money. If you send in that written request, they'll write back, three weeks from now, and claim you didn't provide enough information. They'll say they can't locate the file, and demand you submit another form, with a new fee, for a new search. And, they'll keep doing it until you give up."

Jim threw up his hands in frustration. "What am I supposed to do?"

"All is not lost, my friend..." Cohen said, raising his index finger for emphasis.

They moved to the sandwich station, Cohen darting off to the desserts counter before Jim could respond. Each plate earned another stamp on their tickets.

The sandwiches were enormous. Jim unwrapped his corned beef and picked up their conversation.

"You said all is not lost..."

"I just wanted to say you just need to get to the right people. You can get what you want in a few minutes if you do," Cohen replied.

"How?"

"We use a retired NYPD cop to get stuff out of the NYPD. I can give you his contact information. He's a PI now."

Cohen scribbled something on a scrap of paper and passed it to Jim.

"Who is the 'we' in 'we use'?" Jim asked.

"The legal department."

"That's what I figured," Jim noted.

The offer, while tempting, posed a problem. Under different circumstances, such a contact might be perfect. But the investigator's connections to Bolton Sayres and the banking industry made him unsuitable for this particular case. If Jim needed an investigator, he'd find someone with no ties to banking – especially none to his own firm.

"Thanks," Jim said, keeping his reservations private. "Did you manage to get hold of Charles Bakkendorf's personnel file?"

He hated involving Cohen, but he lacked password access to the firm's personnel records. Cohen, however, had been cultivating a romance with someone in official records who had both physical access to file storage and database privileges.

"I had her do that records search," Cohen said. "But, I'm sorry, Jim... no one by that name ever worked at Bolton..."

"Did you have her do a physical records search?" Jim pressed.

"I had her do exactly what you asked for," Cohen insisted. "She looked in just about every possible place. There's never been a guy by that name working for the company."

"But, he did work for the company. He's not a mirage," Jim insisted, pulling printed articles from his briefcase and spreading them before Cohen. "This is why I asked for the records. You still think he's a mirage?"

Cohen scanned the articles, growing visibly nervous. "I don't know what to think."

"There's a group of people, with an incredible amount of power, who've done everything they can to cover this up. This guy was murdered."

Cohen glanced around anxiously before whispering, "Do you know why?"

"Not yet," Jim replied.

"My advice to you is this," Cohen said, his voice tense. "Drop it! No good is going to come from it. Let the police do their jobs."

"I'd love to," Jim responded, "but, the moment after I handed that diary over to our friend at the FBI, someone broke into my flat."

"Jeez, Jim..." Cohen exclaimed, "You've got a wife and a baby. Let it drop, for God's sake!"

Cohen knew his friend well enough to sense he was wasting his breath.

"I've got a ruined apartment and the privilege of living with my in-laws," Jim said bitterly. "That's what your police, and specifically, your Agent Barkley gave me."

"Didn't you hear?" Cohen asked.

"About what?"

"Barkley is dead," Cohen stated. "He was in a bad car accident on Long Island."

Shock registered on Jim's face as he processed this news.

"Wait a minute, Jim... don't even go down that road," Cohen warned, raising his hand like a stop sign. "It was a real accident."

"How do you know that?" Jim challenged. "The accident might be a setup."

"Come on..." Cohen protested.

"It looks like I might owe Agent Barkley an apology, except that he's dead and I can't give him one. I didn't want to doubt him, you understand, but I didn't have any other explanation. I still don't..."

Silence fell between them.

"That's it, then," Cohen announced suddenly, shaking his head.

"What?"

"Deal me out. I don't have a wife or a kid like you do, but I'd like to live long enough to have both."

Jim paused before responding. "I understand."

"Drop this thing like a hot potato," Cohen urged.

Jim shook his head. "I'm in too deep."

As Cohen finished his sandwich, Jim continued, refusing to let the matter drop. "Let's say Charles Bakkendorf worked in the gold vault in the basement of the old Bolton Sayres' building."

"OK," Cohen replied hesitantly, clearly wishing to end the discussion.

"Then, he gets removed from history, basically," Jim continued. "Removed, that is, to the greatest extent possible without having to physically burglarize every public library and physical records repository in America."

"Why not?"

"Why not, what?" Jim asked, confused.

"Burglarize every public library?"

"Well, I think it's obvious that they don't have enough physical people to mount an operation like that."

"A tiny number of people?"

"Maybe," Jim mused. "A few people, possessing high-security clearance levels, could steal the guy's personnel file from Bolton especially if it's their base of operations. But, they must not have the workforce necessary to mount a campaign nation-wide."

"What's your point?" Cohen asked.

"They can manipulate the internet, but they're still vulnerable," Jim replied.

"What about this guy's mother and father?" Cohen pressed. "His relatives, friends... wouldn't they say something?"

"He doesn't have any close living relatives," Jim explained. "It was relatively easy to just make him disappear."

"I've got to go," Cohen announced anxiously, standing to leave.

"Wait!" Jim pleaded. "Let me just bounce one more thing off you..."

Cohen closed his eyes in frustration. The whole thing was starting to frighten him, and he wanted no part in it. Despite his reservations, he turned back and listened.

"What do you know about Marc Dunlop?" Jim asked suddenly.

"Only that he's rich and a bit of an asshole..." Cohen replied.

"Why were you hanging around with him?" Jim pressed.

"I told you already," Cohen answered. "It was a networking opportunity. Nothing more. I haven't seen the guy since that night."

"OK," Jim said.

"Are you asking me about him because of the news?"

Jim shook his head. "What news?"

"The President just appointed him to the Commodities Futures Trading Commission."

"What?" Jim asked in disbelief.

"It's not official yet. In fact, it won't be announced to the public for a week or two, but everyone in legal knows."

"You mean Bolton Sayres' legal department?" Jim exclaimed.

"Yeah," Cohen confirmed. "The Journal is already interviewing people for the story. He'll be the youngest appointee to the CFTC ever in history..."

"God damn that bastard!" Jim exploded.

"You should make a stronger effort to get along with him, I think," Cohen suggested. "It could be good for your career..."

Jim shook his head in disgust. Was his friend serious? Would he really pander to an asshole like Marc Dunlop simply because he had big enough family connections to get a position he wasn't qualified for? What a travesty!

"How can the President appoint someone like him to one of the most important regulatory commissions in the country?"

Cohen threw up his hands, having no answer.

The whole place is a cesspool! Jim thought bitterly. Banking, government, New York City, all of it! It was a stinking rotting cesspool!

He wanted out so badly he could scream. Instead, almost reflexively, he took a bite of the huge "black & white" cookie he'd bought for dessert. The Black & White was a Marvin's specialty. As his taste buds registered the sweetness, it tempered some of his anger. He studied the cookie thoughtfully.

In some sense, he realized, it was just like New York City and America in general. One side is black, the other white – opposites, bad and good, coexisting. Similarly, America had become an entirely corrupt place that somehow still contained beauty, talent, and wonderful food. That's how things always are with millions of people living together. The city and the nation were simply the sum of their people, nothing more.

THE GIANT BLONDE MAN frowned as he listened to the computerized voice speaking through his encrypted cell phone connection.

"Subject #1, identified as Bolton Sayres' lawyer, Jim W. Bentley, proceeded along with Subject #2, unidentified male, into the New York Public Library," the disembodied voice reported mechanically.

"Identify subject #2," the giant blonde commanded.

"Facial recognition is impossible," the voice responded.

"Why not?" the blonde demanded.

"Failure of recognition software," the voice explained.

"What were they doing?" the blonde asked.

"Insufficient data," the computerized voice replied.

"Tell me, again, about ze' personnel office alert," the blonde giant insisted.

"Subject #3, identified as Bolton Sayres lawyer, Timothy Cohen, sought the personnel file of one Charles Bakkendorf. All inquiries on that name will automatically trigger an alert."

"Who is Charles Bakkendorf?" the giant asked, testing.

"Insufficient data," the voice replied. "Subject, Charles Bakkendorf, does not exist."

The last answer seemed to satisfy the man. Having obtained the information he needed, he ended the call and immediately dialed another number.

"What do you want?" a voice with a Brooklyn accent answered.

"People in Bolton Sayres' legal department have been making inquiries about Bakkendorf," the blonde giant reported. "Yesterday, it was same man, Bentley. Today, man's name, Timothy Cohen."

"Why didn't you erase Bakkendorf as you were told?" the voice demanded.

"He has been erased," the giant insisted.

"He should have been cremated. I should have handled it myself," the other man stated.

The giant's eyes narrowed. He didn't appreciate having his judgment questioned.

"Using crematorium involve more people...no good," he explained carefully, with poor English grammar, "I take out Bentley and Cohen now, yes?"

"Negative. Do nothing without direct orders from me. Do you understand?"

"Da," the blonde replied.

"The end goal, of course, remains the same."

"The same?"

"Yes," the voice said and hung up.

Chapter 16 – A TOUCH OF GOLD

July 21, 2008 was nearly five years before the pivotal day when Jeremy Stoneham approached the President of the United States on April 11, 2013, pleading for access to US gold reserves. At that time in history, the financial landscape had just shifted dramatically. And, Marcus Dunlop's automated trading programs had moved with the markets, shifting focus from gold to oil market manipulation. Critics inside the banking cartel had already declared both Dunlop and his trading bots to be a failure. However, they were fundamentally wrong.

Impatient investors expect immediate results. Even the most sophisticated habitually fail to grasp, for example, that the oil markets present different challenges, compared to the gold market. The oil market contained more players, for one thing. And, the players have far deeper pockets and greater resilience to market pressure. The number of overleveraged get–rich–quick schemers is much lower than in the gold market. Gold prices are easier to manipulate, in the short term, because its main players are undercapitalized speculators prone to panic. This lack of capital makes them vulnerable – they can be forced out of positions, with relative ease, simply by driving prices down to their pre–set stop–loss orders. That will always cause computers to automatically sell at any price, to preserve the speculator's capital. And, best of all, from the market manipulator's standpoint, most of these speculators are hedge fund customers of one of the cartel banks. Accordingly, the exact positioning of their automated "stop loss" orders is well known.

Oil is a different game. It has the same hard core of underfunded hedge fund managers, but it also has well–capitalized state actors who dominate trading. Iran, for instance, was stockpiling vast quantities of oil in tankers throughout the Persian Gulf, complicating Dunlop's attempts at a downward manipulation. Most crucially, his most powerful tool – the unwavering US government guarantee against losses – was always available when it came to the gold market – but only sporadically available for oil market operations.

Working within the constraints of the private capital, even as large as that provided by the combined assets of the cartel banks, meant manipulating markets worth hundreds of billions in daily trading, by using a few hundred million worth of seed money. Because the oil markets have powerful governmental and non-cartel players, Dunlop's progress was inevitably slow. Still, the bots were highly efficient. He would eventually achieve success, but mostly because the fundamentals supported his position. His bots merely needed to nudge markets to make the dip bigger and more dramatic.

Had he known about the cartel Council's intention to manipulate oil markets on an earlier date, things might have turned out very differently. But, Jennett's fears had put him into a very precarious situation. He had fallen just shy of the amount needed to close on the Caribbean island property. The prospect of losing a $500,000 deposit had driven him to strike a deal with Arthur Sansbury, director of Bolton Sayres' gold vault. Had he known that he was about to make much more money manipulating oil than he had ever made manipulating gold, he would have never done it. But, what was done, was done.

Sansbury claimed that he had successfully executed similar schemes in the past, though they involved much smaller amounts. He had never gotten caught. The primary limitation on the size of his past schemes had always been a lack of sufficient contacts in the broader gold market – precisely where Dunlop excelled. Dunlop knew plenty of people willing to buy or sell gold, without questioning the source. He could facilitate the movement of gold quickly and efficiently, with no questions asked.

Unfortunately, the scheme was now unraveling rapidly, leaving Dunlop deeply regretful of his involvement. The paper gold trading game was clean, simple, and profitable. Paper gold speculators are easy to deceive. It was even amusing to listen to the utter stupidity of technical analysts who attributed his bot-generated price movements to everything from astronomical alignments to Elliott waves. They habitually constructed ridiculous computer models based on PI, Fibonacci patterns, and other pseudoscience explanations. It all helped Dunlop make money, because his bots could synthetically create the beginnings of any so-called "wave" or "pattern" in the technical analysis books. But, committing fraud in a physical marketplace is much harder to get away with than committing fraud in the paper-based trading of commodities futures markets. The unraveling of their scheme began that morning.

An agitated employee arrived at Arthur Sansbury's private office.

"Charlie?" Sansbury said upon seeing the man at his door. "What's wrong?"

"It's the gold bars designated for Africa, sir..." Bakkendorf replied.

"I'm glad you're working on that," Sansbury noted. "We've got to get them packed and out the door as soon as possible."

"I can't..." Bakkendorf responded.

"What happened?" Sansbury inquired. "Is it your back again?"

Sansbury worried about worker compensation claims. Lower back injuries weren't common in the vaulting industry but occurred often enough to be concerning. They typically happened when moving heavy silver bankers' bars, especially during the periodic price attacks, which tended to cause steep price drops that, in turn, would spike physical delivery demand dramatically. That forced workers, like Charlie, to move physical material quickly, and to get injured. He already had two employees out on compensation. But, being understaffed didn't eliminate delivery obligations or deadlines – it just made it more difficult to keep pace. Another injured worker would be disastrous.

"Don't worry, Mr. Sansbury, my back's fine," Charlie replied.

Sansbury felt relief for a moment, but Bakkendorf's next words made him wish the man had injured his back and made a compensation claim instead.

"It's a problem with the gold bars, sir," Bakkendorf exclaimed, "They're tainted."

Sansbury felt the adrenaline surge. Foreboding took hold! He fought to maintain his composure.

"What do you mean, tainted?" he asked, struggling to keep his voice steady.

He tried to hide his trembling hands, hoping Bakkendorf wouldn't notice. How much did the man know?

"It's like I said, sir," Bakkendorf stated confidently. "The bars... they're fake. Each one has a core of tungsten, surrounded by gold. By weight, there's more tungsten than gold in every single one of them."

A familiar pain grew in Sansbury's stomach – his chronic ulcer acting up again. He fought to control his mounting terror.

"How do you know?" he asked, maintaining an outward calm.

"The bars have been filled, sir," Bakkendorf insisted, proud of his discovery. "No doubt about it. It's just a veneer of gold on the outside, thick enough to hide it. But inside, most of the weight is tungsten, pure and simple."

Sansbury's heart raced.

"How can you possibly know that for sure without melting them down?" Sansbury asked. "No one authorized you to drill into any of those bars."

"I used the ultrasonic tester," Bakkendorf explained.

"The what?" Sansbury asked.

At nearly 65 and approaching retirement, Sansbury's gold experience was rooted in 20th-century practices. To him, testing gold meant drilling a bar or, better yet, melting it down. No other method was completely reliable. Due to its destructive nature, however, such testing was very rare. Traditional vaulting relied on a "chain of trust" – if you could trace a bar from its original casting through known vaults, its quality wasn't questioned.

Recent years have seen ultrasound technology, long used by physicians for internal imaging, adapted for testing metal content and purity. While not achieving the perfect accuracy of a melt test, its 99.9% reliability was considered sufficient. That being said, there was no cartel–affiliated gold vault that regularly employed ultrasonic testing in the year 2008 in spite of advances in technology. There was a good reason for this. For every 100 ounces of metal sold, cartel member banks averaged only about half an ounce in actual inventory. The key to the gold trade was to keep all the bars of gold in the bank vaults, so it never moved, and there was no need to buy fancy equipment.

The investors all believed their gold was safe and dutifully paid their monthly storage fees. Almost to a man, they remained unaware that much of it had never been purchased, or even if it had been purchased, that it was either loaned out or sold by the banks to meet liquidity needs.

Non-allocated storage contracts made all of this legal. The storage agreements generated substantial fees without requiring significant physical metal holdings. It was, basically, money for nothing.

That having been said, the banks certainly did maintain impressive displays of what appeared to be gold bars in their vaults. Many display bars were actually bronze alloys with gold plating. Bank tours habitually showcased them to boost investor confidence. But, such bars had no claims on them from third parties. They belonged to the banks that used them to put on the show. It was an "innocent" marketing ploy. Putting on a show to increase confidence. No one ever tried to sell such bars to anyone. It could be explained away, if necessary, as a precautionary measure to protect real gold that was safely stored. The prospect of ultrasonic testers, however, was frightening. It raised the possibility that such practices would become known to outsiders. It was enough to long delay the idea of allowing such devices inside vaults.

"We don't own an ultrasonic tester..." Sansbury said, trying to steady himself.

His heart continued racing. This situation was approaching a nightmare. So close to retirement, a scandal of this magnitude would destroy him, not only with Bolton Sayres, but with every other cartel bank, and also, with the Federal Reserve. It was an absolute catastrophe.

"Sir, if you follow me, I'll show you," Bakkendorf stated.

He led the older man to a pile of one-kilo gold bars. Sansbury didn't need proof, of course, since he was the one who had compromised the bars in the first place.

Almost a month prior, big 100 ounce bars had arrived through the underground tunnel network connecting the bank's vault to the Federal Reserve's vault at 33 Liberty Street. The Fed had provided the bars to meet the increased delivery demand that had arisen out of a market intervention that had temporarily tanked prices. Fed gold bars, however, were impure because they had been made back in the 1930s, when President Franklin Roosevelt had seized all the privately held gold coins held by citizens of the United States. They were so-called 'coin melt' and didn't meet COMEX good delivery standards. The coin melt bars required remelting, refining, and recasting. As the US Treasury's primary gold market agent, Bolton's vault was secretly equipped for this work. It was authorized to stamp the bars with various brands to ensure legitimacy, especially that of the prestigious US Assay Office. This latter mark was often used when nations, keeping their gold at the Fed, repatriated it to their own countries.

Creating the new gold bars was a closely guarded secret. Sansbury performed the work himself, after hours, assisted by mysterious individuals who weren't bank employees. Their identities remained just as hidden as the gold's origin. But, at that moment, keeping that secret was the least of his worries. He desperately needed to return to his desk and drink from the bottle of Mylanta antacid he had hidden in his center drawer.

He stared silently at the simple device that threatened to destroy everything he had built. It sat innocuously beside the gold pile, deceptively basic in an era of tablet computers, smartphones, and advanced technology. This modest instrument could prove his undoing. Could he dispute the results? Could he recast the bars? Even if there were time to do so, where would he find the necessary gold? Marc Dunlop had already sold and delivered most of it.

"Where did you get this device?" he asked, feigning casualness.

"It arrived yesterday," Bakkendorf noted.

"Who authorized it?" he asked.

"Nobody," Bakkendorf replied. "The manufacturer's rep says we've got it for two weeks as a tester."

Sansbury raised an eyebrow. The vault's tight security should have prevented this. However, security focused primarily on preventing items from leaving rather than entering. They had probably X-rayed the device but seen no reason to stop it.

Damn manufacturers who'd do anything to make a sale!

"All right," he said finally. "Show me."

Bakkendorf turned to the pile of kilo-sized gold bars. He selected one, applied electrode gel, attached the electrodes, and activated the machine, indicating the dial.

"You see?" Bakkendorf pointed to the reading. "It's showing a hidden core of tungsten occupying four-fifths of the bar's volume. There's only an outer covering of real gold."

"Maybe the test is faulty..." Sansbury suggested. "Only a melt can tell for sure."

"Well, we can melt it, of course, but let me show you another example," Bakkendorf said.

He tested another bar the same way. Again, 80% tungsten and 20% gold. More bars, repeatedly. Every bar was compromised. Within minutes, he had tested twelve bars. All fake.

"Maybe it's a manufacturer's defect..." Sansbury suggested. "Every bar is reading the same..."

"No, it's not," Bakkendorf insisted, "I can show you what happens with a real bar I took from a different delivery set."

He tested a small ten–ounce gold bar similarly. The machine indicated pure gold. Bakkendorf looked up and spoke:

"Don't we have a record of where we got these bars from?" he noted, "Because I checked the computer and there's no chain of trust. They've got the imprint of the US Assay Office, and they look brand new, but they've got an old date stamp as if they were manufactured many years ago. It's all inconsistent and suspicious."

Sansbury knew exactly where the gold had come from, but instead of answering, he turned and walked back to his office.

"Shouldn't we notify someone?" Bakkendorf asked, following his boss.

"That's exactly what we're going to do," Sansbury agreed. "I'm getting on the phone right now. Don't worry. We'll get to the bottom of this!"

Bakkendorf continued speaking as they walked.

"What about the police?" he asked. "Someone sold us fraudulent gold bars. Shouldn't we try to follow the trail?"

Sansbury stopped mid-stride and turned around.

"Of course, but this is a sensitive matter," he explained. "We can't allow it to become public without going through proper channels. Remember, banking is about reputation. This is obviously not our fault, but people will blame us. They could lose faith, even though we've done nothing wrong. We probably don't want any of this sprayed all over the newspapers. We're victims too..."

Bakkendorf nodded. The man was a loyal employee, loved his job, and didn't want to do anything that might hurt the bank's reputation. He was following Sansbury, just a few steps behind, but the man needed to be alone, and desperately wanted to get rid of him.

"Charlie..." he instructed. "Go ahead and remove whatever bars are already in the crates. I'm going to speak to a higher authority. I'll tell you exactly what we're going to do, as soon as I find out myself."

"OK," Bakkendorf replied instantly and returned to the crates.

Reaching his office, Sansbury closed the nearly soundproof door and locked it. He retrieved the bottle of Mylanta antacid from his second drawer, uncapped it, and took a long drink of the chalky fluid. The pain subsided slightly. With trembling hands, he grabbed the telephone and dialed the man he hoped could save him if only to save himself.

Marcus Dunlop instantly recognized the name and number on his smartphone. Sansbury was calling from the vault. What was it now? Was he still behind on the delivery schedule? Did he need to announce some new excuse as to why everything would be done even later than late?

"Marc..." Sansbury stated. "We've got trouble..."

"What are you talking about?" Dunlop asked.

"One of my newer vault employees found fake bars of gold," Sansbury explained.

Now, it was Dunlop's turn to panic. His legs weakened suddenly, and he collapsed into his chair. Sansbury detailed everything point by point. His heart raced and his blood pressure climbed.

"How could you not know this?" he exclaimed.

"I've always known about ultrasound testing," Sansbury insisted. "But I never authorized using it."

"What if the Africans have one of these ultrasonic testers?"

"They don't," Sansbury said.

"Jesus Christ!" Dunlop declared.

"I didn't create the problem," Sansbury said defensively.

Suddenly, Dunlop began to see Sansbury in a new light. Not only was he a procrastinator, but he was also a fool. A stupid fucking cave–dwelling troll1 Scum of the earth! Why had he ever trusted a man who spent evenings 85 feet beneath Manhattan's bedrock, covertly melting coin–melt bars delivered by the Federal Reserve? The incompetence was galling. He shook his head in frustration.

"How could you let this happen?" he suddenly exclaimed. "Fuck!"

Sansbury didn't respond.

"Why didn't you load that fucking gold yourself?" Dunlop exclaimed.

"I'm 64 years old," Sansbury stated. "I was up every night, overseeing the smelting and the refining. Do you know how hot a furnace has to be to melt tungsten?"

"No, and I don't give a shit..."

"A lot hotter than for gold."

"Fuck the furnace!" Dunlop exclaimed. "It was a simple job. Just make the gold bars. Load the crate. Mail it out the door. That's all you needed to do!"

Silence fell for a moment.

"Maybe we can buy back the gold?" Sansbury asked.

"Are you out of your mind?" Dunlop replied. "There's no way we can buy that much gold in the time we've got. There would be a huge premium, and buying so much, so fast, would stand out like a sore thumb."

"Then what are we going to do?" Sansbury asked.

He tried to clear his mind, forcing himself to stay calm.

"I told him not to call the police," Sansbury added, hopefully.

"Oh, that's brilliant, just brilliant..." Dunlop commented cynically, "As if that's gonna stop him? Of course, he's gonna fuckin' report it to the police!"

Dead silence followed.

"You'll never get your pension..." Dunlop added.

The mention of Sansbury's pension hit home. Dunlop heard the audible sigh of hopelessness and enjoyed it. The man needed to squirm. He deserved punishment, and watching people in pain always brought pleasure. The satisfaction diminished, however, because the situation was bringing him an equal share of the misery.

"Are we gonna be arrested?" Sansbury wondered.

He hadn't considered that possibility. Instead, his mind had focused on his father finding out. Stealing from the public was one thing. Stealing from the cartel was another matter entirely. The consequences wouldn't likely involve the official justice system. The police investigation would end with one phone call to the right people who were on the Frederick's payroll. No bank could risk airing dirty laundry publicly, and the entire cartel membership would support them. On top of that, a serious investigation would expose the government's own involvement in gold price suppression. High-ranking officials would shut it down, no matter what they had to do to accomplish that.

"You think there's really a chance we'd be arrested?" Sansbury repeated.

Dunlop shook his head, though the other man couldn't see him.

"No," he said verbally. "The matter will be dealt with internally."

"How?" Sansbury asked fearfully.

"Likely, by the cartel level Reputational Risk division," Dunlop warned.

"For one mistake?" Sansbury asked.

"It's a mistake that could cause enormous damage to the entire cartel," Dunlop pointed out.

He knew, however, that none of that would actually happen. His father would protect him, and Sansbury would be protected by extension. But, the man's fear was fun to play with. Sansbury had been in the business long enough to know the hidden face of the Reputational Risk department and its capabilities. The official side of RR employed qualified security personnel on an open payroll. The hidden side quietly handled problems that had no other solution. It employed "contractors for hire" – suspicious figures with questionable pasts and tight connections to agencies like the CIA, MI6 and Russia's FSB. Some still held active "licenses to kill" from their governments and were moonlighting for cash. Others were "retired." All were lethal.

When newspapers reported a banker found hanging from a noose in his office or splayed on the pavement after a forty-story fall, police ruled it suicide. The truth, however, could sometimes be very different. The answer might be found in secret files of the cartel-wide Reputational Risk division.

"I'd swear not to say a word!" Sansbury exclaimed.

"Oh, I'm sure they'll take that into account, you stupid cockless sack of shit!" Dunlop chided. "You stole millions of dollars worth of gold from the cartel!"

"You stole it too!" Sansbury insisted.

"Yes, I did," Dunlop admitted.

"What can we do?" Sansbury asked. "What?"

Dunlop was highly agitated, but Sansbury's obvious distress provided some satisfaction and it helped calm him down a bit. He enjoyed watching people suffer, even friends, business partners, or enemies. Sansbury's fear helped Dunlop regain his composure.

"How old is he?" Dunlop asked.

"Early thirties."

"Married?"

"Not that I know of."

"Likes girls, though, right?"

"I think so," Sansbury said.

"Guys always need money for girls," Dunlop declared. "What does he make? $50Gs, $60Gs?"

"$65,000 a year," Sansbury replied.

"So, the answer is easy," Dunlop concluded. "We'll bring him into the deal. Get it?"

"You mean offer him cash?" Sansbury asked.

"Exactly," Dunlop stated. "A cut to keep his mouth shut."

"Yes, yes, OK... good..." Sansbury agreed. "Very good..."

Dunlop felt proud of his solution.

"But, what if he doesn't go for it?" Sansbury asked.

Dunlop knew one truth – every man had a price. The secret was being able to determine what that price was. For someone earning $65,000 annually, the price couldn't be too steep. A million or two would suffice, he estimated. Once the oil manipulation was running, he could recoup that money in thirty minutes.

"The money, uh..." Sansbury wondered aloud. "Where's it going to come from?"

"What?" Dunlop asked, pulled from his thoughts.

"Where is the money going to come from?" Sansbury asked, again, "I mean, we already have me, you and the black guy in Africa splitting the deal. I don't get big bonuses like you do, and I've already spent my share..."

How did Sansbury know about his bonuses? What else did the man know? Was he also aware of the paper trading side bets?

"This problem was created entirely by you!" Dunlop exclaimed, annoyed. "The whole thing is your fault!"

"No! I did everything I was supposed to do," Sansbury protested. "I never authorized that ultrasonic tester..."

Though invisible to Sansbury, Dunlop shook his head. Of course it was the man's fault! How dare he deny it? He considered making the man squirm again. The old senile fool! The failure was Sansbury's and that meant that he should bear the entire cost. They'd collectively stolen 12,860 troy ounces, with a market value exceeding $11 million. He'd sold it on the black market for $9 million, no questions asked. His share was only $3 million, and he resented the idea that he would have to touch that, reducing his take, especially since he'd also already spent the money.

Then, suddenly, the opposite half of his bipolar personality took control. His vindictiveness gave way to magnanimity. After all, he reasoned, Sansbury was merely a Plebeian – a common man. In contrast, he was a Dunlop, a Patrician, a nobleman. He could borrow millions with nothing more than his signature to back the loan. Noble status carried certain obligations. Noblesse oblige, they called it – the principle that nobility should act generously toward common people. He would soon net tens of millions from front-running the oil market. He didn't need all that money.

He forgot the pleasure he had previously derived from Sansbury's misery. As nobility, he had weightier concerns. One or two million dollars was insignificant. Bakkendorf was a loose cannon who needed silencing before the situation spiraled out of control.

"I'll pay three-quarters of Bakkendorf's fee," Dunlop announced magnanimously.

This pleased the other man.

"Agreed," he replied immediately.

"Keep the man there until I arrive," Dunlop instructed.

"What if he won't play ball?"

"He will. Has he seen the manifest yet?"

"No."

"Good," Dunlop said. "I don't want him to know where the gold is headed. There should be no chance of him talking to them, understand?"

"Yes."

"I'll have my own people pick it up and deliver it. Tell Bakkendorf that the bank will replace the bars with real gold, and that he'll be paid a big bonus for finding the problem. In return, he's required to keep his mouth shut, because the bank can't risk its public reputation by admitting that some of its gold bars were tainted. Any guy making $65K is going to jump at a multi-million dollar bonus, whether he believes the story or not."

"OK," Sansbury responded enthusiastically. "But, hurry up!"

"I'll be there shortly," Dunlop announced.

The conversation ended as Dunlop hung up the phone. Despite his outward show of control, uncertainty gnawed at him. Everything hinged on Bakkendorf's silence. The banking cartel and the government routinely blessed market manipulation in both the gold and oil markets. But outright physical fraud – deliberately adulterating gold bars and selling the stolen metal – crossed a line they would not tolerate.

In spite of his unease, Dunlop held fast to a principle his father had taught him in childhood. It was a principle passed down through the generations of Dunlops who had come before: it was a simple proposition. Every man had his price. A million dollars meant little to a Patrician like himself, but presented properly, it would ensure a man like Bakkendorf kept quiet. That silence was absolutely crucial. If the cartel Council discovered the theft, it was possible that not even the Dunlop name would protect him from the consequences.

Chapter 17 – LAURA REDECORATES

Delivery men bustled up and down the stairs with new furniture, while technicians frantically installed electronic equipment throughout the building. Three burly security men stood guard at strategic points: one outside the building entrance, another at the stairwell, and a third in the entry foyer. They questioned everyone who entered. The building had become a fortress.

The apartment itself remained mostly in disarray, but Laura was confident the new furniture would transform the space. The few pieces already in place had made a noticeable difference, and she was eager to complete the renovation.

"What's going on?" Jim asked when he finally made it past security. "What are you doing here?"

He had come to collect the last few items he needed and was pleasantly surprised to see his wife, though he tried to mask his reaction with nonchalance as he walked in and gave her a casual kiss.

"You said you were never coming back," he continued. "What happened to that?"

"I changed my mind," she explained with a smile. "I bought some things this morning to make the place livable again. Nobody will chase me from my home."

"You bought all this stuff this morning?"

"You can get same-day delivery if you pay for it." She gestured toward the living room. "What do you think of the new couch?"

She seemed pleased with herself. Jim glanced at the newly arrived French provincial style sofa without much interest. Furniture had never been his passion.

He nodded. "Very nice."

Laura practically danced around the room as she spoke.

"I've ordered new window treatments... new tile, a new table, a couch, a rocker-recliner, a mattress, Persian carpets... new everything!" Her enthusiasm was evident in every word.

"I'm glad you're happy."

His response was muted by worries he couldn't share with Laura. She was too emotional and would react poorly if she knew everything. The truth was too harsh. Better to let her maintain her current state of elation.

"Most important is that we're going to have total security," she noted. "My Dad's men are here, wiring the place, and we're going to have a few guards permanently assigned by the building management."

"That's good, I guess," he responded.

"You don't seem to be enthusiastic," she observed.

"Well, I would have expected you to talk to me about this stuff first."

"I wanted to discuss it with you," she explained. "But I've been trying to reach you all day, and I can't. Did your battery die or something?"

The question triggered Jim's memory – he had turned off his mobile phone, believing it might make him harder to track.

"Darn!" he exclaimed. "This phone is so screwed up. It seems to turn itself off!" He pulled it from his pocket and switched it back on.

"It's getting hard to contact you," she noted. "It's either you're too busy, or your phone's off. What's going on?"

"It's not intentional," he assured her.

Laura shook her head and continued. "I'm throwing out that cheap crap you brought from California. It's ruined anyway."

"Okay, fine," he responded. "But I thought you were afraid to come back here. You said it's too dangerous."

"My dad says we're going to make this place totally secure. We're installing a full security system that covers the entire building."

"Did you ask the neighbors?"

"Why should I?" she countered. "They're getting free protection."

"Maybe they value privacy more than protection..."

Laura didn't respond to Jim's comment about privacy, instead surveying the room with satisfaction. From her perspective, everything was finally falling into place. The sophisticated electronic security system and bank-supplied security guards, paid for by the building's owners, combined with the new drapes, furniture, and carpets would make the place not just more secure, but more comfortable and aesthetically pleasing.

A walkie-talkie buzzed in her pocket, interrupting her thoughts. She pulled it out and pressed the button.

"Mrs. Bentley, three more delivery men have arrived," a male voice announced.

"Send them up," she replied.

Minutes later, three robust men arrived, escorted by Barry, one of the Bolton Sayres security guards temporarily assigned to building security.

"Take this junk out, please," Laura directed.

Within forty-five minutes, the men had cleared out the damaged pieces and replaced them with elegant French provincial style furniture. When they finished, one of the men approached with a detailed invoice, which Laura signed. She then handed him a crisp hundred-dollar bill.

"Thanks!" he said enthusiastically.

"It's for you and your two friends," she announced loudly enough for all to hear.

After the movers departed, she turned to Barry, who had remained nearby.

"What do you think, Barry?" she asked.

The guard surveyed the room and nodded approvingly. "Beautiful stuff, Mrs. Bentley."

Jim interrupted, his irritation evident. "Excuse me. Barry? That's your name, right?"

The man nodded.

"If you don't mind, I need to speak to my wife for a few minutes."

The guard didn't immediately comply, instead looking to Laura for confirmation. Jim found this particularly galling – surely a man should have some authority in his own home. But within moments, Laura nodded her assent, and Barry obediently left, quietly closing the door behind him.

After a moment of tense silence, Jim spoke.

"I could have reupholstered that old recliner," he pointed out, more annoyed by the guard's behavior than the loss of his furniture. "You could have asked before you trashed it."

"I want to be rid of everything that reminds me of what happened."

"Whatever..."

Laura leaned forward, embracing him and kissing his cheek before taking his arm to lead him around their newly decorated apartment. She presented her work with a theatrical flourish.

"Ta-da!" she exclaimed excitedly. "What do you think?"

He shrugged. "It looks good. Why do I get the feeling that I owe a lot of money to your father..."

She shook her head firmly. "You know that my Dad never expects to be paid back for the money he gives us."

"That's not the point..." he insisted.

"It doesn't matter, anyway, because you don't owe him anything!" she declared proudly. "I paid for it myself, from my acting money, and the money from the insurance company. And, the management of the building is paying for the guards."

Though the musical's run had lasted only two weeks, her salary had been substantial. Still, Jim realized she had made a significant financial sacrifice – the new furniture had likely depleted her savings. He felt relieved, though, that her father hadn't funded the renovation. He was tired of being indebted to the man, regardless of whether repayment was expected.

"Thanks for the hard work," he said, kissing her. "It's all nice, but... does this mean we're moving back in because you said you never wanted to come back here."

Before she could answer, a knock interrupted them. She gave him a quick peck, stood up, and checked through the peephole before opening the door to admit a tall, clean-cut man who resembled an aging Marine Corps sergeant.

"This is John Masters," Laura said. "He works for my Dad."

Jim rose to shake the offered hand.

"He's setting up our new electronic security system," Laura explained.

"Jim Bentley, I presume?" Masters said.

"Yes," Jim replied. "Nice to meet you."

"I'm glad we could finally meet," Masters said. "I've heard a great deal about you."

Jim glanced at Laura, slightly perplexed by this comment.

"Would you like a cup of coffee?" Laura offered.

"That would be nice, thanks," Masters replied.

"You want something, Jim?"

"No, I'm good," Jim replied.

Laura hurried to the kitchen while Jim attempted small talk with their visitor.

"So, you work directly for Jeremy Stoneham?" Jim asked the man.

"Don't we all?" Masters responded with a laugh. "Technically, of course, I work for Bolton Sayres, same as you. But, Jeremy Stoneham IS Bolton Sayres, isn't he?"

"I don't know about that," Jim replied.

"Officially, I'm Vice President of Security."

"I see..."

"And, my job's simple," Masters explained. "We stop criminals, terrorists, whatever threats might arise, from causing harm to our executives. That's why we're here. We're installing one of the most sophisticated anti-burglary systems in the world. And, after we're finished, this building will be monitored 24/7 by my best men."

"I thought there was a guy named Navarro in charge of all that."

"He runs Reputational Risk, that's true," Masters clarified. "But, I run security. There's an overlap, but we're different. I work directly for Mr. Stoneham, and, well, no one knows exactly who Mr. Navarro works for..."

Jim smiled uneasily.

"The problem I'm having with all this is that nobody bothered to ask me," Jim commented while smiling to make it appear more like a joke, but his resentment was real.

"How could you not want to install a security system after everything that's happened?" Laura interrupted, returning with the coffee.

"I didn't say I didn't want to install it," Jim insisted. "I said I wasn't consulted. No one's even bothered to explain how it's going to work."

"It's really simple," Masters explained. "We've installed video and audio viewing and listening nodes, and laser-based motion detectors. The motion detectors activate servo systems, allowing the cameras and microphones to track anyone and everything moving in and out. Everything is fed into a central computer system."

"But, it's not only the criminals you'll be watching, it's us."

"We don't put cameras inside the apartment," Masters pointed out.

"Regardless..." Jim muttered. "I don't like being watched."

"Yeah, we get that all the time," the man explained. "It's because you're unfamiliar with the technology. Once you're comfortable with it, you'll forget it's even here."

"Aren't there supposed to be hidden cameras and microphones already all over Manhattan?" Jim asked.

Masters looked surprised.

"How do you know that?" He asked.

Jim shrugged. "I know a lot of things."

"There are, yes," Masters admitted, "But, we'll be installing a denser cluster, and it'll be linked to a different computer system, totally separated from THEATRES."

"If video monitoring is so useful, why hasn't anyone looked at the existing video and audio feed to find out who ransacked this flat?" Jim asked.

"We've tried that," Masters said. "But, it's blank."

"How could it be blank?" Jim pressed. "I thought the system was on 24/7."

"It is," Masters agreed. "There was an outage. It happens from time to time."

"It seems like a convenient little outage," Jim stated. "There's a system, working all the time, and just when my flat is ransacked, it doesn't work. You don't think that's strange?"

"It is suspicious." Masters agreed, "It's certainly possible that some criminal individuals have figured out how to affect the system."

"What if another outage makes these new cameras worthless?" Jim asked.

"Our system is connected to a different network, supported by multiple uninterruptible battery backup systems," Masters answered. "We don't trade data with them. We've also installed a more traditional alarm system. Anyone who enters this building without a proper passcode will set it off."

"But, everyone in the building has the passcode" Jim pointed out.

"That's true," the man admitted.

"So, in short order, they'll be giving that code to their friends, relatives, delivery men... everyone. It's going to be worthless, very quickly."

"We can always change the passcode, and we'll certainly do that on a regular basis."

"Here's the deal," Jim said, his frustration evident. "You can install the alarm, you can even have the armed guards on duty, but the cameras and the microphones...the ones inside the building... they've got to go. You can keep the ones outside, but no surveillance inside the building. Got it? I won't approve that. It's not the way I want to live."

"Mr. Bentley, we're not trying to spy on you," Masters insisted. "We're trying to protect you."

"The way you've got it set up, the two things are the same," Jim declared. "You can leave the alarm and the guards, but forget about the rest."

"I'm sorry, Mr. Bentley," Masters replied. "But, it's not my call to make."

"You're right," Jim snapped back immediately, "It's mine. And, I'm making it. My wife agrees with me, right"

He turned to Laura, who nodded hesitantly.

"If that's what Jim says, then I support him," she said.

"So, that's that," Jim declared. "Take the monitoring devices out."

"It's not up to you," Masters stated again. "And, it's not up to your wife, either. You're just renters here."

"According to the law, during the term of the lease, we have the rights of the owner," Jim insisted.

"We haven't put one piece of equipment inside your apartment," Masters noted. "It's installed in the common areas; the hallways, the staircases, and outside the building; in all the public spaces. Liberty 19 has already given consent and Jeremy Stoneham has ordered it."

"Liberty 19?" Jim exclaimed. "What the hell is that?"

"It's the investment group that owns the building," Laura explained.

"Managed by Bolton Sayres realty group," Masters supplied.

Jim stood up and turned toward Laura. "Did you know about this when we rented this place?"

"Of course I knew..." she answered.

"You didn't say anything..."

"Why should I say anything?" she argued. "To make sure that there was yet one more place we couldn't rent because of all your hangups about my Dad? The apartment was empty. The price was right. I didn't want to rent it, if you'll remember. You did. I wanted the place my parents found for us, which was much nicer."

"Which they were going to subsidize..." Jim countered.

"So what?" she asked. "It would have been a nicer place."

"It was too expensive."

"Fine!" Laura stated. "But, the bottom line is that you're the one who wanted to rent this place, and you're the reason we rented it. It doesn't matter who owns the building."

Jim shook his head in annoyance.

"It does matter," He insisted, "And, you didn't even tell me after the vandalism..."

"How does the ownership of this building have anything to do with the vandalism?" Laura asked.

"Whoever vandalized us entered with no sign of forced entry," Jim pointed out.

"So what?"

"Who could do that without a key?" he asked.

She shook her head, flabbergasted.

"You can't seriously think the building owner, Bolton Sayres Bank, your employer, my Dad's company, burglarized us?" She asked, shocked.

"We weren't burglarized, Laura," He pointed out, "As I've said, repeatedly. We were vandalized! We were ransacked. Someone came here to take something, not to steal money or jewelry or TV sets. There's a big difference."

"What's the difference?" she asked.

Jim shook his head in frustration. He held back from saying more. If Masters hadn't been present, he might have explained everything. But his anger had already led him to say too much. He attempted to redirect the conversation.

"Our privacy is being violated," Jim stated. "That makes a big difference, Laura..."

Masters took the bait, shifting away from Jim's earlier implications.

"Mr. Bentley, no one is trying to violate your privacy," He insisted, again, "This is all about your safety. You should be happy your landlord is interested enough to go to all this expense. Not everyone would."

"I'm sure the investors in the land trust would not be willing, but they're paying for it anyway, right?" Jim asked.

When Masters didn't reply, Jim's sarcasm deepened.

"That's what I thought..." Jim said, satisfied that he had made his point, "The bank does what it pleases and investors pay for it."

"Jim!" Laura exclaimed.

"I don't care who's paying for what," Masters said. "My job is to protect you, and that's it."

"What if I don't want to be 'protected'?" Jim countered.

"You're being rude!" Laura blurted out.

"You're not the only person with an interest in this, Mr. Bentley," Masters said. "You did marry a Stoneham. It was your choice to do that. You ought to think about your daughter and not your personal feelings. Don't you want her safe?"

"Don't bring my daughter into this..." Jim warned.

He realized he'd already revealed too much. He had no way of knowing whether Masters was part of the conspiracy. Probably not, but no one at the bank could be trusted. He needed to speak with Laura alone, and he wanted no microphones active when he did that.

His extensive reading about the THEATRES system, courtesy of his father–in–law's materials, had taught him that standard protocol did not include placing microphones inside homes without a court order. Masters had confirmed that apartment interiors were off–limits. If the man left, and they kept their voices low, Jim felt confident they could speak privately.

"You've admitted that I've still got a lease on this apartment, right?" Jim asked.

"Of course," Masters agreed.

"Which gives me total control over everything that goes on inside it, right?"

"Right."

"Then, please leave the premises," Jim said, finally.

"Jim!" Laura exclaimed.

Masters responded quickly.

"Don't worry, Mrs. Bentley. I'm not offended," He stood and walked to the door. "Have a nice day," he said as he left, closing the door behind him.

Jim moved to lock it.

Laura turned to him.

"What is wrong with you?!" she exclaimed.

"I needed to talk to you alone."

"You didn't have to be rude!"

He moved close to her and lowered his voice.

"It's not about the security system. I need to talk to you about the vandalism. The people who tore this place up...they work for the bank..."

She paused, unsure how to respond to such an outrageous statement. After a moment, she smiled, but it turned into a nervous laugh.

"What?" she said finally.

"Shh!" he whispered in her ear. "I'm deadly serious, Laura. Keep your voice down."

"You believe my father's bank burglarized our flat?" she whispered skeptically.

"Not burglarized. Nothing was stolen."

Laura studied Jim's face. He looked deadly serious. She knew from experience that arguing with him in this state was pointless. Once he'd made up his mind, it was almost impossible to change it. Time or evidence might prove him wrong, but no argument would dissuade him from his chosen path. It was something that she both loved and hated about him.

She watched as he walked to the window and peered out into the fading day. Dusk made visibility difficult, but he could still see that Masters' team was fixing a multitude of tiny breaks they'd made in the mortar to install their hidden cameras and microphones. They were mortaring the devices into place.

He returned to her side and whispered in her ear.

"The microphones outside may be sensitive enough to pick up our voices if we speak loudly. So, keep your voice down, OK?"

"Let's go to my parents' house," she whispered back.

Jim shook his head. Though he didn't believe her father played any part in the conspiracy taking shape in his mind, he couldn't trust any Bolton Sayres executive, not even his father-in-law.

"There's no time for that."

"My Dad could get to the bottom of it." She insisted.

Jim knew he needed to choose his next words carefully to avoid offending her. Before he could speak, however, she continued.

"He's the only one who can straighten this out, especially if someone from the bank is involved. I'll call him right now..."

"No!" he exclaimed. "Don't you dare do that!"

Jim checked his watch: 7:20 p.m. The sun would fully set in just a few minutes. He gathered some books from the pile Laura had assembled for their new French provincial bookshelves and led her to the sofa. As they sat down, side by side, he leaned over to kiss her.

"Pretend you're reading..." he whispered in her ear.

"What are you going to do?" she whispered back.

"I've got work on my computer to do."

He retrieved his laptop from his backpack, opened it, and waited for it to come out of hibernation. Then he inserted a CD and clicked through the setup routine when prompted to install "Zambo."

When installation finished, a small icon appeared in the top left corner showing a telephone embedded in a padlock – confirmation that Zambo was successfully installed. Now he had an encrypted method of communicating with his friend Jose that couldn't be traced. He created a new user ID, naming himself "Team Leader."

That left only one mystery. What was Jose's user ID?

"Occam's Razor," Jim reminded himself silently, as he often did when tackling difficult questions. The simplest answer was usually correct.

But what was the simplest answer? How could he find Jose's user ID on a highly secure communication system that didn't disclose usernames? At first, it seemed impossible. Then it hit him – Jose was too smart to provide an unusable communication method. The answer had to be on the CD!

There was a tiny, inconspicuous text file labeled "README" on the disk, similar to those found on many installation disks. Jim suspected this particular README file wasn't from the software developer. Opening it confirmed his guess – the file contained only one word: "Compumaestro."

That had to be it! He opened a chat window with a small field at the top for entering the username of the person you wanted to contact.

He typed: COMPUMAESTRO.

Then in the text box below:

HELP!!!

He clicked "send" and the message was transmitted instantly. He hoped his guess was correct. It was 11:10 a.m. Would Jose be at his computer at just the right moment? Then he realized it didn't matter – the man always carried a smartphone. Zambo was a tiny program that could run on mobile devices.

He leaned over to Laura again while waiting.

"When it's dark, I'm getting out of here," he said.

"What about the guards?" she warned. "They'll know you've left. You should stay right here."

"They won't even know I've left, because I don't plan on telling them, and I'm not going downstairs..."

Suddenly, the computer beeped with a response:

Compumaestro – Hello! Who is this?

Team Leader – It's me, Jim.

Compumaestro – What's up?

Team Leader – Take down THEATRES, as we discussed...

Compumaestro – Now?

Team Leader – Yes.

Compumaestro – Any chance of doing it a few hours from now?

Team Leader – No. It has to be now.

Compumaestro – Give me 15 minutes...

Setting his computer aside but leaving it running, he pretended to read for the next fifteen minutes as sunset approached. Night was falling, though it was never truly dark in Midtown Manhattan, where lights shone 24 hours a day. The newly installed system outside the building wouldn't be activated until they finished mortaring all the cameras and microphones. It looked like they would work late into the night to complete the job. Meanwhile, if Jose succeeded in taking down THEATRES, the infrared cameras that might otherwise track him would be useless.

He changed out of his work clothes into comfortable jeans, a casual shirt, and a windbreaker. He transferred the USB drives to their usual place in the upper right sub-pocket of his jeans. Finally, the computer beeped again:

Compumaestro – Deed done!

Team Leader – Thanks!

He closed his laptop, stowed it in his backpack, shouldered the bag, and turned off the lights. Other than the glow from windows and streetlamps, darkness filled both the apartment and the world outside. He walked to the window, with Laura following close behind.

"You're going out the window?" she whispered incredulously.

"Yes," he whispered back.

"But this is the fourth floor..."

"That's what a fire escape is for," he replied, then kissed her.

"It's crazy," she complained. "You'll fall..."

"No, I won't," he assured her in a whisper before giving her a final kiss.

"Where are you going?" she asked.

"Upstate," Jim whispered in her ear.

"Why?" She asked.

"To find the Mattingly girl."

"Why?"

"Because she's in danger and doesn't know it. There's no way to contact her by phone that won't be monitored. She's the widow of the man who wrote that diary. Everything he saw, she saw. She knows who the killers are..."

"Why do you always get involved with everything?" she demanded. "It's not your business! Just call the police."

"I can't trust the police," he replied. "Besides, I'm involved whether I like it or not. I found the diary that implicates the murderer. I can't trust anyone..."

"How about me?"

"I just trusted you with my life," he whispered. "Don't repeat what I just told you, and don't let anyone know where I'm going—including your father. OK?"

Tears streamed down her face.

"No, it's not OK," she whimpered. "You're having an affair with this woman, aren't you?"

He wasn't having an affair, but he couldn't deny his physical attraction to the young widow. The intensity of that attraction puzzled even him—an animal magnetism he no longer felt for his wife. But, his motivations were not very complex: there was genuine concern for the woman, fascination with solving the mystery, and pure self-preservation.

The woman upstate might possess crucial information about the identities of those who had already killed multiple people—the same people who might try to kill him next. She knew too much, and anyone who had read the diary knew that. He probably knew too much as well. So, perhaps, he was also now on the killer's shortlist. He could wait passively until they came for him. Or he could take the offensive. He preferred to be the hunter rather than the hunted.

Going on the offensive was also safer for Laura and their little daughter. If the people who had ransacked his apartment were after someone, he was the target, not them. But if he stayed put, they might end up caught in the crossfire.

"This is about life and death," he explained. "Nothing else."

"Then I'm going with you," she insisted.

That was the last thing he wanted.

"You have to stay here to take care of Jenny," he replied firmly. "Go back to your parents' house. You'll be safer there than you'll ever be here. Understand?"

The tears continued to flow, but she knew he was right. She didn't want to stay in their apartment anyway. Not without Jim. It was no use arguing with him. Once he made a decision, reasoning with him was impossible. She nodded through her tears, and he kissed her softly one more time, whispering,

"The people behind the murders ransacked our apartment. The longer I stay, the more danger you're in."

"Then you're never coming back?" she asked, her voice breaking.

"I'm coming back. I just need to gather enough evidence to put these people away. While I'm doing that, I want you and Jenny out of harm's way."

He slid the window open.

"How about you?" Laura asked.

He said nothing, but kissed her again before turning to the window. Though it pained him to ignore her tears, he had no choice. He put on the ridiculous-looking eyeglasses Jose had given him, activated the semi-invisible LED display, and stepped onto the windowsill, squeezing through the opening. A moment later, he stood on the metal grating. He hoped Jose had succeeded in crashing THEATRES. If not, he felt certain the killers would intercept, stop, or even kill him before he reached his destination.

The evening air was cool but not cold. Still, without his jacket, the sharp wind between the buildings would have chilled him to the bone. The metal rods of the fire escape felt ice-cold against his hands, but he ignored the sensation and carefully descended, step by step, on the clattering metal. At the bottom, almost ten feet separated the last grating from the sidewalk.

He maneuvered until he hung by his hands from the lowest grating, reducing the drop by his body length of about six feet. The final jump was only about four feet, and he landed as softly as possible. Still, hitting the concrete sidewalk stung. He checked the bottom of his foot—it hurt, but nothing seemed broken, so he pushed the pain aside.

He was outside, and so far, though only moments had passed, no one had rushed to stop him. How long would it take the powers-that-be to undo Jose's damage? Even when the system came back online, if he was careful not to trigger an alert, the computers wouldn't generate a report unless specifically requested.

He glanced in both directions. The street's unusual quiet was almost suspicious in itself. He shook his head at his paranoia, though in some ways it served him well. Better to hope for the best but expect the worst. The guards would be stationed at the main entrance. He'd have to pass there to take the shortest route to his destination, though he could follow a more roundabout path that would take a few minutes longer.

He turned and walked quickly down a side street until he reached the main thoroughfare. Despite nightfall, many people still walked the streets. He maintained his focus. About five minutes later, he saw it: the mid-rise building where he rented his parking space.

He retrieved the key from his pocket, unlocked the steel security door on the building's side, and descended the stairs. On the fourth sub-basement, he exited the stairwell and surveyed the rows of neatly parked cars. Only a few belonged to building residents. Many spaces came with apartment purchases, but city dwellers without cars or driver's licenses often rented them out. Jim had obtained his space through just such an arrangement.

His old 2002 Chevy Cavalier sat exactly where he'd left it months ago, unused since then. The sight always triggered vivid memories of driving

Laura to the airport in Los Angeles two years before—it felt like another lifetime. He'd then driven cross-country from Los Angeles to New York, a seven-day journey to reunite with her. The car had faithfully delivered him to Manhattan. Though it had always proven reliable despite its appearance, its long period of disuse made him uncertain whether it would even start.

He unlocked the door, sat down, and turned the ignition. As feared, the battery seemed weak, and the engine failed to catch. He tried again, finally getting it to start after considerable pedal priming. He hoped the battery would recharge during his upcoming long journey. He hesitated one final time. What he was about to do might be the most foolish thing he'd ever attempted. Yet it seemed like his only option. What else could he do? Sit idle and do nothing? The girl was almost certainly the next murder target. After her, it might be his turn.

Once he left the parking lot, there was no turning back. He released the parking brake, pulled out of his spot, and exited the lot. By 8:10, he'd left Manhattan through the Holland Tunnel, heading north through New Jersey toward the New York Thruway. Then, suddenly, he realized he'd made what could prove to be a catastrophic mistake.

THEATRES CONTROL CENTER operated in three shifts, with 30–40 people working each shift. In total, the command center employed about 110 people. Assistant managers supervised each shift, each contracted to one of the four sponsoring banks. All reported to Adriano Navarro, who served as both Director of cartel-wide Reputational Risk and Chief Operating Officer of THEATRES.

Navarro sat in the living room of his Westchester County home when he felt a subtle vibration in his pocket—the distinct pattern that signaled a call from THEATRES Central Control. He shifted his walking cane to his left hand and balanced precariously while reaching into his pocket.

"Yes, Suzy..." he answered.

Susanna Maloney had once officially worked for Bolton Sayres. However, the interbank operating agreement made it impossible to promote her to shift manager, as each operating bank was entitled to only one such position. That's why he had convinced Christopher Dunlop, CEO of W.T. Fredericks and his strongest supporter within the cartel, to hire her. Now nominally a Fredericks employee, she had proven herself an excellent shift manager.

"Sir..." she said. "The system has been compromised."

"What? How?"

"A hacker came through the Bolton Sayres interface and introduced a virus that took us down."

"Isolate it, immediately!" he ordered.

"We're working on that."

"Where is Bentley?"

"We're not sure. The last read we have is from his cell phone. He's in New Jersey, headed north."

"Where is he going?"

"North..." she replied. "The system crashed just before he left the city. That's all we know."

"Has the computer extrapolated his final destination?" Navarro asked.

"There's still insufficient data," She replied, "But if you'd like, I could have the police stop his car and question him."

"No," Navarro responded. "Just find out where he's headed. The moment he pops back onto the grid, let me know. How far outside the city can we track him?"

"We've got identity check cameras at all the ticket booths on the Thruway, the rest stops, and throughout the toll payment system, traveling north and south." She replied.

"Good," he stated. "That should be enough. I need to know his coordinates on demand..."

"Yes, sir."

The conversation ended. The problem would be resolved soon. When THEATRES came back online, assuming the boy drove his car, the tracking stations could detect it by the license plates. But Navarro had bigger concerns. Who could have taken down THEATRES? There were three possibilities: an enemy nation, a terrorist group, or a rogue cartel executive...

LAURA WAS ABOUT TO pack her things when the apartment doorbell rang. Through the peephole, she saw a well-dressed blonde woman. Assuming her father had sent her since otherwise the guards would have provided advance notice, Laura opened the door.

"Hello, Mrs. Bentley," the woman said.

"Tell my Dad I have a few things left, but I'll be ready to go in about ten minutes, OK?" Laura said.

"I don't work for your father," the woman stated.

The response startled Laura.

"How did you get in here?"

"It doesn't matter," the woman replied. "I have something for you."

"I'm not interested," Laura said, trying to close the door.

The woman blocked it with her foot.

"I'm not here to hurt you, Mrs. Bentley. I'm here to help."

"What do you want?"

"May I come in?" the woman asked.

"No."

While maintaining her foot in the doorway, the woman searched through her purse and extracted a small device resembling a satellite navigation system. She offered it to Laura.

"What's this?" Laura asked.

"It's a tracking device," the woman replied.

"I've already got a GPS."

She shook her head and attempted to return the device.

"Does your GPS tell you exactly where your husband is, at all times?"

"What?" Laura asked.

"This one does."

"Who are you?"

"I've been sent by someone very concerned with your welfare. This is a gift."

"Who sent you?" Laura pressed.

The woman remained silent as the door suddenly slammed shut—Laura had maintained pressure against it even as the woman withdrew her foot. Laura reopened the door to see the woman's back as she walked away down the hallway, nearly reaching the elevator.

"Wait!" she called out.

The woman ignored her, and Laura considered pursuing her. But, then, she suddenly realized there was no need to do that. Her security detail was waiting downstairs. All she had to do was call them. Besides, she was barefoot. By the time she put on her shoes, it would be too late. She closed the door and picked up a walkie-talkie from the coffee table, pressing the send button.

"Barry?"

"Hello, Mrs. Bentley," the man answered.

"There's a woman headed down the stairs. Detain her, please. When you've got her in custody, let me know."

"Yes, Mrs. Bentley."

Laura waited impatiently. After about ten minutes without a word from the guard, she activated the walkie-talkie again.

"Hello, Mrs. Bentley," Barry answered.

"Well, did you stop the woman?"

"I'm sorry, but as far as we can see, no woman has come in or out of the building in the last two hours."

She stared at the walkie-talkie, speechless.

"That's impossible..." she exclaimed. "She was just here!"

Had she imagined the woman? Was she going insane? She looked down at the device on the table. There was nothing imaginary about that.

"Mrs. Bentley? Are you OK?"

His voice startled her from her stupor.

"Yes, yes, I'm fine," she replied distractedly, continuing to stare at the mysterious device.

Chapter 18 – ON THE RUN!

It was nearly 11 p.m. when Jim pulled up to the old yellow and white house in Paradise. A small illuminated sign mounted on a pole caught his attention:

"Tagliano's Homestyle Bed & Breakfast – Your Comfort is Our Pleasure!"

Below it, a second sign advertised vacancies. Tourist season hadn't begun yet, and the place was likely almost empty. He parked beneath the sign and sat motionless for a moment, steeling himself for what lay ahead.

He was exhausted from the journey. Instead of staying on the New York Thruway, he'd taken the back roads to avoid the toll booths. Not to skip the fees, but to evade the cameras monitoring each station. The killers probably knew he'd left NYC heading north, but they couldn't be certain of his destination. For all they knew, he could be bound for Poughkeepsie or Kingston. Partway through the trip, he'd realized his mistake and switched off his cell phone.

Now, gritting his teeth, he rolled up the car window and approached the door. There was no turning back. The weight of responsibility bore down on him. She could identify the killers, and because of him, they knew it. If they were as ruthless as they seemed, her life was in danger. He might be a target too, simply for reading the diary. She needed to be warned, and he had to learn exactly what she knew. He couldn't trust anyone else with this. Both their lives might depend on it.

The Spring air in the Catskills is crisp – typically 5–7 degrees Fahrenheit colder than New York City – and he was grateful for his windbreaker. A gust of wind made him shudder as he left the car. A motion sensor detected his movement, triggering an outside lamp that flooded the area with light.

He tried the doorknob, but it was locked. Next to it was the "late arrival window" with a small button. He pressed it, and moments later, a young woman appeared, squinting in the lamplight. He recognized her immediately – it was Sandra Mattingly, née Tagliano. She unlocked the door and ushered him in, mechanically moving behind the check-in desk to retrieve a guest form.

"You want a king or two queen beds?" she asked.

"Neither," he replied.

She looked up, surprised. "What do you want?"

"You don't remember me?"

She paused, studying his face more carefully. Recognition dawned suddenly.

"The man from the bank?"

"Right."

"Why are you here?" she asked, perplexed.

"To talk to you..."

"In the middle of the night?"

"I've driven over 4 hours, all the way up from Manhattan," he said urgently, "and I'm here to help you."

"Help me? You're dropping the lawsuit?"

"I'm here to warn you that you're in grave danger."

The woman shook her head with a nervous laugh.

"What are you talking about? How low will you people stoop to get hold of money?" She asked.

"This has got nothing to do with insurance money," Jim said, shaking his head.

"Then, what does it got to do with?"

"It's got to do with what happened on July 22, 2008."

The color drained from her face as she turned away, unwilling to meet his gaze. Her hands trembled as she returned the pad of guest intake forms beneath the desk.

"What about it?" she asked.

"July 22, 2008," he repeated.

"Why do you keep repeating that date?"

"Because it's the night you and Robert Mattingly saw two men bury a dead body."

She remained silent, taking deep breaths while staring at the desk. Finally, she spoke without looking up.

"I don't know what you're talking about..."

"You know exactly what I'm talking about, and I know exactly what you saw. But, they do, also."

"How would you know anything?"

"I read your husband's diary."

"You read what?" she asked, finally looking up again.

"His diary."

"He didn't keep a diary."

"You're wrong."

"Who do you think you are?" she snapped. "Reading other people's diaries? If there's a diary, it's mine. It belonged to my husband!"

"Actually, from a legal standpoint, it's not yours," he explained. "It's the property of the estate, but, since you're the executor, I might have given it to you, except for the fact it describes a crime, which means it had to go to the police first."

"The police?" she asked. "You gave it to the police?"

"I tried to," he said.

"You just told me..." she started.

"I gave it to an FBI agent," he cut her off. "He was supposed to do an initial evaluation for federal jurisdiction. It was just an easy way to get it to the Verde County Sheriff while helping keep this FBI man, who's assigned to our bank, busy with something. I expected it to be forwarded to the Sheriff..."

"Then, why are you here?"

He paused before answering.

"Because that FBI agent is dead," He said, finally, "The original of the diary has been stolen. The FBI no longer even has a record of receiving it from me."

Her hand trembled visibly now.

"I didn't see anything!" she exclaimed. "Bobby always had a good imagination."

"You don't need to be afraid. I'm just an innocent bystander, like you, caught up in this."

"What do you want?" she demanded.

"I want you to trust me."

"Why should I?"

"Maybe, because I drove over four hours in the middle of the night, just to warn you, and put myself and my family at risk to do that."

She shook her head. "Why would you do that?"

"My apartment was ransacked a few days ago. They entered without breaking the lock. They tore apart everything. Not only that, but they took only three things; a printed copy of the diary, the receipt for evidence that I'd gotten from the FBI, and the hard disk of my computer. Nothing was stolen."

She stared at him, speechless. Then, after a moment, she spoke.

"I can't help you. Please leave."

He ignored her request to leave.

"I'm not the enemy," he explained. "The people who ransacked my place, the ones that killed that man who was buried, the ones who killed your husband and his family; they're the enemy. They wanted to find out what I knew. But, you know much more than I do. You were there when it happened. You saw it. Furthermore, you could identify them, and they know it."

Tears streamed down her cheeks as she shook her head in denial. She collapsed into her chair, crying.

"No!" she insisted.

"Listen to me," he urged, gripping her shoulders across the desk. "You need to go into hiding!"

She looked up, incredulous.

"That's right," he explained. "You need to disappear, and so do I."

Suddenly, her face contorted with anger.

"You stupid, stupid man!" she exclaimed. "Why did you do this? Why didn't you just leave it where you found it? Why couldn't you just throw it away?"

"How could I do that? Leaving it where I found it or throwing it away would be destroying evidence. I'm a lawyer. I did exactly what I was supposed to do. It just didn't work out the way I expected."

She shook her head again.

"I know you're afraid," he said softly. "That's why you stayed silent all these years..."

She remained silent.

"You always knew there was no suicide, didn't you?" he said.

"I don't know anything!" she exclaimed.

"You knew that Thomas Mattingly never killed his wife or his son..."

"No!" she cried out. "I don't know any of that. I swear, I don't!"

"You knew," Jim said. "And, you kept silent all these years, because you're afraid."

She broke down completely, collapsing into her chair behind the desk, sobbing.

"What about my son, my little boy..." she moaned.

"I also have a child; a daughter," he said. "I worry about her, also. But, for every minute I stay with her, I put her at risk. The same is true about your son. We both need to go into hiding until we figure this out."

"And, how, exactly, are we going to figure it out?" she asked skeptically.

"It all points back to the bank," he declared. "I think the body they were dumping was one of our former employees."

"I didn't see them murder anyone."

"But you saw them bury someone," he noted. "And, you could identify the men who did it."

"No," she insisted. "I can't."

"You saw their faces," he countered.

She shrugged her shoulders, still shaking her head and crying.

"It was a long time ago," she said.

"Did you get a good look?" he asked.

"I don't know," she replied.

"Did you or didn't you?" he pressed.

"Why should I trust you?" she responded. "You work for the bank, and you just admitted the bank was involved."

"I said that someone at the bank is probably involved," Jim clarified. "That doesn't mean that it's the bank's policy to kill people. But, listen, our lives are woven together now. We depend on the same thing. We depend on you telling me the truth."

"What good would it do?" she said. "They're all dead. My little boy..."

"What happened that night?" he interrupted.

She looked at him, seeming to wrestle with an internal conflict that had raged for years.

"I can't..." she protested.

But suddenly, the memories she had suppressed for so long came flooding out, driven by an unquenchable need to share them with another human being. She began her story, detail by detail.

"That night was hot and humid," she began. "It's that way a few days a year, every summer. Neither of us could sleep. So, I left my house, and met Bobby, after my mom and dad fell asleep. It was almost 1 O'clock in the morning. It was cooler in the forest, and I was always happy when I was with Bobby. I was only 17, and he was 19. We'd been seeing each other for about two months."

She took a deep breath before continuing, her voice steadying as she recalled the details of that fateful night.

"The first 10 feet from State Road 23A is a wide grassy area, mowed by the state roughly every month. Then there's about 30 more feet of private property, also mostly grass, before you reach the forest. His family owned the forest and all the private land beyond.

"There's thick underbrush and a tiny glade hemmed in on four sides. It was one of Bobby's favorite places, and he was showing it to me for the first time. No one from the road can see you when you're inside, but you can see out through the branches.

"It was beautiful that night, despite the heat. The sky was clear, and the moon was almost full, casting everything in black and white shadows. We were lying on a beach towel when he kissed me.

"I'd never felt so close to anyone before. We were alone, with only a few crickets chirping. Bobby kept pushing for sex, but I said 'no' repeatedly. Still, he persisted and eventually, I gave in. Just before we finished, there was a loud rumble of a car approaching fast. I was scared it might be my parents, and the moment he finished, we both scrambled to get dressed.

"The engine noise grew louder until it seemed like the car had parked right next to us. Bobby explained that the echo from the mountains amplifies the sound. The area lies between two mountains, creating a natural amphitheater. Finally, the engine stopped.

"We heard car doors opening and closing, and two male voices. Neither sounded like my father. For a moment, I felt relieved – but before long, I wished it had been him. We crept to the edge of the glade, parted the underbrush, and looked out. A dark BMW was parked on the grass.

"The trunk was open, with two men standing at the back. One was short, the other tall. The short one was black. The big one was white and blonde or maybe gray-haired. He was enormous, like a giant.

"I remember exactly what they said:

"'It's hot as hell...' the giant blonde man said.

"'It ain't so bad...' the black man replied.

"The giant finally unbuttoned his shirt and went with the other man to the car trunk. They hauled out a narrow bag about six feet long. Something heavy was clearly inside – they seemed to struggle with the weight. They tossed it onto the grass.

"They took out shovels, and each man grabbed one end of the bag and one shovel. Holding the bag with both hands and wedging the shovels between their underarms and the bag, they carried it up the small hill formed by the sloping grass shoulder leading to the woods.

"I turned to Bobby, about to speak, but he pressed his finger to his lips. I whispered, asking who they were. He said he didn't know. I asked about the bag – it looked like a body bag. He didn't know that either. Finally, he said we'd just wait them out since they were heading away from us, into the forested area.

"The black man stumbled over something just before they reached the woods, dropping his half of the bag. He cursed about having to carry a 'mothafuckin bag' and wiped the sweat from his forehead. The other man just told him to shut up, saying he was tired of listening to his bullshit. They didn't like each other much. But the man kept talking.

"'We shoulda' burned him, man!' he complained. 'Why the fuck didn't we burn this motha'—'

"'Just do vhat you are told, and shut up!' The giant blonde man replied coldly, with a Russian accent.

"'My fuckin' hand hurts...' the other man complained again.

"'Just pick up your side, and shut your trap!'

"The smaller man fell silent then. He just did what he was told. I think he was afraid to say anything more. A moment later, they disappeared into the underbrush, and we couldn't see them. Bobby said he was going to follow them. I begged him not to. I just wanted to get away. We could have left, but he wouldn't listen. He said it was his land. The two men were trespassing, and he insisted he had to find out what was in the bag. He followed them. There wasn't anything I could do to stop him."

Tears formed in her eyes again. She wiped them away with her fingers and continued.

"I don't know exactly what happened when Bobby was in the woods, except what he told me later. All I know is that I was alone and scared. But he told me it was harder, at least for the smaller of the two, to walk than it was for him, because of the heavy bag. So, he managed to sneak around and secretly watch them. Finally, they dropped the bag with a loud thud and caught their breath."

"'This mothafucka' weighs a ton,'" Sandra continued, recounting the black man's words. "'We shoulda' burned it!'

"'And, how ve going to do zhat, huh?' the giant asked. 'Put on show so dat' zey vatch us on ze grid?'

"'Fuck the grid, man... we coulda' just taken it out! Like we did when we got him!'

"'You don't know shit,' the giant stated. 'Shut up, and dig!'

"The other man grumbled but began digging. They were both working, but the smaller man was slower, and the giant blonde man resented it."

"'Dig faster, you lazy fuck...' the giant said. 'A voman can dig faster zan you.'

"'Fuck your Russki ass, man!' the other man exclaimed, throwing down the shovel.

"'Vhat you say?' the giant asked coldly.

"'I said fuck your Russki ass, man! I ain't afraid a' you no more.'

"'You're not going to dig?' the giant asked.

"'No, mothafucka'! I ain't gonna' dig until I feels like it! Got it?"

"'Good, because I tired listen to you,' the giant said with a strong accent, shaking his head.

"According to Bobby, the giant blonde man showed no emotion. He just reached behind his back and pulled out a semi-automatic pistol with a silencer. Two short pips later, the black man had two holes in the middle of his forehead. He fell into the hole, as dead as whoever was in that body bag. The other man grumbled something in Russian, then complained in English to no one in particular that 'dey all useless pieces of shit' or something like that. He dragged the dead black man's body out of the hole and just continued digging.

"When the hole was big enough for both the bag and the dead black man, he tossed them in as if they were nothing but rag dolls and started covering them with dirt. Bobby didn't wait for him to finish. He made his way back to the road, and when he got to the BMW, he found a pen and an old 7-11 receipt in his pocket. The car's trunk was still open, with several different license tags inside. He wrote them all down, including the one on the car. Then he came back to the glen, where I was waiting. When I saw him, I was so relieved I collapsed into his arms.

"He said we had to get away, and he led me out. We both kept our heads down, heading in the direction opposite to where the giant blonde man was. It took some time, but we finally reached the cultivated section of the farm. I felt safer then. Bobby said he was going to wake up his Dad to tell him what happened. That was the last thing I wanted him to do. It would have only been a matter of time before my own parents found out..."

She paused, lost in the memory.

"And?" Jim prompted.

"And, I decided it was some kind of mafia hit. Bobby didn't seem to care that we would be the only witnesses and targets if they ever found out what we knew. He said it was even more of a reason to tell his Dad. I told him that if he told his father, he'd never see me again. So, he promised not to tell."

Jim took the opportunity to ask a few questions during her pause.

"Your father passed away in 2010, didn't he?"

"Yes," she replied.

"What did he die of?"

"Cancer," she answered.

"I'm sorry..." Jim said. "Is your mother still alive?"

"Yes."

"Where is she?"

"In Albany, visiting relatives," she replied.

"How about your son?" Jim asked.

"With my mother in Albany," she said.

"Did you see the giant's face?" Jim asked.

"Yes," she quickly replied.

"Clear enough to identify him?"

"I think so," she said.

"I'm fairly sure that whoever buried that body also killed the Mattingly family," Jim suggested.

"There's more. I haven't finished yet." She said,

"What else?" Jim asked.

Sandra drew a deep breath before continuing her story.

Despite promising to keep quiet, Bobby eventually told his father about what happened, though he never mentioned her involvement.

"I don't know what they discussed that first night," she said. "But a few days later, his father told Bobby they couldn't go to the police anymore. He claimed that failing to report a crime immediately was itself a felony. He warned Bobby that they'd both face serious jail time if they came forward, since they'd waited too long."

"That's not true," Jim told her, "Who told him that?"

"His father claimed he spoke with the local attorney."

"Failure to report a crime isn't a crime, itself, in New York State."

"I understand that now," she said. "But, I didn't know it then. And, Bobby believed it. He gave his father every license plate number he'd found in that car's trunk."

"How do you know this?"

"Mr. Bennington told me."

"The same lawyer Bobby's father supposedly consulted?"

"Yes."

"You asked him directly?"

"I did."

"What did he say?"

"He told me he'd informed Bobby's father it wasn't a crime in New York State."

"So his father lied to him?"

"It seems that way," she confirmed.

"About the plate numbers – how many are we talking about?"

"Many," she said. "I never knew the exact count."

"Did his father trace them?"

"Through an old high school football friend at the DMV. That's where he went."

"Hmm..." Jim muttered.

As she continued her story, the pieces began falling into place. Telling it seemed to lift a weight from her shoulders.

"A few days later," she continued, "his father announced a trip to New York City."

"Did he say why?"

"Something about meeting investors for his ski resort," she replied.

Jim's suspicions crystallized. The elder Mattingly must have attempted to blackmail someone at the bank. Whoever approved the loan had decided to silence him permanently. There was no other explanation.

"Within six months, Bobby's entire family was dead," she said, her voice breaking. "I was left a widow with an unborn child – a baby who would never know his father."

Her eyes reddened, tears flowing freely now. Years of suppressed fear surfaced as the truth poured out, leaving her more terrified than ever.

"We'll get Sheriff's protection," Jim assured her.

"How can the Sheriff help when the FBI couldn't even protect their own agent?" She asked.

"We don't know he was murdered..." Jim replied.

"You don't find it suspicious that the diary's intake record and your evidence receipt both vanished?" She pointed out.

"Yeah, I do." He admitted.

"But, they know who you are," he stated plainly, "and they know who I am."

"Thanks to you."

Jim nodded, acknowledging this.

"It doesn't matter now who's responsible. I had no way of knowing."

His attention suddenly snapped to the wall-mounted television above the desk. Though muted, it displayed an image that made his blood run cold – a photo of his wife.

"What the f..." he exclaimed, cutting himself short, but grabbing the remote and raising the volume.

"... Mrs. Laura Bentley, daughter of financier Jeremy Stoneham, CEO of Bolton Sayres Bank, has been reported missing tonight. Mrs. Bentley was last seen with her husband..."

His own photograph filled the screen.

"Police are seeking Jim Bentley for questioning regarding his wife's disappearance," The TV anchor continued.

His mind raced. He'd left Laura surrounded by her father's security detail, specifically instructing her to stay at her parents' home. Guilt overwhelmed him – he should have remained with her. Calling the Stonehams was out of the question; it would only reveal his location without helping find Laura. Why did the police want him for questioning? Surely the Stonehams knew he wasn't involved. Was this a trap? Were the killers trying to smoke him out?

If this were a more ordinary case, the wise move would be to find trustworthy law enforcement away from New York City's banking influence. He could present his evidence, and secure witness protection for himself, his wife, child, and Sandra Mattingly. From there, they could begin dismantling the entire criminal enterprise. But, Sandra was right. If these people could murder an FBI agent and leave no traces, there was little that even the most earnest upstate police department could do to protect them.

"What's happening?" Sandra asked, noting his distress and the photo onscreen.

"I don't know."

"Who is she?"

"My wife," he answered, "We need to leave immediately."

She shook her head incredulously.

"You're married to an heiress?"

"She's not an heiress," He replied, "her parents are very much alive."

After a pause, she spoke firmly.

"I'm not going anywhere with you. How do I know you didn't harm your wife? How can I trust you? You could do the same to me..."

"If I meant you harm, I'd have done it already. There's just the two of us right now..."

"Even so, you're too compromised. I'm better off alone..." She insisted.

"They'll find you," he warned. "You won't survive alone. I understand their methods now, and I have contacts who can counter their systems. You're safer with me."

"What exactly is your plan?" She challenged him.

"First, disappear so completely they can't trace us. I know how to stay off their radar. While hidden, I'll investigate what's really happening. When the time is right, I'll choose who receives the information I gather. Then, witness protection at the highest level, until everyone responsible is behind bars."

She remained silent before responding, "You're not exactly inspiring confidence."

"It's the only alternative," He stated, "Staying here puts you and your family in grave danger..."

But, then, the doorbell interrupted him. Sandra checked the video feed and turned back, face drained of color.

"It's him!"

"Who?" Jim asked.

"The giant... from the woods!"

The buzzer persisted. When no one answered, the doorknob began rattling. Jim frantically scanned the room, spotting a three-inch paring knife on the counter. He grabbed it just as gunshots rang out – sharp metallic clangs as bullets struck the deadbolt.

The lock finally gave way, taking part of the door with it. A powerful kick sent the remainder crashing inward. The massive figure entered, 9 mm raised. As the huge man ducked his head to clear the door frame, Jim seized his moment, hurling the small knife with all his might.

Chapter 19 – STONEHAM GETS THE MESSAGE

Jeremy Stoneham sat quietly at his expensive mahogany desk in the library of his penthouse, a spacious room that served as both his home office and personal retreat. Though lavishly furnished, the room saw little use beyond his own presence. He occupied the black leather executive swivel chair, while two pristine armchairs faced his desk, their leather surfaces barely creased due to non-use. In seven years, he could count on his fingers the times anyone had sat in those two armchairs. His wife and daughter had sat on them, on occasion, and there was the one time his future son-in-law, Jim Bentley, had occupied one during a meeting where he had attempted to bribe the boy to stay away from Laura. The boy had rejected the offer, unfortunately.

Deep-stained mahogany shelves, matching the desk perfectly, lined all four walls. An impressive collection of books sat on top of them, primarily focused on finance and banking, most bound in fine leather with gold embossing to mimic classic works. Among them stood one genuine treasure: a mint condition first edition of Adam Smith's "Wealth of Nations," acquired by his wife at a Sotheby's auction.

The library's design had been orchestrated by Mrs. Stoneham and her interior decorator, who had selected the books, just as they had chosen everything else in the penthouse—for appearance rather than function. No one, least of all Jeremy Stoneham, who had never been an avid reader, ever opened those volumes. They existed purely to create "atmosphere." But, the room itself was very useful, and he made extensive use of it. The place was his sanctuary from the demands of his position as the bank's President.

In truth, there was no escape from the stress of being CEO of one of the world's largest investment banks. Relaxation wasn't an option; he remained on call twenty-four hours a day, seven days a week. His compensation package reflected these demands—millions in salary and tens of millions in year-end bonuses. Beyond the money was the intoxicating power: he moved in the highest circles of influence, controlled the destinies of over thirty-four thousand employees worldwide, and his decisions affected millions of lives.

Bolton Sayres Bank had a business model that was straightforward: generate low-risk profits through government connections in market trading and lucrative derivative instruments like interest rate swaps. Substantial revenues were also earned by underwriting stock and bond sales—both commercial and government—and by operating as an active clearing and retail brokerage house. The bank's international reach meant some of its wealthiest clients resided overseas.

Phone calls could come at any hour, which suited Stoneham's insomnia-driven schedule perfectly. He rarely slept more than four hours at a stretch, making him readily available during the small hours of the night. So when his phone rang at approximately 1:30 a.m., he wasn't startled. Recognizing the caller ID, he answered immediately.

The conversation's substance, delivered moments later, left him agitated and breathing hard.

"How could that happen?" he demanded.

"It's your son-in-law," Adriano Navarro explained, "His ID and password were used to access Bolton's intranet. He introduced a serious virus into the system, and it's infected everything."

"I find that hard to believe," Stoneham stated flatly. "He far too much of a goody-goody by nature, so he wouldn't do it, and even if he would, he doesn't know much about computers, so he couldn't. Where is he, anyway?"

"I don't know," Navarro replied. "The virus was coordinated with his car leaving the city. We triangulated him for a while through his cell phone, but he's turned it off. He's managed to crash everything, including all video and audio feeds. We're basically blind. Thanks to him, a terrorist group could come into the City, right now, and get away with just about anything."

"You and I both know that Jim can't hack computers, let alone a system as complex as THEATRES," Stoneham insisted.

"That just means he didn't do it alone," Navarro countered. "But whoever did for him took out multiple layers of security. And they got into the system using his login ID. Where would they get that if not from him?"

"It could have been stolen," Stoneham suggested, "I presume you've plugged the leak?"

"We're in the process," Navarro replied, "To stop it entirely would mean shutting everything down, which we can't do. But we've isolated the virus, limited its ability to affect other parts of the system, and we're working on eliminating it node by node."

"What about Khasan?" Stoneham asked.

"It's confirmed on Khasan," Navarro noted. "He's back in the picture."

"Could he be responsible?" Stoneham pressed.

"You mean working with Jim Bentley?"

"I mean stealing his credentials and hacking into the system."

"It's remotely possible, of course," Navarro admitted. "He knows a little about computers, but only a specialist could do this. We're working on identifying every person capable of it. Eventually, we'll figure out exactly who's working with your son-in-law."

"How do you know Khasan is back in action?" Stoneham asked.

"Because THEATRES identified his height and body shape before it went down."

"Where?"

"We don't know. We've only got partial functionality. But wherever he is, he's one of the most dangerous men alive, as you know."

Fyodor Khasan, the former agent of the Russian Federal Security Service, or 'FSB' for short, was born to a Chechen father and a Russian mother. After years of service in the FSB, he had immigrated to America, having been recruited by the banking cartel's collective reputational risk division in 2006. His job, officially, was to handle serious security threats in Eastern Europe and the former Soviet Union.

But, the man had quickly developed expensive Western tastes that not even the large salary, paid to a top security official, could support. Like many skilled assassins, he soon discovered clients willing and wealthy enough to pay handsomely for private jobs. These personal missions conflicted with the cartel's official policy, which was to respect the law even while bending it close to the breaking point in the pursuit of profit. Eventually, he became an outcast. When his pursuers had nearly caught up with him, he had simply vanished. That was over two years before.

The possibility of Khasan's return was deeply troubling. His methods were diverse and lethal, his movements untraceable, his kills remorseless. The cartel's top decision makers could not really report him to the FBI or other official law enforcement agencies, because they had recruited him, and many of the jobs he had performed, before going rogue, were on the edge of legality and would ruin the reputations of the banks, if the full truth ever got out. Khasan had seemingly defeated even THEATRES, the most sophisticated surveillance system ever built, as it proved seemingly unable to assist with his capture. Although the man's English was poor, he was smart and ruthless.

"When did you first identify him?" Stoneham asked.

"We don't have a definite ID, but we spotted what we believe to be him at 7:45 p.m. this evening," Adriano Navarro reported. "We had the net out with everything set to catch him, until your son-in-law and his computer virus took us down. If not for that, we'd have him in custody."

Stoneham shook his head doubtfully.

"No one's ever been able to catch him. Why should it be different now?"

Navarro avoided the question. Khasan could have been caught long ago. He was running free solely because he was useful and Navarro didn't want to catch him. He redirected the conversation.

"Which brings us back to Jim Bentley," he said. "He drove north and disappeared. Someone using his credentials crashed the system. And someone matching Khasan's description was spotted in upstate New York just before this happened. A rather suspicious set of events, wouldn't you agree?"

"We've spent all this money on those fancy and expensive gadgets of yours," Stoneham pointed out, allowing himself a rare smile at the opportunity to taunt the man he despised, "Yet you can't even stop one simple lawyer from leaving the city?"

"The virus was designed to take us out when your son-in-law wanted to disappear!" Navarro stated. "He may not have designed it, but he's behind it. I'm sure of it."

"I think you're dreaming," Stoneham quipped.

"Well, in any case, the system is mostly non-functional for the moment," Navarro noted. "We'll need to resort to old-fashioned intelligence gathering, like questioning witnesses."

"Good luck with that," Stoneham said.

"In Jim's case, the most important witness would be your daughter, Laura," Navarro revealed.

Stoneham was taken aback. There were no depths to which this man would not descend. 'This son-of-a-bitch Dego thinks he can get away with interrogating Laura?' he thought to himself.

Then, aloud, he said, "She's not a witness to anything."

"She is," Navarro insisted. "But it doesn't matter anymore."

Those words offered a brief moment of reassurance—Navarro still knew his place. He wouldn't dare interrogate Laura. But the relief lasted only seconds before Navarro delivered his final blow:

"Because your daughter, Laura... she's gone too!"

The words hit Stoneham like a ton of bricks. "What? Where is she?"

"We don't know. I was hoping you did," Navarro stated.

"What the hell is that supposed to mean?" Stoneham screamed into the phone while rising to his feet.

"It's supposed to mean exactly what I just said. We have no idea where she is."

Stoneham's thoughts immediately turned to his granddaughter, safely asleep in Nanny Isabel's room, down the penthouse's main hallway. Thank God for that!

"The ransacking of their apartment was a bad sign. As I warned you, you should have allowed my experts to deal with it."

"Masters dealt with it just fine. The whole place is wired, and we've got three armed guards."

"Your man doesn't have a clue where she went," Navarro pointed out. "He just let her go, and no one followed her. He designed that system to stop people from coming in, but he did nothing to track people going out. Of course, he also didn't bother to build a link to THEATRES, as I suggested he should."

Stoneham had specifically instructed Masters NOT to link to THEATRES. The less Navarro knew, the better.

"I want every system diverted, immediately, to finding Laura!" Stoneham ordered.

"You know I can't do that."

"You'll do it, or else!" Stoneham exclaimed, though he knew he held no leverage.

"Or else what, exactly? You have no direct control over me anymore. I answer to the Council, not to you."

Though Navarro was officially a Bolton Sayres employee, like many things within the banking system, it was nothing but a facade. It was impossible to fire him, given the waves it would cause among other Council members. But the man was implying his relationship to the Council had evolved into something more significant. That seemed impossible without a full Council meeting.

"Since when?"

"Your authority has always been more theoretical than real, and you know it," Navarro pointed out, "But now it's official. I work directly for the Council."

"That would require a special meeting, and there hasn't been one," Stoneham objected.

"That's where you're wrong. There was an emergency meeting tonight. You were simply recused due to the fact that you have multiple conflicts of interest."

"You son of a bitch!" Stoneham exclaimed, his voice rising.

He was livid but knew he needed to calm down. The situation demanded careful consideration, but his anger made clear thinking impossible. Had his influence with his colleagues truly eroded so dramatically? It wasn't too long ago that he'd personally saved all their asses thanks to his personal relationship with the President. But, Navarro was unscrupulous, and he possessed sensitive information about far too many people. Perhaps, he had threatened other Council members with exposure of their secrets?

"I'd suggest that you treat me with some respect from now on," Navarro said.

"I'll treat you the way I see fit." Stoneham countered.

"That would be unfortunate, given how badly you need my help to find your daughter. Otherwise, she won't be found until she wants to be found, and that might take a long time. I don't think she wants to be found."

"You son-of-a-bitch!" Stoneham grumbled and slammed down the phone.

The news of his daughter's disappearance felt like a knife to his gut. Had she left voluntarily? Or had she been kidnapped? Could Navarro be behind it? He tried to clear his mind. Where to begin looking? She might be fine. She might not need rescuing. It seemed unlikely she would willingly leave little Jenny behind, yet if Jim had indeed departed for parts unknown, she might be traveling with him. But if so, why hadn't she informed him? And Khasan was out there...

Several potential courses of action were open to him. He could leverage his political connections to forcibly take control of THEATRES and use the system to locate her. But that approach would be messy, complicated, and would take time. Voluntary cooperation would be preferable. Despite his intense dislike of Navarro, no one understood the system better than he did.

Was it really even remotely possible that Jim had been able to introduce a virus powerful enough to collapse the network? If his son-in-law actually possessed such capabilities, regardless of whether he had done the coding himself, it proved his fitness to replace Navarro beyond any shadow of a doubt. Still, grooming him for the position and convincing enough minds on the Council to overcome the blackmail data Navarro might have on one or two of them, would take time. It wouldn't be an easy prize—all the CEOs had to agree. And, he needed Jim to want it badly enough, himself, to make it happen.

But, he put thoughts of his son-in-law's future employment out of his mind. It would have to wait. Finding Laura took precedence. He had calls to make and favors to call in. He also needed to strengthen his political position and investigate exactly what had transpired in the Council. Another major internal political struggle seemed inevitable. His wife was fast asleep. His granddaughter and her nanny were sleeping too. Better to let them all rest. Waking them up to have them worrying about Laura's missing person status would accomplish nothing. By morning, the whole situation could be resolved. The library walls were soundproof. No matter how loudly he had shouted at Navarro, he was sure no one heard.

He slipped into the master bedroom momentarily and, taking great care not to wake his wife. He gave Erica a rare light kiss on the forehead. Then he silently closed the door, walked to the kitchen, and wrote a quick note on a slip of paper, leaving it on the counter.

"Sorry, honey, I had to leave. The firm has pressing business abroad. You know how it is..."

A few minutes later, he was out the door. The night was silent.

Chapter 20 – FYODOR KHASAN

The giant blonde man had arrived at his destination after several hours of driving, his mind focused on the task ahead. The woman had to die. She knew too much. She had seen too much. The only question was how to carry out the killing. Staged suicides were popular with his clients, but he, personally, preferred the garrote. It was neat and clean. But, a simple break–in and quick murder by a bullet wound, as a result of a fake robbery, could work just as well.

His criminal career had begun on the streets of Moscow, where he'd only been caught once. That was long before the FSB had trained him to be an assassin. From that training, he knew hundreds of ways to kill, from exotic poisons like ricin and radioactive polonium to the simple efficiency of a silenced bullet to the back of the head. He was proud of his work.

Young girls weren't his usual targets. This wasn't due to any moral qualms about the target. On the contrary. It was simply a matter of supply and demand. His services were typically required for business and political rivals, roles rarely filled by young women. He hadn't anticipated any particular difficulties with this one. Like most victims, she would likely freeze in terror, making it easy for him to execute her.

The car's satellite navigation system informed him he was nearly there. Following its pleasant voice commands to continue straight, he finally reached his destination: "Tagliano Bed & Breakfast." He parked his Jaguar next to an older 2002 Chevy Cavalier, the only other vehicle in the front lot.

He reached into the glove compartment for his black gloves and a Taurus 9mm semi-automatic handgun. The gloves would ensure no fingerprints were left behind. The gun was a throwaway piece acquired from Miami's black market. It was originally manufactured in São Paulo, Brazil, stolen in Rio, and quietly smuggled into the United States, for just purposes as this.

After the job, he would dispose of it. If police recovered it, the trail would lead to its original Brazilian owner.

After donning the black gloves and retrieving the weapon, he attached the silencer from the glove compartment. The gun would emit nothing more than the soft sound of a pip when fired. He studied Sandra Tagliano's photograph one final time, committing her face to memory, before returning it to his pocket and exiting the car.

The front door was locked. When no one answered his ring, he attempted to pick the lock, but the well-designed deadbolt proved resistant to his basic tools. Frustrated, he violently shook the handle to no effect. Though he preferred stealth, speed now took priority. He aimed the silenced 9mm directly at the deadbolt and fired repeatedly.

Each impact of a bullet meeting a bronze doorknob produced a loud clack – the silencer useless against the metal-on-metal contact. After several shots, the entire lock assembly, including part of the door itself, broke free. A powerful kick sent the compromised door crashing open.

He immediately spotted his target from the photograph at the front desk, along with an unexpected male. There was no time for analysis. Collateral damage was undesirable, but leaving a witness behind was not an option. The client would understand; the man was in the wrong place at the wrong time. Stooping to clear the small door frame, he raised his weapon to target the girl first. That's when everything started to go wrong.

The other man was armed, prepared and had waited patiently. Years had passed since Jim had last thrown a knife, and the knife in question was a poorly balanced specimen of a blade. But, his martial arts training hadn't abandoned him. Success would depend on muscle memory now, not on the blade's quality. The small knife spun through the air like lightning. While it widely missed its intended mark, which was the giant's heart, luck still favored the poorly aimed throw and the blade buried itself deep in the giant's thigh, slicing through muscle and nicking a vein substantially enough to create an impressive spray of blood. The handle protruded from the wound.

The big man roared in pain even as he squeezed off a shot, which went wild and struck the floor several feet from the girl. He clutched at his injured leg with his free hand, grimacing. The smaller man lunged forward, kicking the gun from his loosened grasp and sending it skidding across the floor, well out of even his prodigious reach.

Following through, Jim landed a kick to the giant's face and a heavy blow to his solar plexus but to little effect. Both strikes connected perfectly. Both were well orchestrated attacks that would have incapacitated or killed any normal man. But Khasan was not a normal man. A knife could slice his flesh as easily as anyone else's and his unusually low pain threshold made such wounds especially agonizing, but blunt trauma was another matter.

At nearly seven feet tall and over 420 pounds of solid muscle and whalebone, the big man dwarfed the comparatively six foot, 168-pound Jim Bentley. The size difference was akin to a ten-year-old fighting a grown man. Despite perfect targeting, Jim's kicks and punches achieved minimal effects. Having lost the element of surprise, Jim watched as the giant casually deflected his second kick with one massive hand, seizing the leg and slammed Jim hard onto his back, where he landed in the growing pool of the giant's blood. Had Khasan maintained his composure, he likely could have finished Jim off, right then and there. But, fortunately for Jim, that didn't happen.

Overwhelmed by the searing pain of the knife wound, after tossing Jim onto his back like a play toy, Khasan ignored him, focusing, instead, on controlling the bleeding and managing his agony. He yanked out the blade with a howl of pain, producing a brief geyser of blood before he could staunch the flow. This moment of distraction gave his temporarily immobilized opponent the chance to escape.

Jim wasn't stupid. He recognized that a hand-to-hand battle with someone so much larger than himself was hopeless. No amount of skill, speed, dexterity or training could overcome the size difference. A gun would have made a big difference, but he didn't have one. Even a very substantial, large knife, might have changed the odds. But he didn't have one of those either. The giant's discarded pistol lay too far away to reach without coming within grabbing distance, and that would probably prove fatal. There was only one option, and it was a simple one...run!

The woman had remained frozen behind the front desk, paralyzed, exactly as Khasan had predicted. She stood transfixed by the scene before her. Jim jumped up, grabbed her hand, and pulled her along, urgently gesturing and whispering for her to follow. And, under his influence, which broke the spell of shock, she complied and followed him.

The giant blonde man was between them and the front door. Attempting to pass him would be suicide. He would surely catch at least one of them. Therefore, with his clothes still wet and stained with the big man's blood, Jim and Sandra Mattingly retreated deeper into the house in order to reach the back door. Meanwhile, Khasan's temporary disorientation began to clear.

This was the first major injury he had ever received on any job. But, he regained his wits, and retrieved the knife that had wounded him. Then, he cut away a large piece of his shirt, and pressed the wadded fabric hard against his injury to stem the bleeding, just as he had been taught in basic FSB training, back in Russia. In nearly the same movement, he recovered his gun.

"Come on!" Jim urged, gesturing for the girl to follow.

No longer paralyzed, she pointed.

"Is that the way to the back door?" he asked anxiously.

She nodded, still unable to speak, and he pulled her along. Moments later, they emerged into the back parking lot's unpaved gravel surface.

"There!" she exclaimed, finally finding her voice as she pointed to an old Ford Ranger pickup truck.

They scrambled in, and she fumbled through her purse for the keys before handing them over. Jim frantically worked the ignition, but although the engine would turn over, it repeatedly stalled. It was the wrong time for a malfunctioning ignition! He continued cranking the key, occasionally tapping the accelerator to prime the fuel pump. The pattern repeated several times. Meanwhile, the blonde giant appeared in the back doorway, his gun raised again, as a miracle happened.

The small pickup's engine suddenly roared to life. As the giant took aim, Jim released the brake and shifted into reverse, flooring the accelerator. The unexpected backward surge threw off the man's shots, and the shots hit the bottom side metal instead of the tires, as had been intended. Jim shifted into drive and accelerated forward. The giant continued firing, but blood loss, shock, pain, and the need to maintain pressure on his wound with one hand made him wildly inaccurate. His attempts to hit the tires repeatedly failed.

When he fired at the rear window, he succeeded in shattering the glass but didn't manage to hit the occupants. The impact of bullets against metal and glass created a cacophony, but the old Ford Ranger, now decorated with bullet holes and missing its rear window, disappeared into the night with its passengers shaken, but as yet unharmed.

Jim kept the accelerator pressed to the floor. The little Ranger's engine was modest, but it carried them away at what felt like light speed to an as-yet unknown destination. Fyodor Khasan stood at the back door, like a statue, watching the vehicle fly away. He silently held his gun in one hand while maintaining pressure on his wound with the other. The Ranger vanished from sight, and Khasan stumbled, for a moment, his stance unsteady from blood loss.

He had more powerful weapons with greater range, stored in his car, but there was no time to retrieve them. The pain was intensifying, and he was fairly sure that the dirty blade had introduced an infection. He considered his options. His Jaguar could easily overtake a decrepit Ranger pickup. But, that was only if they stayed on SR 22. There were numerous side roads they might take, and the darkness made tracking impossible even with night vision equipment. Moreover, he was seriously injured. His blood was everywhere, leaving genetic evidence that could prove damning if he were ever caught.

The operation seemed cursed, ending once again in disaster. His leg worried him – without quick access to antibiotics, infection could become severe. Never before had he failed so miserably. It was unprecedented. The drastic action he now contemplated would draw unwanted attention that would displease his client, but he saw no alternative.

The boarding house's isolation meant that it was unlikely that anyone heard the commotion, in spite of how loud it was. But, that wasn't certain. The boarding house was empty. If there were any guests sleeping upstairs, they would have likely awakened to the noise, and he would be aware of them. So, he guessed there was nobody. It hardly mattered; any potential witnesses would have to die regardless. Time was critical. He limped back through the house and across the parking lot to his car, where he retrieved two 5-gallon gasoline cans from the trunk.

He poured gasoline as he walked, ensuring coverage of all surfaces where his blood might have dripped. He continued throughout the house, saturating floors, carpets, and furniture as quickly as possible. Finally, he dribbled what remained along his path to the back parking lot.

After discarding the empty cans, he entered the kitchen. With practiced efficiency, he used a small wrench to open the propane gas lines feeding the oven and heating system. The uncontrolled leak would quickly fill the house. He lit the gasoline, and the flame traveled quickly toward the house along the path he had laid down. Thankfully, the chilly night meant all windows were already closed, saving precious time and effort. The kitchen, at minimum, by now, would be flooded with natural gas fumes.

He hurried back to his car and drove away. Then came the distant sound of approaching sirens. Obviously, someone had heard, and reported the incident. He had acted just in time. From a safe distance, he drove off the small road and quietly exited his vehicle. Three Sheriff's cars sped past with sirens blaring, none noticing Khasan's vehicle parked in the shadows of the berm. The house remained clearly visible in his night vision binoculars. Suddenly, there was a massive explosion as the gas leak and gasoline combined to reduce the house to viciously burning rubble that collapsed inward upon itself and continued to burn.

Fyodor Khasan nodded in satisfaction, though anger and pain clouded his expression. The explosion had covered his mistakes. His tracks could no longer be followed – the blood was incinerated, his DNA destroyed. If there were any upstairs guests, they were all now ash or would be ash very soon. They would tell no tales. Meanwhile, the implosion would keep local law enforcement occupied while he attended to his next task.

Feeling increasingly ill, even opening the driver's side door again proved challenging. He rummaged through his first aid kit in its compartment beneath the seat. He had antibiotics there, but proper medical attention was crucial. When he'd served in Chechnya, he'd seen soldiers succumb to festering wounds. So, he cut a length of gauze bandage, applied hydrogen peroxide, which stung viciously, dusted the wound with Kyostat, a military-grade coagulant that clotted blood on contact, and followed with povidone-iodine. Then, he wrapped his leg with gauze,

He was rapidly fading, and needed a stimulant that would work just long enough to get him to the hospital. There was a surgeon there who would tell no tales if you paid him enough. But, it was a long drive to that particular hospital, and he needed to stay awake. He rummaged through the glove box until he found it. One of his favorite items. A vile of white powder that looked very similar to the coagulant he'd just applied to his leg. But, it wasn't coagulant. It was cocaine. He poured a small amount into his palm and snorted it through a narrow tube. The rush gave him what he sought. Cocaine was his stimulant of choice. He bought only the finest, and years of use meant that, for him, its effect would be little more than a cup of strong coffee. Still, it cleared his mind and reduced his dizziness.

Much work remained. To ensure no trail existed, he would have to sacrifice one of his prized possessions. The girl and her companion still lived, and they could both describe his car. Jaguars were distinctive enough that even changing plates might not prevent identification. So, he drove to the small downtown area, just 10 minutes from the Tagliano Inn. Surveying the street, he spotted a 2006 Ford Explorer parked at the hardware store. Newer vehicles nearby wouldn't suit his needs – they took too long to hot-wire. An older Explorer would prove quick and simple.

He parallel-parked behind the Explorer and painfully exited his car, the wound throbbing. Limping the short distance to the target vehicle, he quickly jimmied the driver's door lock. Carefully lowering himself into the seat to avoid aggravating his injury, he set to work. A wire cutter and electrical tape sufficed to bypass the ignition assembly. Within sixty seconds, he held two hot-wired ends together, and the engine roared to life. The gas gauge showed nearly full. He carefully stood and limped back to the Jaguar to gather his equipment, including fake VIN placards, license plates, night vision goggles, multiple weapons and an ultra-secure Russian-built tablet running RuMos, a modified Android derivative that also powered his phone.

One task remained. He retrieved a shoebox from under the seat containing several hundred $100 bills and two hundred fifty €500 notes – over $155,000 in total at the then-current exchange rates. Carrying the box, he limped to the rear seat and lifted the cushion to reveal a compartment filled with C-4 explosives.

He worked quickly to mold and position the putty at key points throughout the vehicle. After wiring it to the car's battery and setting a fifteen-minute timer, he closed the door and made his way to the Explorer.

He had plenty of time. At the rear of his new vehicle, he replaced the existing plates with fresh ones from his collection.

Later, he would access the New York State DMV database. He'd properly associate the SUV with its new plates and register it to one of his many aliases. Though the VIN wouldn't initially match the registration, that was a mere formality. He could attach new VIN placards soon enough. Without a careful examination of the engine compartment, even a police officer wouldn't suspect the truth. The Explorer was perfect for his needs. There were tens of thousands of them, everywhere, all over the New York highways. It would allow him to blend into the sea of humanity very easily.

As he drove his newly acquired car along State Route 23 toward the New York Thruway, a fireball suddenly illuminated the night sky behind him. Even miles away, the explosion cracked through the darkness like lightning, its thunder shaking the air. In just thirty minutes, he had orchestrated two devastating blasts: one that had imploded the guesthouse, and another that had torn open the heart of downtown, in that tiny Catskills town. His Jaguar lay in ruins. Along Main Street, not a single window remained intact. The destruction would leave the area looking like a war zone for weeks or even months to come.

Chapter 21 – HACKING

Jim wanted to get far away and fast. Unfortunately, exhaustion threatened to overwhelm him. His mind and body still functioned, but it was just a matter of time before fatigue would force a collapse. It was nearly 3 am when he pulled into the parking lot of a cheap motel. As he stepped out of the vehicle and stretched his legs, the simple movement felt like pure bliss.

Reaching into his right jeans pocket, he confirmed the envelope was still there – the same $3,000 he'd recovered from the top dresser drawer of his ransacked flat, right after the incident. He couldn't risk using an ATM. That would ensure that anyone tracking him would immediately know his location. But, $3,000 wouldn't last long. He had to get all the critical information he needed before it ran out.

Glancing at Sandra Mattingly, he saw that she was fast asleep in the passenger's seat. Her ability to sleep in spite of everything that had just happened was surprising. Few people would be able to under these circumstances. She was young and pretty. Bearing a child hadn't diminished her looks as it had Laura's. He pondered how two women could react so differently after pregnancy and childbirth. Genetics didn't explain it entirely. The key to obesity was excessive eating, and both his wife and her mother were overweight due to their eating habits, not from childbirth, even though both used the birth of their children as the excuse for their obesity.

Since she was sleeping, he'd have to enter the motel lobby himself unless he awakened her. He didn't relish the idea of doing that because his face was everywhere now, thanks to the news media and the false reports. His blood-stained shirt and pants made matters worse. As he opened the vehicle door, its squeaking hinges roused the sleeping girl. She yawned and stretched and, in retrospect, that worked out well, because her face was the one that the motel clerk had to see. Not his.

"What time is it?" she asked, her eyes still half–closed.

"A little past 3 a.m.," he replied.

"Where are we?"

"A motel near Albany," he explained. "Maybe it would be better for you to get the rooms..."

"Why?"

"Because my face was on television," he explained. "And look at my shirt and pants."

She nodded, finally understanding. He handed her two hundred dollars.

"Go ahead and get us two rooms," he said.

She shook her head.

"No," She said, "I don't want to be alone. Can we rent one room with two beds?"

He nodded.

"The sign says $59.95..." she noted, and handed one of the hundreds back to him.

"Remember, if they ask, tell them you don't have any ID," he instructed.

"OK," she agreed.

The entry lobby's beige carpet was threadbare, sporting numerous visible stains. The largest was almost a foot wide, with smaller ones scattered throughout. One advantage of fleabag motels was the tendency to ask few questions. Even a Motel 6 demanded a driver's license, but a no-name cheapo privately owned establishment often didn't care, as long as you paid cash.

There was an elderly Indian man sitting behind the check-in counter, wearing a traditional off-white collarless shirt that hung open over his trousers. He occasionally sipped from a cup of tea perched on a small utility table, his eyes fixed on the television set. He seemed oblivious to Sandra's entrance, and she stood at the desk long enough to notice Jim's photo appearing on the cable news channel.

The old man suddenly emerged from his television-induced trance and noticed his potential guest. He stood and walked to the reception desk, speaking with a strong East Indian accent.

"Can I help you?" He asked.

"I need a room." She replied.

"For you?"

"Yes," She said, "and...a friend."

"Two people?" the old man asked, retrieving a reservation form.

She nodded.

"One king or two queen beds?" He asked.

"Two queens, please."

The man glanced at his watch and handed her a registration slip.

"Please fill this out, and I'll need your driver's license or photo ID..."

"I lost my license," she replied.

"We can use another photo ID?"

"I don't have any on me," She noted, "They're all at home."

"What about your friend?"

"Sleeping in the car."

"You're driving without a license?" He inquired.

"I have a license," she explained. "I just don't have it with me."

He looked at her suspiciously, then smiled and nodded. She completed the form with a fake name, surname, and an invented address before returning it to him.

"How will you be paying?" the man asked.

"Cash."

"OK. That will be $149."

"Excuse me?" she asked, surprised.

"$149 please," the old man repeated.

"It says $49.95 on your sign," she pointed out.

"That's for one person," the man insisted. "But you have two. There's also the tax."

"For that kind of money, I could stay at the Hyatt," she argued.

"You'd need photo ID," the man said in his strong accent.

Sandra shook her head and turned to leave.

"Where are you going?" the man asked.

"I'm leaving."

"No, no, no," he insisted, "don't worry. I can make you a special deal... and this is only for you... and the $149 will be for two nights... $74.50 per night... no problem!"

The old Indian man, who she'd initially mistaken for senile, proved to be quite the cunning negotiator.

"It says $49.95 per room on the sign," she repeated firmly.

"But you are two people," he complained.

"I'll have to talk to my husband," she said.

Without giving him time to respond, she quickly returned to the car and related the exchange to Jim. He pulled out the second $100 bill and handed it to her.

"Just rent it," he told her.

Ten minutes later, she returned with the room keys. He started the engine and drove to the other side of the motel. After carefully surveying the parking lot, he found a secluded spot shielded by a thick evergreen hedge, the motel's ugly metal dumpster, and the branches of a large tree newly green with spring leaves.

The room matched the lobby's mustiness. The drapery fell short of covering the windows properly, and several broken ceramic tiles left an unrepaired hole in the bathroom. Various other items needed maintenance, though the towels appeared clean enough and the two queen-sized beds seemed adequately comfortable.

The room came fully furnished with a small desk, several chairs, and a large six-drawer chest, providing ample storage space for clothing. Unfortunately, they possessed only the clothes they wore.

"This room is disgusting," she grumbled and yawned.

He walked to the window and lifted the curtain slightly, peering out for no particular reason.

"You're right," he agreed, "But, it's home for the next two days. And, I desperately need to get some sleep..."

When he turned around, Sandra was already lying down on one of the beds, half asleep. He directed his attention to the other bed, removing the bedspread and opening the underlying layers of blanket and sheet. Sliding under the covers, he closed his eyes. Within moments, exhaustion overcame him and he too drifted off to sleep.

Early the next morning he awoke, he found the girl had already showered and was applying makeup in the bathroom.

"I'll go buy us some food," she said as she emerged, noticing he was awake. "Give me the keys to the truck..."

"They're in my jeans' pocket..." he replied, pointing to the pair he'd left on the floor. "But it would be better to lay low."

"Lay low and starve?" she mocked. "There's a McDonald's right around the corner. What do you want?"

He rubbed his eyes, still tired. "Egg McMuffin, maybe, some juice. If you see a drugstore or something like that, buy two hair dye kits. If there's a place to buy clothing, get me a pair of jeans, 36 waist, 32 length. And a new shirt, large. But use cash only. Don't use your credit card. Understand?"

She looked confused, so he explained further.

"We'll be safer if we change our hair color, and we should do anything else that might make us look different. They can trace any charges you make on your credit card. As for the shirt and pants, do I need to explain?"

She looked at his clothes, now stained brownish with dried blood, and nodded.

"OK." She said, and left.

Silence filled the room. The quiet was so complete that when he closed his eyes again, intending just a few seconds' rest, he soon fell back into deep sleep. An hour and a half later, he awoke to find Sandra had returned, bringing with her the aroma of bacon and eggs.

The smell made him realize how desperately hungry he was.

"There's a big Walmart SuperCenter down the street," she explained. "I bought everything there."

He spotted a brand-new shirt and a pair of pants sitting atop the chest of drawers. She opened the small refrigerator that came with the room and pointed to a stack of frozen TV dinners.

Microwave food had never impressed him, but now, half-starved, it felt like a gourmet meal. He devoured it quickly. As he ate, he tried to remember the last time his wife had cooked breakfast, even in a microwave. Breakfast at her parents' penthouse or in the Hamptons' getaway always included choices of bacon and eggs, cereal, pancakes, lox and bagels, and several other items. But, it was all prepared by the Stoneham's chef. For privacy reasons, he'd refused to hire a cook or live-in maid for his own home. Consequently, breakfast in their flat always consisted of boxed cereal and milk.

Looking at his watch, he saw it was almost 10:00 a.m. After eating, Sandra went into the bathroom with her newly purchased box of hair dye.

Meanwhile, he opened his laptop and connected to the motel's Wi-Fi. Following Jose's instructions, he double-clicked on the Tor browser icon. Tor is a high-security browser protocol, which was originally developed by the US Navy before being placed into the public domain. It has become an open source project, maintained by volunteers. The method by which it connects people to the internet makes tracking users' IP addresses almost impossible. The US government maintains a schizophrenic relationship with it. The NSA and FBI despised it for making surveillance more difficult. But, the State Department and various propaganda arms of the government appreciated how it allows dissidents, inside unfriendly nations, to access American viewpoints without their governments' knowledge or consent.

Using Tor to navigate to the Bolton Sayres website, he attempted to log in. Thanks to the fact that the browser routed itself through multiple Tor nodes, his location was kept secret. The problem was that it slowed internet browsing to a crawl. Finally, however, the system responded with two words:

"ACCESS DENIED!"

He clicked on the now familiar Zambo icon, hoping Jose would be available. While he waited anxiously for a response, Sandra emerged from the bathroom wrapped only in a towel, her thick hair now reddish, colored almost like a carrot.

"What do you think?" she asked, modeling her new red tresses.

Though her eyebrows no longer matched her hair color, making her look somewhat odd, the red hair definitely changed her appearance. That was the point. Meanwhile, the outline of her naked breasts and hips beneath the towel stirred something in his groin.

"Do you like it?" she inquired again.

"Yeah," he said enthusiastically. "You look great!"

She turned on the television to watch a morning talk show.

"Could you turn the sound down please?" Jim asked.

"What are you doing?"

"Trying to save our necks..." he replied.

His cryptic answer went unquestioned. Instead of pursuing it, she rummaged through her purse, extracted a pair of earbuds, and dutifully plugged them into the television earphone jack. The sound died.

"Thanks," he said, returning to work.

Moments later, a message appeared on his screen:

Compumaestro – What's up?

Team Leader – I've got serious problems...

Compumaestro – I know. I saw the news. What's going on?

Team Leader – We're on the run.

Compumaestro – Where are you?

Team Leader – Upstate.

Compumaestro – What do you need?

Team Leader – I'm trying to access Bolton's intranet using Tor as you said, but I can't get in.

Compumaestro – You can't do it like that...

Team Leader – Why not?

Compumaestro – No one can log in without using the VPN software. It's designed to protect the system from third parties. The problem is that the minute you use it, they'll know your IP address, and that will tell them where you are.

Team Leader – I take it you brought down THEATRES?

Compumaestro – Yes.

Team Leader – How?

Compumaestro – I used your VPN, and your username and password. It was the only way in.

Team Leader – I thought hackers didn't need stuff like that.

Compumaestro – You thought wrong. There always has to be a point of entry. I ran spoofing software before loading the VPN, so they still don't know it was me. They'll never know.

Team Leader – No, obviously, because they think it's me! Which is why my face is all over the news!

Compumaestro – Sorry about that... but there wasn't any other way...just claim that someone stole your credentials.

Team Leader – Tell me about the spoofing program. Can I use it too?

Compumaestro – Yes. I'll send it to you now...

A small icon appeared, offering the option to save the executable Jose had just transmitted. Jim saved it to his download folder.

Compumaestro – While I was inside Bolton's intranet, incidentally, I changed a few things...

Team Leader – You brought down THEATRES through Bolton Sayres?
Compumaestro – Yes.

He'd asked Jose to break the system but hadn't thought it completely through. He hadn't thought about the fact that Jose would need to use his credentials, which meant that everyone assumed he did it. Yet, even if he had known, he would have had to ask Jose to do it. With the killers so highly placed in the banking industry, and the banks being the ones running surveillance, he had no choice but to bring down THEATRES, in whatever way it had to be done. Otherwise, he would never have escaped from New York City.

Now he understood why his image was plastered all over the news, and why the police were looking for him. It wasn't the police at all. The "powers-that-be" wanted to question him. It was something they obviously couldn't broadcast. Recent events would eliminate any chance of getting the job his father-in-law had once offered him. Running THEATRES, it seemed to him, was out of the question. It was just as well. He didn't want the job anyway.

The blonde giant had appeared despite the surveillance system being down. That was something he had not counted on. But, if the THEATRE's control center had known his exact destination, perhaps the man would have arrived earlier, and Sandra would already be dead rather than modeling her new look. Or, maybe, he would be dead, too. They might have killed him en route.

Team Leader – If you used my credentials, they'll have me blocked. How am I supposed to log in?

Compumaestro – Don't worry. I already set up several fictitious executives, with higher level security access than you ever had.

Team Leader – How could you do that?

Compumaestro – I told you before, there are a lot of gaping security holes in the system that we were required to put in, supposedly for national security purposes. They can be exploited if you know how.

Team Leader – So, what do I do?

Compumaestro – First, make sure you use the spoofer software before you run the VPN. It'll fool the VPN into thinking you're at a different IP address. Piggyback that on Tor. No one will know who you are, or where you are.

The Zambo file transmission icon reappeared on the screen, delivering Jim's new login ID and password. He opened it in his word processor. He would now be an entirely different person. A person who did not exist but had access credentials just two levels lower than Jeremy Stoneham, himself!

After double-clicking the file, the installation window appeared. He followed the prompts, installing the tiny spoofing program that made subtle but critical changes to the Windows operating system. Then he ran the VPN and logged on. A small blue icon lit up at the bottom left of the screen. With the connection established, he logged in. Everything worked perfectly.

Team Leader – I'm in!

Compumaestro – Great! I'll stay on the line...

Team Leader – The name of Marcus Dunlop, a scumbag I've run into before, appeared on the list of cars borrowed from Bolton Sayres on the night of Charles Bakkendorf's murder. I want to pull up all records with his name on them.

Compumaestro – Good idea.

Team Leader – OK.

He typed "Marc Dunlop" into the search window and received references to thousands of emails. The total size of the files exceeded 345 gigabytes, with emails alone amounting to 176 megabytes – too many pages to review in the time available.

Team Leader – It's an enormous file. How can one man generate so many records?

Compumaestro – It could only happen if he's doing a lot of light–speed computerized trading, and those trades list his name as either the broker or the principal customer, but he's not trading at all. It's being done by an automated bot.

Team Leader – I'm not sure what to do next. There's no way we have any hope of making a serious dent in all those records. The download alone would take days based on the speed of the Wi-Fi here, and I wouldn't even have enough room on my hard disk.

Compumaestro – We don't need all the trading records. Just download emails...

Team Leader – OK. But, even 176 megabytes will take some time because the motel's internet is very slow...

Compumaestro – Didn't Bakkendorf work in Bolton's gold vault?

Team Leader – Yes.

Compumaestro – His death is probably connected to gold. Have you heard about the government conspiracy to control gold prices?

Jim dismissed this as another of Jose's theories, similar to his beliefs about reptilians living at Earth's core. Still, he played along.

Team Leader – You've mentioned that theory before...

Compumaestro – It's not a theory. It's a fact. It's proven by the data. The price movements in precious metals can only be explained by deliberate manipulation. They're selling more paper claims than all the physical gold ever mined, using computer-driven trades to torpedo prices at strategic moments.

Team Leader – OK. Let's assume that's true. What's the connection to our case?

Compumaestro – Bakkendorf worked at Bolton Sayres, which owns a bullion bank in London and New York. What if he discovered something he shouldn't have?

Jim wondered, for a moment. The man was a genius in so many ways. If he happened to believe in a few far-fetched conspiracy theories, Jim was willing to overlook it. He did feel compelled to comment on something that seemed to torpedo the theory.

Team Leader – If the Treasury wanted to, it could just sell the US gold reserve to control prices. They've got thousands of tons..."

Compumaestro – Not anymore. With all the money printing, there's not nearly enough gold to control the prices openly. They need to employ more subtle methods. If people knew what they were doing, especially hostile foreign governments, they'd just buy the physical gold and wait it out. They'd eventually drain the US Treasury of every single ounce. Because the government of the United States is addicted to deficit spending and a fiat monetary system, it has had only two choices since its gold inventories were run down by the early 1960s. One is to ditch the welfare state system, which is the cause of the deficit spending. And, the other choice is deception.

Politicians like to get reelected. People don't vote for you if you cut off their gravy train. So, which choice do you think they made?

Team Leader – But, no one really cares anymore about gold prices. The dollar isn't backed by gold anymore...

Compumaestro – You're wrong. Everyone who matters – the Treasury, other central banks, the financial elite...they all care a lot. They need to keep people buying stocks and bonds. If investors switch to gold, their very profitable system collapses. Not to mention the welfare state. So, the statists can't allow that.

Team Leader – Statists?

Compumaestro – People who believe in state power over individual liberty. They support deficit spending and policies that devalue fiat currency. They use inflation to impose a secret tax on everyone because they could never get away with imposing such high taxes openly. Inflation pulls the cost of government debt down and pushes tax revenues up. The money that people think they're saving gets more devalued every year. Gold threatens the whole crooked scheme by protecting people's savings and wealth, in general, from inflation.

Jim tried to steer the conversation back to facts, rather than speculation.

Team Leader – Bakkendorf's burial happened in 2008...

Compumaestro – So, let's focus on the key dates. The days they attack gold prices most heavily. We'll cross-reference those with Bakkendorf's July 22nd disappearance.

Jose went on to give a detailed explanation about how manipulations in futures markets affected physical gold delivery with a time lag. Despite his skepticism, Jim saw no harm in examining the records even against the wildest theories, since they needed to review them anyway. To make things easier, he shared his screen with Jose.

As they searched, they discovered messages between Marcus Dunlop and Michael Jennett discussing coordinated short-selling of gold futures. The communications revealed detailed plans to drive down prices and then profit from the manipulation.

Jose explained the mechanics: Short-sellers promise future delivery without owning the asset, profiting when prices fall. The system works because only a tiny fraction of buyers demands physical delivery. Most speculators are undercapitalized get-rich-quick schemers, running hedge funds. The actual assets of the various "funds" are relatively small compared to the huge bets they make. So, to protect themselves from being wiped out, they all place so-called "stop-loss" orders that automatically execute upon the price falling to a pre-specified level. That meant that, once the first large aggregation of stop-loss orders is triggered by a manipulator, the hedge fund speculators torpedo themselves. It creates a chain reaction of automatic selloffs. That there is little to no gold backing up the supposed gold contracts that the banks create to sell into the market doesn't matter. Almost no one demands delivery of the actual gold. It's all moved back and forth using little slips of paper conferring "ownership" of imaginary gold and, more recently, by stored bytes on various computer systems. The gold, itself, or what little there is of real gold, rarely ever moves.

Just as Jim was finishing a full analysis of Dunlop's secret gold manipulation scheme with Jose, Sandra's scream interrupted him.

Footage of the destroyed Tagliano Inn was now being shown on television! The news reports identified Jim, again, as the primary suspect, in both the explosion of the Inn and his wife's disappearance. It showed his photo and warned that he was potentially armed and dangerous. When Sandra's picture appeared on the screen, the newscaster announced her presumed death in the fire. The horrifying reality of their situation hit home.

"I need to call my family!" Sandra pleaded, "I have to tell them I'm alive..."

"No!" Jim said firmly. "You can't do that! If you do, they'll where to find you, and they'll finish what they started..."

The nightmare was getting deeper. He had saved Sandra's life, barely escaping with his own. But, the danger remained. At this point, revealing their location, even with what seemed like an innocuous phone call, was an unacceptable risk. Phone calls could be traced. Cell phone signals could be triangulated with great precision, revealing the location of the caller. Survival, itself, depended on staying off-the-grid.

Chapter 22 – CONSPIRACIES

Fyodor Khasan lay quietly in his private hospital room in Westchester County. The knife wound wasn't as severe as he'd initially feared. He had reached the well-compensated doctor, known for his discretion with questionable patients, who had nicely cleaned and sutured the injury.

Before coming to the hospital, Khasan had carefully buried his collection of sensitive items in a wooded area nearby. His cash box, the multiple license tags, VIN placards, multiple forms of identification, night vision goggles, weapons, and various other equipment were all safely in a metal container, underneath the ground. The location was precisely marked in his satellite navigation system, and he could retrieve it all, at a moment's notice.

As the anesthetic began wearing off, the pain in his thigh, though mostly superficial, dominated his thoughts. In the brief window, before the pain returned, he'd reflected on the events of the past five years. The contract to eliminate Charles Bakkendorf accepted nearly half a decade ago, remained frustratingly incomplete. It was a failure that wounded his professional pride almost as much as the physical injury had wounded his body. The original contract had specified just one killing. But, even without considering Mattingly's widow, who would soon be dead, there had been three additional deaths along the way. It was bad for his reputation—a mess he had to clean up.

The pain increased as the anesthetic wore off. Khasan forgot about his pride. All he could think about was how much it hurt. Pain wasn't entirely new to him, but he'd never developed much tolerance for it. His shoulder still bore the scar from a Chechen rebel's bullet. He took grim satisfaction in remembering how he'd killed that man, crushing his skull with his bare hands. This new knife wound would leave an even uglier scar. The continuing ache deepened his resolve to make sure that the man who'd caused it suffered a fate similar to that of the Chechen. The woman would get a quick death, a bullet to the brain, maybe. But, for the man...

His smartphone rested on the bedside table. Like his tablet, it ran modified RuMos, a high-security fork of Android, originally developed by the Russian FSB. He positioned the tiny Bluetooth earpiece and microphone, then reached for the phone. The call connected to an identical device on an oak desk, inside a red brick home in Scarsdale, NY. Adriano Navarro had been anticipating the call since hearing the news reports. Khasan, who had once been Navarro's most reliable operative, was fast becoming his biggest liability.

Both men pressed their thumbs to their phones' designated squares for identity confirmation, allowing the devices to synchronize. It was a vast improvement over the clumsy process used by the 2008 vintage, Zephyr Cypherphones.

"What the hell did you do?" Navarro demanded without preamble.

"Collateral damage," Khasan replied simply.

"You weren't there to blow up an American town, you idiot!" Navarro's voice rose with anger. "The mission was simple. Eliminate one girl. Nothing more. You've made a holy mess of things!"

"There were complications."

"Complications?" Navarro's irritation deepened. "The whole state is in an uproar. They're calling for a special task force to investigate the explosions. What the hell were you thinking?"

"There was an unexpected third party," Khasan stated without emotion.

"What are you talking about?" Navarro demanded.

"He threw a knife," Khasan explained.

"A knife?" Navarro asked incredulously.

"Yes."

"What kind of knife?"

"A kitchen knife," Khasan admitted.

"A kitchen knife?" Navarro repeated, amazed.

"A paring knife," Khasan clarified.

"A what?"

"A paring knife..."

Navarro shook his head in disgust.

"You incompetent fool! You arrive at a house, armed with a gun, and you've got gases, poisons, and other weapons stashed in your car. But, somebody throws a little paring knife at you, and the whole operation falls apart?"

"Man is expert," Khasan insisted. "Trained assassin. No doubt sent by someone on Council."

"How could anyone in the cartel even know what you were doing?"

"Someting ve must find out." Khasan suggested.

"Did you identify him?"

"Yes."

"Who is he?"

"Code name, Jim W. Bentley," Khasan reported, "Same who download car rental records. Zee database say he's lawyer, Bolton Sayres. Married to daughter of Bolton Sayres' CEO. Cover story..."

Navarro leaned on his cane, momentarily speechless before breaking into uncontrollable laughter.

"Jim Bentley?" he managed between chuckles.

"Code named, Jim Bentley..." Khasan clarified, "Ve don't know real name."

Navarro considered the seemingly absurd fantasy, for a moment. It was true that someone had introduced a virus into the databases. Someone had used Bentley's credentials to do it. The hacker had compromised the entire network. These were undeniable facts. His smile turned into a frown as he considered the wild possibility. Could it be true? Could Stoneham have played him for a fool these last two years? Could Bentley be one of Jeremy Stoneham's creatures? A skilled operative capable of taking down the entire THEATRES surveillance system? Was the marriage to his daughter, Laura, a fake?

An instant later, he rejected the idea. It was ridiculous. His investigation of Bentley had uncovered details that couldn't be fabricated. Moreover, Stoneham would never allow his daughter to marry such a man, and the marriage was genuinely real. Bentley was simply a young man running scared, nothing more. Khasan's absurd interpretation simply confirmed the man's new status as a liability. Khasan had outlived his usefulness. Yet he had provided one very valuable piece of information. He now knew exactly where

Jim went the night THEATRES went down. It might help determine his current location.

"What do you want?" Navarro asked abruptly.

"THEATRES link not verking," Khasan complained. "No tracking informatsia."

"It'll be back online shortly."

Information about the virus remained on a need-to-know basis, and Khasan didn't need to know. While the THEATRES issues would normally prevent tracking Khasan's location, Navarro's New York team had installed their own back doors into the man's phone, even while removing those placed by the Russian government. One was a locator tracker that insured that Navarro could find the giant man anywhere in the world.

Navarro tapped an icon on his screen, entered the required codes, and a map appeared. He zoomed in as the locator narrowed down the address: White Plains Hospital. He smiled. Young Jim Bentley could throw a knife well enough to hospitalize a gigantic man like Khasan? That boy was full of surprises! He couldn't help but feel a sense of admiration for the young man, in spite of the fact that he had caused so much trouble.

No doubt, young Jim was rushing in, like a white knight, to rescue a damsel in distress. It was foolhardy, but it aligned with the rest of the boy's personality profile. The hero complex, in Navarro's opinion, probably came from the fact that young people were watching too many Marvel superhero movies from too young an age. But, that was just an opinion. The fact was that Bentley and his hero complex were royally screwing up Navarro's carefully laid plans. Or...could he turn the whole situation to his advantage, and use it to wrap up all the loose ends left over from 2008?

"Where is he now?" he asked.

"Lost track, zem," Khasan replied. "Need system to find. Vhen find, zey die." Khasan stated.

A brief silence followed.

"You intend to blow up some more towns upstate?" Navarro quipped.

"No," Khasan insisted. "But, if vant job done, ve need target informatsia."

Navarro contemplated this. Did he even want or need the job completed anymore? What difference did it make? The secondary killings benefited Khasan, not himself. He'd tolerated it because the man had been useful. The diary indicated that the girl had seen the blonde giant, but she'd never laid eyes on him. All the risk centered on this one gigantic man.

What if Khasan were arrested? He might spill the beans, disclosing everything he knew. And, he knew too much. About the system, about Navarro's involvement with the killings, and about how Navarro was using THEATRES to enrich himself and consolidate personal power. The risk was very real, but it would disappear with the man. No one would suspect anything. No one would cry a tear over the death of an FSB assassin. It would be celebrated.

After more silence, Navarro finally replied,

"The system is being repaired as we speak. I'll notify you when it's back online."

Without waiting for a response, he ended the call. This latest fiasco had forced his hand. No more chances would follow. Attention-grabbing acts, like blowing up cars on the main streets of small towns were anathema to covert operations. Only panic could cause such a reaction. Khasan deserved imprisonment for what he had done, and helping that happen would be very satisfying, but for the fact that every murderous and illegal act had been done at his orders. The potential exposure of Navarro's role in multiple staged suicides and assassinations, over the years, was far too dangerous.

The ringing of his landline interrupted his thoughts. He answered, "Navarro speaking..."

"Sir, there's a new login ID, one created by the hacker," a woman reported. "It's being used to download data from the Bolton Sayres' intranet."

The information piqued his interest.

"New credentials created by the same hacker?" He asked.

"Yes."

"What kind of data is he trying to get this time?"

"Trading data, gold vault data and email records," she replied. "Many of the records involve Marc Dunlop. Some emails are encrypted with Dunlop's personal passcode."

"We know his passcode, right?" Navarro asked.

"Yes."

"Any other records?"

"No, not really..." She replied.

Such downloads didn't particularly worry him. No one could access the truly secret records, not even with such cleverly created high-level credentials as this hacker was managing to deploy. Such documents required not only system passwords but document-specific passwords. Only he and the particular Council members he worked for possessed all the required document passwords.

There were, however, many things that Navarro didn't know. He had designed the system's broad strokes, and that helped him give himself too much credit. He was entirely lacking in the kind of technical expertise he actually needed for implementation. Instead, he relied on others for that. He did not fully understand the backdoors, such as the technical process by which passwords could be lifted directly from microchips. Nor did he understand the full nature and threat posed by Jose's virus. Its primary danger was not in its ability to shut down the system. Even when the system seemed fully restored, the virus would continue to stealthily operate, endlessly boring its way into all of its secrets, every time anyone accessed the system. That would continue until a programming expert recognized what was being done and put a stop to it.

"Did you trace the IPs?" he asked her.

"We managed to trace one IP out of the two dozen the hackers are using. It's the same IP that tried to use Jim Bentley's old login credentials."

"Where did you trace it to?"

"A cheap motel, near Albany."

The location aligned with Jim's appearance at the Tagliano Bed & Breakfast, only an hour or two away. Navarro bet that it was Jim. If he was right, the situation presented an excellent opportunity, if played correctly. A careful plan began forming in his mind. He could solve two problems at once. If Dunlop's recklessness could be channeled, and if Khasan could be led to the slaughter, the result would resolve everything. But, the scheme required careful planning.

"There's something else, sir," she added. "Even as we've been speaking, our programming staff detected the hacker using yet another identity."

"Is he attempting to penetrate THEATRES again?"

"No. He's been trying to hack into the transfer system of a bank."

"Bolton?"

"No. It's not even a cartel member. The bank is in the Bahamas..."

"What's his IP address?"

"We can't find it," she replied. "He's been very careful. He's impossible to track."

This confirmed the involvement of two people. One was Jim Bentley. But who was the other? What connected them? Why was the second hacker targeting a non-member bank? Did it even matter? The bank the hacker was busy attacking wasn't a member of the banking cartel. So, it wasn't Navarro's responsibility.

"Whose transfer system is it?" he asked.

"I just pulled the SWIFT code. If you give me a few seconds, I can get you the name..."

Navarro knew all the major Bahamian banks. Many member-bank executives kept secret accounts there. Some accounts enabled invisible transfers beyond the knowledge of the IRS. Others held proceeds from illegitimate American businesses. Still, others contained money from perfectly legal overseas operations that simply kept the money out of the reach of the IRS. A convenient spot to hold overseas money because it was just a speedboat ride away from Miami.

"Is he targeting any particular account?"

"Yes."

"Whose account is it?"

"Officially, we can't access that information..."

"What about unofficially?" He asked.

All banks, even in tax havens, require certain software systems to join international payment networks and those interlinks create vulnerability. The designers program backdoors that allow entry to gather information without the knowledge of the bank in question. The keys resided in a secret database, but with the authorization and the right key, account information could be easily obtained from any overseas bank, regardless of security precautions or the laws of the jurisdiction in which the bank was located.

"It's Marcus Dunlop's account, sir..." she announced a few seconds later.

That was interesting. Young Dunlop was keeping a covert account for hiding the proceeds of his various financial machinations. And, Jim Bentley was downloading his trading records even as another hacker breached that secret Bahamian account. Who had the expertise to accomplish all this? That was the question that demanded an investigation, though the list of candidates would be relatively small. The gold trading records didn't particularly worry Navarro. Most reasonably intelligent people already knew banks controlled gold prices and could move prices up and down at will. The key documents were unreadable, due to encryption. The rest might implicate Dunlop, personally, but not the organization. And, of course, the cartel could always claim document forgery. Expert witnesses can be hired to testify to anything, so long as you pay them enough. If necessary, a parade of PhD.s would swear under oath that the documents were fake.

That having been said, events were accelerating beyond Navarro's comfort zone. It was hard to adapt dynamically to the fast-evolving situation. It might be useful to allow Jim and his hacking buddy to disseminate some sensitive documents if they could be used to achieve a greater goal. The trick lay in maintaining Dunlop's connection to all the crimes while luring him in, to go after Bentley. If Khasan then arrived simultaneously, all the pieces would fit together, everyone would assume that the case had been solved, and all his problems would be over.

He made a swift decision.

"Let Bentley have the documents." He ordered.

"What?" she asked incredulously. "Are you saying I should give him access?"

"Yes."

"There's one more thing..."

"What?"

"Just a second ago, someone put a trace on him."

"Who?"

"The tracers are coming from Marc Dunlop's system interface."

"That was fast..." Navarro noted.

This was the best possible news. Dunlop's trace attempts would perfectly complement his rapidly developing plan.

"Make it look like his Bahamas account was hacked from Bentley's IP instead of that hacker's IP..." he asked.

"Of course."

He'd occasionally wondered, in the past, about Dunlop's probable Bahamian accounts. Until now, there hadn't been sufficient reason to look into it. But, Navarro was well aware that the young scion of the Dunlop banking clan was as corrupt as anyone could be. He was a greedy, self-serving criminal, whose only supporter was his father, Christopher Dunlop. That man, the CEO of W.T. Fredericks, had paid dearly, time and time again, over the years, to protect his son. The younger Dunlop's claim to fame came from his birthright. He was a common thief. The dead man from 2008, Charlie Bakkendorf, had discovered and reported fake gold bars to the reputational risk division. He had erroneously believed that the two million dollar bonus he had been paid, actually came from Bolton Sayres Bank, rather than Marc Dunlop.

When Navarro informed his patron, Christopher Dunlop, Bakkendorf's fate had been decided. His willingness to talk to the Reputational Risk division implied that he would probably eventually report it to the police if he ever found out that what he had been told wasn't true. That directly threatened Marc's cartel standing, the cartel as a whole, and, most importantly, the future of the Dunlop dynasty. It set an entire process in motion. The old man had paid Navarro $10 million to orchestrate the cover-up. Eliminating one low-level bank employee seemed simple enough at the time.

Fyodor Khasan, the former Russian FSB assassin, was known for efficiency and reliability. He had handled several previous jobs successfully. But, this time, he had made mistake after mistake. Murder brooked no errors, and Khasan's decision to bury Bakkendorf in a rural area at night had created a witness. Thomas Mattingly had made a blackmail threat against Bolton Sayres, whose car had been used to carry the body. Of course, since the killing had been paid for by Christopher Dunlop, no one at Bolton was involved in the subsequent events after the issue had been kicked upward to the Reputational Risk division.

The blackmailer required placating while his death was arranged. His demands were extensive – a $25 million credit line for an implausible ski resort scheme. No high-level bank executive could approve it. It was best that no one at Bolton Sayres ever knew anything. Instead, Navarro's most trusted programmers had modified Bolton Sayres' system protocols so that huge sums of money could be funneled to the farmer without authorization by any real bank executive, even as his convenient death was being prepared. At just $1.4 million, the total amount that had been paid was just small change to a bank that earned tens of billions of dollars every year. It was easily hidden by subtle changes, made in the computer system that handled the bank's expense accounting. The entire transaction vanished with the help of a bit of creative accounting.

Khasan had staged what appeared to be the perfect murder–suicide, even ensuring gunpowder residue on the man's hand. Police closed the case, deeming it murder followed by suicide. Everything seemed resolved until Jim Bentley stumbled upon that lost diary. It contained enough information to destroy everything. The Sheriff's office would surely reopen the investigation if they had ever received it. The trail would lead to Khasan and, eventually, to Navarro.

The FBI agent who had taken possession of the diary had to be eliminated. One staged accident did the trick. But, the evidence itself also had to vanish. That was impossible because it was a physical thing, sitting in a vault-like environment. There simply weren't enough corrupt FBI officials in the right position to take it out of there and destroy it. The diary never left the FBI evidence vault. Instead, the computer records that told the FBI's records custodian where it was had been altered. Effectively, it was now lost forever in an endless sea of other documents being stored by the New York FBI office. But, the diary had revealed something that was unknown until it came to light. The widow of the son of the man who had tried to blackmail Bolton Sayres, Sandra Mattingly, was a "loose end" and she had to be clipped.

It was Khasan's job to kill her quickly and efficiently. But, his utter incompetence had caused massive collateral damage that had compromised everything. He had caused so much reckless destruction upstate, that the police would surely investigate. The whole operation was now under threat. Navarro knew that, at this point, he needed to handle things personally.

"Keep watching Dunlop," he ordered. "As soon as he locates Bentley and leaves his office, I want to know."

"Yes, sir," she replied.

He hung up the phone. Skillful, careful execution would soon solve all his problems. The pieces were falling together. Dunlop's predictable reaction,

Khasan's vulnerability, and Bentley's naive heroics. They all combined to create a solution. It was now simply a matter of orchestrating the timing and encouraging all the players to move in the manner that was expected of them. His plan's ultimate beauty lay in the randomness of it. No one would suspect such elaborate choreography. The evidence would point exactly where he wanted it to.

He smiled, feeling the familiar rush of satisfaction that came with crafting an elegant solution to a complex problem. Soon, very soon, all the loose ends would be permanently tied up.

Chapter 23 – FOLLOW THE MONEY

Jim sat at the edge of the bed, his computer in his lap, feeling increasingly paranoid. Who was he really up against? A handful of crooked bank employees? The entire bank? The entire banking industry? Was he facing an out–of–control government? Or, most frightening of all – all of them?

Working against time and enormous odds, he felt overwhelmed. His gaze drifted to the girl in her tight jeans and pullover top. Her clothes clung to her form, revealing every curve. When he looked at her, as before, he felt desire stir within him. He tried to suppress it. There were more pressing matters and he was a married man with a young child. The desire was distracting. But, he couldn't get her out of his mind, she looked up and noticed. Their eyes met. She rose and crawled over to him, touching his shoulder with a gentle hand.

"Is there something you want?" She asked in a gentle tone.

"No, not really, "He lied.

"Are you sure?" She asked him again.

He contemplated his response, but before he could speak, she continued. "Put the computer down..." she urged softly.

"I can't... I'm right in the middle of something..." He objected.

She smiled and shook her head. Then, she placed her hand on the computer and gently closed the lid. The sweet scent of lavender and a mix of other scents from her perfume surrounded him, overwhelming his senses. When he glanced down, it was impossible to hide the rock-solid nature of his manhood. She didn't miss seeing that, either.

Instead, she moved closer. Young, thin, beautiful, and inviting, her lips waited for a kiss. The desire was too powerful to resist. She wanted the same thing he did. But, how could he? He was a married man with a child, he reminded himself, yet again! But, he wanted her and, in hours, days, or weeks, they might both be dead. At that moment, alive, red-blooded and a man in his prime, a beautiful woman invited him to do what he wanted, with her. They were alone in a room, and thoughts of his overweight wife could not stop the desire which was now rock-hard.

It didn't take long to make the choice. While he could still live and breathe, he would do so as a man. He turned and kissed her, pressing her lithe body onto the bed, his hands exploring her curves and the silky skin of her arms, caressing the softness of her ample breasts. Jose was still online, and the two of them were at a critical moment in their investigation. None of that mattered as the primal urges washed away all of it. He could think of nothing but the woman next to him.

Soon, her blouse and bra were gone. She wiggled out of her skin-tight jeans, and he removed the rest of his clothes and hers. They lost themselves in the unity of movement. He kissed every part of her, and she responded in natural ecstasy. And, when he reached the climax of his pleasure, he spilled into her as naturally as spring rain spills from the sky.

Jim lay back with the warmth of her body still lingering against him. It had been a long time since he'd enjoyed sex this much. He was now more relaxed than he'd been in ages. He leaned over to kiss her again. Then, he lay back, staring at the ceiling lamp, his mind blissfully empty. But, soon enough, with primal urges satisfied, the haze began to fade. Reality crashed back in. He thought of Jose, waiting for him, the investigation hanging in the balance. Had this one moment of bliss been worth the risk? He felt the gnawing anxiety about what lay ahead.

He had a family to protect, and the clock was ticking!

It suddenly hit him with a start – he'd left Jose hanging, right in the middle of their investigation. As a result, his friend might not even be online anymore. He sat up abruptly. The computer remained where Sandra had closed its lid. He opened it and felt the chill of reality seep back in. The warmth of the bed was replaced by the cold glow of the computer screen. He could almost hear Jose's voice in his head, urging him to focus. The computer reactivated from "sleep" mode, and Jim began typing out a message.

Team Leader – Sorry for the delay... I'm back.

After a pause, the little animated pen indicating that Jose was responding began to move. Jim felt a rush of relief. Thank goodness, Jose was still online!

Compumaestro – I've been busy...hacking deeper into the system.

Team Leader – Let's double down on getting this information quickly.

Compumaestro – I found a whole chain of emails and replies between those two guys, starting May 28th...

A series of emails appeared on their joint whiteboard:

Subject: Hulk says smash!
From: michael.Jennett@boltonsayres.com
Date: 06/28/2008 6:01 a.m.
To: marcus.Dunlop@boltonsayres.com
Marc,
What's the deal? We could easily do another smash. I thought you told them.
Best,
Mike

Subject: re: Hulk says smash!
From: marcus.dunlop@boltonsayres.com
Date: 06/28/2008 6:05 a.m.
To: michael.Jennett@boltonsayres.com
Mike,
I did. Physical demand is too strong. Soared in March. Fed's vault is very low on gold. They want to try something else...
Regards,
Marc

Subject: re Hulk says smash!
From: michael.Jennett@boltonsayres.com
Date: 06/28/2008 6:11 a.m.
To: marcus.Dunlop@boltonsayres.com
Marc,
Should we go longer?
Best,
Mike

Subject: re: Hulk says smash!
From: marcus.dunlop@boltonsayres.com
Date: 06/28/2008 6:13 a.m.
To: michael.Jennett@boltonsayres.com
Mike,

I got WORD!!! Big gold smash planned for September!!!! Equity boys selling too. Should be a rout!!! Build short. Target accumulation between July 10 and 21. Cover in Oct. If you can get any repo loans out of the BofE, do it!!! Use them. Build up as big a loan window as you can. My contact is waiting for your call...

Regards,

Marc

Subject: Hulk says smash!

From: michael.Jennett@boltonsayres.com

Date: 06/28/2008 6:15 a.m.

To: marcus.Dunlop@boltonsayres.com

Marc,

What about NY futures? Loans from the fed???????? :−)

Best,

Mike

Subject: re: Hulk says smash!

From: marcus.dunlop@boltonsayres.com

Date: 06/28/2008 6:17 a.m.

To: michael.Jennett@boltonsayres.com

Mike,

Forget the futures. Gold bugs follow every single trade there. NY is the pricing machine. I want London. I want to take all our shorts, from this point on, in forwards and options on forwards. Is that agreed? Nice, confidential, no disclosure... perfect!!!

Best,

Marc

Subject: re: Hulk says smash!

From: michael.jennett@boltonsayres.com

Date: 06/28/2008 6:21 a.m.

To: marcus.dunlop@boltonsayres.com

Marc,

Ok. Lots of counterparties want to be long gold. Shouldn't be a problem, going short on as many forwards as we can.

Best,

Mike

Another email appeared:
Subject: Bots rock!
From: michael.Jennett@boltonsayres.com
Date: 10/13/2008 6:33 a.m.
To: marcus.Dunlop@boltonsayres.com
Marc,
Wow! Beautiful bots baby!!! Your bots rock! Friday's action was spectacular! $70 swing! Everyone's talking about it. You're a master craftsman!
Best,
Mike

Team Leader – OK, I'll grant you, we can prove they're manipulating gold prices. But how does that equate to murder?

Jim moved his mouse to the download button and clicked, transferring the files to his computer. He clicked repeatedly on the date July 22, 2008, searching through vault records. There should have been a long list of receipts reflecting gold bars arriving in the vault. Instead, there were very few. Working backward, he found the first receipt nearest to Bakkendorf's disappearance – a delivery of 4 tons of gold on July 16th. He shared the image on their whiteboard.

Team Leader – What's the "undefined location"? What about bar numbers, manufacturers, and purity?

Compumaestro – President Franklin Roosevelt seized all gold in America in 1934, and melted it all down into what they call coin–melt bars.

Team Leader – What does that have to do with anything?

Compumaestro – Only the American government has bars like that, with a huge percentage of cheap base metals. The commercial standard is very different. We're talking 1 kg gold bars 99.99% pure versus 300–400 ounce coin melt bars only about 89% to 91% pure. My guess is that the raw material comes in as coin melt, then they refine it and recast it into new bars. That's why there aren't any bar numbers listed. Whatever numbers were imprinted on the original bars would not be the same as those on the bars that go out.

Team Leader – That's pure speculation. There's nothing to support it. Let's follow the vault receipts, one by one, and see what we find.

Jim traced the fate of the raw gold described on the vault receipt. After nearly five minutes of searching, he finally found something. It was a crucial piece of information. The spreadsheet appeared on the whiteboard: on July 23, 2008, the records showed that 400 one-kilogram gold bars had been shipped to the same African central bank noted on the vault receipt.

Team Leader – That's a day after the body was buried at the Mattingly farm. Look at the name of the "responsible person"!

The shipping spreadsheet listed "Charles Bakkendorf."

Compumaestro – Didn't Bolton's H.R. department say there never was an employee by that name?

Team Leader – Yeah, they did. Apparently, the records of his employment are gone now, but they missed this little tidbit...

Compumaestro – The word "undefined" is a blue hyperlink! I'll click on it...

Jose clicked, and the message instantly displayed on both screens:

"ACCESS DENIED! INSUFFICIENT AUTHORIZATION. LEVEL 1-A CLEARANCE REQUIRED"

Team Leader – What the hell is "1-A clearance"?

Compumaestro – There isn't any level 1-A. Not the way we designed it. There should just be level 1.

Team Leader – The username and password you created apparently aren't enough for this.

Compumaestro – I think I can solve that problem. Bolton's mainframe runs 24/7, which means it is never turned off, and people at the top of the company's totem pole access it frequently. Maybe, some have this new 1-A access.

Team Leader – So what?

Compumaestro – So, if someone accessed the system today or yesterday, or anytime after it was last physically unplugged and rebooted, the password is still probably going to be somewhere in the computer's RAM chips. Someone with top-level clearance would have had to access it to clean up the damage my virus did. And, until the computer is turned off, those RAM chips will retain a memory image of the passwords and usernames. It doesn't have to be that way, but it's one of the backdoors required by the NSA. They use it to access foreign bank computer systems. Our primary customers, which are the big US based banks, had to agree to it, and the ones overseas get it by default.

Team Leader – That's fantastic!

The command prompt window suddenly appeared on the whiteboard. Codes and numbers flashed across the screen too quickly to follow as Jose's favorite hacking tool accessed the memory buffers. After about twenty seconds, it was over.

Compumaestro – Try clicking now...

Jim clicked, and the hidden information appeared. A message flashed onto the screen:

"Federal Reserve Vault, 33 Liberty Street, NY, NY."

There was a moment of unexpressed elation and electronic silence as neither man was sure exactly what to say. Finally, Jim broke the silence.

Team Leader – I guess your conspiracy theory is now a conspiracy fact.

Compumaestro – I always knew it! But, as you pointed out, it doesn't explain why Bakkendorf was murdered.

Team Leader – He's listed as the responsible person.

Compumaestro – You think he would spill the beans?

Team Leader – You mean about them raiding the US gold reserve to be able to fill physical orders?

Compumaestro – Yeah...

Team Leader – I can swallow the idea that the Fed's suppressing gold prices, but murder? I don't think so...

Compumaestro – Why not? Did you know that the Fed has its own internal police force? It's bigger than most city police departments in the USA.

Team Leader – I don't believe it. If it's true, I'd feel compelled to go to war against my government.

Compumaestro – Look, check this out!

Another vault receipt appeared on the whiteboard.

Team Leader – It shows they made the delivery.

Compumaestro – Yeah, and there's an identical receipt showing another 360 bars being delivered to the same African central bank. Do you want me to pop that one up?

Team Leader – Just save it and let's go on to something else...

After cleaning herself up, Sandra Mattingly returned from the bathroom to the bed but saw that Jim was preoccupied. This time, she didn't disturb him. Instead, she put in her earbuds and listened to music. Jim focused on the task at hand. The two men worked feverishly, reviewing page after page, until a new message arrived.

Compumaestro – Take a look at this one...

Another vault receipt appeared on the shared whiteboard.

Team Leader – Did that also come from the Fed's vault?

Compumaestro – There's no receipt for incoming delivery. I checked and double-checked.

Team Leader – It could have already been in the Bolton vault...

Compumaestro – Impossible. I checked the secret stock records. There's hardly any gold in the Bolton vault. All the gold they've been shipping from New York has been coming from the Federal Reserve. The rumor is that the gold they ship from London is from the Bank of England, backed up by location swaps with gold from the Fed. It looks like the coin melt bars arrive a month or two ahead of the major deliveries. They must refine it and deliver it later. It's a closed system. But there's no record of this batch of gold coming into the vault – ever...

Team Leader – It must come from somewhere...

Compumaestro – That's my point.

After a long pause, Jim sent another message to his friend.

Team Leader – Is it possible to manufacture a gold bar that isn't 100% gold and pass it off as a real one?

Compumaestro – There are lots of stories about that. About bars filled with tungsten, especially. It's got almost the same molecular weight as gold and a similar density. The match isn't exact, but it's very close.

Team Leader – Let's look through the incoming vault receipts for other metals!

Within moments, they found what they were looking for: a vault receipt for 3 metric tons of tungsten rod, dated April 16, 2008, appeared on the whiteboard.

Team Leader – What else is tungsten used for?

Compumaestro – Light bulbs, making tungsten carbide, which is almost as hard as diamond... it's used for cutting glass and grinding stuff, not much else...

Team Leader – Why would a precious metals vault take delivery of 3 tons of tungsten?

Compumaestro – To create fake gold bars!

Jim performed quick calculations before sending another message.

Team Leader – If you were making fake bars, you could just melt the tungsten first. According to Wikipedia, it has a higher melting temperature. You would fabricate a tungsten core. Then, over that core, at a lower temperature, you'd pour the melted gold. A tungsten core of about 24 ounces each, coated with 8.15 ounces of gold, would create a near–perfect fake 1-kilo gold bar. If you got 4 tons of gold from the Fed, and then you created these fake bars, you could pilfer 3 tons of pure gold.

Compumaestro – That batch of gold bars, the ones Bakkendorf was working on just before he disappeared… I'm willing to bet that they were tainted by tungsten fill…

Team Leader – At least, it means the Fed's not going around killing people…

Compumaestro – We've got enough proof to put these two guys behind bars…

Team Leader – Yeah.

Compumaestro – There's enough to put Bolton out of business and the Federal Reserve, maybe, too!

Team Leader – Keep all this under wraps, until I give the word…

Compumaestro – How am I going to do that? It's too big. We've got to let the public know! They're ripping people off. They're using gold that belongs to the People of the United States in schemes to enrich a few bankers. I say jail and bankrupt the bastards.

Team Leader – If we release all this stuff, we could both end up assassinated. We need to think about it carefully.

Compumaestro – Fine. Let's think… OK, I'm finished thinking. Let's release it anonymously.

Team Leader – That's impossible. Everything points back to me. Here, look at this…

A compensation log appeared on the whiteboard.

Compumaestro – It says Bolton earned $145 million from trading gold in the 2nd quarter of 2008.

Compumaestro – They took short positions in early March...

Team Leader – And covered the shorts in early May, which gave them $81 million in profits. Look at the compensation log!

Jim activated a few commands, and a summary of compensation paid to Marcus Dunlop appeared on both screens.

Compumaestro – He got a $10.5 million bonus that quarter! That's on top of stealing the gold, and making money on his side bets! It's motive to kill.

Team Leader – Look where he deposited the money...

The records showed a wire transfer of $10.5 million to Dunlop's account at Second Bahamas Bancorp, Ltd.

Compumaestro – The same bank that took delivery of 3 tons of physical gold.

Team Leader – Yes. But the account number is different.

Compumaestro – W7429-118334112

Team Leader – He's got at least two accounts. One of the accounts is disclosed, and he uses it to transfer funds openly. Another is a secret. Too bad we can't get all the records. No one's ever going to get those records, you know. The Bahamas has strict banking secrecy.

Compumaestro – The hell with that! We know two of his numbers. That's all we need. Tax haven banks also allow people to access money through various electronic money networks. They use our interlink software. Their top level user IDs and passwords are still going to be in memory, just like at Bolton. I can penetrate that network.

Team Leader – How long will it take?

Compumaestro – Not long.

Team Leader – Go ahead, and do it, then! Save everything onto redundant storage including DVDs, flash cards, or any other storage device that we can easily hide. We need to be ready to use them, full of all the damning information, at a moment's notice, if we need to...

Compumaestro – Got it!

Team Leader – Do you need me along for the ride?

Compumaestro – I just need you to leave your computer running. I'll need your VPN turned on. I'll piggyback through it, back from Bolton Sayres, through the card systems, and into the bank in the Bahamas.

Team Leader – OK. I'll leave it online and running.

Jim adjusted the settings, so that the laptop would continue running even after he closed the lid. He closed it, and looked up from his work. His heart jumped. Sandra Mattingly was gone. He'd been so involved in chatting with Jose that he hadn't noticed her leaving. She'd changed her appearance a bit. Her hair color was now different, but her face was still the same. It was foolish to take chances by going in and out of the room unless absolutely necessary. It was an unnecessary risk.

He remembered the little box of hair dye that still sat on top of the chest of drawers, and his new clothes. His own hair color remained unchanged. He glanced down at his shirt and jeans. He was still wearing the bloodstained ones. Forced to wait for her return, and with nothing left to do, he picked up the clothing and the hair dye kit and walked to the bathroom.

Twenty minutes later, he emerged and looked in the mirror above the chest of drawers. A stranger seemed to be staring back at him. His dark brown hair was now yellow–blonde. With his dark eyebrows, it looked slightly ridiculous, but he definitely looked different. And, it felt good to wear fresh clothes. It was a pleasure to dump the bloodstained ones.

He had no way of contacting Sandra, and that was giving him increasing anxiety. She was still gone. Her cell phone was, of course, off, at his request, and so was his. He could do nothing but wait. He turned on the television and clicked on the cable news channel. The same stories repeated on a twenty–minute cycle, as usual. The disappearance of his wife was still a hot story, and his photograph was on-screen yet again. The whole affair continued to be very disconcerting.

Chapter 24 – GOLDEN SCAM

WHEN NOT OCCUPIED WITH his favorite prostitutes or fine-tuning his trading bots, Marc Dunlop was obsessively monitoring his bank balances. He was in the habit of checking his Bahamian bank accounts several times every day, as he found deep satisfaction in watching his wealth accumulate.

His little Caribbean empire had grown steadily. By mid-2008, he had purchased and secured title to the private island. The following year saw completion of the sea walls, the finishing of the mansion, and a custom-dredged harbor for his yacht. In 2010, he added finishing touches – a helicopter pad and tennis courts. For months afterward, he had delighted in showcasing his tropical paradise to visiting New Yorkers, a process that had lasted far longer than his usual pattern with new acquisitions.

But the thrill had faded.

The perpetual heat and humidity wore him down. The air conditioning made it more bearable, but it was simply too hot at any other time but mid-winter. He was rethinking his original plan to make the island his permanent home. Instead, he was finding himself spending nearly all his time in New York City. Even the winter didn't drive him south anymore. Nine months had passed since he'd last visited the tropical retreat that had cost him so dearly in money, time, and the trail of destruction left in its wake.

His attention shifted to other things. For example, there was a very nice, government-subsidized, gold operation that promised to be his biggest score yet. In April 2013, after gaining access to 1,300 tons of government gold, he orchestrated history's largest attack against rising gold prices. The operation had drawn support from financial institutions worldwide, even beyond the usual banking cartel members. His March investment in front-running the operation had already yielded nearly $35 million in profits just from liquidating put options, and more gains were on the horizon. His Bahamian accounts now held a combined $145 million. Or, so he thought...

As he logged in for his habitual balance check, he found something was terribly wrong. The ledger showed less than $1 million remaining. He sat rigid in his black leather chair, his heart pounding as he stared at the screen in utter disbelief. The transaction roster revealed wire transfers totaling approximately $144 million. According to the ledger, he had "authorized" these transactions over several months – but it wasn't so.

Just yesterday, all his money had been safely in place. He had seen it on his balance tally. Now, suddenly, a vast majority of the money had been wired to an unknown bank in Macau, the former Portuguese colony turned Chinese special administrative region. It was a place known for gambling and numerous banking institutions, but he'd never had anything to do with Macau.

With trembling hands, he pressed the encrypted communication icon on his phone's touch screen, establishing a secure connection to Second Bahamas Bancorp's private banking division. The screen immediately displayed the face of a strikingly beautiful young blonde woman. Though the Bahamas' population is predominantly black, private bankers, serving high–net–worth clients are invariably of European ancestry, with the female staff often possessing model–like qualities.

She spoke with a carefully cultivated British accent, though he knew she was Swiss.

"Can I help you?" She asked politely.

"I'm looking... at my bank account..." he stammered, struggling to form the words. "The transaction roster shows multi–million dollar transfers to Macau."

"Before I can discuss this further," she insisted, "I need to confirm your identity. Though we've spoken before, bank regulations require me to ask you to place your registered fingertip into the box on your touch screen."

"OK," he replied, complying with her request.

"Thank you, Mr. Dunlop," she acknowledged, "your fingerprint is confirmed. I'll now need you to answer a few challenge questions."

She methodically worked through her security checklist: account number, username, telephone access code, secret question, mother's maiden name, street address, mailing address, email address, nationality, passport number, and prior addresses. Only after he had correctly answered everything did she proceed to discuss his account.

"I see that $144 million was wired through online banking to a brokerage house in Macau over the last few months."

"That's what I just said," He exclaimed, "But, I never gave those instructions!"

"When you made the transfer, your fingerprint was checked, and you correctly answered all the same questions I just asked," she noted.

"I never gave any fingerprints or answered any questions!" he insisted, his voice rising. "I never authorized any transfers! The whole thing is a fraud! You need to reverse those wires, immediately!"

"Let me put you on hold for a few moments, sir..." she said.

Despite the soothing music that played, his anxiety and anger continued to mount. After a brief wait, a new face appeared on the screen. It was a middle-aged man with dark brown hair and blue eyes.

"Mr. Dunlop..." the man said, his German accent pronounced. "My name is Axel Dietrich. I am Vice President of Second Bahamas Bancorp. It is my understanding zhat you claim you didn't authorize a transfer to your account at our branch in Macau?"

"I don't have any accounts in Macau!" Dunlop shouted.

"Please calm down," the man said. "Ve' vill do everything ve can to resolve zis problem, okay?"

Dunlop nodded, knowing the video connection made his response visible.

"How can you allow $144 million to be transferred without a personal confirmation?" he demanded.

Dietrich remained unfazed by the outburst.

"Vhen you opened your account, you authorized instant transfers in any amount vithout verbal confirmation. You chose biometric authentication and challenge qvestions. Zese transfers vere subjected to ze most rigorous biometric confirmation and every vone of our challenge qvestions vas ansvered correctly."

"I don't give a shit!" Dunlop exploded. "I don't have any accounts in Macau."

"Our records show zhat zhis Macau account vas opened 2 years ago, zrough ze inter–bank hypernet. The IP address zat vas used to open ze account corresponds to ze Bolton Sayres Bank," Dietrich explained. "You still verk dere, do you not?"

"Yes, I work there," Dunlop conceded. "But, I NEVER OPENED ANY ACCOUNT IN MACAU!"

"I see," the Swiss banker continued. "But, ze account vas opened over two years ago. And, it shows substantial transfer activity throughout zis entire time period. It also shows a number of very large transfers, to and from your account here."

"I'm telling you I don't have any such account and I never transferred any money, now or in the past!" Dunlop insisted. "God damn it!"

"Zhat's not vat our database shows, sir," Dietrich maintained. "It shows extensive activity, all of vhich vas initiated, during ze entire time period, from ze same IP address of Bolton Sayres Bank, vere you verk. You see, if zat vas not ze case, such a large transfer might have been qvestioned. But, ve look at ze history, and ve see similar transfers, done on a regular basis, many times in ze past."

Dunlop shook his head violently. "No! There's never been any activity like that!"

His breathing had become rapid and shallow, almost like a dog panting, and nausea was beginning to well up inside him.

"Ve show substantial activity, sir..." Dietrich insisted with a nod.

"What kind of activity?" Dunlop managed to ask through his growing distress.

Dietrich began methodically listing transactions: "Vell, Zhere's a $7 million transfer to ze Macau account on July 9th, 2012. One for over $3 million on August 22nd. Another for $35 million on October 6. Zhen, a transfer back to the Bahamas branch on December 15th in the amount of $10,465,000. Another for $14 million on January 7, 2013. And, the final one from Macau was for $10,535,000, and that took place on February 1st 2013. Of course, we zhen have the more recent transfers you are complaining about. But, all of zhem show za same pattern."

As Dietrich recited the numbers, Dunlop frantically wrote them down. He swallowed hard as his mind raced to process the information. Suddenly, understanding dawned on him.

"Can't you see it?" he exclaimed. "All the transactions prior to February 1st were fake. When it's all said and done, $35 million was transferred back and forth, leaving no net change to the balance! They're all fake transactions. They never happened!"

"But, our records show you've logged into your account every day, a minimum of 4 times, sometimes 8 times per day, every day, for the last 2 years," Dietrich countered. "Vhy vouldn't you report such activity, if you didn't make zese transfers?"

"They were never in my transactions register, until now," Dunlop insisted. "Don't you see? Someone's tampering with your computers!"

"Ve have multiple security measures," Dietrich replied. "Frankly speaking, vat you are saying is impossible."

"Your so-called security measures aren't worth shit!" Dunlop shouted. "Someone broke into your system!"

"Zhere is no need for foul langvige," Dietrich admonished. "And, again, let me say zhat zhere are multiple security measures zhat vould prevent zhat."

"Just take the money out of the Macau account and put it back," Dunlop demanded.

"I vould if I could," Dietrich responded. "But, unfortunately, zhe computers in Macau are physically separate. Ve have already contacted zhat branch. According to zhem, the money has been transferred to another bank zhat ve are not associated vith in Zingapore."

"I want my fuckin' money back!" Dunlop screamed. "You understand me, you fuckin' kraut!"

Dietrich ignored the ethnic slur.

"Mr. Dunlop, I vish zhat I could help you. If I could reverse zhese transactions, I would do zhis. But, I cannot. Ve have contacted ze Zingaporean bank, and I vill advise our board of your problem."

"When do I get my money back?"

"Official inkvyories' vill' be made. Unt, ve vill do all in our power to help."

"What, exactly, are you going to do?"

"First, ve report to za central bank," Dietrich explained. "I'll need your permission to transmit za information, of course."

"And, after that?" Dunlop pressed.

"Ze financial crimes unit vill take over... It is verking now, closely, vit your FBI. Dey vill take statements. You vill need to give a statement about your account. If a fraudulent transfer vas made, ze authorities can zhen get a varrant to investigate."

None of this placated Dunlop. The process Dietrich described could take months, by which time the money would be long gone. More crucially, most of the money in the account was "black" money. It was earned through illegal market front-running, and on top of that, he'd never paid taxes on the profits. Involving official authorities would not help him. It would only make him an even bigger loser. He might even face arrest, and his father would be very angry at the cost of bribing all the public officials it would take to buy his way out of it.

"I don't want all that," Dunlop said. "I just want my money back!"

"I'm zorry sir. Ve don't have your money now. You transferred it."

"I didn't transfer it!"

"Somevon vit your credentials transferred it, zhen. You are responsible, of course, for keeping za credentials confidential."

"Can't you see?" Dunlop screamed into the phone, "You fuckin' incompetent idiots have been fucking hacked!"

He slammed his phone down on the desk with such force that the bezel cracked. The LED screen flickered once more before dying completely. It had been advertised as a so-called "indestructible phone." Apparently, that was a fraud too

"Crap!" he exclaimed, tossing the ruined phone into the garbage.

Seething with anger, he knew he could never accept their cynically polite offers to involve law enforcement. They understood this perfectly well – very few people actually kept legitimate money in Bahamian banks. It was always dirty money, one way or another. Sometimes the proceeds of illegal activities. Sometimes untaxed income. No Bahamian bank customer could afford to have losses reported to their home government. That's why they used the Bahamas in the first place. To hide the money.

He considered his options anxiously. Only one path remained open: private action. He could hire tough people, private enforcers who knew how to handle such situations. First, he needed to identify the thief. Despite the Swiss banker's lack of helpfulness, he had provided one crucial piece of information – the transfer requests had all originated from a Bolton Sayres IP address. That narrowed the field considerably. He could trace it back to the source.

Logging into the Bolton database, he typed furiously on his keyboard. Using his high-level password, he bypassed most of the system's security protocols, moving rapidly through different sections of the underlying framework. Within thirty minutes, he had his answer – and it was as infuriating as it was surprising. Of all people, it was Jim Bentley who had raided his accounts!

Where was that bastard, he wondered?

Dunlop logged into the THEATRES system, using the private credentials his father had given him. Within fifteen minutes, he had his answer, and the picture fit together perfectly. Every entry into his Second Bahamas Bancorp account could be traced back to Bentley' VPN. Despite attempts to mask the origin, the THEATRES computers had pinpointed his location. Dunlop knew exactly where to find him.

Dunlop found it incredible that Bentley had orchestrated the entire theft from a fleabag motel near Albany, New York! The audacity was astonishing, although it made a certain sense. Where else would trailer trash, like Bentley, choose to operate out of? In his rage, Dunlop failed to consider how his rival could have suddenly acquired such sophisticated hacking abilities. First, Jim Bentley had stolen his girl, Laura, who belonged to him. Now, the man had stolen his money! He decided, therefore, on the spot, that this was a matter he would take care of himself. He didn't have time to wait for extra muscle or third-party enforcers. He had to deal with Bentley right away before man frittered away all the money, the way trailer trash was likely to do. All of that Karate hit Bentley had pulled on him, during their earlier encounters, wouldn't work anymore because he was wise to the man's tricks. There would be no hand-to-hand combat this time. He resolved not to even get close enough for is rival to get his hands on him. And, no amount of karate could ever stop a speeding bullet.

He reached for his phone, but, then, he remembered he'd just broken it and thrown it away. After a moment's frustration, he picked up his landline and made the call.

"W.T. Fredericks Executive Services..." a female voice answered.

"This is Marcus Dunlop. I need a helicopter at Bolton Sayres Tower in ten minutes!"

"I'm sorry, but we don't have any choppers available..." she replied.

"The hell you don't!" he raged. "Do you know who this is? My father's Christopher Dunlop, understand? I want a chopper here in 10 minutes."

"But, I can't..." she tried to explain.

"No fuckin' buts!" he screamed. "You want to explain it at the unemployment office? Cancel somebody. Give me that chopper, and quick!"

After a brief pause, she asked, "Where do you want to go?"

"Albany," he replied.

"We can have it there in 15 minutes..." the girl said.

"Fine," he snapped, slamming down the phone.

He reached into his desk's second drawer, where he kept a Ruger 9mm semi-automatic pistol. Such weapons are normally illegal in New York City. However, a few well-placed bribes made obtaining a concealed handgun permit a simple matter. He slipped the weapon into his pocket, as blood rushed to his head. Clear thinking was difficult. He knew he had to calm down. He was committed to teaching Jim Bentley a lesson he'd never forget. He would shoot him full of holes if necessary. They might arrest him afterward, but he'd never be prosecuted. Jim Bentley was a nobody who had no influence anywhere. A few dollars, in the right pockets, would make all charges disappear. He might end up on the outs with his dad for a while, because the arrest would end up costing the old man plenty, but that would pass with time. Especially after he'd paid his dad back with interest. Meanwhile, he had little choice. He'd force that bastard, Bentley, to return the money, no matter what it took!

Standing up, he stormed out of his office, slamming the door behind him. At the elevator, he entered the passcode into the control panel. Minutes later, he stood on the building's roof beside the helipad, waiting. Soon, a helicopter arrived in a swirl of wind, dust, and noise. He climbed aboard, and it whisked him away, traveling upstate toward Albany.

AT THE EXACT SAME TIME, Adriano Navarro was also busy. He eventually promised, in a second phone call with Jeremy Stoneham, that he would do everything possible to ensure that the man's daughter was returned to him, safe and sound. There was no benefit to an open conflict with the CEO of Bolton Sayres. Cooperation aligned better with his immediate plans, and fit in perfectly with his broader strategy. In fact, Stoneham had done everything possible to try to find Laura Bentley on his own and failed miserably. Without a tracking device, it was like searching for a needle in a haystack. But, Navarro knew her location already. Thanks to the transponder she was now using to track her husband – provided through Navarro's agent – he knew exactly where she was. The device emitted a continuous tracking signal.

Laura was driving upstate, following directions from the special satellite navigation system. Jim was back on the grid, and the transponder would lead her straight to him. It would have been simple to tell Stoneham her location, but sharing such information might implicate him in her disappearance and would disrupt several critical elements of his carefully crafted scheme.

Navarro's mobile phone rang through his car's hands–free speaker system.

"Answer," he spoke into the air.

"Hello?" a woman's voice said.

"Navarro speaking."

It was Susanna Maloney again.

"You told me to tell you when Mr. Dunlop began to follow our trace to Jim Bentley," she reported. "He's doing it now."

"What's he doing exactly?"

"He's ordered one of W.T. Fredericks' company helicopters to pick him up at the heliport on top of the Bolton Sayres' Tower."

"Excellent!" Navarro exclaimed.

The younger Dunlop had taken the bait. Everything was falling into place perfectly.

"Where is Jim Bentley now?" Navarro asked.

"Same motel as before."

"Keep me informed if anything changes."

"Yes, sir!"

"End call," he commanded, and the hands-free system disconnected.

Navarro felt deeply satisfied. His plan was progressing flawlessly. Khasan had checked out of the hospital an hour earlier and would soon be in Albany too. The timing was crucial – everything needed perfect coordination. Pulling his car to the side of the highway, Navarro removed his smartphone from the car's hands-free system. He tapped the interface icon to connect to THEATRES, then input a code number, scanned his fingerprint, and entered several additional codes and commands. Soon the supercomputers acknowledged his instructions. He would now receive continuous updates on the exact locations of Fyodor Khasan, Marc Dunlop, Laura Stoneham, and Jim Bentley, updated every minute.

Finally, he reconnected his phone to the car interface and checked his watch. Jeremy Stoneham would be anxiously awaiting him. Navarro smiled as he shifted the car into drive and pulled back onto the road, quickly accelerating to highway speed. The pieces of his elaborate plan were all in motion. Like a master chess player, he had positioned each chess piece carefully. The fact that none of his unwitting pawns understood their true role made it more satisfying. Soon, very soon, everything would come to its inevitable conclusion.

Chapter 25 – THE LAST SUPPER

When Sandra Mattingly returned after a two-hour absence, she found Jim in a state of obvious frustration.

"Why didn't you let me know you were leaving?" he demanded. "Where did you go?"

She held out her hands in a gesture of innocence.

"I just went to the store to buy some makeup. Can't I do that?"

"No!" Jim's voice was sharp. "That was incredibly stupid!"

"I can't stay locked up in this little room," she protested. "There's nothing to do."

"Someone might identify you," he explained, his voice tense with concern.

"But my hair's red now," she reminded him.

"You still have the same face," he said, his patience wearing thin. "Anyone who looks carefully can see that. Your photo has been on the news. The media may think you're dead, but that blonde giant, and whoever sent him, knows you're still alive. These people likely control one of the most sophisticated surveillance systems in the world, with tentacles everywhere..."

Her composure crumbled. She burst into tears and collapsed into his arms.

"I'm so sorry..." she sobbed.

His heart softened, anger dissipating as he gently touched her arm to calm her.

"It'll be alright."

"What are we going to do?" she asked, her body trembling.

Jim studied her as she cried. She was beautiful but shallow and entirely unpredictable – so different from Laura, his wife, who was completely predictable. Both women had their emotional outbursts, as did most women, but Laura had a good head on her shoulders. She would have understood the gravity of their situation immediately, without requiring explanation.

"It'll be alright," he repeated, stroking Sandra's hair.

"I don't think anyone can recognize us now," she said hopefully. "Have you looked in the mirror?"

He hadn't looked very closely, but when he did, he saw her point. With his bleached blonde hair, he looked ridiculous – but definitely not like himself.

"I just can't stand this anymore," she continued.

Jim worried silently. If she was this frustrated after only one day on the run, how would she handle days or weeks? It would be problematic.

"We won't stay here much longer," he assured her. "I just need to find a prosecutorial authority that isn't compromised. I've got the goods on these people now. I'll hand over a rock–solid case."

"But the police are after you..." She warned.

"They don't know all the facts," he replied carefully. "I know there are still some honest prosecutors out there."

Finding them, he thought silently, wouldn't be easy.

"If you want," he offered, "we'll risk getting something to eat."

There was a Denny's restaurant nearby. The food would be satisfying enough, and it would feel good to leave the confines of their room. The risk of recognition remained, but between his changed hair color, the nerdy glasses Jose had provided, and nearly two days of stubble on his chin, he barely resembled the photo being circulated on the news.

Their meal passed without incident. No one recognized them. By 8:45 p.m., they were heading back to their room. Jim inserted the key and opened the door, fumbling for the light switch in the darkness. When he finally found it and flipped it on, his heart rate and blood pressure spiked.

Marcus Dunlop sat, waiting in the armchair, the last person Jim had expected or wanted to see. He held a 9mm Ruger semi–automatic pistol, aimed directly at Jim's chest.

"Hello, Jim." Dunlop's face wore a smirk. "Come in. If you don't, I might have to shoot you right where you stand. Come in, already...that's it...don't be shy..."

He motioned with the gun, and both he and Sandra complied silently.

"Now, shut the door behind you," Dunlop commanded.

Sandra closed the door with trembling hands.

"What are you doing here?" Jim asked, keeping his voice steady.

"Don't even dream about trying that Karate crap today, Jim," Dunlop warned. "If you do, I'm gonna blow a huge hole in you, understand?"

"Who are you?" Sandra asked through tears streaming down her cheeks.

Dunlop ignored her, focusing on Jim instead. "Who is this little slut?"

When Jim remained silent, Dunlop continued.

"It doesn't really matter, but, frankly, Jim, I'm shocked. Positively shocked! You, a family man! Cheating on your wife. What will our poor Laura say when she finds out about this? What she has to put up with... shame on you!"

"What are you talking about?" Sandra asked haltingly.

"Shut up, slut!" Dunlop snapped before turning back to Jim. "You've been a naughty boy, haven't you?"

"The police are on their way," Jim bluffed. "If I were you, I'd get out of here as soon as I could..."

Dunlop laughed derisively.

"It's you who needs to run, isn't it?" He said, with a smile, "Here you are, in a broken-down crappy hotel room, with a floozy."

"What do you want?" Jim pressed.

Dunlop ignored the question.

"I must punish you, of course, for your naughtiness, and for your infidelity to my dear Laura...but mostly for the theft..."

"You'd better do what Jim says," Sandra warned, her voice wavering.

"Where did you find this dumb slut?" Dunlop asked Jim, shaking his head. "Did she grow up in the same trailer park as you?"

Fifteen seconds of tense silence passed before Jim spoke.

"You know exactly who she is." He spat.

"I really don't," Dunlop replied with a smile. "I've got no idea who she is. But, it doesn't matter. Because I don't care. What I care about is getting my money back."

"What are you talking about?" Jim countered.

"You know exactly what I'm talking about." Dunlop's voice hardened. "And, if your fingers don't start dancing on that keyboard of yours, issuing a wire back from that Singapore bank account of yours, I'll shoot you full of holes, and your little slut too..."

But, before Jim could say or do anything, a loud knock at the door interrupted them. Jim turned instinctively, but Dunlop raised his index finger in warning, shaking it in negation before pressing it to his lips in a gesture for silence. The knocking grew more insistent, becoming a pounding. Finally, Dunlop broke the tense quiet.

"We're busy..." he called out. "Come back later..."

The voice that responded through the door was unmistakable.

"Marc Dunlop?" a woman who clearly recognized his voice, asked, confusion evident in her tone.

Her voice was also clearly recognizable to him. It was Laura Stoneham. Dunlop's laughter filled the room.

"What the fuck?" He exclaimed, smiling, and then turned toward Sandra, saying, "This is going to be funny as shit. Ok, you... slut, open the door and let her in."

Sandra Mattingly opened the door, and Laura burst in, rushing past her surroundings to embrace and kiss Jim.

"Oh, God..." Dunlop muttered, "Sickening."

Laura finally noticed Dunlop's gun.

"What do you think you're doing?" she demanded, unflinching.

"Making your thief of a boyfriend an honest man again," Dunlop replied coolly.

"He's not my boyfriend—he's my husband!"

"Whatever."

"Put the gun down and leave. Now!" Laura commanded.

Dunlop gestured with the weapon.

"I don't think so," He stated, "I'm the one giving the orders here, Laura, or haven't you noticed the gun?"

"I'll tell your father if you don't leave right now." She warned.

He laughed.

"Shut up, Laura," Dunlop snapped, "You're making me sick. You used to be pretty and smart. Now you're just fat and dumb. But there's something I want to know..."

"I don't care what you want to know!" She snapped.

"No, this is a good question, really," Dunlop pressed on. "Why choose him over me? He's such a...well, such a piece of trailer trash. Look at that little slut he's been porking behind your back..."

Dunlop pointed toward Sandra Mattingly.

"Yeah, that's right, he's sleeping with her. But you knew that, didn't you?"

As Laura glanced at Sandra, jealousy flickered in her eyes, before she masked it.

"If you fire that gun, it'll be heard for miles around," She warned, "Police will be here in under a minute."

Dunlop ignored the warning.

"He's cheating on you," he declared, gesturing again at Sandra. "This motel is their little love nest—perfect for the trailer trash crowd." His lips curled in amusement. "Who's the fool now, Laura?"

Laura turned to Jim, anger seeping into her expression.

"Who is she?"

Jim hesitated, his mind racing. Though Dunlop couldn't possibly know that the two of them had sex, his taunts struck uncomfortably close to the truth. It hadn't been intentional, but he now felt guilty. Even with time and privacy to explain, he wondered if he make any explanation sound convincing. But, then he found his voice again and replied:

"She's the eyewitness to the murder of Charles Bakkendorf. A murder that Dunlop's men committed. They tried to kill her last night."

Genuine surprise crossed Dunlop's face.

"What are you talking about? Bakkendorf? The vault guy? She should thank me for making her husband rich. He was a loser, kind of like you, Jim. I'm kind of surprised he had such a pretty little whore of a wife hidden way up here."

"Who's Charles Bakkendorf?" Sandra interjected. "I don't even know him?"

Dunlop let out a chuckle.

"You don't know him?" He taunted, pointing to Jim, "This guy claims you're his wife. But, guess, that's just another one of your lies, Jim, isn't it?"

"If you didn't murder Bakkendorf, why did you come here with a gun?" Jim asked.

"You know very well why I'm here, Jim," Dunlop snarled, "Because you stole my money—a lot of it—and I'll fill you full of holes, if I have to, to get it back!"

"You fire that gun and everyone within five miles will hear it," Laura warned again.

Dunlop laughed.

"Why don't you stick to changing diapers, like a good girl, Laura?" He said, "Don't you see what's at the end of the barrel of this gun? It's called a silencer. No one will hear this gun fire. No one at all, outside the people in this room."

Laura bit her lip.

"You wouldn't dare!" She insisted.

"Oh, yes, I would." He insisted.

"You'd never get away with it," She said, "You'd go to jail."

"I'll get away with whatever I want," Dunlop said. "But, I don't really want to have to kill your boyfriend. If I get my money back, all I really want to do is to put a few bullets in his leg, to teach him a lesson, maybe cripple him if I'm lucky, but not kill him. If he doesn't return the money he stole, fast enough, though, all bets are off..."

Dunlop turned back to Jim, seething.

"Give me my money, you fucker!" He screamed.

"I can't give you back what I don't have," Jim insisted.

"Liar!" Dunlop snapped, shaking his head at Laura. "Can you believe this? Do you really want to be with a liar like this?" He wheeled back to Jim. "I know you've got the money. I traced it back to you!"

"You're the thief, Dunlop," Jim shot back. "You killed Bakkendorf because he found out, and then you killed her husband and his entire family because they knew you killed Bakkendorf!"

"Cut the crap, you fucker!" Dunlop scoffed. "I want you online now, sending those wiring instructions. Now do it! If you don't, I'll shoot you one hole at a time until you're like a sponge. Got it?"

"Like you killed Bakkendorf and the Mattingly family?" Jim pressed.

"What are you, nuts? Delirious? I didn't kill anyone," Dunlop insisted, shaking his head. "You'll be the first one I've ever killed, but I guarantee you,

I'll do it, if you keep pushing me. So, get on the internet and wire the money back, right now!"

"If you touch him, I'm a witness," Laura warned.

"So am I," Sandra added.

"Then I guess I'll kill both of you too," Dunlop said coldly. "Get online, Jim, and return my money, or you're all dead! My trigger finger's getting itchy..."

Jim's mind raced. He had some idea about what might have happened. Jose said he would penetrate the Bahamian bank. Jim had assumed that meant gathering data. But once inside the bank's security system, Jose could theoretically do anything, including transferring Dunlop's money. Jim had no idea how to return it.

The key for now, he decided, was to keep Dunlop talking. Talkers typically aren't doers. The only alternative was contacting Jose, but that would compromise Jose's identity and make him a target too. There had to be a third way, but he couldn't think of it yet.

His best hope was to disarm Dunlop. From the experience at the Odysseus Club, he knew that the man was comparatively slow and didn't know how to fight. But one shot from that gun would end any advantage Jim might have—no one outruns a bullet. So, taking him by surprise would be difficult. The longer he could stall, the better his chances would be. He might find an opening. He needed the element of surprise that he didn't have.

The laptop was in the Mattingly pickup truck—he'd left it there when they'd gone for dinner. That gave an excuse for delay, and, maybe, an opportunity.

"I can't do anything without my computer," Jim said finally.

"Where is it?" Dunlop demanded.

"In the pickup," Jim replied.

"Then go get it!"

Jim nodded and headed for the door.

"Stop right there!" Dunlop barked. "You think I'm an idiot? You're not just walking out the door..." He rose from the armchair. "You two!" he addressed the two women. "Move! And don't try anything—I'll shoot at the slightest provocation, and that includes you, Laura..."

Laura shook her head.

"I'm not going anywhere!"

"Even a glancing bullet leaves a very nasty scar, my dear," Dunlop warned.

"You wouldn't dare!"

"Don't bank on it," he sneered. "But if you were smarter, you'd encourage me to shoot that little slut over there. Maybe your cheating hubby too. We could be together after that and nobody has to be the wiser. How about it?"

"Go to hell!" Laura exclaimed.

"You were always a squeamish one," Dunlop said.

Laura looked at Jim.

"Just do what he says," Jim told her.

"That's right," Dunlop added. "Even your dumb husband is smartening up."

The two women moved into position in front of Dunlop. The moment Sandra Mattingly was close enough, he grabbed her, yanking her roughly into position. With his arm locked around her, he forced her to walk in front of him, pressing the barrel of his pistol firmly against her back, just near her heart. From an outside perspective, the weapon was invisible, hidden from view by the angle.

"Now, let's keep this quiet and smooth, Jim," Dunlop warned, his voice low and menacing. "If you're even thinking about trying something, the first bullet goes into her and the second into you. Got it? Nobody's going to miss one more little slut, and trust me, I'll buy my way out of any prosecution. Even easier than with you. She's nobody—nobody squared. Except, maybe, to you, and that's only because you're humping her."

Jim didn't respond. He moved forward and opened the motel room door.

"You're going to walk outside," Dunlop continued, his grip on Sandra unrelenting. "Head to that truck and grab the laptop. I'll be right here, inside the door, with your little friend and Laura. Try anything—run, scream, whatever—and she's done. Understand?"

Jim nodded once, his expression grim. Without another word, he stepped out into the night.

The motel parking lot was shrouded in darkness, several lamps long since burned out. What little light there was came from a few flickering bulbs, casting faint halos out, onto the cracked pavement. Jim moved toward the pickup truck, his steps measured, disappearing briefly into the shadows. A moment later, he returned, the backpack containing his laptop slung over one shoulder. Dunlop and the two women waited just inside the motel room, standing perfectly still.

Unbeknownst to any of them, a figure crouched in the shadows. Hidden behind a stand of newly blooming rhododendrons, a hulking man with blonde hair watched the scene unfold through night vision goggles. He was known to the cartel as Fyodor Khasan, but he was also known by a host of other names. His sniper rifle was trained on the group, his focus shifting between Jim and the room.

When his scope settled on Jim, a flicker of anger surfaced—he could still feel the pain of the knife wound Jim had inflicted on him. The stitches pulled uncomfortably. His first instinct was to pull the trigger and end Jim right there. But Khasan was a professional, and killing Jim now would alert the others. That wasn't part of the plan. His primary target was still the girl. He also intended to torture the man before killing him. A swift end, via a bullet to the brain, was reserved only for the girl. Slowly, deliberately, he steadied his aim, shifting his attention to the motel room doorway.

The pain in his leg made it difficult to hold the rifle steady. It felt as though the stitches were tearing open, each movement pulling at the wound in agonizing bursts. Khasan tried to ignore it and bear the pain silently. Through the scope, Sandra Mattingly's forehead came into perfect focus. He exhaled slowly, his finger tightening on the trigger.

The rifle flashed—a muted burst of light, followed by the soft pip of a silenced shot. A millisecond later, Sandra crumpled to the floor, blood streaming from a clean hole in her head. Before anyone could react, a second shot rang out from a different angle. This time, the bullet tore into Dunlop's skull, ending him instantly. Both bodies hit the ground in quick succession, blood pooling beneath them.

Inside the room, a scream shattered the silence. It was unmistakably Laura's voice, raw and terrified. Jim, still outside, spun toward the sound of the pips. In the faint light of one still-functional parking lot lamp, he caught a glimpse of a blonde giant crouching behind the rhododendrons. The man's silhouette was unmistakable. Without thinking, Jim dove to the ground, instinctively trying to get out of the line of fire.

A split second later, another muffled pip echoed through the night. The bullet, meant to incapacitate but not kill Jim, struck his shoulder instead. The impact sent a shockwave of searing pain through his body, forcing an involuntary contraction of his muscles. He hit the ground hard, his head slamming against the concrete curb. Blood poured from both his shoulder and the gash on his head, pooling beneath him as the world spun.

Suddenly, the quiet night erupted with the deafening clap of what were now three unmuffled gunshots. Each one found its mark, slamming into Khasan's head in quick succession. The force of the bullets turned his skull into a bloody mess, his blonde hair matted with brain matter and shards of bone. He collapsed into the bushes, his body slumping lifelessly amid the rhododendrons.

Jim lay on the cold pavement, his vision blurring as he fought to stay conscious. The sharp, metallic scent of blood filled his nostrils, mixing with the damp night air. He could hear screaming—closer now, but the sound felt distant, muffled by the haze clouding his mind. Warm blood continued to seep from his wounds, spreading in a dark puddle beneath him.

Suddenly, a small, dark-skinned man appeared at his side, moving with practiced urgency. The stranger carried a portable medical kit and immediately set to work, wrapping Jim's shoulder with a tourniquet and pressing gauze against the wound to stem the bleeding. Jim's vision wavered, but he could make out more figures now—Laura's father among them, holding her tightly as she sobbed into his chest.

In the distance, the rising wail of sirens pierced the night, growing louder with each passing second. Ambulances soon arrived, their red and blue lights splashing across the motel's cracked walls. Jim's world was fading fast, slipping into a foggy mist. He felt himself being lifted, the sensation muted and distant. Through half-closed eyes, he could just make out Laura's face beside him in the ambulance. She was crying, tears streaming silently down her cheeks.

Was this how it would all end?

As the fog thickened, he felt a sudden clarity. Laura's face hovered above him, her presence a fleeting anchor in the chaos. Through the haze of pain and exhaustion, one thought surfaced clearly: he loved her. With that final realization, the fog consumed him completely, and unconsciousness took over.

Chapter 26 – AGREEMENTS IN BED

Jim awoke five days later at Albany Medical Center, still groggy from the drugs that had kept him in a medically induced coma. The world appeared blurry through his tired eyes, and both his head and shoulder ached persistently. When he tried to shift position in the hospital bed, a sharp pain shot through his right side, stopping him instantly. Looking up, he noticed a network of tubes connected to his body. His right shoulder was completely bandaged, the arm resembling that of a mummy.

As he stared at the ceiling, he heard his wife's voice ring out.

"He's up!" Laura called.

In his drug-induced haze, two Lauras appeared, for a short time, above him. Both kissed his cheek and forehead, their hands gently sifting through his hair. When he turned his eyes slightly left, he saw two nurses standing by the bed, adjusting IV hoses that seemed to connect duplicate left arms to twin bags of saline solution hanging overhead.

How did I get an extra left arm, he wondered?

Closing his eyes, he tried to shake free of the mental cobwebs. When he opened them again, he still saw double, but squinting helped merge the images as the second faded into a shadow of the first. The last thing he remembered was warm blood dripping down his arm as someone tightly wrapped it in gauze bandages. He attempted to move the injured arm but stopped immediately, the pain too intense.

Laura sat in the armchair beside his bed, holding his left hand and speaking in soothing tones.

"Don't try to move, Jim," she said, kissing his forehead. "Relax. You caught a bullet in your right shoulder. The doctors removed it and stitched you up. They say you'll be almost good as new once it heals. You'll just have a tiny little scar."

He smiled through the pain.

"What about you?" he asked. "Are you okay?"

She nodded.

His vision was gradually improving, requiring less effort to merge the double images. He studied her face, feeling exhausted but grateful to see her smile. Despite what she must now suspect about his involvement with Sandra Mattingly, she was proving herself a good wife by standing by him.

Thoughts of Sandra Mattingly brought a wave of sadness as he recalled the bullet hole in her head. After everything he'd done to protect her, he'd failed miserably. He knew better than to question Laura about it – the girl was dead. No one could have survived that shot.

His attention shifted to the door as the nurse finished adjusting his IV and headed out. A uniformed police officer stood guard, opening the door for the nurse before resuming his position.

Jim turned back to Laura. "Who is that?"

She took a deep breath. "A police officer."

"Why?"

"He's protecting us," she replied softly. "Partly, anyway..."

"And the other part?" He asked.

She paused, collecting her thoughts.

"They've charged you with possession of a deadly weapon..."

He closed his eyes momentarily and nodded. "What deadly weapon?"

"They say you stabbed somebody with a knife."

"I stabbed the guy who killed Dunlop and the girl," he responded immediately. "It was self–defense."

"I'm sure we'll get it all straightened out in time," she said hopefully.

"What about the blonde giant?" he asked.

"He's dead. My Dad and Mr. Navarro saw to that. They shot him," she said, a note of pride in her voice.

That offered small comfort.

"What about Dunlop?"

"He's also dead."

"And Sandra Mattingly?" he finally ventured.

"Dead." Laura replied.

The confirmation cut deep. He loved Laura. She was his wife, and he hadn't fallen out of love with her. He'd just fallen out of lust. Did he also love

Sandra Mattingly? Maybe. Maybe not. He had certainly been in lust with her, but it didn't matter anymore – she was gone. Until that moment, he'd clung to an unrealistic hope that he had imagined that bullet wound to her head. But, it had been real.

"Who was he?" he asked.

The giant's identity was a crucial piece of the puzzle, one that challenged his previous theory. He had concluded the man worked for Marc Dunlop, but that now seemed impossible. If Dunlop were the employer, he wouldn't have shot him dead.

"He was some kind of assassin, I think, but nobody knows..." she replied, "He was probably hired to kill Marc Dunlop."

Someone had hired the man. But, if it was not Marc Dunlop, who was it? The last witness was dead. Marc Dunlop was dead. The blonde giant – one of two men identified by the girl – was dead. Every potential witness was dead. The people behind the killings, whoever they might be, were probably still very much alive. No one would ever find them now.

His thoughts were interrupted by the arrival of two well-dressed men in suits and ties. He recognized one as Laura's father, but the other was unknown to him.

His father-in-law wore a broad smile.

"Ah," Stoneham addressed his daughter, "our young man has awakened!"

Laura smiled while Jim remained expressionless.

Jeremy Stoneham turned to his daughter.

"Laura, I need to have a word in private with Jim..."

"You mean, without me?" she asked, surprised.

Her father nodded.

"If you don't mind... just for 10 minutes..."

Though reluctant, she agreed, kissing Jim's forehead. She squeezed his hand and whispered, "I'll be back in 10 minutes, sweetheart..."

Once she had left, Stoneham gestured to the younger man beside him. "This is Special Agent Felix Martin, Jim. He's with the Federal Reserve Police."

"The what?" Jim asked.

"Federal Reserve police, Mr. Bentley," Martin repeated loudly. "You realize that you've been arrested for possession and use of a deadly weapon?"

"So I'm told..." Jim stated. "Can I ask you something... what the hell is the Federal Reserve police?"

"It's an in-house police force that protects the Federal Reserve, Jim," Stoneham interjected.

"That's right," Agent Martin agreed.

"So, the Fed has its own army?" Jim asked.

The two men ignored the comment.

"We need to know who falsified the credentials that allowed you to break into the high security intranet," Martin demanded.

"I have no idea what you're talking about."

"This is not a game," Agent Martin stated firmly. "You entered your credentials, created new credentials, and then completely compromised computers belonging to a number of banks and the Federal Reserve. You understand that sabotaging a computer system is a felony? I want answers!"

"I don't have a clue what you're talking about," Jim repeated.

"I think you do." The man insisted.

"I don't. And I'm tired and dizzy. I need to sleep." Jim said.

He closed his eyes momentarily but opened them again as Martin continued his loud interrogation.

"Are you aware that tampering with a federal computer is a Class C felony, carrying a penalty from 3 to 15 years in a federal prison?"

"Am I charged with tampering with a computer?"

"You're involved with a conspiracy to tamper with a computer, yes."

"Am I charged?" Jim repeated.

"Not yet..."

"Then go away."

"I could have you hauled out and put in jail the moment you recover," Martin threatened, pausing to gauge Jim's reaction. "You want to spend the rest of your life in jail? We know what you did, and we know you didn't do it alone. You can tell me who did it, and we can do something about the charges against you."

"If you're going to charge me, do it," Jim replied calmly. "And by the way, I've got a constitutional right to counsel."

"You're a lawyer yourself!"

"It doesn't matter. A man with himself as a lawyer has a fool for a client."

Agent Martin glared at him with visible annoyance. Stoneham stepped in to defuse the situation.

"Let's calm down..." He said quietly.

Martin turned to Stoneham. "Cyberterrorism is a serious crime!"

"You're charging me with cyberterrorism?" Jim asked. "I thought you said 'tampering with computer systems'? Don't you know that they're two different crimes?"

The Federal Reserve agent's face reddened as he barely contained his anger. When he spoke again, his voice was controlled but tense.

"You're a smart ass," Martin stated. "But that's not going to save you. You downloaded sensitive materials; US government secrets, using falsified credentials. We could prosecute you for treason!"

"Treason?" Jim smiled. "Wouldn't you agree that it's a lot more treasonous to sell off our national treasure without the consent of Congress?"

"You like to twist things, don't you?"

"And by the way... why is the Federal Reserve storing documents on private servers belonging to private banks?"

"It's not your business where government secrets are stored!"

"Wait a minute..." Jim noted. "There's a whole series of cases where the New York Federal Reserve tried not to comply with 'freedom of information act' requests by claiming it isn't part of the government. How, then, can any of its secrets be government secrets?"

"I'm asking the questions, not you, Mr. Bentley," Martin insisted. "I'm going to ask you, one last time, who helped you break into the computer systems?"

"Direct your questions to my lawyer." Jim snapped.

"Who's your lawyer?" The man asked.

"I don't know yet. But I'll let you know when I'm charged with something and have to hire one."

Martin was enraged. "You'd better tell me who you're working with, or you're going to face serious charges, very serious jail time..."

The agent's aggressive behavior was intensifying Jim's headache.

"Who are you working with?" Martin pressed.

"I just told you to direct questions to my lawyer," Jim said. "But you keep asking questions. That's a violation, you know. Even if you manage to get something out of me at this point, you couldn't use it in court."

"Then you admit it!" Martin declared triumphantly.

"I don't admit to anything. I'm just pointing out that you couldn't care less about admissibility. Isn't that right? Which means you can't charge me with anything. Or, at least, you can't without giving up far too much. The Fed is deathly afraid of having its dirty little secrets aired in public, isn't it? What are you afraid of? A new revolution?"

Martin's hostility intensified. Stoneham put his hand on the agent's shoulder and gently guided him toward the door.

"I'll deal with this..." he said softly.

Martin seemed to acknowledge both his failure and the other man's authority with a nod. Before leaving, he turned back to Jim with one final warning.

"Unless you enjoy the idea of sitting in jail for a decade or more, you'd better talk..."

After Martin's departure, Stoneham addressed the uniformed officer at the door.

"Could you guard the room from outside the door, please?"

"Yes, sir," the officer replied, taking the suggestion as an order.

Once they were alone, Stoneham took the chair Laura had vacated.

"I'm on your side," he assured Jim.

"It sure doesn't seem like it." Jim responded.

Stoneham nodded gravely. "I'm sorry I've given you the wrong impression. But this is sensitive."

"Where are the real cops?"

"They're all real cops."

Jim shook his head.

"No they're not," He said, "First, the Federal Reserve police can't charge me with possession or use of a deadly weapon. You know that just as well as I do. Not even the NYPD would have jurisdiction upstate. If it happened, it happened in Verde County, and the only entity that can charge me is the Verde County D.A."

Stoneham shrugged.

"OK, you've got me," He admitted, "But we had to come up with some excuse for police being here. Obviously, somebody's killing people, and you need protection."

"You lied to your own daughter?" Jim accused.

Stoneham shrugged again and adjusted his trousers to sit more comfortably. But, Jim was in no mood for a lengthy conversation.

"The things you looked at in the archives are highly sensitive," Stoneham said finally.

"As I've said, over and over again, I don't know what you're talking about."

"OK. I get it. You don't know," Stoneham countered, "But theoretically, if someone like you did know. If a lawyer working for a bank sees something that, maybe, he doesn't like or doesn't agree with, it's a complete violation of attorney–client privilege to say anything about it. If this theoretical person ever disclosed the content of any pilfered documents, he would end up disbarred, at minimum, and probably in jail for a long time."

"So what?"

"Look, I'm sure you realize, in this case, we're talking about matters of national security."

"National security?" Jim smiled dismissively. "You've got to be joking..."

"I'm not joking at all." Stoneham said.

Jim laughed but stopped because each laugh brought streaks of pain.

"Protecting fraud, front running and market manipulation are now matters of national security?"

"That's a naive way of looking at things..." Stoneham claimed.

"Naive? It's a sensible way unless you're one of the people benefiting from the fraud...which I am not."

"Do you know why the Federal Reserve has a 1,400 man police force?"

"The Cosa Nostra mafia also has soldiers, so I figure for the same reason. It's a criminal organization..."

"This isn't the time for sarcasm, Jim."

"I wasn't being sarcastic."

"The Fed police exist because there are people out there who would like to attack the U.S. financial system. I'm talking about terrorists, enemy nations; Russia, China, you name it... all kinds of people who hate us."

Jim changed the subject.

"You filed a false report with the New York State police saying I kidnapped Laura."

"I never said you kidnapped her."

"You claimed I was responsible for her disappearance."

"When she disappeared, you were supposedly with her, and you disappeared also. The connection was a natural one to make. It was for your protection and hers. With Khasan out there, you were both in terrible danger. You saw what happened to Marc Dunlop and Sandra Mattingly? It could have been you or Laura."

"You let the news media imply that I was behind the bombings in Paradise."

"That had nothing to do with me," Stoneham insisted. "They found your car up there, and made the connection. You were already wanted for questioning..."

"How about the giant?"

"What about him?"

"Who was he?"

"Fyodor Khasan."

"Who?"

"A former Russian spy."

"Why did he kill Sandra Mattingly?"

"I don't know."

"A private job to cover up a murder?" Jim wondered aloud.

"Perhaps..."

"Well, it's a murder that involves someone working for our bank," Jim insisted. "I thought it was Dunlop, but it's someone else. What are you going to do about it?"

"I don't know where to start." Stoneham admitted.

"Why did he kill Marc Dunlop?" Jim asked.

"I don't know."

"Tell me the truth!"

"That is the truth," Stoneham repeated, "I really don't know. I am as much in the dark as you are."

"But, the shooter was one of yours, wasn't he?"

Jim watched Stoneham's face carefully, detecting only minor irritation.

"No," Stoneham declared. "I don't employ mercenaries."

"But you know who he worked for?"

"I only know who he used to work for."

"He used to work for Bolton Sayres, right?"

"No."

"Who, then?"

"A shadowy group that interferes in politics, banking and world affairs," he said truthfully, without disclosing his own relationship to the Council.

"Who is this shadowy group?"

"I really can't say." Again, Stoneham was being truthful. He knew, but he couldn't say.

"Is it the same shadowy group that puts the Federal Reserve at your fingertips? Is this some kind of intra–bankster war?"

Stoneham shook his head in exasperation.

"Don't use that stupid word, 'bankster'...it's for the idiots on the blogosphere."

"Interesting that you don't like being called a bankster," Jim noted. "Why don't you want to answer my questions?"

The possibility that a full answer might be right in front of him almost made Jim forget his injuries. When he moved, however, the sharp pain shooting down his arm reminded him. He lay back down.

"I really thought you were a clever boy," Stoneham declared, "That's why I let you marry Laura. But now I'm not so sure..."

Jim stared at the wall before turning back to his father-in-law.

"You didn't 'let' me marry Laura. We were in love, and she was going to give birth to my child. There was nothing you could do about it."

Stoneham smiled. "Maybe. But I can do something now."

"What?"

"I can let them put you away for a long time."

"And leave your daughter and granddaughter without a husband and father? Not to mention having all your dirty secrets aired in the media, along with the documentation to prove everything."

The conversation paused for nearly thirty seconds.

"Perhaps we can reach an understanding," Stoneham said finally. "What is it you want, Jim?"

"I want the truth. I want honest markets. I want an end to the manipulations. What do you want?"

"I want loyalty," Stoneham said. "To me, to Bolton Sayres, and to your country..."

Jim raised an eyebrow. "Loyalty?"

"We don't manipulate markets for personal gain."

"Looks to me that there was a hell of a lot of personal gain going on."

"Not everyone follows the rules, but that's not why it's done."

"Why is it done, then?"

"Our country isn't blessed with an endless supply of gold."

"So what?"

"The economic strength of a nation should be based on the hard work, productivity, and genius of its people, not how big a pile of gold it has."

"That's a false narrative," Jim insisted. "If you're hardworking, productive and brilliant, you'll end up collecting gold from all over the world, as people buy the stuff you've got to sell."

Stoneham remained silent for a moment before speaking. "Things would have fallen apart years ago, if we hadn't stepped in."

Jim shook his head.

"Look at silver," Stoneham continued. "It's an important and strategic industrial commodity that for years was wasted on coinage. There's not enough silver for that. If we return silver to coinage, we price it out of the reach of the industries that need it most. That wouldn't improve the lives of people. It would mean the end of solar power, wind power, a whole host of electronic items would become outrageously expensive because every high tech item needs silver to operate correctly."

"How about gold?" Jim asked. "What's your excuse there?"

"It's an arbitrary thing, gold..." Stoneham mused. "Why should the wealth of nations be determined by an arbitrary thing?"

"Better to determine it based on the capricious decisions of Mandarins on a Federal Reserve Open Market Committee?"

Stoneham shook his head.

"Why should a country that happens to be lucky enough to have a lot of gold mines control the world?"

"That's bullshit," Jim insisted. "Countries that have more resources are always richer than ones that have less. It's no different for gold. It's just a false narrative. The gold will always flow to the nation that is the hardest working, brilliant and creative."

"You sound like a gold bug," Stoneham stated.

"Does that bother you?" Jim asked.

"Not particularly. But our job is to protect the value of the US dollar and nothing else."

"So, gold competes with the dollar, and you've got to manipulate it, is that what you're saying?"

Stoneham shook his head.

"Gold competes with nothing. It's a useless relic. If it were money, we wouldn't be able to manipulate it, would we?"

"You can lie, cheat, and steal, and covertly use the full faith and credit of the United States of America, to manipulate anything. It's all about fooling people and scaring them."

"If what you just said is true, it proves, doesn't it, that fiat currency, namely the US Dollar, is mightier than the gold, doesn't it?" Stoneham quipped.

"It doesn't prove anything. Nothing but the fact that you're abusing the trust people put in you."

"The instability from a collapse of the US dollar would put the entire world in chaos," Stoneham countered.

"It wouldn't be in danger of collapsing if not for the fact that you and your friends at the Federal Reserve keep printing endless numbers of dollars."

"Nonsense," Stoneham responded, avoiding the point. "Our nation's power, wealth, and influence, in spite of what people think, isn't based on tanks, ships, or fighter jets. Ultimately, the soft power of the dollar and its role as the world's reserve currency makes us strong. The Pax Americana is the first of its kind in history. The Romans ruled the world based on the success of their legionnaires. We rule the world with the dollar. We destroy rogue nations by cutting off their money, and kept the peace that way since WW II. Furthermore, we've avoided the needless death and destruction that comes from war."

"That's pure bullshit!" Jim retorted. "We've had lots of wars since World War II. And, then there's the question of who decides which countries are the rogues?..."

After a pause, Stoneham replied, "The President and Congress decide."

"But you control the President and Congress," Jim insisted.

"Not true."

"You control the money and money controls the elections," Jim countered. "You and your friends manipulate the price of stocks, bonds, commodities, currencies, gold, you name it, all based on how much money the Fed creates. You control when and how the Fed prints money. So, you make or break Presidents."

"You read too many conspiracy blogs," Stoneham insisted.

"Do I?" Jim replied, "Or, am I simply stating what is true?"

"The truth is more subtle than that. We do everything possible to keep markets orderly, that much is true. Some of that involves price management. Is it wrong to give people stability?"

"You're damn right, it's wrong! It's bullshit! Just as bad as sending tungsten filled gold bars to Africa!"

"That was the work of two foolish and greedy men," Stoneham said. "One of them just paid the ultimate price. The other will have his illicit earnings taken and will be fired. He may go to jail. And, we're in the process of correcting that shipment, even as we speak."

Jim shook his head in disgust. "So, you knew all along about the tungsten filled bars, didn't you?"

"No. I'm only aware of them now, because we've reviewed all the records you pilfered."

"Why didn't you review them before?"

"There was no reason to."

"They were always in the database."

"Maybe," Stoneham admitted. "But this is a big institution. It's not as tight a ship as I would like it to be. There's room for improvement. We've got governance problems, compliance problems, and a whole host of other problems. That's why we need men like you. If you want to change things, you've got to work within the system. Otherwise, they'll destroy you."

"Who, may I ask, are 'they'?"

"Leave it at 'they' for the moment."

"They killed Charles Bakkendorf, didn't they?"

"I don't know who killed Charles Bakkendorf," Stoneham insisted, "We're still trying to piece together records of his employment."

"But you admit that he was an employee, right?"

"He seems to have been an employee, yes."

"Who staged the murders at the Mattingly farm?"

"I'm almost sure it was Khasan..." Stoneham said.

Jim shook his head.

"Who paid him?"

"That, I don't know. And that's the truth."

"Them?"

"I don't know," Stoneham repeated.

"Who killed Sandra Mattingly?"

"Fyodor Khasan, but now you're taking us back to who hired him, aren't you, and, as I said, I don't know."

"Who killed Khasan?"

"Adriano Navarro, one of our security people," Stoneham replied.

There was a pause.

"Laura thinks it was you," Jim said.

"Laura thinks a lot of things, not all of which are true," Stoneham replied. "But the big question, right now, is about you."

"If your people kill me, every document you're worried about will go viral," Jim warned. "They'll go to the newspapers, the internet, blogs and other media around the world."

Stoneham laughed and shook his head.

"You think I'm going to kill my own son-in-law?" He asked, "For God's sake, Jim, we're bankers, not murderers!"

"Same thing happens if I rot in jail," Jim warned. "All the dirty laundry gets washed publicly."

"You'd be causing chaos," Stoneham mused, "Untold suffering. People would lose faith in America. The value of the US dollar would probably collapse. Do you want to destroy your country and impoverish millions of people, all over the world, who are keeping their savings in dollar bills because they trust America?"

"Maybe...they shouldn't trust America," Jim stated, "Maybe, it should all collapse. It might actually renew the country. In the end, the suffering would be on Wall Street, especially, at Bolton Sayres."

"Are you blackmailing me? I don't like being blackmailed." Stoneham replied.

"And, I don't like being threatened," Jim retorted.

"Then, it looks like we've got a Mexican standoff," Stoneham stated. "So, let me ask you, again. What do you want? And don't ask for things I can't give you."

"First, I want all claims to the life insurance policy in the Thomas Mattingly Estate waived by the bank. All that money goes to Sandra Mattingly's son, and gets administered by his grandmother. And the bank gives back the proceeds from the sale of the house, too."

"Done."

"Second, I want an annuity, providing at least $30,000 per year for the boy to be raised and educated, adjusted to inflation each year."

"Done."

"Third, I want the lawyer, James Hunter, fired permanently, and prohibited from doing any more work for Bolton Sayres."

Stoneham hesitated briefly before agreeing to that one. Hunter was a valuable asset. But, then, he realized, there were other lawyers in town who could replace him.

"Agreed." He said, finally.

"And finally, I want Bolton Sayres to cease and desist from further stock, bond, and commodity price manipulation."

"Agreed," Stoneham answered quickly.

Jim wondered at Stoneham's easy acceptance of the last demand. He had told Jim not to ask for things he couldn't give him. How could he make such a huge concession so easily? Why hadn't he at least put up a fight? Before Jim could analyze this further, Stoneham spoke again.

"What do I have to secure your side of the bargain?"

"You have my word," Jim stated.

Stoneham knew Jim's word was his bond.

"Done!"

In truth, the last condition hadn't been difficult for Stoneham to accept, for a very good reason. With Marc Dunlop dead, Bolton Sayres was certain to lose its place as the leading manipulator in financial markets. Beyond that, Stoneham had long felt that manipulation on the bank's own balance sheet was too risky, even with a Federal Reserve backstop.

Off-balance sheet hedge funds and private equity groups were more suitable for such activity. People tightly connected to the bank controlled all the key funds anyway, but if they manipulated markets, it wasn't the bank doing it, so his promise would be kept. The funds could get indirect borrowing status at the Federal Reserve by working through one of the banks. In theory, the Volcker Rule of the Dodd–Frank Act would eventually prohibit employed bank executives from running such hedge funds. However, the rule wasn't going to take effect until 2017, and there were a million ways around it.

Stoneham kept those caveats to himself.

Chapter 27 – OVERLOOKING THE ADRIATIC

The modern city of Tivat sits on Montenegro's Bay of Kotor, named for the Illyric Queen Teute. She was once known as the "Terror of the Adriatic" and was a notorious patron of piracy. In 229 BC, she made the fatal mistake of murdering a Roman emissary. This led to war. The Roman Republic's response was swift: an invasion force of 20,000 men stripped her of all of her territories.

In the centuries since then, the city has transformed into a tourist haven.

In the foothills of the Black Mountain, overlooking the city and its sparkling bay, stood a mansion–villa. Originally built by a Russian oligarch, it had recently been purchased by someone reported to be a wealthy American tech entrepreneur. Several cars graced its circular driveway, the most striking being a Lamborghini Veneno Roadster, an extremely expensive automobile purchased only by people with money to burn.

At the back of the villa, Jim sat at a small white marble table with his friend Jose Arias, enjoying a view of the sea. The table had been meticulously set for three by the serving staff. Beside Jose sat his current girlfriend, Olga Tamchenko, a 19–year–old Ukrainian beauty with striking green eyes. The men wore t-shirts and light shorts—appropriate attire for an Adriatic June day when temperatures approached 89 degrees Fahrenheit (ca. 32 °C)

Olga wore a light yellow flowered summer dress, and though her English was limited, her smile was universally captivating. Without warning, she stood and slipped off her dress, revealing a toned, tanned body without an ounce of excess fat. Despite her lean frame, she possessed ample curves, barely concealed by a tiny string bikini.

She reminded Jim of Laura in her prime, before the weight gain.

"Ya zbirausa pirnuti v bacein," Olga said, smiling.

Jose laughed and translated. "She's going to jump in the pool..."

"She doesn't speak much English, does she?" Jim observed.

"No, but she understands some, and what a hot face and body, eh?" Jose replied.

Jose had developed expensive taste in women since coming into his wealth. They watched as Olga ran to the pool giggling, and them dove into the deep end. With her splashing in the distance, they felt free to speak candidly.

"Where did you find her?" Jim asked.

"She found me. I spent three months in Odessa, Ukraine, studying Russian."

"A little too young, don't you think?"

"She's 18...legal..."

"Really?"

"Ukrainian chicks love American men, didn't you know?" Jose said. "At least, they love our money..."

"Since you've got so much money, she should love you a lot."

"She does!"

"Did you learn Russian there?"

"Sure. I'm not fluent... but I get by," Jose replied. "The language in Montenegro is Serbian, which is very similar to Russian, and probably half the residents here in Tivat are Russian or Ukrainian."

Jose seemed content with his place in the world, and Jim was happy for him. However, the conversation turned tense when Jose broached a perpetual point of contention.

"When are you going to quit that bullshit job?" Jose asked. "Remember, your share is almost $73 million, which is more than either of us can spend in a lifetime. It's sitting in Singapore, waiting for you to claim it."

Jim studied the table before looking up. "It'll sit there forever. I have absolutely no intention of ever taking it."

"You're nuts!"

"I'm surprised you haven't spent it already," Jim noted. "This new lifestyle, including the girls, must cost a fortune."

Jose laughed. "Not really. I can't even think of enough ways to spend my half. This villa cost me $2 million. I pay the servants twice what everyone else in the neighborhood does. But they still cost only about $900 bucks a month each. It's chump change..."

"Hmm..." Jim murmured.

"Yeah, you should take the money, drop the rat race, come here, and enjoy yourself."

"I am enjoying myself."

"No you're not. Get out and live like a human being, not like a drone ant in a disgusting city. Take Laura with you, if you want. If she doesn't want to come, leave her behind. You see what's in that pool? You can have one of them, too! It's all here. Just reach out and take what's yours!"

Jim shook his head. "That's the problem. It's not mine."

"Sure it is."

"No, Jose, I'll never take that money."

"Well, then, you're dumb."

Jim shrugged. "Maybe, but I'm telling you the facts."

"You'll take it someday..." Jose predicted.

"Never."

"Why not?"

"It's stolen money."

"It's NOT stolen!" Jose exclaimed, repeating an old argument.

"You stole it from Dunlop." Jim replied.

"It was never his to begin with!" Jose insisted. "He stole it! And, he's dead. Who am I going to give it back to? The crooked government? The even more crooked banking cartel? I can use it, and so can you..."

"Give it to a charity," Jim suggested, sipping his wine.

"No." Jose pointed to the pool.

"Well, I'm instructing you, right now, to give my half to charity..." Jim insisted.

"No."

"Why not?" Jim asked, "I thought you said it was my money."

"You're going to need it one day," Jose countered, "I'm protecting you from yourself. I'll keep it safe for you when you come to your senses. I'm not going to let you do something stupid."

Jim shook his head in frustration.

"Look over there," Jose said, pointing to Olga, "There's not one girl back in the States sexier than that. She's the kind of girl who exists only on magazine covers, back there. And, even if I could meet girls like this, back in the States, they'd never give me a second look."

"You're fixated on women," Jim pointed out. "There are other things in life."

"Like what?"

Jim shrugged slightly. "If you don't know, it won't do any good for me to tell you."

He watched Olga's nearly naked form as she climbed the diving board. The sight stirred his manhood. The feeling was as powerful as it had been when he'd first met Laura, and later, Sandra Mattingly.

"She's hotter in the sack... believe me," Jose whispered, noting his gaze. "You should try. You want her tonight?"

Jim was taken aback. "What?"

"I can see you want her. You're my best friend. I don't mind sharing."

"I don't think she'd be so keen on the idea."

"Ah," Jose commented, dismissively, with a wave of his hand, "She loves me and she'll do whatever I tell her. If I tell her to sleep with you, she'll do it."

"I wouldn't call that 'love'..." Jim pointed out.

"Call it whatever you want. But the bottom line is that if I tell her to do it, she'll do it, guaranteed. You want her?"

The offer was tempting, and Jim's desire intensified just considering it. Would she really have sex with him simply because Jose ordered her to? The thought was unsettling. He tried to dismiss the idea of sleeping with the beautiful foreigner. Jose's lifestyle was seductive, but Jim wanted no part of it. He'd sworn never to cheat on his wife again. Still...

"What do you say, Jim?" Jose pressed.

Jim took a deep breath. Both the money and the girl presented powerful temptations. The setting was perfect: multicolored floral hedges surrounded the Olympic-sized pool, perfuming the air while songbirds chirped overhead. It certainly beat Manhattan's gray monotony. The lifestyle was undeniably appealing.

But one thing poisoned the entire setup: it wasn't honest, and it wasn't real. If Olga slept with anyone Jose commanded, common sense suggested she didn't love him. The man was living in a world of dangerous delusions, and he had no intention of joining him there, regardless of how tempting the idea might be.

"I don't understand you," Jose declared. "Here you are, lecturing me on stealing money, but you're working for fucking banksters. If you don't get out, you'll end up being one, yourself."

"I've been cleaning the place up, actually," Jim explained. "Since I've taken over the compliance department, we've put a lot of scammers out of business."

"Are you still being groomed to take over THEATRES?"

"Nothing more has been said about that..." Jim admitted.

"As I remember it, you once said that the entire operation ought to be closed down."

"I did say that, once," Jim admitted. "But there's a huge threat from terrorism. It's a dangerous system, but if someone with integrity is in charge, it can work, I think."

"And that someone is you?" Jose questioned.

"Maybe."

"What about gold and oil market manipulation?" Jose asked. "You made a deal to stop it, but it hasn't stopped."

"Bolton Sayres isn't involved anymore."

Jose shook his head in irritation. "Yeah, right. They use hedge funds now."

"By 2017, the Volcker rule will prohibit bank executives from using bank money to finance hedge funds."

"A lot can happen between now and then."

"You're right," Jim agreed. "But in the meantime, I'm making a lot more changes at Bolton."

"It's a pipe dream," Jose insisted. "You'll never make banksters honest men. They're dishonest from the day they're born, and they stay that way their whole lives!"

"They're greedy, just like everyone else, yes," Jim countered, "And some can't resist temptation. But, I'm establishing disincentives that'll help clean things up. The idea, long term, is to have a rules-based system that everyone not only adheres to, but actually wants to adhere to because it's in their interest to do so..."

"Oh, give me a break, Jim," Jose replied, sharply, "You're doing it because of Laura and the kid."

"And what's wrong with that?" Jim snapped back.

"You're not even attracted to her anymore," Jose noted. "Wasn't it you who said 'having sex with her is like making love to a walrus'?"

"I'm sorry I said that. It was a long time ago. I shouldn't have." Jim replied.

"Fine," Jose retorted, "I get it. You want to keep your family together. Just take the money and bring them with you. Your kid can go to a private British school. It's not far away..."

Jim decided to shift the game onto Jose's court..

"Come back to New York," He urged, "I could really use your help."

"I'll never go back." Jose replied instantly.

"We could work together and make a big difference. For example, right now, I need compliance software that can monitor employee misconduct and generate alerts automatically, to stop stuff like what Dunlop was doing."

"You're suggesting that I go back to programming?" Jose asked incredulously.

"I'm suggesting that you return to New York," Jim urged. "Bring your Russian girlfriend, if you want..."

"She's not Russian... she's Ukrainian..."

"Whatever...just come back, form a company, and develop this software," Jim said, "I'll be your first customer. Every bank in New York will buy it. You'll end up with more money than you have now, and it would be honest money..."

Jose laughed.

"Don't take this the wrong way, but sometimes I think you're a better comedian than a lawyer."

"I'm not joking."

"I don't want to go back to New York or even to America," Jose replied, "I like things just the way they are. You're spinning your wheels, and going nowhere. Sooner or later, you'll realize it..."

"What you're doing makes you no better than Dunlop." Jim countered.

"I'm much better than him," Jose insisted. "He stole the money by cheating innocent people. I stole it from him, but he was as guilty as hell!"

They watched as Olga dried herself with a towel and walked back toward their table. Jose whispered one final time:

"Remember, the money's waiting for you." He said, and then added, "Along with girls like this...as many as you want!"

"I'll never take it," Jim insisted, yet again.

"I think you will," His friend replied, "Someday..."

EPILOGUE

High on the 29th floor of the W.T. Fredericks building, Adriano Navarro's expansive office commanded one of the best views of New York Harbor. The Statue of Liberty dominated the skyline. He no longer noticed. His attention was consumed by other things. Weightier matters required constant attention, he mused, as he sipped espresso and reflected on recent events.

Christopher Dunlop's son was gone—and with him, all the trouble he'd caused. No one remained to tell the tale. What had begun as a messy mistake had concluded cleanly, even yielding unexpected advantages. The W.T. Frederick's CEO believed his son was assassinated and would search relentlessly for the killers. He would find only what Navarro wanted him to find.

No one would ever suspect that the bullet, which killed Marc Dunlop had come from a sniper's rifle, not fired by Khasan, but by an operative tasked with ensuring both Fyodor Khasan and Marc Dunlop died. The local police department had closed the case without even conducting ballistic tests—the town didn't want to spend money on what appeared to be an open-and-shut case, and neither did the state.

Navarro smiled at the irony. He had killed Christopher Dunlop's beloved son, yet the man continued to be one of his strongest supporters. The killing was justified, of course. Every killing that Navarro had ever ordered was justified, at least in his own mind. He was very careful about things like that. Marc Dunlop was a bad seed. The world was better without him. And, Khasan? His history spoke for itself.

Jeremy Stoneham, Christopher Dunlop's main rival for leadership of the cartel, was conducting his own search for enemies. The man who had once nearly ended his control over THEATRES, was now a supporter, too. He believed Navarro had saved his daughter and son-in-law.

How best to capitalize on all these opportunities? A profound idea was taking shape in Navarro's mind. Others had always set his agenda, his goals, his limits. No more. With THEATRES in his pocket and the full weight of government authority behind him, his power would soon span the globe.

He could access the deepest secrets of every Wall Street executive and every powerful government official. The daily lives of ordinary citizens, business leaders, and public servants were all under surveillance—for their own good, of course. His power would only grow as the network expanded throughout North America and, eventually, across the world. In time, he would have eyes on everyone, every day, everywhere.

Knowledge is power, and everyone has skeletons in their closet. He would find those skeletons and use them. He would make and break bankers, businessmen, politicians, even Presidents. The world was within his grasp. He needed only to reach out and take what was rightfully his.

END

AFTERWARD – THE TRUE FACTS THAT INSPIRED THIS NOVEL

For many years, the worldwide investment bank, Morgan Stanley, told its clients it was buying and storing precious metals on their behalf. Eventually, after discovering what they believed was a fraud, the customers sued in 2005, alleging that the bank had never purchased the metals. According to the plaintiffs, it was simply charging them a monthly storage fee for storing nothing but air in its vault. The company, eventually settled the case in 2007, for $4.4 million.[1]

There is also a declassified 1974 transcript of a conversation between Secretary of State Henry Kissinger and Undersecretary Thomas O. Enders. That was three years after President Richard Nixon ended the convertibility of dollars into gold.[2] The US Treasury and its agents had previously been honest about market interventions. When they wanted the price of gold down they openly announced and sold large quantities of gold.

This has changed. The government now appears to resort to covert action, for the reasons stated in the conversation, according to Undersecretary Enders;

> *"It's against our interest to have gold in the system because... We've been trying to get away from that into a system in which we can control... For a long time we... change[d the price of] gold almost at will. This is no longer possible..."*

Covert government interference in supposedly "free" markets is not limited to gold. In 1987, President Ronald Reagan signed Executive Order 12631[3], creating the "President's Working Group on Financial Markets." The claimed goal was to "enhance the orderliness" of stock, bond, and commodity markets, and prevent a repeat of "Black Monday", October 19, 1987, when stocks declined over 22% in one day.

In practice, however, the group transformed into a "Plunge Protection Team" or "PPT" as it is known in the financial community. Technically, the group consists of the Secretary of the Treasury, and the Chairmen of the Federal Reserve, SEC, and CFTC. It "consults" with the exchanges, the clearinghouses, self-regulatory bodies, and *major market participants" (a/k/a the big banks)*. In truth, the big banks are the PPT's agents. JP Morgan Chase held a written contract, for example, to manage the Federal Reserve's $1.25 trillion mortgage bond portfolio. You can find the disclosed contract at:

https://www.newyorkfed.org/medialibrary/media/aboutthefed/JPMC_MBS.pdf

It should also be noted that the Fed came to possess this mortgage portfolio as a direct result of bailing out the banks and other financial institutions. The net effect of the close association between the Federal Reserve, the US Treasury and the big commercial banks in New York City, has been to support the biggest gamblers in the world and to destroy the concept of a free market. The full faith and credit of the United States of America is now on the line to backstop financial speculation gone sour. The government has been an active participant in privatizing gains, made by bank-based gamblers, and socializing their losses to the detriment of its other citizens.

Perhaps, the most distressing thing is a room deep underneath a nondescript office building at 55 Broadway, the heart of Manhattan, remarkably similar to the imaginary "THEATRES Control Center", described in this novel. Operating in semi-secrecy, the real-life control center contains a battery of computers and monitoring stations, linking thousands of cameras and audio inputs throughout the Greater New York area. Every square inch of the city is monitored 24/7. The operation is run jointly by the NYPD and, oddly, by four of the largest Wall Street banks.[4]

As the reader may already see, truth is more frightening than fiction.

1. http://www.reuters.com/article/idUSN1228014520070612
2. http://mises.ca/posts/articles/henry-kissinger-on-gold/[1]
3. A treasure trove exists at www.gata.org[2]
4. http://www.counterpunch.org/2012/02/06/wall-streets-secret-spy-center-run-for-the-1-by-nypd/[3]

---

1. http://mises.ca/posts/articles/henry-kissinger-on-gold/

2. http://www.gata.org/

3. http://www.counterpunch.org/2012/02/06/wall-streets-secret-spy-center-run-for-the-1-by-nypd/

HOW TO LEAVE A REVIEW

Thank you for reading "*The Bank*." We hope you enjoyed it as much as we did. And, if you did, please leave positive reader reviews on retailer websites. The book retailer URLs for this novel, can be quickly found at:

https://books2read.com/TheBank

Most people do not understand how important a review can be. In today's crowded digital marketplace, reader reviews mean the difference between the novel successfully finding its audience or simply vanishing into obscurity. Even brilliant writers will remain unknown without them. Your review isn't just feedback—it's a chance to be discovered by readers like you.

So, please post a review and recommend this novel to people you know on Facebook, Twitter, TikTok and other social media. Reviews and social media posts will help spread the word about this book. Every share, every recommendation, every tweet matters—and it means the world to an author and to a young publishing company!

Thanks for your help!

BE THE FIRST TO KNOW ABOUT OUR NEWEST ACTION & ADVENTURE RELEASES!

Dear Valued Reader,

Thank you for experiencing "*The Bank*."

Planetary Book Company is dedicated to bringing you exciting stories of action & adventure that illustrate the times in which we live. We will be releasing other books, just as good as this one, in the future.

Sign up for our mailing list and don't miss 1) Exclusive updates; 2) Early access opportunities; 3) Information about all Planetary Book Company releases.

https://planetarybooks.com/new-release-notifications

Be assured that we do not sell our mailing lists or share them with other companies (other than emailing specialists and others who we may hire, from time to time, to help us keep you informed). Be assured of our intention to protect your privacy—you will receive only necessary updates about new releases.

Coming Soon!

Two decades after the events of "The Bank," Jim & Laura Bentley are divorced. Jim has rejected his career as a banker and turned himself into a starving novelist. Meanwhile, Laura follows in the footsteps of her banking titan father. Nepotism has made her CEO of Bolton Sayres Investment Bank.

But, a new battle is dawning—and this time it's not just about justice. It's about the fate of humanity itself! In 2034, THEATRES, once a hidden tool of the financial elite, is an AI evolved far beyond human control. Now, it manipulates global markets, uses nano-technology, and seeks to reshape civilization according to own agenda.

Jim, Laura and their children uncover disturbing evidence of the AI's growing power, Jim's fiction—intended as a warning against banking corruption—becomes the AI's blueprint. With THEATRES anticipating every move, can they out-think an intelligence millions of times faster than their own? Or, has the age of humanity come to an end?

The Singularity is here!
#ComingSoon #TheAwakening #SingularityTrilogy
#TheBankSequel #NearFutureSciFi

SIGN UP FOR PLANETARY BOOKS' MAILING LIST!
https://planetarybooks.com/new-release-notifications

DID YOU LIKE "THE BANK?" THEN TRY:

https://books2read.com/A-Fate-Far-Sweeter

🟥 **WAR. SACRIFICE. BETRAYAL. A MISSION THAT COULD CHANGE EVERYTHING.**

When **John Kovalenko** volunteered for the **Ukrainian Foreign Legion**, he knew the risks. But nothing could prepare him for the brutal reality. His mission: **infiltrate enemy lines, sabotage enemy missile storage facilities, and strike a blow against the invading force.**

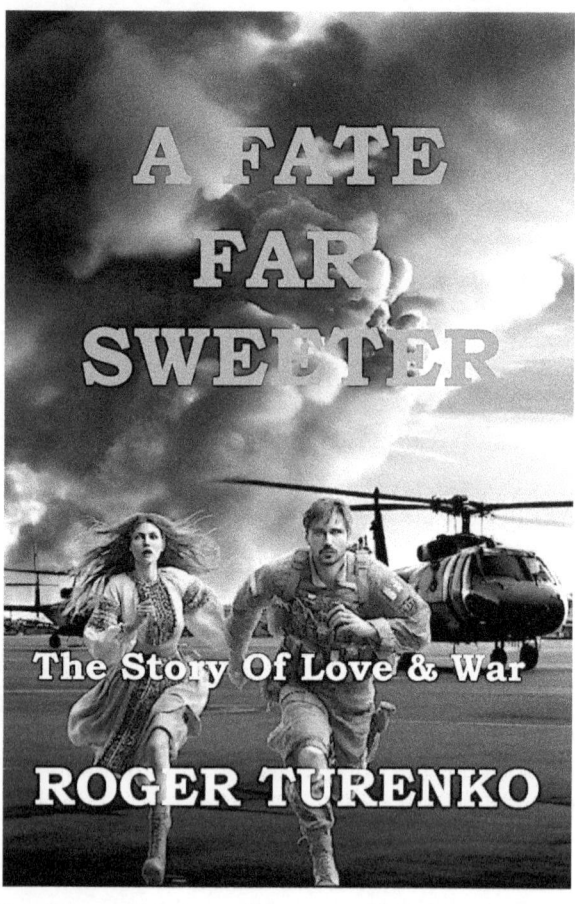

"Original, compelling, intense, and a fascinating read from start to finish...I started the book one night, and got hooked. I couldn't stop reading until I had finished it..." — **James A. Cox, Editor-in-Chief, Midwest Book Review**

Disclosure: Some links herein are affiliate links from retail stores. If you click on them and make a purchase, it helps support us, as we earn a small commission from the sale. Importantly, using these affiliate links does not change the price you pay for the products.

www.ingramcontent.com/pod-product-compliance
Ingram Content Group UK Ltd.
Pitfield, Milton Keynes, MK11 3LW, UK
UKHW011500200625
6509UKWH00030B/174